Innocent

Sebastian Swan

All rights reserved.

No part of this publication may be reproduced or transmitted, in any form or by any means, without prior permission from the author.

Copyright: David Mattches, 2015

Dedicated to my dearest brother

Douglas

1938 - 2015

Aefre

Thanks to:

Bob Watson, for all the help he has given to me. Bob is the only person I know who ISN'T – an expert.

Pat: She's been priceless.

Carolyn: For her constant encouragement and support.

Michelle Mattches: For her special insight… into matters beyond my ken x.

And especially June, for all she has suffered for the sake of literature.

The Price of Honour

This book is a work of fiction and should not be understood in any other sense. It is set in the context of history to give the story literary credibility. Many of the place names in this book are real, but their descriptions do not necessarily portray accurately the places mentioned. Most of the characters are fictitious. All thoughts or comments, speech and opinions are from the author's own imagination and should not be attributed to any third party, unless otherwise stated. Historical information has on occasion been adjusted to fit the story

The cover artwork is by the author.

If the reader has any comments about the book, the author would be pleased to hear from you.

Sebastian Swan was born in the North East of England not far from Bamburgh, he lectured in Yorkshire then, as the salmon returns to the place of its birth, he returned to the North East when he retired and began writing. All his life he had struggled with the written word, being dyslexic. Where he did excel, was his artwork, he drew and painted from being a small boy.

He had cancer, which forced him to retire, while he was ill, he started to read for pleasure, he couldn't do much else for a while. He found that in reading he could be transported away from the pain to another place, a "Dream World".

One day he thought he could create his own dream world, he would do it through writing, with a little help from his friends, and draw from the vast resources of history and beauty on his doorstep. Writing, he thought, was only an extension of his childhood games. The only limitations were down to imagination.

Most of his books are played out in the beautiful North East of England, where the places in the books can be seen and touched.

Come to the North East, sit on the quiet beaches, close your eyes, and be transported into the world of Sebastian Swan.

David Mattches BA

Briton A.D. 620

Reference Notes

[1] Ælla: The king of the southern half of Northumbria from the River Tees to the River Humber, known as the kingdom of Deira.

[2] Din Guyaroi: Bamburgh, Northumbria, northern England.

[3] Ulfberht: A rare Viking sword, made from 800 to 1000 AD, of crucible steel, the quality was not matched until the industrial revolution.

[4] Wōden: The earliest written documentation of Wōden as an ancestral figure for royalty is in Bede's *Historia ecclesiastica gentis Anglorum* (*HE*) and later in the *Anglo-Saxon Chronicle*.

To understand the nature of Wōden's role in royal genealogies, it is necessary to understand his role as a deity. Most of what we know about Wōden is in fact taken from thirteenth century Icelandic sources about his Norse counterpart Oðinn. These are far from ideal and in fact refer to a potentially very different god in a different country, many centuries after the Anglo-Saxons converted to Christianity.

[5] River Tes: Now known as the River Tees. The name; is thought to be derived from the ancient Welsh word "Tes" meaning "Sunshine and heat."

[6] Gododdin: A people living in the land of Hen Ogledd an area of south-east Scotland.

[7] Monkchester: In Saxon times, Newcastle fell into obscurity when the old Roman fort of Chester was occupied by a small collection of monks and the place came to be known as Monkchester. Newcastle acquired its present name fourteen years after the Norman Conquest when Robert Curthose, the eldest son of William the Conqueror came north on a military expedition into Scotland. Robert stopped at Monkchester where he built a wooden castle, which he called the New Castle.

[8] Eoforwic: The city of York, pre-Norse name of Jorvik.

[9] Abhainn Dubh: River Forth in Scotland.

[10] River Hymbre: The earliest *name for the River Humber* Hymbre – The Anglo-*Saxon* Chronicle

[11] Thwart: A plank forming a structural crosspiece, making a seat for a rower in a boat

[12] Thunor: An Anglo-Saxon god of the sky and thunder and who was a friend of the common man.

[13] Hibernia: Anglo-Saxon name for Ireland.

[14] Grendel: Grendel and his mother are both hunters and guardians of a burial mound in marshland and are given an aquatic aspect to match - *brimwylf*, for instance, meaning "Water-wolf". Picturing bodies of water - usually rivers, but sometimes a lake or sea.

[15] Mete: Saxon word for general food.

[16] Brýdgifu: The **brýdgifu** or the bride's dowry was to be paid by the bride's family and was to belong to her and to be untouchable by her husband. Like the morning gift, it was to ensure, in event of the husband's death or divorce that she and her children were provided for.

[17] The Weofodthegn: The priest officiating at the ceremony, he would call on the gods to hallow the site and would make a statement as to the purpose for gathering. Of the various gods the goddesses Freya and Frige would be particularly invoked as those most involved in weddings, love, marriage, and fertility.

[18] Lôgna: Lôgna has many names throughout the Germanic cultures of that period in history. *Lôgna* is his Anglo-Saxon name. The Vikings called him *Loki Laufeyiarson;* he was not a god at all but rather the full-blooded Giant Lord of mischief who resides with the Gods of the Aesir. He is a son of Farbauti and Laufey and is described as the "Contriver of all fraud". Loki is Blood brother to Odin. With his first wife, Glut he was the father of Einmyria ("Embers") and Eisa ("Spurt")

Loki or Lôgna is also an adept shape-shifter, with the ability to change both his sex and form. As such, Loki represents a random factor, an unpredictable element that, combined with all the other (more stable) forces of nature, produce unknown results that no one, save the Norns themselves can quite foresee. Once while in the form of a mare, Loki accidentally became impregnated with Odin's eight-legged horse Sleipnir by the giant horse Svadilfari "Unlucky traveller".

[19] Ēostre: Goddess of thanksgiving, joy, springtime, and renewal.

[20] Degsastan: The exact location of this battle is not known, but it is recorded by Bede and thought to be near Liddesdale in Scotland.

[21] Taemwerh: Tamworth in Staffordshire, England, located 14 miles (23 km) north-east of Birmingham city.

[22] Pengwern: The exact location of *Llys Pengwern* - the Court of Pengwern - is not known, and the problem is compounded by the fact that several other Pengwerns exist in Wales.

[23] Ella's sons: Ellingham lies in north-eastern Northumberland, close to the North Sea coast. Its landscape is varied and falls from moorland in the west to rolling farmland in the east. The village of Ellingham lies roughly at the centre of the parish and is surrounded on most sides by remnants of its medieval field system. The name Ellingham probably means, "The home of Ella's sons".

Book 1

The Price of Honour

Chapter 1

The Battle of Catraeth
(Catterick) **600AD**

EHIND YOU,' Leofwine yelled as a shining bloodstained war axe descended in a perfect arc towards Wulfstan's spine. Wulfstan instinctively bent his knees on hearing the warning. His warrior's inbred sense of survival energised the muscles in his leg, powering down on his foot and exploding against the resistance of the ground, propelling his weight to the right and pushing him clear of danger. He was now facing the axe-wielding giant Briton, and, in one flowing movement, he delivered a scything slice with his sword, just below the skirt of the man's mail byrnie, slashing ruthlessly across his unprotected thighs. The blow cut through the taut muscles into the bone. The pitiful wretch did no more than throw back his head; squeeze his eyelids together, and groan – either at the sudden pain – or the realisation of his now *certain* fate. The axe continued its travel and buried itself harmlessly in the soft earth beyond Wulfstan's foot. The Briton's legs buckled – and he slumped helplessly to his knees, and his once green leggings turned instantly black from the haemorrhaging wounds.

Wulfstan was a born warrior and he was now on his feet, having turned defence into attack, and he delivered a second stroke to the exposed neck of the Briton kneeling before him. It was delivered with such force it severed the man's spine separating head from body and leaving it swinging macabrely before him, attached only by a sliver of skin. For a second – all was as if frozen in time – and then the body folded – slowly – forward into a twisted grotesque heap.

Wulfstan was momentarily distracted from the horror and the blood-curdling curse swirling mayhem of the battle. His eye had caught the glint of an exposed sword blade in the dead man's belt. It had the strangest markings set into it. Reaching down he tugged it free and pushed it into his own leather scabbard, to examine later when he had a moment. From what he glimpsed in the short time between tugging it from the man's belt, and sliding it into *his* scabbard, he could see it was a fine weapon, and it felt unbelievably light. Such a sword was wasted on a man who obviously preferred his war axe.

The Briton was clearly a man of some consequence, whoever he was, by the look of this sword and his lavishly engraved and gilded helma. Wulfstan hadn't time to take the helma, though tempted, for the battle was raging mercilessly, and distraction's friend this day was certain death. His younger brother Leofwine called, Wulfstan turned, stepped to him, linking shields with him and Cedric, Ælfweard and Godric, and they pushed forward into the thick of the action. Once shoulder-to-shoulder with his brother and these blood-sworn friends from childhood, he felt invincible.

The fighting was vicious, merciless; the grass was slippery with a shimmering coat of red. The stench of death was everywhere, it was stifling, corrupting the air he breathed; he could taste the butchered flesh, it was on his lips and in his mouth. He suddenly retched and vomited. This decaying pollution would be part of him for days; he knew that bathing would not remove this sour metallic tang of blood and corruption. It was all part of the charnel house of offal, in which he was now wallowing. Weariness descended like death upon him and he knew, in the days to come, the horrors of it all would haunt him like a revenant of the night. Some warriors were empowered by the frenzy, but not he. This defilement was contrary to all that he was. *Yes*, he was a warrior, and a warrior that men heralded as an example to follow; he knew fine well how able he was. He was taller than most and built to match. Yes, he could kill, but that was not really the man he was, he was gentle by nature, a farmer, a poet, a builder, not one who destroyed.

The battle seemed to be – *suddenly* – all over. He stood panting, yet, even in this short space of time, while he attempted to still himself and gain some control of his body and mind, the well named carrion crows – had settled and were now feasting on yet warm – dead – eyes.

The Saxons in their vastly greater number had slaughtered the Britons. In their struggle to regain land lost, the Britons had greatly misjudged the Saxons' resolve and had paid the ultimate price. Wulfstan knew there were many factions set against them, tribes and warlords, Celts from the west and south, Picts, and Brythonic people from Hen Ogledd in the north, but as far as he was concerned, they were all Britons and the Saxons were now their masters.

Wulfstan and his four friends touched hands and made their way towards King Æthelfrith.

Æthelfrith lifted his head and watched them as they stepped over the dead and dying, which blocked the path to him. King Ælla of Deira, [1] was standing next to him, both men were clearly exhausted.

'Ealdorman Wulfstan,' Æthelfrith said when he saw Wulfstan. 'So, we have been victorious it appears, my fine warrior. I saw you fighting, and you are indeed all that men say of you, not that I ever doubted it. You are worth ten men, and with these noble friends by your side you are an army,' he laughed, 'pray God you never stand against me.' The five men bowed in response to the King's generous praise.

'You honour us, Lord – as to *victorious*, if that be the word for this bloody day's work, I'll let you proclaim it thus. They fought bravely, but we must have outnumbered them three to one, the fools. If what I have heard be the truth of it, this bloodletting has been a year in the planning,' Wulfstan wearily reached to the outstretched hand of King Æthelfrith.

Æthelfrith grasped it and drew him into an embrace. King Ælla laid his hand upon Wulfstan's shoulder.

'You and your friends are indeed great warriors, Ealdorman, as your king this moment has declared.'

'Whatever this day has spawned, I am glad you are safe my friend. Have you seen or heard what has become of their king?' King Æthelfrith asked, releasing Wulfstan from the embrace.

'No, I've not heard or seen anyone like a king. He may lie on that rise yonder,' Wulfstan nodded to a spot where the last of the fighting had taken place and King Æthelfrith cast his eyes in that direction.

'Aye… perhaps; he would attract the most ferocious fighting and his warriors would try to defend him, and there is surely a hellish mound of dead on that hillock.'

'I warrant that even his mother would be sore pressed to recognise her son's face amongst this, this bloody butchery.' Wulfstan offered, gesturing with a sweep of his hand towards the dead and dying before them.

'Aye, you speak the truth of it, Ealdorman, I will be glad when we are home, safe and sound at Din Guyaroi, [2] and drinking away this glorious victory from our thoughts. Time and ale are great healers and manipulators of the truth. No doubt I will thank Wōden for this day soon enough.'

'Perhaps their king may be identified by the quality of his clothes and weapons, surely they will be finer than that of anyone else.' Wulfstan glanced at the fine cut of what King Æthelfrith was wearing.

'True, I will see for myself before the corpses on that rise are stripped, anything of value will soon vanish.'

'Oswald take some men and guard that ridge until we can take a look. None of the dead lying there are to be touched,' King Ælla said turning to the warrior behind him.

'Yes, Lord,' replied the man who was obviously one of Ælla's huscarls, and he and some other warriors made their way to where the King had directed them.

'I rejoice that you are not hurt my Lords. I will leave now, with your permission, and take stock of my men.'

'Granted, we will meet later.'

Wulfstan and his friends bowed and returned to where they had been fighting. Wulfstan knew it would be several days before they left for home. The men would be searching for whatever they could find of value from the bodies of the fallen. They'd be in no hurry to leave before they'd fed their ever-hungry purses.

There were all manner of weapons and clothing to be taken from the vanquished. Expensive to buy; if good fortune was their friend this day, gold rings and jewellery would be found on the bodies. Wulfstan knew even he was not above taking something of worth from the battlefield. He would try to find the giant with the fine helma; if he was quick and luck was with him, he would make it his own. At the very least, I have a fine sword he thought, as he stood by his standard. He pushed the tip of *his* sword into the soft soil to free his hands and withdrew the Briton's sword from his scabbard.

He carefully examined the weapon. The balance was perfect; he had never held a sword like this. He already had a fine sword of his own; a snake like pattern ran up the blade where the smith had twisted strips of metal together, and at the same time adding strength to the blade. However, this blade was just one piece of metal, longer than usual. He bent it, and it sprung back into shape.

Looking closely at the strange markings on the blade, he tried to make sense of them, +ULFBERH+T. [3] He ran his finger over the slightly raised letters, and he wondered what they meant. He recognised what he guessed were symbols of the Christian Gods, if that is what they were. Then he wondered if it was the name of an old Briton god, but discounted that because of the two crosses and he knew that most of the Britons were Christians, but it was the mighty Wōden, [4] the ancestor of Æthelfrith who had ruled this day. If it *was* the name of the weapon, it was no use to him for the word was meaningless.

'I will call it... Mmmm,' he thought for a while staring into the distance while massaging his chin. One could only dream of a sword like this. 'Perhaps it has come from the world of dreams. Yes – I will call it – Dream World – *yes* that's it, *Dream World*, perfect.'

'A fine sword you have there, brother,' Leofwine said as he walked to Wulfstan.

'One moment Leofwine,' Wulfstan quickly responded, gently moving him to one side with his hand, trying to see beyond him. '*HEY, FELLOW!*' he called to a man he saw with a helma in his hand, he was sure it was the one belonging to the giant Briton he'd slain. 'Where did you get that?'

'What... the helma? I found it, Lord,' he shouted back, apprehensively.

'And what of the head that was in it?'

The man was uneasy now; his Lord knew of his trophy and was about to claim it for his own. 'I hoped to sell it, Lord.'

'What, the head, or the helma?'

'I don't know what you mean Lord,' the man said, reluctantly walking towards Wulfstan.

'Never mind, I will give you my gold arm torc for it.' Wulfstan slipped the torc from his arm and passed it to him. The man stared at it for a moment in disbelief, and then smiled, the smile of a man well pleased.

'The helma is yours Lord, it's too big for me anyway.'

Wulfstan knew that he could have taken the helma without payment, but for the barter, he would gain respect and that had no price upon it. The man bowed and walked off examining his bargain; he knew none of his friends would have a torc like this.

'What to do with you, Brother, that was yours for the taking, you will forever be poor,' Leofwine added and laughed.

'Only in hacksilver and coin, my dear brother, but there are other riches that are beyond price, such as friendship and loyalty.' Leofwine threw back his head, laughed once more, and slapped Wulfstan's back.

'Aye, and you have a king who calls you his friend, so you are rich indeed, Brother. Lesser mortals, such as I, will be happy with hacksilver, friendship with kings can carry a price too great for me, I fear.'

Chapter 2

The Conqueror's Feast

Just as Wulfstan suspected it would be, it was days before the army had had their fill of looting and were ready to make tracks for their homeland of Bernicia, north of the River Tes, [5] and on to their home of Din Guyaroi.

They had buried the body of a man whom King Æthelfrith decided was the Gododdin's dead King, [6] though how his name was pronounced was beyond Wulfstan. It seemed of the few Gododdins who'd not been killed, each spoke the King's name with their own dialect and from one person to the next, the versions were so varied, Wulfstan was not even certain they were speaking of the same man. The best sense Wulfstan could make of what they said, was that their king had been a Briton from the south-west; in the land, some called, Wælisc. However, "A" man had been buried and honoured as a king, and that was enough to satisfy King Æthelfrith. Wulfstan knew that King Æthelfrith set great store by royal lines knowing his ancestor Wōden, was the god of kings.

He knew kings were more than ordinary beings and thus even enemies should be afforded due respect. Otherwise, lowly slaves might see fit to challenge them, imagining that they be their equals.

Once on their way, the army travelled at walking pace, though the leaders were mounted, most of the warriors were on foot. The King insisted that the army be kept together. He wanted to be sure that there were no factions of Britons yet roaming the remote countryside, who might take advantage of fewer numbers if they were spread out.

It took several days travel up past Monkchester, [7] at the end of the old wall, then on to the settlement of Wick on the River Aln, before they descended from the higher ground towards the coast and their capital of Din Guyaroi, with its fort set on the black whinstone rock overlooking the beach. It was a relief to all to be once more within breathing distance of the fresh sea air, after the memory of the rotting stench of decaying flesh they'd left behind. They had buried some of the dead, but most had been left to rot where they'd fallen.

Having bought and paid for his new helma, Wulfstan had not yet tried it on. He would let the gruesome image fade for a while, and he'd set a servant to thoroughly clean it before he tried it for size. It was indeed a work of great beauty. The craftsmanship was remarkable, it was even inlaid with gold. He'd never seen anything like it. In addition to the helma of course, he had a sword, which he'd gained, and *it* – was almost magical. Once in the hand it mystically drew him forward into action. A thing of extraordinary beauty though it was, this was no passive adornment.

Wulfstan spent a great deal of the journey in the company of King Æthelfrith. The King seemed to want his companionship, and Wulfstan found the King to his liking, so it was agreeable to them both. His father had often met with Æthelfrith, but *he* had only had fleeting conversations with him. Since his father had died of a bloody flux the year past, Wulfstan was now the Lord of the estate and directly answerable to the King. He had a feeling though that the King was deliberately endeavouring to get to know him better as if assessing him, which unnerved him slightly.

The Beast of Bamburgh

King Ælla of Deira had said his farewells at Catraeth, and then he set off south with his men for his capital at Eoforwic. [8] He said as he held Æthelfrith's hand, that he hoped for even closer ties in the months to come. Ælla must have been –

almost – old enough to be Æthelfrith's father, Wulfstan speculated.

When they were within a day of Din Guyaroi, riders were sent ahead to warn the stronghold to be prepared for King Æthelfrith's arrival. There would be feasting and celebration to welcome him after his great victory over the Gododdins.

The border between Æthelfrith's kingdom and the Gododdins had always been a contentious divide. The River Tweid was the token separation. That division was no more, the savages who dwelt to the north, were now subject to a new *undisputed* Lord, King Æthelfrith of Bernicia – Lord of all.

His new kingdom stretched as far north as the river Abhainn Dubh. [9] Since his great victory at Catraeth, Æthelfrith was King of a vast empire.

As they neared the settlement of Din Guyaroi, there was great cheering by ceorls and thralls standing on the roadside. The bulk of the army made camp at the foot of the great rock whilst the leaders rode on up the rocky path into the stockade, and dismounted, bond-servants welcomed them offering ale.

Edgar, a thegn, whom Æthelfrith had left in charge, bowed, and informed him that a feast had been set out in the long hall, as he'd been commanded.

The King was in high spirits and set his arm around Wulfstan's shoulder. 'This is a fine welcome for us,' he said as he passed, casually tearing a piece of flesh from an ox turning on a spit in the yard. He swore and tossed the meat back and forth in his hands for it was hotter than he'd expected, but even this shock didn't upset his good temper. 'Come, join me at the high table, Ealdormen, for you are all worthy of honour.'

Once the King had taken his place, he beckoned Wulfstan to be seated by his side. No sooner had they seated than the food came, and mouth-watering it was.

The horrors would not be remembered this night, with the help of a surfeit of fine ale and good food, just as Æthelfrith had predicted.

'Do you wonder why I am eager to have you seated next to me, Ealdorman?' Æthelfrith asked as he sank his teeth into a leg of mutton, grease, and fat soaking into his beard which he wiped with the back of his hand. 'Other than the obvious pleasure of your good company that is,' he laughed.

'Is – there *another* reason you honour me, Lord?'

'Indeed, there is… I am looking for a man, a noble man, whom I can trust, someone like you. I have been watching you and I see how others try to imitate you. Even warriors with greater experience talk about you with admiration and respect. For the work of such importance that I have in mind, I need such a man, Ealdorman Wulfstan. I remember your father and his faithful service both to my father *and* me.'

'You are generous, my King.' Wulfstan said bowing his head. 'I am sworn to you. I will do whatever you ask of me, and I pray to the great Wōden that I will never fail your trust.'

'From the likes of you, Ealdorman, I know that to be the truth.' Æthelfrith took a long drink from his bejewelled golden chalice. 'This is the work I have for you… King Ælla – has offered me the hand of his daughter, the Princess Aefre, and I want you to go to Eoforwic to fetch her.' Wulfstan was quite at a loss, and Æthelfrith laughed at his obvious unease.

'This is a great honour and responsibility you would entrust to me, Lord.'

'Indeed, but I have given it much thought over the last days. King Ælla is not young and when he passes on our Kingdoms will be one, and all the stronger for that.'

'What of King Ælla's son, how does he feel about this, if I may ask Lord?'

'Aye… *Eadwine* – mmm – we'll see where that lonnen leads us when we come to the fork in the track, *but* in any event our position will be strengthened, *and* – she is very beautiful, – so I'm told,' Æthelfrith said prodding Wulfstan with the mutton leg that was in his hand, laughing lecherously. 'How say you, will you do this for me, Ealdorman Wulfstan?'

'If it is your wish, I will do as you ask, I am your servant, Lord.'

'*Excellent,* – good fellow, I know I have chosen wisely, we will talk about the details when my head's once more mine to own. Besides this is a night for forgetting this world,' he laughed again.

The feasting and drinking went on until the early hours, most slept where they collapsed. Wulfstan was no different; he'd slipped from his chair and lay contentedly amongst the rush floor covering. He was awoken early, not by the sounds of a new day, but by the pain of an overfull bladder and an urgent need to relieve himself.

At first, he had no idea where he was; someone was lying on his head. He struggled from under the weight and with some effort clambered unsteadily to his feet, rubbing his eyes and blinking. It was yet dark, and he stumbled in the darkness over the bodies. He felt his way along the edge of a table towards the faint moonlight coming through the open door, when suddenly his hand touched the tail of a dog dangling over the tabletop where it slept, such was his shock his bladder nearly released its contents. He was trembling now, if his need for relief were not so urgent, he would have strangled the animal with his bare hands. Once outside he gave a long slow sigh of relief, as the pressure eased.

A shiver ran through him as the cold night air began to work its magic on his bewilderment and he slowly began to make sense of the swirling confusion in his brain. As the pain in his bladder subsided, he had time to take note of the familiar surroundings. He stared down to the beach, and his eyes caught sight of the blue light from the moon flickering across the top of the waves as they lazily tumbled onto the sandy beach.

He fastened his britches, rubbed his eyes once more, and decided to walk out of the fort and down to the shore. Hesitating for a moment, tempted to return to the hall to find a warm spot and more sleep, but he knew his head would be better for the fresh air, so he set off towards the beach.

'Ahh, I love this place,' he said to himself, filling his lungs with the salty sea air as he clambered down the hill onto the soft sand. He walked for about half a league to the rocky outcrop at the far end of the beach, sat on the rocks for a while glanced one more time out to sea, then made his way back to the fort.

By the time he climbed up the rough steps hewn into the rock, walked through the gate and up to the long hall, the settlement was beginning to come to life. Servants and slaves were already at work preparing food for the new day.

'Here fellow, fetch me something plain to break the night's fast, bread and cheese and ale will suffice,' he instructed a sleepy-eyed bond-servant who had probably never slept all night.

'Yes, Lord.' Wulfstan took his seat once more at the high table. He felt better for his walk and smiled at the groans and curses of those returning to the land of the living. The King was nowhere to be seen; Wulfstan guessed he would probably be emptying his bladder, which would be the first thought of most who were now stirring.

Chapter 3

In search of a Queen

While Wulfstan waited for his food, he thought again on the work he'd been asked to do for the King and wondered what such employment might entail. He glanced up and saw the King coming towards him, no smiles this day, merely a grunt of acknowledgement as he took his seat next to Wulfstan, he banged his knee on the table as he did so and cursed.

'*Some ale,*' he called out impatiently to a slave as he vigorously rubbed his knee, and she scuttled quickly to him with a jug. The King grunted once more then gulped greedily from his now full chalice. 'Ah, that's better, my mouth tasted as if I'd been licking your backside, Ealdorman.' Wulfstan smiled. 'Feeling as I do, it does not please me to see you looking so irritatingly well this morning, was the night past not to your liking?'

'Aye… it was a fine enough night, Lord. I've been awake for some time, and I went for a walk on the beach, it's cleared my head.'

'Ah.'

'Is it too early in the day to talk about this mission you wish me to undertake for you, Lord?'

'What mission's that?'

'Your bride, you wanted me to fetch her.'

'I mentioned, that did I? Æthelfrith smiled, 'I don't remember.' Wulfstan's question seemed to focus Æthelfrith's thoughts. 'Aye, I want you to go to Eoforwic within the month, even sooner. You can sail in my longboat, up the River Ouse into the heart of Eoforwic. I want a show of wealth and my fine longboat, will do that. Also, it will be a more suitable way for the Princess to travel here. She needs to see how I honour her.'

'Would it not be more fitting for *you* to go Lord?'

Æthelfrith looked at him as if it was the most foolish of questions. After a moment's hesitation, he shrugged his shoulders; he must have decided that the question was well-intentioned.

'No, no, that would never do, you are an innocent, Ealdorman. I'm a great king, people come to *me*, I do not go to them, King Ælla understands this; we talked on it. It is a great honour for his daughter to marry me.'

'I'm sure his daughter will see it as such, Lord.'

Æthelfrith laughed and grimaced then squeezed his eyelids together; laughter was not what his aching head needed at this moment. 'Too early for laughter, my head's not in a fit state for such disturbance this morning… In truth, I've never seen the girl, and she's never seen me, but she will understand her duty, and I'm not a bad fellow, what say you?'

'Indeed Lord, as kings go,' Wulfstan smiled, and Æthelfrith *almost* laughed once more but curbed the instinct just in time to spare himself more throbbing misery.

'Here, drink to a fine bride with broad childbearing hips, Ealdorman,' and Æthelfrith clumsily lifted his chalice to touch Wulfstan's drinking horn.

Having eaten what was set before him, Wulfstan went to find his brother and friends. After their brief recollections of the night past were exchanged, he gave orders to his brother Leofwine, to see to the work on their estate while he was gone. He explained the employment he'd been given by the King, and bade farewell to Leofwine and his friends, apart from Cedric; he would take Cedric with him. The rest of the men whom Æthelfrith had chosen to go to Eoforwic, were little more than faces to Wulfstan, so he'd be thankful for a loyal friend whom he knew and trusted.

'If we don't see you again before we leave, I know you intended to return home this day, and we will go as soon as we are ready, you take care. You will be as aware as me, of the responsibility you now shoulder.'

'Aye, I know well enough, Leofwine, but it will benefit our family and people to do this for the King.'

'Just take care, that's all I will say.' Wulfstan embraced his brother and friends and left them to prepare for their journey home.

He was busy for the next days; there were stores to organise for the voyage and gifts to be safely stored, an oak chest had been provided for the purpose. There was a bearskin coat for King Ælla, a seax with a gold inlaid bone handle for Prince Eadwine, and for the Princess Acha a gold penannular brooch. Princess Aefre was given a magnificent richly woven purple winter cloak, also a gold necklace, and a ring set with large pieces of amber. Truly, gifts fit for a future queen.

Wulfstan enjoyed sea travel; though he was the leader of this mission, he was thankful he was not the one responsible for sailing the longboat.

This was indeed a fine boat, it was built by a Norseman who had fled from Zealand to Bernicia and thrown himself on the mercy of King Æthelfrith. Æthelfrith, seeing the potential of having such a guest, welcomed him. Wulfstan didn't know the full story, but whatever it was, Æthelfrith had ended up with a beautiful vessel, unlike any other Wulfstan had seen.

They sailed down the coast to the mouth of the River Hymbre [10] and into King Ælla's kingdom, up the Hymbre then onto the River Ouse.

Wulfstan insisted his men made a visible show of arms when they sailed up the Ouse. They would be noticed and may well be seen as a threat. He hoped that the sight of fighting men would be enough to let them pass by unhindered. Whoever saw them would not want to fight unknown warriors unless forced.

Wulfstan breathed a sigh of relief when he saw the landing stage at Eoforwic; clearly, Ælla had been informed of the approach of an unknown longboat, which was not a trading vessel, for there were armed men at the landing to meet them. Wulfstan knew he would need to quickly make his intention known to avoid a bloody conflict.

On drawing near, Wulfstan was relieved to see Oswald, Ælla's huscarl, who he remembered from the battle at Catraeth. He stood at the prow of the longship so that Oswald could see him, and he hoped, recognise him. Oswald must have remembered him for the welcome party made a show of putting up their weapons, Oswald even waved.

The longboat bumped and scraped along the timbered side of the landing; the side of the longboat thankfully was protected by well-positioned rope for that very purpose.

'Greetings Ealdorman,' Oswald offered, bowing, as Wulfstan leapt from the boat, 'King Ælla has been expecting you.'

'We come as friends, it's good to see a face I know. We have gifts for the great King from my Lord, King Æthelfrith. Can you see that such is taken to his palace?'

'My men will see to all your wishes, while I take you to meet my Lord. It's not far we can walk.'

Wulfstan spoke to Cedric; telling him to see that all was done as he would wish, 'Make sure no one is tempted to open the chest Cedric, see that all are fed, and keep our men together.' Wulfstan turned once more to Oswald, 'I will leave Cedric,' he gestured to him, 'he will be in charge in my absence,' Oswald bowed and led Wulfstan in the direction of a large timbered longhouse he assumed was Ælla's hall.

By the time they had walked the short distance to the great hall, he saw King Ælla, two girls and a young man, waiting to welcome them. Wulfstan assumed one was the Princess Aefre, the other her younger sister Acha, and her brother Eadwine. Wulfstan bowed, and King Ælla introduced his family. Wulfstan bowed to each as they were introduced. He took particular note of the Princess Aefre, for she was the purpose of his visit. This girl is indeed extraordinarily beautiful he thought.

Chapter 4

Welcomed to Eoforwic

Wulfstan was warmly welcomed, Ælla generously made known to all around Wulfstan's prowess as a warrior, but *Wulfstan* was distracted by the shy beauty of this Princess. King Æthelfrith would not be disappointed by this girl as his Queen, he thought. She was every inch a Queen, her whole manner and bearing denoted her as such. She was slender, tall, above average height for a woman, with fair hair, which shone as if sprinkled with gold.

Her features were exquisite, she was tanned, obviously someone who liked to be outdoors. Perhaps the court was not her preferred habitat. He couldn't see the colour of her eyes, as she didn't look at him directly. Her brother was also a fine looking fellow, who smiled liberally, her elder, Wulfstan guessed. Princess Acha was obviously the youngest but was also destined to be a beautiful woman. He glanced at their father and smiled... his children clearly favoured their mother.

Wulfstan was shown into the hall and food was set before him, as he was about to take the seat offered, he looked up to see two men carrying Æthelfrith's oak chest into the hall.

'My King, your friend, has sent gifts for you and your family, Lord,' Wulfstan pointed to the chest as it was set down before the King. Wulfstan rose and went to open it; he passed the gifts to each in turn. These were gifts of great cost, and that would be noted by Ælla.

'My friend, King Æthelfrith, honours us.'

'He considers this naught compared to the honour you afford to him, my Lord.' Wulfstan smiled in the direction of the Princess and was certain he detected a slight blush on her face at the meaning of his compliment.

King Ælla smiled, 'this is a covenant between two friends, which will strengthen our kingdoms, now and in the future. There are no ties like blood ties, Ealdorman.'

That night Wulfstan was honoured as the representative of King Æthelfrith and sat next to King Ælla, who had ordered a lavish feast for his guests. Prince Eadwine sat to the right of his father with Wulfstan to his left and next to him, was seated the

Princess Aefre and, her sister, Acha. It was as if in the absence of King Æthelfrith he was to be understood as the embodiment of his Lord.

Wulfstan was obliged to make conversation with the Princess. It was difficult at first, but as the night went on, she relaxed. She told him her mother had died recently from a fall; she'd broken her leg, and the wound had turned putrid. Wulfstan told her how sorry he was to hear such, and that he had some understanding of her loss, for his father, had not long been dead. He told her how close he'd been to his father, because his mother had died when his brother was born, he'd been only three. She furrowed her brow and told him she was sorry for his loss, at least she yet had her father, brother, and sister.

'Did your brother live?'

'Yes, he is called Leofwine and is at our home taking care of our people while I'm away. We are very close.'

She asked him about his home. Wulfstan knew that she really wanted to ask about King Æthelfrith, but she probably did not think such a question appropriate.

Wulfstan told her about her new home of Din Guyaroi and went on to talk about Æthelfrith. He told her how handsome and generous he was, how he was loved by his subjects, *which* – was the truth, but Wulfstan was not sure that the Princess believed him.

She asked how old Æthelfrith was, Wulfstan said he did not know his exact age, but he thought he was perhaps a little older than he was by two or three years, that seemed to please her.

Out of the blue, Wulfstan asked her if she was afraid, and regretted his over-familiar question. She hesitated and stared at the table for a while then in a soft voice, said, 'A little.'

He wanted to take her hand and reassure her; instead he said, 'don't be afraid my Lady, you will always have a friend in me.' For the first time, she looked into his eyes, only for the briefest moment, and smiled.

'Thank you.'

King Ælla nudged his arm and told him that on the morrow, they would ride around Eoforwic, and he would show him his capital. Wulfstan thanked him and said that he would like that.

'All have heard of the fine trading centre of Eoforwic, you have built a place to be envied, such is down to your wise counsel, Lord.' Ælla acknowledged his compliment with a smile and slight dip of his head.

After the meal there was music and dancing, not by those on the high table, they only watched.

'Do you like to dance, my Lady?' Wulfstan asked Aefre.

She laughed, exposing beautiful even white teeth. 'Indeed, I do, and you, Ealdorman?'

'I love to dance, but that does not mean I am any good. Ladies do not rush to be my partner, fearing for the well-being of their feet.'

'I can't believe that. I'd imagine that you have ladies aplenty, vying for your attention.' She again blushed. After collecting herself, she added, 'perhaps one day I will be honoured. I will wear my winter boots,' she said and they both laughed.

It was late, and King Ælla rose, saying that Wulfstan and his men would be tired after their long journey, and he must be a considerate host. He beckoned a servant and told him to show the Ealdorman and his men where they would be sleeping. Wulfstan stood and took the Princess' hand to politely raise her to her feet. She bowed, and Wulfstan went off with his men. They had been given a house to themselves. Once it was known where they were to sleep, Wulfstan and Cedric walked to their longboat to see it was adequately guarded.

'What did you make of our new Queen, Wulfstan?'

'I liked her.'

'I'm sure King Æthelfrith will be well pleased. If I find a wife the like of her, I will feel like a king, she's a rare beauty for sure. I see she has a sister, has she any other near kin who would wish to be wed to a handsome huscarl?'

Wulfstan laughed and pushed him, 'I'm sure she has, but if she wants a handsome huscarl – that excludes you.' Cedric laughed too and playfully punched his arm.

On the morrow, as King Ælla had promised, Cedric and Wulfstan were shown around the city. It was bigger than they expected, it was indeed a city of trade.

There were ships from across the sea and merchants on the quay selling all manner of exotic merchandise, even silks from the east. Wulfstan wondered if Princess Aefre might find Din Guyaroi very drab, after all she had here.

There were many stone buildings from the time of the Roman conquest; though most had fallen into disrepair, it was clear that they had once been magnificent. Wulfstan was shown floors decorated with scenes made from coloured stone pieces, he'd never seen anything like these wonders. King

Æthelfrith might have a larger kingdom than King Ælla, but he doubted if it was as wealthy.

Chapter 5

The Storm

Wulfstan was not exactly *eager* to be on his way home to Din Guyaroi, but he thought he ought to be leaving soon. Aefre seemed to be dragging her heels. If he was being honest, he was enjoying the Princess' company.

Eventually, he suggested to King Ælla that King Æthelfrith might be anxious for the well-being of his future bride. It was now three weeks since he'd arrived. King Ælla said he would see that they left by the end of the week. He seemed to be as reluctant to say goodbye to his daughter, as she was to leave.

King Ælla was as good as his word, and by the end of the week, they were packed, and all had gathered at the quay to say farewell to the Princess. There were no tears; Wulfstan assumed all the tears had been shed in private.

Wulfstan took the hand of the Princess and helped her into the longboat, smiled and told her once more that he would look after her. His kindness almost broke her brave resolve, and her lip trembled, but she managed to retain her dignified appearance so as not to make this parting any more difficult for her family than it already was.

The ropes holding the longboat were loosened and thrown to them, oars pushed against the timber of the landing, and she glided gently… away from the past and into the future.

The moment was starkly reinforced when her silence was sharply invaded by the sound of the master's voice, "*PULL*". The oars dipped as one into the river, and the boat came to life.

Aefre staggered at the sudden change of direction and Wulfstan took her arm to steady her. She quickly grabbed hold of the side, but her eyes never left her family, and she continued to look back until they were swallowed up by the distance.

Wulfstan patted the thwart [11] where he was sitting. 'Here, be seated Princess, it's a fair journey, too far to stand I fear.'

She smiled sadly at his attempt to lighten her mood.

'Thank you,' she said and sat down next to him.

'There are some sheepskins over there,' he pointed, 'where you may lie down and rest if you wish.'

'Thank you, my Lord, but I don't imagine I will be able to sleep.'

'You will be surprised, the gentle motion either makes you sick or sleepy and for you, I hope it's the latter.'

'I have never been on the sea before.'

They both turned their heads to the sound of the great square sail being hoisted. She gazed forlornly at the significance as if she was staring into her future, helpless to the vagaries of the wind of fortune, which would fill and shape it to its will. She lowered her gaze, and Wulfstan gently touched her shoulder.

'I'm not without any understanding of how difficult this must be for you, my Lady. At least you have your two maids, so they are two familiar faces. What are they called?' he asked, at a loss as what to say.

She looked up at the two girls leaning over the side, idly laughing and talking to each other. 'That is Edith with the dark hair, and as you can see Rowena is fair, which is the meaning of her name.'

'Have they been with you a long time?'

'Yes, we have grown up together.'

He tried to engage her in conversation on their way down the two rivers to the sea, hoping to occupy her mind on other things rather than dwelling on all she was leaving behind.

The day changed once they left the mouth of the Hymbre and were on the open sea heading north. The sky became overcast then quickly darkened, and the swell increased. The longboat sank into troughs, so the sea appeared above them, then they rose up onto the crest of the wave and the sea was below them. There was an unnerving silence from those onboard. Wulfstan didn't want to make his ward fearful, but he was not sure what to say to put her mind at rest. This was a new experience to him too; he was not an experienced sailor by any measure.

It began to rain; at first, it was light, no more than a shower. Wulfstan ordered that a spare sail should be rigged across the boat to give the Princess and her maids some shelter. No sooner had that been attended to than the heavens opened, and all seemed to *suddenly change*.

That gentle sea which had been merely but an element of nature, its single purpose for being was to provide an ideal surface for the sailors to guide their graceful vessel upon. Not now, now it was wretchedly different from that calm shining pond of laughter and leisure on which they made south for Eoforwic but three weeks past. The waves were now thrashing white horses of ferocity bursting over the side; and the ship was taking on water quicker than they could bail it out.

'It is my suggestion Lord, that we try to beach just south of the River Tes, and let the storm blow itself out. There are some fine sandy beaches there, and we have a shallow draft, made for such a landing. We can re-float her after the storm settles,' the master shouted to Wulfstan, hoping that the howling wind was not stealing his words from Wulfstan's ears.

Wulfstan had heard him. 'You know better than me Godfread,' he shouted back, 'we will be guided by you, you must do what is best for the safety of the Princess.'

Wulfstan ducked under the makeshift shelter and wrapped *his* cloak on top of the one Aefre was already wearing, desperate to protect her from the bitter cold.

'Ealdorman, you need your cloak to keep yourself dry and warm!'

'No, I might be needed to help; I will be hampered by it. Can you swim?'

'No!'

'Well hang on to me if the worst comes to the worst, do you hear? Just hang on, come what may. The Master, Godfread, is going to try to run the boat aground on a sandy beach he knows, not far north of here.'

All were watching with bated breath, as the boat was being driven ever closer to a large cliff off the lee side.

'If we make it around the headland, Lord, there are beaches just beyond,' Godfread yelled.

The gale was howling, and the salt spray was lashing the faces and eyes of the sailors. Suddenly there was a sound like a roar of thunder, and the sail tore loose and flapped wildly, casting one sailor over the side into the boiling foam, he disappeared from sight in seconds.

'Catch hold of those ropes and bring that sail under control or we'll be dragged onto the rocks.' Godfread was screaming out an endless stream of orders and men were being thrown from side to side as they tried to do what he commanded.

One poor fellow fell, and his arm snapped like a dry twig. Wulfstan reached for him and dragged him howling under the cover beside them.

'Keep still you fool, or I'll toss you overboard and be done with you, I might do that anyway.' The man reduced his cries to a pathetic whimper. Wulfstan broke the shaft of a spear over his knee for a splint and bound it to the sailor's arm with a shawl from one of the maids.

It would have to do for now until they were safe on land, if they didn't make it, it wouldn't matter anyway. The man fainted and was unconscious long enough for his arm to be straightened and bound. The ice-cold water swilling around where he lay soon revived him. Cedric wedged him against one of the ribs of the boat and a tool chest. He groaned miserably, but for now, he was safe.

Wulfstan and Cedric did what they could to keep the three women secure by forcing them into a corner. He felt helpless; he pushed his back between some timbers and held onto the Princess for dear life.

The sailors had managed to fasten down the sail. Aefre watched them over Wulfstan's shoulder, hardly daring to breathe.

Wulfstan and Cedric were more concerned by the view to the lee, as they inched perilously around the rocky outcrop.

'Thank Wōden we've made it beyond that point. We are now being swept toward the beach as Godfread hoped. I can just make it out, look there, at the waves powering up the shore.'

Aefre twisted her head round to see where he pointed, 'Yes, you're right, I see it,' she responded with relief.

Godfread never ceased pushing and pulling men *and* ropes, to do all he could to save them, and then he turned to them and shouted.

'When we hit the beach, the longboat will stop suddenly, and sea will try to turn us over. Hang on like never before, the impact will be enough to rip your arms from their sockets. If you don't have a good hold onto something solid, you'll probably be tossed about like a bit of flotsam and likely break your neck. Look out for each other; get clear of the boat and up the beach as soon as possible. There will be no time to waste.'

Godfread's advice was hardly necessary; fear was in control of their limbs at this point. Suddenly their paltry shelter was ripped from its fastenings and blown over the side. Not that it mattered; they were all soaked to the skin.

'Get ready, here goes, hang on...' Godfread shouted his last order before they beached.

There was the most deafening scraping and creaking as the boat struck the shore... the boat stopped instantly. Pain shot up Wulfstan's arm as he resisted the impact by hanging on to an oarlock with one arm, and Cedric with the other, encircling the women. Aefre was nearly strangling him she clung to him so tightly. Just as Godfread had said, the waves were now trying to turn the boat over, and it trembled in shuddering spine-chilling spasms.

'Help us with the women, we must get clear and up the beach,' Wulfstan shouted to a sailor about to jump for his life, to another he ordered him to help the man with the broken arm.

In an impulsive moment of reassurance, he pressed his lips to Aefre's head and told her to stay with him, he grabbed a piece of rope and tied it around her waist and through his belt with enough slack for him to get over the side.

'Now hang on,' he shouted to Aefre as he jumped into the roaring surf. His head went under the water, and he surfaced coughing and spluttering trying to wipe his eyes so he could see. He reached up for her, and she clambered over into his arms, as he turned to carry her ashore, a spar, which had broken loose, struck him savagely on the side of his head. He was stunned and stumbled back against the boat, blood pouring down his face. He managed to cling to the Princess and carry her to the shore then tumbled with her yet in his arms falling headfirst into the surf. She shook herself free of him and lifted his face clear of the water, all the while screaming for help. Cedric, who had seen to the safety of the other girls ran to her side and dragged Wulfstan up the beach clear of the merciless waves.

'Dear mother of Wōden no, no, he's dead!' She cried burying her face in her hands.

'Still yourself *woman*, he's not dead.' He spoke to her so sharply that it shook her from her moment of panic. Cedric took Wulfstan's wrist with one hand, slipped his other arm between his legs, and lifted him onto his shoulder. 'Come with me, we'll make for the shelter of the dunes and try to get a fire going somehow.'

As they neared the dunes Aefre spotted a hut, perhaps it belonged to fishermen.

'There Cedric, *look*, make to that hut.'

Cedric was struggling now his muscles were on fire. She pushed open the door for Cedric, and he tumbled onto his knees gasping for breath. Aefre dragged Wulfstan from him, wrapped him in her arms and covered them with their cloaks.

'Cedric, see if anyone has a steel to make a spark, we need a fire, there is dry wood enough in here, we must get him warm.'

'Yes, my Lady, I will be as quick as I can,' he pushed himself to his feet and left them. Aefre tore a strip from her dress and bandaged Wulfstan's head. She was fearful for him; he was drained of colour, and cold as any corpse.

Chapter 6

The binding of friends

Cedric returned with Godfread who had the means to make a spark. They made a pile of dried chippings and quickly got a fire going, which brought warmth and light to the cramped space. The small hut soon warmed up, even if Cedric was compelled to open the door to vent the smoke before they all choked.

Wulfstan coughed and gradually opened his eyes, 'Thank God,' Aefre whispered, yet holding him in her arms.

'My Lady, Cedric, Godfread, what's happened?' he croaked and coughed once more.

'You were struck on the head by a spar from the boat, and Cedric carried you here. How do you feel?'

'I don't know… my head is pounding fit to burst. What of the men and the boat?'

'We are all safe and sound; bar the one we lost overboard when the sail broke loose. Even the fellow with the broken arm made it, and lives to tell the tale.'

'Thanks be to God, and the longboat?'

'Fear not, it is secure; we have fastened it with ropes tied to stakes driven deep into the shore. It will need some repairs, but we will attend to that when the storm blows itself out.'

'Cedric, you must organise some guards, we don't want to be attacked before we understand our position.'

'I have already done that Lord, it was my first thought.'

'I'm sorry my friend, I should have known that you would think of that. It seems I am not needed, then I am a fortunate man to have cracked my skull.'

'*What*,' exclaimed Aefre.

'Who would not wish to be cared for by such a nurse?'

Suddenly she felt very awkward holding his head in her lap.

'I had to force her to care for you, she was for leaving you to drown,' Cedric laughed.

'But, but…'

'Pay no heed to us, my Lady, we are savages next to you,' Cedric reassured her, and she smiled at their teasing. She liked these men and knew, that this day, they had been bound together having shared the cusp where life and death met.

Wulfstan tried to brush off his injury, he wanted to alleviate Aefre's concerns, but in truth, he didn't feel well. He felt nauseous, had a constant headache, and all he really wanted to do was sleep.

Despite his efforts, Aefre was concerned, but Cedric reassured her that this was all normal. He had seen many warriors who'd had worse blows to the head, and they'd made full recoveries.

'Do not fret my Lady; Wulfstan always makes a fuss when he is injured to gain the attention of beautiful ladies. Don't spoil him, he's a baby.'

She smiled; Aefre had insisted that he and Cedric remain in the hut with her and her maids.

Once the storm had abated, Cedric and Godfread were able to take stock of their location. They walked to the top of the dunes to survey the surrounding land and saw that there was a village no more than half a league from the shore, and guessed that the huts, for there were three in all, belonged to men from the settlement.

They contacted the elders of the village; some had even fought at the Battle of Catraeth as part of their levy to their King, Ælla, and had heard of the great warrior, Ealdorman Wulfstan. They were taken to the thegn, who knew that it was in his interest to see that King Ælla's daughter was given care. He insisted she was brought to *his* house and given the best room. Aefre made sure that all who were with her from the longboat were housed and fed. She was adamant that Wulfstan came with her so she could personally see to his care until he recovered.

The Thegn, Edgar, would do as she wished and Wulfstan was carried to his longhouse. She wanted him to have the framed cot in the room, and she would sleep on the floor with her maids, but he drew the line at that. He would join the other men as soon as he was able. They'd been given a hut in the village.

All who had been shipwrecked were cared for generously, as she had ordered. Edgar was determined that there would be no tales of shabby treatment of the daughter of King Ælla; she would have the best he could offer.

Cedric arranged with Edgar that riders would be sent to both King Ælla and King Æthelfrith, to tell of the storm, and give them assurance that all were well and safe.

While Wulfstan rested, Godfread managed the repair work on their longboat. Wulfstan slowly recovered, as Cedric knew he would. He spent a great deal of his time with the Princess whilst he regained his strength. Wulfstan thought that they were even becoming token friends. However, she was above him, and would no doubt forget him once she was Queen. They went for walks, sometimes down to the sea to watch the men working on the longboat.

The work was almost completed now, and the boat was once again seaworthy, much to Wulfstan's relief. He knew how proud Æthelfrith was of his longboat and he didn't want to be the one to tell him it had been destroyed.

He had enjoyed this time with Aefre, perhaps *too* much. He was sure that she had also been contented in *his* company, but it was never spoken of in so many words. Such pleasure had deadly barbs, which were for a fool to own.

They would leave Edgar and his village on the morrow's first tide. Channels had been dug so that when the water rose, they could easily re-float the longboat.

Wulfstan walked back from the shore to the longhouse to tell the Princess of his plans, but he couldn't find her anywhere, then he spotted her maid, Rowena, hanging out washing and went to her.

'Where is the Princess?' She turned to the sound of his voice.

'She's walked up the hill behind the village, Lord,' Rowena said nervously, removing a peg from between her lips and pointing in the direction Aefre had gone.

'*What*... on her own?'

'Yes, Lord.'

'You, foolish girl, how could you allow such a thing?' Wulfstan was furious. The girl was terrified and began to cry.

'I'm s-s-sorry Lord, I begged her not to go on her own,' she blurted out in between sobs, 'but she bade me stay here. She said she *wanted* to be alone. I tried to find you or Cedric, to tell you, but you were nowhere to be found.'

Wulfstan listened impatiently; he knew that the girl had probably done her best to dissuade Aefre. Yet, he still *growled* without any sympathy for her tears and stormed off in the direction the maid had pointed.

Chapter 7

The price of fate

As Wulfstan neared the summit of the hill overlooking the bay, he spotted Aefre sitting with her back against a stone cairn, staring out to sea. She seemed totally oblivious to her surroundings or any threat, as if in another world.

He decided to walk round to be in front of her so that she would see him and not be startled. Even when he was in view, it was a moment before she responded to his presence.

'*Princess*,' he called to her and bowed.

'*My Lord Wulfstan!*' she was clearly surprised to see him suddenly before her.

'I was worried, my Lady, it is not safe for you to be so far from the village on your own.'

'Forgive me, I didn't mean to cause you any concern, it was thoughtless.'

'Well… you are safe – that's all that matters to me.'

She frowned as she looked up at him. 'Is that *really* all that matters to you, Lord?'

He hesitated for a moment, thrown by her odd question. 'I have sworn to take you safely to my King, your safety is everything, my Lady.'

'Mmmm, your loyalty does you credit,' she turned from him and stared once more out to sea. 'Can you give me a moment longer before we walk back, sit with me for a while… I know you are anxious to be on your way home, to fulfil your employment. I suppose now that our boat has been repaired, there is nothing to keep us here.' This time it was she who hesitated... 'Has there been – *no* – pleasure for you in your work, *no* memories you might treasure from these days past?' She drew her legs up, rested her arms across her knees, laid her brow forward onto her arms, hiding her face from him, and waited silently for his response.

He sat down by her side as she'd directed, reached forward, picked up a rock from the ground, and examined it thoughtfully for some time before he spoke. It was a piece of pink granite with white quartz lines running through it.

'So many facets to this one rock in my hand... so many ways to look at it... beautiful though it is. Yet, it is a hard thing, and in the hands of an enemy, it could easily take the life of a loved one. Aye... I have memories, memories that a wise man would best not dwell on,' he said lifting his head and turning to her... 'We ought to return, people will be worried. I was harsh to your maid when she told me you had gone off alone, I should make it right with her.'

He set the rock down, stood, and offered his hand; she took it, rose to her feet, and brushed the grass from her dress. Without looking, she stepped forward, trod on the stone Wulfstan had been holding, and stumbled into his arms.

'*Forgive me*,' she said lifting her eyes to meet his, but it was *too* late. This chance accident was about to empower the very demon she'd hoped to exorcise. Neither made any attempt to move, their faces were almost touching. She could feel the warmth of his skin, and the warmth seeped into her.

This was a new place; a place with which *she* was not familiar, nothing mattered, but the person before her. She lifted her lips to his as if this moment had been ordained from the beginning of time. Their kiss was tender yet passionate, she felt him move back on his heels to keep his balance as she pressed her body unashamedly against him.

Slowly the enormity of the moment broke into their passion, and their lips parted. Yet, they held each other's gaze still. Wulfstan could feel her trembling as his fingers slowly moved from her neck and spread out gently into her hair.

'Forgive me,' he whispered, pressing his lips to the top of her head.

'What is there to forgive? I *wanted* you to kiss me. I came up here on my own, to fight my demons. Who knows, perhaps

I deceive myself, and I hoped that you would come to find me. I just don't know the truth; I feel to have lost my senses. I do know, if this had not happened now, it would have happened later.'

Holding her at arm's length, he slowly shook his head in despair. 'Sit down,' he said releasing her, not really knowing what to say; the words just tumbled mindlessly off his tongue.

She knelt holding her face in her hands. He slumped down next to her, leant back, pressed his head against the pile of stones, and closed his eyes.

'We shouldn't have done this. We must forget this moment. We will walk back to the village, and leave this foolishness here by this cairn, and hope no one saw us. I will take you to your future husband and return to my home. This is what we must do. This was merely a moment of utter madness, I was anxious about your well-being, and *you* are worried for your future. Fate took advantage of our vulnerability and has played a cruel trick, we must see it for what it was.'

Aefre hung her head and cuffed a tear from her eye; clearly, he did not feel like she, or he would not say this.

'You are stronger than I, Lord.'

'No, I'm not, you have no idea how I feel… It is merely that I care more for you than *my* worldly wants. Such would mean exile or worse, death for you, even war between our two peoples, many who are innocent would die. You are not simply a woman; you are a princess who is promised to a king. You *must*, you *will*, forget me, and I you. My master is a *good,* kind, fair, man. Come, let us return now, we leave on the morrow's first tide, and this will be all forgotten.'

'You think I am without understanding? If you believe this moment can be so easily swept aside as you have said... you are a fool. For what I feel for you is no ordinary thing, not a morning haze which disappears with the changing hour of the day.'

Wulfstan could not even contemplate such talk and chose to discount what she said. He couldn't clear his thoughts; his head was spinning; she was addling his brain. He got up but did not offer his hand to her as he might have done.

'Come,' he said, and they walked in silence down the hill. Even though she stumbled more than once in the long grass, as she tried to keep up with him, he made no move to help her.

When they entered the village, Aefre's maids ran to her. Wulfstan totally ignored them, with not so much a word or a glance he strode off in the direction of their beached longboat.

It was clear to both Edith and Rowena that the Princess had been crying; they looked awkwardly to each other. Aefre paid little attention to them; *her* eyes were following Wulfstan in desperation. They were pleading to him, begging him to look back as he walked off, but he did not, and she lowered her head once he'd disappeared from view.

'Are you well my Lady, are you hurt?' Edith asked. Aefre only shook her head.

'Perhaps you would like to go to your room for a while and rest?'

Aefre nodded.

Cedric was on the beach and looked with concern as Wulfstan walked at some pace towards him.

'Hello, my friend,' Cedric called to him. 'Did you find the Princess? I was told she'd walked off and you had gone to look for her.'

'She's well enough, is all done here as I ordered?' he asked curtly.

'Yes... you seem troubled.'

Wulfstan's response was again sharp, 'concern yourself with *your* work, and *not* with things that are no concern of yours. I have had enough of your presumption. I am your Lord, you seem to forget that,' and he walked away from Cedric, shouting, and cursing at the men loading the boat.

Cedric watched him; he was taken aback by his friend's strange uncharacteristic aggression. He wondered what had occurred to bring about this dark mood.

It seemed as if Wulfstan's life was now one of attending rich feasts, for once again, he was seated at a high table as an honoured guest, their host's farewell gift to them, but this was a feast like no other. He was seated next to Aefre; neither had any appetite for the lavish spread set before them. Their feasting consisted of constantly repositioning the food on their wooden platters. Suddenly, Wulfstan reached for his cup and gulped greedily at his ale, then he nodded to a servant to refill it, hoping perhaps to deaden his brain.

Aefre watched him out of the corner of her eye. He rolled the cup back and forth between the palms of his hands and stared into the sweet brown liquid as if wishing to glimpse his future – and at the same time – fearing that he might.

He was tormented by her wretched sadness, he could feel it without looking at her. Then like the mad fool he was, he impulsively slid his hand under the table and tenderly squeezed her fingers, and she responded by pressing his with her thumb. Her face never betrayed them, but he understood fine well that such action had given her some comfort, and he cursed his weakness. He knew there would be a reckoning; from now on, every touch, glance, or word carried with it a price, and he feared that the price might be his honour.

Hell, of hells, he said in his head, how to rid myself of this. It was clear to him that if he had any feelings for her, he must turn away, damn, damn and damnation.

Eventually, Wulfstan could sit no longer and rose from his chair. He thanked Edgar and his wife, saying that King Æthelfrith would hear of this kindness to his future queen, but they must leave now, rest was needed for the morrow's journey. This talk of tomorrow fell like rotten clay from his lips, and he felt sick to his stomach. He took Aefre's hand and led her towards her room.

In the passage outside her door, she stopped and whispered, glancing in the direction they'd just come, to be sure they were alone. She said that she *knew* he was right, but nevertheless thanked him for his kind touch at the table and told him how much it had meant to her.

Please – kiss me – her eyes begged, desperate for his touch, but her voice was calm and only asked that he would not ignore her; and that he would yet be her friend.

He felt sick but nodded. In *heaven's* name, he could not imagine how he would ever fulfil such a doomed bargain. His lips made the shape of a smile, and he left her.

When he returned to the main hall Cedric was waiting for him, he said nothing, he did no more than stare into Wulfstan's eyes. The two left the hall and walked in silence to their hut. Before they went inside, Cedric took his arm.

'You know my life is ever yours, my dearest friend,' he said.

Chapter 8

The measure of love

Whether it was because Edgar was relieved to see them going or not, Cedric wasn't sure, but he was in high spirits, embracing Wulfstan like a long lost son.

They waved politely once they were afloat and those sailors who'd been manhandling the longboat to make the best advantage of the rising tide, had scrambled aboard.

It may not have been noticed by Thegn Edgar, but it was clear to Cedric that there was some problem between his friend and Princess Aefre. Until yesterday, they had been constantly laughing and seemingly happy in each other's company. Now, there was a clear change.

Cedric leant casually against the gunwale of the ship next to Rowena and asked offhandedly if the Princess was well.

'I think she misses her home, Cedric. Your Lord seems to be ignoring her, and I believe she found his company distracting. Perhaps they had some disagreement yesterday.'

'Well, he has much responsibility,' he said, feeling the need to defend his friend, not wanting Rowena to think badly of him.

'Indeed, it is merely that my princess is not usually so unpredictable.'

As they were speaking, Wulfstan went to where Aefre was sitting and sat by her. Both Cedric and Rowena turned simultaneously and faced out to sea, obviously not wanting to give the appearance that they were watching and discussing them.

'It's kind of you to come and speak with me Lord,' Aefre tried to say as indifferently as she could.

'It's not for the lack of wanting, but I am in a place that I have never been before, and I am at a loss as to what to say, or how to behave.'

Aefre had never looked at him since he'd joined her, 'We are both standing on the same unfamiliar ground.' She now turned to face him, 'I don't know how I will be able to hide this, all I want is you Wulfstan, to be near you, to touch you; I can't pretend.'

'Please, don't say these things. Apart from anything else you may be overheard.'

'If I am to be so bound, then I wish the sail had caught *me* and cast *me* into the sea instead of that wretched sailor, for that would be preferable to a life without you.' Wulfstan leaned forward onto his sword hilt, which he'd removed from his waist for convenience. 'You say that King Æthelfrith is a good man, tell me, is it right that I do this to him, a *good* man?'

'You know as well as I that your match has naught to do with love, it is for the good of our people, and King Æthelfrith knows that too. Perhaps you will grow to love him.'

'And you would be content with that? He will not be my brother; he will be my husband, and all that means. He will expect children, what then?'

'You are asking me, what I do not know, Princess.'

'Do not call me *Princess*, I am Aefre, the woman who loves you, who wants to be with *you* forever.'

'Aefre we have only known each other for, but a few short weeks, you can't be so certain of the things you profess so.'

'Oh... so tell me Wulfstan, do you feel differently? You have only known me for but a few short weeks, as you put it. Tell me you do not feel the same as me, for I know that you do. It is no ordinary thing that the gods have touched us with. They have seen fit to sprinkle their magic onto us, and are *you* such a bold warrior, who is strong enough to fight against the will of the gods? For this Princess is not, and believe me, I have tried.'

'Aefre, do not say these things, you don't seem to have any notion of what will happen if what you are saying is allowed to flourish.'

'You fool Wulfstan; I ask you again, do you really think you can stand against the will of the gods? Try if you must, I will be here waiting for you when you fail, for fail you will.'

He chose to ignore her and turned away. 'The Master tells me we are making good time,' he said quickly, wanting to change the subject as he spotted the Master coming towards them. May the gods have mercy on us, for this is living hell, he said to himself.

The Master, Godfread, came to them and bowed, 'It seems it will be as I said Ealdorman; we will be home by nightfall. You will be glad to see your new home Princess, it's a fine place,' he said laughing without any awareness of the shards of ice he threw into her face.

The cold, sharp reality drew guilty blood; her head was spinning. *Somehow,* she managed to remain seated, she nodded and smiled, and the Master left them, content that they were delighted with his news.

'I can't do this, Wulfstan.'

He was desperately trying to find some words of comfort, to be strong for her, but he could not.

'We are being left alone, have you noticed?'

'*No*, what do you mean?'

'Cedric and your maids have not come near. It is only a matter of time before Cedric realises the cause of our malady. He knows me better than I know myself, *sometimes*, and I fear this will be one of those times. People are not complete fools.'

'Well, hold me now, kiss me, be honest with your friend, for I care not, all will know of this sooner or later of that I am certain.'

'*No*... that would be madness, it cannot be; I am sworn to my king.'

'Do you think that the gods sprinkle their potions so their gifts might be hidden? Do you *really* think that is possible? For if I were a god, I would want the world to know of my generosity and benevolence.'

'Would you really want a man without honour, a man despised for the pathetic weak wretch he was? A man who put *himself* above all else, for that's the sort of man I would be. I must be alone, to gather my wits or we will all suffer?'

'*Please* don't leave me to sit here on my own, I beg you!'

'I must...'

'Well take that sword of which you are so fond, and use it on me, for that would be less painful than your words, and death would be a mercy,' she snapped back.

He cast his eyes to those nearby, fearful of her imprudence, but thankfully her anger seemed to have been lost in the wind. He was quickly reaching the point where he didn't care either way. He stood and pushed his way to the bow of the longboat, clambering over those seated on the thwarts taking their ease until they were again needed to pull on the oars.

I am desperate, and he does not understand, she was furious with him. She watched him clinging to the prow. He never moved a muscle, oblivious to the spray lashing into his face. She furrowed her brow and her eyes burned into his back. Glancing momentarily in the direction of her maids, who avoided her gaze, she wondered if perhaps they did know. Wulfstan was right, she hadn't noticed, but no one came to her, as if they were afraid to approach her, was her ordeal seen by all?

The night was drawing in. How much longer would it be? How could a lifetime pass so quickly?

'*LAND!*' A sailor shouted, and a cheer went up amongst the crew as their home was sighted. It was dusk now, and Wulfstan had never moved from his position at the prow. At the call he slowly turned to her, his face was as stone, water dripped from his hair, he was wet through, and his eyes were red from the salt spray… then… she realised – that he had done this to mask his tears – and she felt ashamed.

He would not fail her no matter how broken he was. He'd never burden her with *his* suffering. She knew she must be as strong as he. She understood for the *first* time that sacrifice of *self* was the truest measure of love.

Chapter 9

To meet a King

Wulfstan knew, whatever he felt, he had now to stand at her side, and he pushed past the excited men to where she was seated. He could see that mounted guards had been sent to greet them; obviously, they'd been spotted from the fort.

King Æthelfrith was not amongst them on the shore, but they had by them a beautiful roan with a richly decorated saddle-cloth, which looked as if it was a gift for the princess.

Wulfstan could feel her trembling; he wrapped his arm around her and drew her tightly to his side on the pretext of supporting her when the boat struck the shore.

As it happened, the landing was gentle. Wulfstan leapt over the side into the shallow water, and she clambered carefully down into his arms, and he carried her the few steps to dry land. In those few steps while he held her in his arms, she had pressed her lips to his neck, and whispered that she was sorry, he all but dropped her, but yet he managed to lower her to the ground, bowing gracefully.

'A gift for you, my Lady, from our King.' The warrior said smiling and passed the rein to Wulfstan, 'my Lord.'

Wulfstan nodded and made a stirrup with his hands to help Aefre mount. 'I will lead the Princess the short distance.'

'Very good my Lord, our King is waiting for you.'

Wulfstan sighed, took a deep breath and set off walking slowly towards the gates. He wanted to look back at Aefre but couldn't. As soon as they entered the stronghold, they saw Æthelfrith in all his finery walking towards them smiling.

'*Princess*, welcome,' and he reached up to help her from her saddle, embraced her and kissed her cheek. 'I hope you are satisfied with my gift?' He patted the horse.

'It is a beautiful horse, Lord; you have been very generous to my family. My father sends his thanks and best wishes to you.'

Wulfstan's eyes burned as he watched every move and gesture. He could hear the deferential words from Aefre, but they were dead words – devoid of any life – spoken from nervous eyes. Æthelfrith seemed oblivious.

'Come, Princess, we have food and warmth to welcome you to your new home of Din Guyaroi. I hope this untamed fellow here has been good to you, he is a little wild, but the best of men.' Æthelfrith said laughing.

'He is indeed the most honourable of men, Lord, and your most loyal subject, who puts *you* before himself in *all* things even those he loves. A man who would take on the gods and defy his fate for *your* well-being.' Aefre narrowed her eyes as she glanced at Wulfstan.

Æthelfrith smiled, wrapped his arm around Aefre, and led her to the stone keep on the summit of the hill. Wulfstan followed as they walked into the great hall, it was ablaze with candlelight and warmth from the roaring fire. It seemed a lifetime since he'd been here.

Æthelfrith beckoned servants and ordered them to take the princess to her rooms. 'You will want to wash and change before we eat, Princess,' he said to her, 'and you my friend, you look as if you have swum here, I have instructed that there be clothes ready for you.'

'Thank you, I am a little wet, Lord.'

'Be quick, so we might eat.'

Wulfstan and Aefre were led off to their rooms. Aefre touched his hand briefly as they climbed the stone spiral staircase. This is never going to work was all he could think, but the alternative was unthinkable. The servants opened the door to her room, Wulfstan bowed to her, and Aefre and her maids disappeared from him, and he was taken to his room.

There were already clothes laid out for him as Æthelfrith had said there would be. He was a favoured warrior of the King and was to be treated as such. He washed and dressed, no time to bathe thoroughly. Æthelfrith would be waiting, and he wanted to get down before Aefre. She was plainly terrified, and in no small measure, because she feared he intended to simply leave her to fend for herself. He was anxious that she would do or say something in her state of confusion, which could not be undone. He walked briskly thinking of how, or what he could say to convince her that he would not now, or *ever* desert her.

'Poor Aefre,' he whispered.

He paused momentarily, as he passed her door then dashed down the stair. He immediately noticed that Aefre had not arrived and was thankful. Æthelfrith was sitting at the table evidently in high spirits laughing and talking to servants and warriors alike.

'Wulfstan – my friend, come sit by me and tell of your adventures. Thanks, be that you sent me news to give some peace to my fears.' Wulfstan bowed and was seated by the King.

He proceeded to tell of the storm and their escape. Æthelfrith listened with some interest, but his eye was ever turned to the staircase. Eventually, he was rewarded with the appearance of his bride-to-be. She wore a plain dress, which fitted perfectly to her figure. Its lack of adornment seemed to accentuate her beauty even more.

Æthelfrith stood, reached out his arms, embraced her, and kissed her cheek. It was Wulfstan's turn to tremble now and he clumsily knocked over his drink. The wine splashed onto his new tunic and dripped onto the floor. He signalled to a slave, she came, wiped his clothes, and the table. If Æthelfrith noticed he paid him no heed, his vision was preoccupied by a beautiful woman, soon to be his bride.

'Welcome my Princess, take your place, you are truly the great beauty I have been told about. I am honoured that you have consented to marry me.'

She smiled dutifully.

'I would marry you tomorrow, but I am a considerate man, we will take time to get to know each other a little, and you must become familiar with your new home.'

'Thank you, my Lord, Ealdorman Wulfstan has told me of your kind and generous ways.'

'He is my most faithful friend, I would not have trusted another soul to bring you here.' Aefre noticeably breathed a sigh of relief, as did Wulfstan, who desperately tried to still his agitation and smiled at her as reassuringly as he could.

'I have chosen to honour you, my friend,' Æthelfrith said turning to him after helping Aefre to her chair. 'I do not forget loyalty and service. It is my wish, Ealdorman, that on my wedding day, you will be the one to pass the bride to me. For you who have born her thus far; so, it is right that you be the one who gives her to me. What do you say to that?'

Aefre was hardly breathing as she stared ahead. Wulfstan had to steady his voice before he spoke. It was to be *he,* who would have to *physically* give Aefre away. Æthelfrith had no idea what a spiritual reality would be undertaken in this physical act.

Wulfstan swallowed and tried to calm his voice before he spoke, 'You do me a great honour, my Lord.'

Aefre never moved.

The following days Aefre spent with the King, riding around Din Guyaroi, they even sailed to Lindis Feorna and the islands.

These were hard days for Wulfstan. He'd ridden home with Cedric to see his brother Leofwine and was greeted warmly.

He knew this was his future and he must make the most of it. Try as he might he could not laugh and be what all expected of him. Leofwine talked excitedly about all that had been done in his absence, plainly seeking his elder brother's approval. Wulfstan tried to be enthusiastic, but it did not seem to satisfy Leofwine. He *would* have been greatly interested at one time for he loved his home, and the people, but this day, his mind had more pressing concerns to occupy it other than new pigsties, or repaired barn roofs.

Poor Leofwine, I know he is feeling disappointed with my lack of interest, and I'm sorry for that, but he has no idea of the turmoil in my head at this moment. Why does it seem that everyone wants me to be something for *them*? I'm sick of it, I just want to be *me*, would it be too much to ask just to love Aefre and be with her, the woman I love? A pleasure that the humblest of ceorls enjoy. *No* – the one thing *I* want, is deemed by my honour to be wicked. Wulfstan grumbled to himself and threw his gauntlet at a tree in frustration. 'I am no better off than a slave who does the bidding of others.'

In the evening, Wulfstan heard Leofwine asking Cedric what was wrong with him.

Cedric only shrugged his shoulders and said, 'your brother changed shortly after the blow to his head when the longboat was washed ashore.' He told Leofwine about the storm and the shipwreck, how they'd been helped in a village just south of the

River Tes in Deira. He said that since they'd left after the longboat was repaired, that he could not recall him smiling. 'On the journey here to visit you, Wulfstan barely spoke. He will mend, I have seen such before from a blow to the head.'

That seemed to satisfy Leofwine. 'I know you will watch over him old friend, you love him almost as much as I do, he is everything to me.'

While he was at his home, Wulfstan had walked onto the moor above their village, with a girl from his past, called Meghan. He realised that he'd never even thought about her, not for months, ever since his father had died, he'd simply been too busy.

She was kind and wanted to know all about the new princess, what was she like? Was she beautiful? Strangely, she was easy to talk to; it was the first time he felt able to speak freely to anyone without feeling threatened.

His lightened mood suddenly changed when she told him it sounded as if he was in love with the Princess. The words numbed his soul. He was so shaken that he couldn't gather his wits, what had she seen, what had he said?

He turned to her, and she wrapped him in her arms, her embrace brought some comfort to him. She *was* beautiful, and her eyes were filled with laughter, he'd always known how she'd felt about him. Before he could gather his senses, her lips were pressed to his and *he* responded. Her kiss was sweet, sensual and her hair had the fragrance of honeysuckle; they lay down in the warm grass – and made love, *but* the release from his torment was brief, and he felt even more wretched than before, *defiled*, as if he had defiled her. He had shamefully used her love to relieve his suffering.

Wulfstan lay on his back and rested his head on a soft tuft of grass. Meghan smiled up at him, laid her head on his chest, and gently twisted the short coarse hairs around her finger. He was conscious of her skin touching his. He wanted to push her from him; he was struggling to breathe. This was living purgatory and he was actively sealing every possible way of escape, *hellbent* on self-destruction. Not only was he betraying his king, he was betraying Aefre's love and now Meghan's. What sort of despicable wretch was he?

'I love you Wulfstan and have for as long as I can remember.'

It was another voice that replied, detached from him, a voice, which spoke kindly to Meghan. He helped her with her clothes, even lovingly picked a leaf from her hair. Surely, she could see the liar's damned soul behind his eyes.

They spoke little as they made their way back to the village and she seemed content with that. This day, he had sunk to new depths of wickedness even for him.

Chapter 10

To tell a friend

Cedric and Wulfstan left the next day to return to Din Guyaroi. Wulfstan could hardly look at Meghan, to add to his self-loathing he kissed her, and she smiled. She said she would wait for him and waved as they rode off.

To his eternal *shame*, he wondered what further blocks of disgrace he had added to the house of dishonour where he now dwelt.

In his madness, he drove his horse as if the devil's hand was clawing at his back. The poor beast was stumbling and gasping for breath, pungent foaming sweat flew from its withers. The pace was going to kill the wretched animal, and the brutal cruelty sickened Cedric.

'WULFSTAN, cease this, it's wickedness, look what you are doing to that poor creature,' Cedric shouted. Wulfstan didn't hear him or chose to ignore him, Cedric was furious. Whatever tore at *his* soul, that animal did not deserve this treatment. Cedric pushed nearer to him, tore the rein from his hand, and drew them both to a trot. Wulfstan's fury was now directed at Cedric, he leapt from his saddle and onto him, and they crashed in a tumbling heap to the ground. Both were stunned by the fall. Cedric was first to recover, shook his head, got up, grabbed Wulfstan's hair and viciously slapped the back of his hand across his face, whipping his head back. Wulfstan pushed up on his elbows and shook his dazed head. He touched his lip, saw the blood on his fingers, and staggered to his feet drawing his sword.

'WELL, what are you waiting for?' Cedric pressed his chest against the sword point. 'Go on, *do it*. Whatever possesses you – it cares naught for friendship, *do it* I say.'

Wulfstan stared at him; he lowered his sword, and threw it angrily to the ground, fell back against a tree trunk and slid jerkily down the rough bark as it snagged on his clothes. He sat quietly between two large roots with his face in his hands. Cedric picked up Wulfstan's sword and drove it into the sod next to him.

'Wulfstan, what in the name of hell ails you? You can't go on like this.' Cedric slumped down next to him.

'I'm sorry Cedric... are you hurt?' he muttered in a pathetic weary voice.

'*Yes*, is the answer, and not due to the fall from that horse,' he said, sweeping his hand agitatedly in the direction of the sweating animal. 'We have been the closest friends since boyhood and yet I am not worthy of your trust. That wounds me more than facing the point of your sword.'

Wulfstan was quiet for some time; he squeezed his head between his hands as if he would crush it.

'Out with it, man.'

'The Princess – and – I – are – in love...'

Cedric pressed back against the tree next to Wulfstan, determined not to state the obvious.

'And you think that changes how much you mean to me. I half guessed as much the night of the thegn's feast, before we left for home, but discounted such as...'

'Aye... who would imagine such folly?'

'You say – *"And I"*, I take it that means that the Princess is also in love with you?'

'Yes...' he answered in a whisper.

'I can see why your brain might be as it appears, a blow to the heart is ever worse than a blow to the head. What do you intend to do, have you given that a thought? *And* – what about Meghan, she has loved you for as long as I can remember?'

'Ah... Meghan, she is *nothing* to me.'

'Wulfstan, I am your friend, nothing will change that, and part of that is telling you what you might not want to hear. As for the Princess, I am at a loss, but for Meghan, she is innocent. To extend – *your* – suffering to her, is – *not*, "*Nothing*", as you put it, or something to be so easily discounted. Don't forget, she is your good friend Ælfweard's sister. We have all been friends since we were children. There was a bond formed of trust and loyalty, and that means something to me, and I thought it did to you. Are you telling me now that I was wrong?'

'No, it's the truth; forgive me. Forgive me seems forever on my lips. I can no longer think; my head is all confusion. I wish I'd broken my neck as we fell just now, for I care not one bit for my life. Death is the only reward for those who rail against the gods, and I delight in that hope.'

Cedric had to admit if only to himself, he was unable to think of any good in this. They were both quiet, Cedric picked up a pebble and threw it into the nearby stream where their horses were now standing, they shied at the sudden disturbance of the water, then settled once more. Wulfstan scratched in the dust with a twig.

'I didn't seek this Cedric, it just happened, and I have, *am*, trying to battle against it, and failing miserably, as you see.'

'Aye, I see that clear enough. I could say, you should have done this or that, but I know fine well how we can all make the right decisions and be strong for someone else. So, I will say naught… only that this does not change how I feel about you my friend. To be honest Wulfstan I have *no* answers but come what may I will stand next to you, shield to shield, as I have always done, certain that you would do the same for me, this I promise.'

'I thank you for that; I suppose one of the fears is that all will reject me, shame desires only its own company. *Tell me*, what is this feeling which drives one beyond all sense, that swoops and devours any ability to function even certain death does not quench its resolve?'

'Ah, don't ask me, Wulfstan, I have never known such a thing, but the scalds tell of such in their winter's tales, and we are all gripped by the stories of undying love and great deeds of valour. Perhaps we all dream of the like, but only the giants among us can ever walk with those gods. We lesser mortals must satisfy ourselves with the stories, and judge jealously those who have tasted its fruits.'

'Well, I am no giant or god, and I am not equal to this. I can't even walk from it; it clings to me like a serpent, devouring my every moment. I am tormented by the voices of the righteous and condemnation fills my head.'

'Have you been able to talk to the Princess of your feelings?'

'A little, but the fire is hot and burns fiercely, the flames devour reason. Perhaps there may be a chance to talk when we return to Din Guyaroi but being alone together is a dangerous occupation. I doubt that the King would be over understanding if he were to catch wind of this.'

'No doubt you are fearful for the Princess' safety.'

'Aye, she has been near losing her wits more than once, she needs my strength, not weakness.'

'If you feel able, please assure her of my friendship.'

'Thank you, Cedric, this moment of kindness has given me hope, and believe me, hope has been a stranger to me these last days.'

'Let us ride back now, it will be dark when we get to Din Guyaroi.'

'Aye…'

Chapter 11

Out of the darkness

It was dark by the time their horses' hooves clattered over the whinstone cobbles, through the gates and into the stockade. The guards acknowledged Wulfstan and Cedric as they passed; they rode to the stable and dismounted. Two stable boys ran to them and took the reins of their exhausted mounts.

'I will leave you Wulfstan I'm tired. This day has been a lifetime of bad days rolled into one.'

'Aye… days are days until they're not. I'm not yet for sleep, I might walk to the beach and ease the muscles in my backside before *I* can hope for some rest.'

'As you like.' They embraced, and Wulfstan watched him walk off. Wulfstan turned and followed the horses to the stables. Leaning on the half door, he watched the two boys as they loosened the girths and carefully removed the hot saddles. They stood them on the rack next to the stall and set about their work by the dim light from a rush lantern.

'It will be enough this night to see they are wiped down, watered and fed. The light is too ill to do more until morning.' Wulfstan suggested, knowing that the two young boys would be tired.

'Aye, we will do what we can to make them comfortable, Lord,' one of the boys said looking towards the door.

As Wulfstan made to go, he heard footsteps and stepped back into the shadows, suddenly fully alert. He instinctively laid his hand to his seax, and all but collided with Aefre. Grabbing hold of her, he placed his hand over her mouth. She struggled wildly for a moment, but he held her securely.

'*What* – on – earth, are you doing here, girl?' he said bending down close to her ear so no one would hear.

She ceased her wriggling when she realised who her captor was. 'By Wōden's beard, you scared me half to death.'

'You've not answered my question,' he whispered drawing her deeper into the shadows between the two buildings.

She turned and clung to him, 'I heard the horses, looked out and saw you. I sneaked down, I had to see you.'

'Aefre, this is beyond danger, what if you were seen?'

'WHO'S THERE?' A guard called as if to reinforce Wulfstan's point. He pushed Aefre behind him and stepped out of the shadow.

'Fear not, it's me Ealdorman Wulfstan; I have been attending to my horse.

'I see you, Lord,' the guard replied and acknowledged him with a token salute.

Phew… Wulfstan blew from his pursed lips and turned once more to Aefre. 'This is folly girl return to your rooms.'

'First kiss me, I have been *desperate* to see you.'

'No – you must return now, for mercies' sake.'

She stood defiantly for a moment, and he lowered his head and kissed her… There was no kiss like this kiss, there never could be, there was no woman like this woman. 'I love you…' the words were from his lips before he knew it.

'And I you, I will go now,' and she pulled up her hood.

'Shush, listen…' he laid his finger across his lips and reached his arm to block her way.

Suddenly Aefre could hear her heart pounding fit to burst from her chest.

'What is it?' she whispered.

His breath stilled, not a muscle moved, his eyes widened as they – slowly – traversed the darkness… 'It's – all – right… I thought I heard some footsteps… I must have imagined it. You take care; I'll wait here and give you a moment before I make my way to the keep. Don't run; walk normally, then if you are seen it will not look suspicious. If you are challenged, tell the truth. You could not sleep, saw us coming home and you came to see that we were both well, but by the mercy of Thunor [12] I beg that you're *not* seen.'

She kissed him once more and silently disappeared into the darkness.

But... there *had* been other feet and other eyes. The night was ever the realm of those who preferred to look at life from the shadows.

There was no sign of Aefre at the morning table, King Æthelfrith entered and welcomed Wulfstan, asking about the journey to his home. Wulfstan told him all was well, and was compelled out of politeness, to ask what *he'd* been doing, but all the while dreading to hear. He was expecting a painful account of his time with Aefre, but no, Æthelfrith's concerns were for his kingdom.

'There are invaders Ealdorman, Áedán mac Gabráin, King of the Dalriada Scots has been joined by a large force from Hibernia. [13] The Dalriada Scots mostly come from that wet miserable land of bogs, only fit for their bald-headed priests and suffering saints. They have settled at a place called Degsastan near Gretna, to the north-west. It is many days trudge, but I intend to face them and defeat them.'

Wulfstan was distracted by this news. 'When do we go?'

'Now the Princess is here I will marry first and then go.'

Wulfstan was silent.

'All is in place, the Princess knows, I will marry today, and I will leave with my army on the morrow's first light. The fryd has been rallied, as you well know, I demand them ever to be ready. Our kingdom might depend on their readiness, many will join us as we go.'

'I must send word to my brother, we could be gone for weeks,' Wulfstan said endeavouring to gather his wits.

'No need, you are my most trusted warrior; *you* will remain here. I need to know Din Guyaroi is safe. I do not know what has been planned; perhaps this is a trap to lure me away from here. Once I am gone, they may swoop down and devour the town. No, I need to have someone I can trust completely. to guard my home – *and* – my new bride. To have her carried off by some brigand in my absence would be a woeful thing,' he laughed and slapped Wulfstan's back. 'She may even be with child after this night,' he said and laughed even more.

He had *no* idea how such a frivolous jest could destroy another's soul. Wulfstan gripped his horn cup so fiercely he crushed it, and the shards tore into his flesh. The King was shocked and jumped as the blood sprayed from Wulfstan's lacerated hand. Æthelfrith grabbed his wrist and pressed it to the table, blood poured from the wound quickly making a pool on the polished surface and dripped from the edge.

'Hold still a moment,' Æthelfrith shouted, 'there is a piece of horn sticking in your palm.' He didn't need to tell Wulfstan to be still for he had never moved. He was oblivious to the blood. Æthelfrith plucked the shard of horn from the deep gash, 'Quick girl fetch the cunning woman with her needle, this needs her sewing skills, cloth, cloth, quickly, we need to staunch the bleeding.'

'Did something disturb you Ealdorman,' Wulfstan heard a voice whisper in his ear. By the time he had enough sense to turn around, there was no one to be seen.

Chapter 12

Those who walk in the night

Wulfstan wrestled with the tantalising phantom and her promise of oblivion, but she forever slipped from his grasp and left him a dishevelled heap of exhaustion. The more he tried, the more sleep mocked him until he refused to rise to her taunting, and *yet* she danced and weaved seductively, teasing him, beckoning him with her finger.

'Ah to hell with you,' he shouted, and bundled the twisted bed rugs in his arms and flung them across the room. He slipped on his leggings, boots, slung a cloak across his naked shoulders and left his room; he didn't even close his door.

It was black dark when he stepped out from the doorway. He had no idea of the hour; the place was like the grave. He walked to the gates, which led to the beach.

One of the guards at the entrance was leaning against the large oak frame on which the doors were hinged. It was obvious sleep was befriending him although it was a stranger to Wulfstan, the poor fellow was so shaken when Wulfstan spoke he staggered and dropped his spear.

'Open that,' Wulfstan pointed to a small door cut into the large gates to allow some access without opening the main gates. The guard fumbled with the batten securing it and swung it open. 'If you value your hide, be awake when I return. Now close it behind me.'

The man averted his eyes when he glimpsed Wulfstan's naked torso.

Wulfstan walked with some intent, his cloak streaming out behind him. The two guards watched him in fear as he stood on the edge of the hill before he descended to the shore. There was now sufficient moonlight to add terror to the vision spied by the onlookers. His silhouette took on the likeness of Grendel [14] from the underworld with his cape and jet-black curly hair swept back by the up draught from the beach. Suddenly he vanished from view, and the two would swear he'd flown off with his mother to join Wōden's wolves. The door was slammed, and the batten replaced, any thought of sleep now a distant memory.

Wulfstan would have welcomed the company of Grendel and his mother this night, but he was alone. *Yes*, he was alone with all that stark reality, darkness ever smiled upon. He threw off his cape and waded into the ice-cold water, the spray lashed him and burned his skin like a whip, but even this deluge of utter numbness could not quench the roaring furnace within.

He turned to face the stone keep, there was one light at a window, and he wondered if it was Aefre. 'Come to me,' he screamed, but the wind swallowed up his cry. Wading back to the shore, he fell to his knees and wept.

He could hardly move by the time the dawn touched the horizon, he had no idea how long he knelt there and cared less. He staggered as he stood up and stumbled his way back to the stockade. He kicked the door and swore at the guard as he nervously edged it open.

'Get out of my way fool,' was the best greeting he could manage to the terrified guard, and he strode off to the keep. 'Bring water to my room to bathe,' he ordered a slave as he passed, 'and be quick, you idle lackwit.'

Once in his room, he slumped down into his chair to wait. He was taken aback by the speed, which a tub and hot water appeared in his room. Two terrified girls came to bathe him, and he stripped, and stepped into the warm water. They nervously began to wash him; he never spoke or made any attempt to aid their employment. When he'd had enough, he stood without warning, and they wrapped him in towels.

'Go, leave me… what is it, girl?'

'Clothes have been laid there for you Lord,' she pointed to his bed, 'will we return to help you?' She asked fighting back the tears.

'You think me a child that I need help to dress, get from my sight.' The two girls all but ran from the room, leaving the tub where it was. He sat once more in his chair, his exhaustion was overcome by the warmth, and his eyes – slowly – closed.

When he awoke, it took several seconds to gain some understanding, and then the reality of what was before him this day enveloped him afresh. He was cold now, and after a while, he stood and let the towels fall from him. He looked at the clothes laid on his bed; they were splendid, richly decorated.

'How in the name of the darkest place beyond the Hellmouth did I get here? Well devour me now dragon for I am already damned.'

There was a faint knock on the door, which he ignored, it slowly opened, and a servant peered around the edge.

'Lord, the King wishes to see you in the long-hall,' he said nervously, and quickly closed the door. Clearly, Wulfstan's ill humour had been spoken of amongst the servants and slaves alike.

When he rose from his chair, he was trembling and was having difficulty focusing his eyes. He steadied himself by taking hold of the back of his chair, took some deep breaths, and blinked several times. Eventually, he felt able to walk, and slowly made his way down to the long-hall.

'My, you look a handsome fellow,' the King laughed. 'Here, ale and mete [15] for the Ealdorman,' he called. 'A great day is it not, my friend?'

'Aye… a great day Lord.'

'Well, you say the right words, but I have seen happier faces lighting a funeral pyre. Has the night not been kind to you?'

'I had little sleep Lord.'

'There will be other battles, do not fret that you are left behind. My young cousin, Hering, will be here to keep you company.'

The prospect of Hering's company did not delight Wulfstan, he couldn't stand him, and he suspected Hering felt the same about him, but Hering would never say the like of that, he was far too sly for such directness. He was forever deferring to the wisdom of his elder cousin. It sickened Wulfstan, and he suspected that Æthelfrith didn't like him much either as he clearly didn't want him as part of his army.

Hering's father was King Hussa, Æthelfrith's uncle. When Hussa died, it was Æthelfrith who was named King. Wulfstan wondered how Hering really felt about Æthelfrith being *his father's* heir. It was difficult to tell what Hering thought about anything, he was always the perfect subject.

Also, among the guests was, Æthelfrith's brother, Theobald, who was everything Hering was not, open, friendly and clearly a warrior.

Chapter 13

The sealing of fate

Æthelfrith left on horseback for the village with a small band of nobles and retainers.

The marriage ceremony would be held on the green, at the standing stone by the old holly tree, which had been a holy place since the beginning of time.

Adhering to Saxon tradition, King Æthelfrith had not seen his bride this morning and would not until she arrived at the green.

Wulfstan had been given the great honour of representing King Ælla, Aefre's father. None of her relations would be at the ceremony, they might have been, but because of the threat to Æthelfrith's kingdom, there was an urgent need to seal the bond as quickly as possible before he left.

Wulfstan, in his role as "Father" of the bride, would be responsible for the brýdgifu [16] and handing the gift of a new sword to Æthelfrith.

He walked wearily to Aefre's room, paused, and sighed. Resting his forehead on the cold stone, he tapped the toe of his boot against the wall to give his mind time to assemble itself. It was something he always did when he was unsure. His father had said that it was because he kept his brains in his boots, and it helped rouse them. He pressed his eyelids together, sighed again, and then reluctantly knocked on her door. Rowena, Aefre's maid, opened it almost before his hand had fallen to his side. She bowed and gestured for him to enter.

Aefre was ready and waiting in her wedding garments, which included a floral bridle crown. It all seemed matter-a-fact, he felt so beaten and numbed seeing her had no effect, whatsoever. If Aefre wanted some comment or words of reassurance, she was to be disappointed for he had none.

'Are you ready, my Lady?'

'Yes, Ealdorman.'

'We must make haste; the King has gone and will be waiting for you.'

He bowed as she walked past. It was as if he simply did not care what happened now, to him, or her, he was bereft of all feelings. He picked up the marriage tokens, the sword, and the coffer containing the brýdgifu, passed them to a servant, and followed Aefre down the stairs and onto the courtyard.

Her new pony awaited her. It had been groomed to perfection, and it was richly decorated with garlands and ribbons. There were even small silver bells attached to the harness, which jingled as it moved its head.

Wulfstan helped her into the saddle, she nodded to him that she was ready, and he led her pony out of the gates, down the hill then up the short incline from the fortress to the village green, where the people gathered to welcome them.

He and Aefre never spoke; some feeling of concern returned as he caught sight of the Weofodthegn [17] standing in all his robes before King Æthelfrith. He had enough sense to wonder if this deadening of his wits was the gods' way of preventing him from simply taking hold of the Princess and riding off, and to *hell* with honour.

At the edge of the green Wulfstan drew her pony to a standstill. He reached up and lowered Aefre from the saddle. His hands encircled her waist, and he gently lowered her until her face was level with his; she set her fingers lightly on his shoulders and tried to smile into his eyes. The moment was an eternity; he was holding his very life, *inches* from his lips.

What cruel jest of fate made *him* the one to give this woman into another's hands? She was his to hold and forever should be.

This was the *darkest* of nightmares, where the screams of tormented souls were driven into one's sleep by a swirling vortex of horror from the Hellmouth of the underworld. The sort of terror that crawls over the morning's cold, clammy skin, and lingers long after one has escaped the clutches of the night's world of dreams. He didn't belong here in this place, this day; he was a stranger in the land and knew not these people. There were no smiling faces where he now dwelt.

Nobles were waiting on the green *for him*, nobles from all the neighbouring earldoms. They would understand that, due to the impending war, there had not been time to organise the lavish spectacle that might have been warranted by the coming together of two great dynasties.

Wulfstan caught sight of his brother and his friends, Cedric, Ælfweard, Geodic, – *and* – Meghan; she smiled at him. For the first time that day he felt something, he couldn't fix a name to the feeling, but it was the most wretched. Was he feeling fear, shame, horror, embarrassment, self-hatred? He didn't know what.

'My Princess,' Æthelfrith bowed, and she acknowledged him.

What is this game that the gods are playing, where they touch the lives of two humans with their magic love concoction then open an uncrossable chasm between them?

He had not asked to fall in love with Aefre, and Aefre had not asked to fall in love with him. Gods were not good, but malevolent, spiteful, wilful, parasites that were intoxicated by the anguish of the innocent.

The ceremony began with the exchange of swords. Æthelfrith gave Wulfstan his ceremonial sword, which would now belong to Aefre, for her to pass on to their son. Wulfstan, in turn, gave Æthelfrith a *new* sword, which Ælla had sent with him for this very purpose. It was all part of the customary ritual observed by the people of nobility.

The Weofodthegn now lifted his hands to the sky; his loose sleeves slid down to his elbows revealing his long scrawny tattooed arms. With his supernatural voice, he called out to the goddesses Freya and Frige and begged that they would be generous to the most-high King Æthelfrith of Bernicia, and his bride. Bringing them eternal love and fertility to their marriage, blessing such a union with warrior sons.

Their oaths were made, and rings were exchanged.

Nothing seemed to touch Wulfstan, – *until* – the priest spoke twice to him in an irritated manner, demanding his response. It was as if suddenly by magic, sound and vision had returned to him.

'*Lord*, is it you who gives this bride?' The Weofodthegn asked him, '*Ealdorman Wulfstan.*'

Wulfstan paused for a moment all eyes turned to him, and he responded.

'I give you this *brýdgifu,* and this woman. She is yours to have and hold...' he hesitated; he couldn't say the words. The priest spoke the words to prompt him, assuming he'd forgotten them. Yet, he was dumb, there was a moment of hush amongst the crowd, and then he went on in a whisper, '... to hold all your days, to the *exclusion* of all others.' Once more, a grey impenetrable silent world descended upon him.

The villagers cheered, and Æthelfrith bent his head and kissed Aefre on her lips.

The King and his new Queen now walked as man and wife to where their horses were standing, and Æthelfrith helped his bride into her saddle, swung gracefully onto his and they rode slowly up to the fortress, passed their subjects lining the track and on to the celebrations.

Leofwine, Wulfstan's brother came to his side, as did Meghan, she took his arm and kissed him.

'What does it feel like to be a King and a Father then?' Leofwine asked jovially.

'The Princess is indeed beautiful Wulfstan, but she does not have what *we* have, I would not change places with her for a *thousand* kingdoms, with all their riches.' She smiled, reached up to his ear, and whispered, 'I am with child.'

Wulfstan turned slowly to face her with a look of utter horror on his face. Fortunately, Meghan was distracted by a horse riding close by them, and she didn't notice his reaction.

'Excuse us for a moment, brother,' and he roughly pulled Meghan to one side. 'What are you saying Meghan, that you are with child and the child is mine?'

She was clearly hurt, 'what are – *you* – saying Wulfstan, do you doubt that it is yours? I thought you would be pleased, for sure *I* am.'

He let go of her hand and leaned back against a tree. 'By all that's sacred, what a mess I have made, a life undone, in but a few days. All lives that come near me are consumed by the scorching heat, hell of hells.'

'I don't understand, Wulfstan, I thought that you would be pleased and that you wanted to marry me. I have always thought that' Meghan, turned from him and folded her arms.

'Forgive me, Meghan, I simply don't know what to say.' She looked dejected, confused. He managed to be sensitive enough to take her shoulder and turn her into his arms. 'Who knows of this?'

'No one.'

'Give me time to think Meghan; my head is spinning this day. The King is leaving for battle tomorrow, and he will be gone for weeks. He is leaving me here to guard the fortress and the village. My thoughts are full of responsibility. Come, I must go to him I will be expected to be with him and his new Queen. You stay with your brother, there is ever danger at such frivolity as this. People drink too much, and fights start, I should not like you to wander on your own. I must speak with *my* brother too, he may have to go to war.'

'No, the King has taken many men from our village, word came a day past by rider. I thought you would know, but your brother is permitted to stay and be here if there is an attack, the King is not taking all that he might as part of the fryd.'

'Ah… I have no idea what's happening it has all been thrust upon me, and I seem to have been distracted.' He kissed her cheek and took her to her brother.

Ælfweard was talking to Cedric when he spotted Wulfstan and his sister coming towards him. He reached out a hand to Wulfstan as he approached wrapping his arm around his shoulder.

'And a most gracious welcome to the man who is now King of Deira. You have made great advancements while you have been absent from us, my friend,' Ælfweard made a play of bowing with great flourish at Wulfstan's new position as the Princess of Deira's Father.

'You think so? My life is not one of enhancement believe me, *never* did a jest fall so far short of the truth.' Ælfweard looked thrown, Wulfstan cast a glance at Cedric, who remained expressionless. 'I must go now, take care of Meghan, I don't know when I will see you again.'

'That is the truth for sure, we go with the King on the morrow's first light, *except* for Cedric, he's to stay here, as are you, so we've been told,' Ælfweard said seriously.

'Yes, you take care Ælfweard we have never been separated before; we who are left will see to the care of your family. The four of us have always fought as one. Are you going too Godric?'

'Aye, I'm going as you can see my dress is not for a wedding.' Wulfstan nodded.

Wulfstan squeezed Meghan's shoulder, 'Take care of Meghan this night Ælfweard, there is much activity, and where there are armed men in high spirits prepared for battle, there is also a danger for young women. I promise I will see that she is returned safely to our village.'

'I will see she is safe this night,' said Cedric. As a leader Ælfweard, you will have men of the fryd to organise.'

'Thank you, Cedric, we will talk later,' Wulfstan said, and walked away in despair. He didn't think his life could get any worse, but it apparently could.

Chapter 14

Freya's dance

Wulfstan was seated next to Hering and to his right was Æthelfrith. He didn't really know what it was about Hering, but he made his flesh crawl. His voice was emotionless, and he had narrow rat-like eyes that never seemed to blink. He was the very last person Wulfstan wanted to be near this night.

The King was in high spirits, laughing and joking with all who would listen.

'Are you not entertained, Ealdorman, you seem in poor humour?'

'You are entrusting me with great responsibility, and I am conscious of the honour, you will be gone on the morrow and people will look to me.'

'I did not make my choice lightly, you are more than equal to all I have asked of you, all will be well. Here dance with my wife,' he laughed and slapped Wulfstan's back. 'She would lighten the load on any man's back. I'm sure she will do this for me.' He turned to Aefre, and she looked horrified at the thought, but the King rose and took her hand giving it to Wulfstan. 'Bring some cheer to this fellow my love, for he carries the world upon his shoulders.'

On stepping from the dais, Wulfstan spotted Meghan with Cedric; he was shocked to see her, he wasn't expecting her to be here, Cedric must have brought her. Perhaps Cedric wanted to remind him.

'Shall I send for my sturdy boots, Lord? You said I might need some protection for my feet when we last spoke of dancing, do you remember?' she tried to smile.

'Pardon!' he had momentarily forgotten where he was as if that were possible. 'Ah yes, I recall,' he mumbled. He flicked his head without smiling in acknowledgement of her attempt to lighten the moment. They stood looking into each other's face, after all the raucous dancing which had been the order of the night; they had taken the floor as the musicians slowed their rhythm to the heartbeat of Freya's dance, the dance of young love.

They were compelled to embrace so that their faces touched. Wulfstan felt that every watchful eye in the hall *burned* into his soul, what care he, to hell with this world of tears and mourning. *This* moment was a token from another time and space, and they were suspended on the breath of the gods.

Wulfstan knew eternity was theirs in this dance of lovers. This was the work of those gods, who controlled and manipulated the swirling powers that give life to what mortals called fate.

Suppose he had to pay the gods with his life's blood, for this glimpse of time without end, it would be worth every drop.

'I love you,' he said, and Aefre trembled as his whisper stole the air from her very breath.

She stared into his eyes, then pressed her lips to his ear, whispering in response to his confession, 'I have always been yours and forever will be. I swore this on the holy stone this day, even as I wed another. Aefre and Wulfstan are one, naught will separate them, not in life or death.'

They were both entranced, their eyes locked and they moved as one, careless, even that the music had ceased. All watched in silence fearing to understand what was before them, and *suddenly* the spell was broken as the onlookers applauded the lovers. They were both startled at the realisation, and from nowhere, perhaps some latent warrior's sixth sense of survival, Wulfstan shouted at the top of his voice, 'The gods blessing on our King and Queen,' and the hall erupted into shouts of acclamation, much to the liking of Æthelfrith.

Wulfstan then led Aefre to her seat, 'Am I not right Ealdorman, she is a gift from the gods?' Æthelfrith asked, clearly enjoying the approval of his guests.

'Indeed Lord, a gift from the gods, as you say, none will ever compare to my Queen…' Æthelfrith had not the slightest inkling of the true intention of Wulfstan's words, but Wulfstan knew Aefre would.

When Wulfstan took his place, Hering leant to him and whispered, 'I must commend you, Lord, on your presence of mind.'

Wulfstan heard him but endeavoured not to show any reaction. He would not be played for the fool by this lackwit, but the sinister implication shot fear through his veins and chilled him to the bone.

'Lord, if I may have your permission to leave, I would be neglecting your trust if I did not ensure that all was ready for your departure on the morrow.'

'We are sorry to lose your company, but yes you may go, perhaps Hering will go with you.'

'No need, your cousin will want to share this evening with you…' Hering gave his usual chilling smile.

Hering was the last person he wanted for company this night. Wulfstan bowed and stepped from the dais.

A hand touched him, 'Will you not dance one dance with me?'

He was startled, '*Meghan*, I was at this moment on my way to attend to work, but yes, and gladly for I have neglected you. Forgive me, my life is not my own. There will be time once the army has taken its leave of us on the morrow to speak with you.'

Their dance was not the dance of lovers it was fast and wild. He had to throw Meghan into the air, she laughed as she fell into his arms and kissed him. He knew that such a kiss would not go unnoticed by Aefre, for it was not the kiss of one friend to another.

'I must go now Meghan, stay close to Cedric.'

'I will, I love you,' she said and kissed him once more.

As soon as he stepped from the hall, he vented his frustration on an innocent dog, kicking the poor beast in the ribs, it howled with indignation and ran off with its tail between its legs. *And yet* – his passion was not satisfied, he bent down, grabbed an empty bucket by its rope handle and flung it with all his might against a wall, it exploded into a shower of splinters, and the two buckled metal hoops, which had held it to its shape, clattered to the ground.

Two armed guards ran to the sound and faced Wulfstan with their spears raised, for it was dark and they didn't recognise him. He ignored the deadly points, walked straight between them, and bundled them both to the ground as if they were naught but two sheaves of dried wheat.

'By the breath of Wōden's mother, Bestla, what ails him?' one of the men asked, picking up the broken spear he'd fallen on.

There were campfires everywhere, at the foot of the fortress hill, in the dunes, on the beach, warriors sharpening weapons, horses being groomed, and stores being loaded onto carts. He looked for his friends, but he could not find them. He saw some thegns he knew, sitting around a fire and eating what looked like smoked fish. They hailed him, and he walked towards their fire.

'Have you had enough of the feasting Ealdorman, and come to envy us warriors, preparing for war? Wishing you were coming too is my guess, there will be riches to fill our pockets, and we'll return covered in glory.'

'If... you return! I am walking round to see if there is aught, I should bring to the notice of the King.'

'You jest, Lord, he will not want to hear aught you have to tell him this night, suppose his army has run off and left him,' and they all laughed heartily at the bawdy jest – but their warrior's humour only served to multiply Wulfstan's misery.

He stared at them until they ceased their laughter. 'It's true, I do envy you, but not for your riches. A warrior may never return, and that would suit *me* fine.'

He left them looking bemused by his grim aside, and he strode off to the far end of the beach.

'Now, there's a happy fellow I'm glad we are leaving behind. I wouldn't want to know he's standing at my back when we face the Gaels,' and they laughed once more.

As always, the salty wind off the sea cleared Wulfstan's head, as he knew it would. Not that he had drunk too much ale for he had not. What thickened his head was an altogether different type of intoxication, which did not lessen its hold come the morning light. As he sat on the rocks at the far end of the sandy beach, he felt resigned.

He watched Æthelfrith's longboat bobbing in the calm water, he got up, waded out the short way to it, and clambered on board. Stepping over the rowing thwarts, he made his way to the stern and sat down at the place he and Aefre had been seated on the journey north. Twisting his head to the side, he saw the sheepskin rugs that had been taken for Aefre's comfort when they sailed from Eoforwic, and he swung his leg over the thwart and lay down on them. Linking his fingers behind his neck, he supported his head and stared up into the jewelled darkness. How beautiful, he thought, and he wondered how many of his ancestor's eyes had spent a moment just like this, staring into the same endless forever. Perhaps *his* sons might do the same, 'Aye, *my* sons.'

He knew he would have to tell Aefre about Meghan, he wondered what she would think on that.

'No doubt we will find a moment to talk when Æthelfrith has gone. I will *have* to marry Meghan. I will do my best for her, but there will only ever be room for Aefre in my heart,' and he shook his head slowly from side to side. 'Perhaps I should tell Æthelfrith, and Meghan how I feel, be honest. If Meghan would still have me, we could go south to Mercia or West Seaxe, I know people there; they would welcome me. Would that not be the honourable thing to do?' He frowned and pursed his lips, 'But never to see Aefre again… mmm, what would you advise Freya, goddess of love? Show your bond-slave what you would have him do.'

As the new day pushed itself free of the horizon, he was awoken by movement at the prow of the boat; he reached for his seax and rose quickly to his feet.

'*Who's there*? Come out, if you value your life.' Two trembling young lovers crawled from below some sailcloth.

'We're a sorry Lord, we were afeared to come out; we thought that you were talking to someone, and we fell asleep. We meant no harm, Lord.'

Wulfstan smiled, 'Fear not, perhaps it is I who should apologise. I must go, I have work which will not wait.'

'I has to go too Lord; I goes with the army today. I hopes for treasure, and we will wed on my return. I wanted to say goodbye to Lydia.'

'And have you said your goodbyes?'

'Aye,' he smiled.

Wulfstan smiled too, reached into his purse, and withdrew a silver penny. He tossed it in his hand and then flicked it to the young lad.

'Here's a start, and may it bring you good fortune, and you, Lydia, don't be fearful to speak to me. I will be the Lord here when the King leaves today.' She bowed her head.

The lad caught the spinning coin, 'Bless you, good Lord. My name is Dudda, I will remember this kindness.' Wulfstan gave a quick wave of his hand and disappeared over the side.

Chapter 15

A question of right

There were warriors everywhere, shouting and swearing at slaves, bondsmen *and* each other, tensions were high. Smiths who had worked all night were yet putting the finishing touches to arms of every imaginable shape and size, turning everyday workers tools into deadly weapons of war.

The preferred weapon was the long spear, favoured by mounted warriors and foot soldiers alike. The elite warriors, the huscarls, had swords, axes, *and* spears. They wore fearsome *steel* helmas, and on their upper body, heavy mail. They – were professional warriors employed by the nobles as their personal guards, they had the finest armour and weapons they could afford.

Wulfstan had to push his way through the hoards beyond the gates, and up to the keep, it was mayhem. It ever amazed him that such apparent chaos could be turned into a credible fighting force, but he knew that come the time, they would form into an awesome screaming shield wall of hell and destruction.

He made his way to the King's rooms, there was no need to knock, his door was wide open, and Wulfstan saw that servants were busily trying to dress him. All the while, he ate what looked like a mutton pie from one hand and drank ale from a silver-rimmed horn in the other.

Aefre stood nervously next to him, her eyes cast to the floor.

'Ealdorman, come in, Wulfstan, my friend. How goes it out there?'

'The best I can make of the men, it seems that the smell of blood is in their nostrils and they are eager to be on their way. All they need now is their great warrior King to lead them to victory.'

'Ha… I will be with them directly, brave warriors to a man. What of my horse, Warrior?'

'He stands at the door, I have this minute walked past him, and as always another servant holds a spare for fear it be needed.'

'All is well then. Come, my Queen, we will go down and take command.'

Wulfstan set his arm on Theodbald's shoulder as he passed, 'take care of yourself and your brother the King; you are a great warrior. May the arm of Wōden wield your sword.'

'We will meet again soon my friend, here or in the great hall at Wōden's never-ending feast,' Theodbald laughed.

Aefre took Æthelfrith's arm, and the two walked down the stairs into the courtyard; a cheer went up when they saw him. He kissed Aefre passionately and mounted his warhorse, which skittered slightly at the sudden weight on its back. Æthelfrith reached down his hand to Wulfstan, he took it firmly and wished him well.

Then he shouted to Aefre, 'Farewell my fine wife and pray to the gods that I have news of a son on my return,' she blushed, and he laughed. Æthelfrith was a man in high spirits. He put spur to flank, waved once more and rode off.

Aefre had never spoken since Wulfstan had entered the King's chamber. As soon as Æthelfrith disappeared from view, she turned and walked briskly into the keep followed by her maids, Rowena and Edith, without so much as a glance in Wulfstan's direction.

Wulfstan stared for some time at the stillness around him. All that remained to show that this place had, just moments past, been the scene of such frenetic activity was the settling dust. He turned to see Hering standing against the wall by the door of the keep, watching him. Wulfstan intended to ignore him and walk past him, but Hering touched his arm.

'As the King's blood relative and most royal son of King Hussa, I have given orders that the Queen is seen as my ward and guards have been instructed to that end.'

Wulfstan was unsettlingly quiet, instantly transformed from the past moment of despair; he suddenly appeared to grow physically before Hering's eyes. He did no more than stare at Hering for several seconds, so implacable was his gaze Hering was compelled to avert his eyes. His ever-present smile disappeared as Wulfstan stooped slightly over him.

'*I* – will take your words as merely information as to your personal history and – *not* – a challenge to my authority, for, believe me, only a fool would make such an error of judgement. There will not be any orders issued without my express authority. Do – you – understand?'

Hering visibly shrivelled and trembled, at the raw intensity of Wulfstan's words, which were all the more threatening because they were spoken in such a fearfully calm voice.

Wulfstan waited for some response from Hering, but he was silent. Wulfstan not bowing or acknowledging Hering in any way, turned on his heels, nodded to the guard at the keep entrance and the door opened before him.

He went straight to Aefre's room; the two guards crossed their spears before him.

'No one is to see the Queen without the permission of Lord Hering,' the guard said with all authority.

Wulfstan offered not a word; he drew his sword with such speed the guards didn't even have time to blink. The keen edge of the Ulfberht fell exactly at the point where the two spear shafts crossed, severing both shafts with the single blow and the now useless pieces of iron clattered to the stone floor at their feet. The guards were awestruck and looked in disbelief at their headless spears.

'Do *not* ever stand in my way again, or next time I will remove *your* heads with equal ease. I am the only Lord you will ever have while our King is at war, barring the Queen. That weasel, Lord Hering is forever subordinate to me. Now re-arm and thank Wōden that you are not carrying your heads under your arms when you make your way to the armoury. Step aside,' and he pushed the two paralysed soldiers roughly out of his way.

Wulfstan knocked on the door, and Edith nervously opened it having heard the furore. She stepped to one side, curtseyed and Wulfstan entered.

Aefre was standing statuesque gazing from the window. She didn't turn but bade her servants leave. The two maids curtseyed even though she stood with her back to them and paid them no heed. They left, carefully closing the door behind them.

'My Queen!'

'*Yes*... I am now your Queen and may carry within my body the *future* King. What feelings do you have now for me, Lord?' Her voice trembled and she bowed her head. Though she made no sound, he could see the irregular movement of her shoulders.

He stepped to her and gently took her arms in his hands and turned her to face him. Her head was yet bowed as if in shame. He set the crook of his finger under her chin and lifted her head, but she looked to the side rather than into his eyes. He could see that her eyes were red and swollen; tears streamed down her face and onto his fingers.

'Aefre, my dearest, sweet treasure, do you not yet understand that my love asks nothing of you. It is not something that you have to earn, or even something, which *I* choose to give or withhold. My heart is yours to do with as you wish, torment and torture it as you will, but it will remain forever yours.' She now looked into his eyes and then pressed her lips passionately to his, and he held her tightly in his arms.

'Thank you, thank you, I feared that you would reject me, I told you the night past that Aefre was yours completely, forever – *love* me.'

'I cannot stay, there are eyes upon me, and blades set to my back, we must take great care. Hering has my downfall at his heart, and yours too, perhaps even the King's. He watches and suspects, we must take great care.'

'Can this be true?'

'Yes, I am without any doubt. I will leave you now we have many days to be together, remember my love. Now bathe your face and I will send in your maids, so that they can tell of your innocence, if questioned, *and* – they – will be questioned, believe me.'

'Rowena and Edith will never betray me, they have been with me all of my life, we played together as children.'

'Aefre, trust me, the viper charms his innocent victim before it strikes, *we* – have a viper in our midst and your maids are innocents. Come, let me, your loyal devoted subject, bathe your face,' and he took Aefre's hand and led her to the washstand.

Wulfstan poured water from the ewer into a bowl and tenderly bathed Aefre's face, 'There, as new,' he said, dabbing her face with a towel, and kissing the tip of her nose.

'How is it possible that such a giant of a man with the great hands of a warrior can be so gentle?' They both smiled, he bowed most courtly with an exaggerated flourish and left her.

Her maids were standing outside the door, the two guards had re-armed and stood very straight as Wulfstan stepped from the room.

'Be kind to your mistress, she is distressed and concerned for the King.'

'Yes, Lord, we love our Lady,' Rowena replied.

When Wulfstan came from the keep he called to a servant, 'Where is my huscarl, Cedric?'

'He went towards the beach with a girl, Lord.'

Wulfstan stared hesitantly towards the shore for several minutes, sighed, and walked off in that direction

Chapter 16

Meghan

Meghan waved as she saw Wulfstan coming down the dunes towards them; he withdrew his hand from his cloak and returned her wave.

'We came down here for some peace and quiet, time to reflect, my friend,' Cedric shouted as he neared.

'Aye, did you manage to say farewell to your brother Meghan?' Wulfstan asked when he reached them.

'Yes, only briefly, he and Godric were too busy for much talk, so Cedric brought me down here out of all the activity for safety's sake. The horses were trampling on anyone or anything which got in their way.'

'Very wise Cedric; you were much safer out of it. Has Meghan told you that we are to wed, Cedric?'

'No, she has kept that news to herself, I'm glad, it is as it should be,' he smiled and kissed Meghan.

'Come, let's sit over there against the rocks, the wind is getting up and blowing the sand.' Wulfstan took Meghan's hand, and they walked to his favourite seat at the rocks by Æthelfrith's longboat. The three sat down on the sand and leant against the smooth basalt rock. Meghan snuggled into Wulfstan, and he wrapped his cloak around her, protecting her face the best he could from the blowing sand.

'I have many things to attend to here. That maggot Hering is up to something, he is angling after my position.' The mention of Hering ensured Cedric's full attention. 'I have a dilemma, Cedric, I need you here, but I also need you to see that Meghan is taken safely home...'

Cedric butted in, 'Hering has already been questioning Meghan about her friendship with you.'

'What, when!' Wulfstan's eyes burned with fury.

'When you left the dancing the night past, he introduced himself as one concerned for *you*, and said if he could ever be of help to Meghan, she must come to him.'

'Over my dead body...'

'He sent a shiver down my spine, Wulfstan, his voice alone sounds like it's from the place of the dead.'

'You have the measure of that man Meghan keep well clear of him. If he ever approaches you again ignore him and come to Cedric or me. Take Meghan home Cedric, she's better away from here. She will have much to occupy her at home and return to me as quickly as you can. Bring huscarls, if there are any left, I need friends around me here. I will come as soon as I can to seek your father's permission for your hand, and we will be married. I will not see you shamed. Explain to your father, that I wish it were different, but I can do no more.'

'We will go this day, and I will return with men by the fall of night the next day.'

'Thank you, Cedric, it is a difficult balance for our home needs men to protect it too, but I trust this to your wisdom.'

'Come, you must go if you are to be home by dark.' Wulfstan stood and offered his hand to Meghan.

They walked back quickly to the stockade and while Meghan bundled together her belongings, Cedric, with Wulfstan's help, saddled their horses. The stable boys tried to help, but Wulfstan bade them be about other work, he would help his friend.

'What about the other lady…?' Cedric asked avoiding names.

'The other lady?'

'Yes, the other lady, your feelings for her?'

'Ah… they have not changed, for her or me.'

'Then I am sorry for you my dear friend. I will not judge, but I am always here for you come what may, it's difficult when such wedges are driven between friends, you know Meghan is a friend too.'

Wulfstan gripped the front swell and the cantle of the saddle having positioned it on the horses' back, and while he held it, he laid his head forward onto the seat. He often did this before a journey. It was as if climbing onto a horse signified leaving and moving on, and he needed to pause for a second to consider. On this occasion, it was not him who would ride the horse, but it was him who was setting his toe into the stirrup of change.

'Aye, well, I am honour bound to Meghan… you tell me what you would do, she is with child.'

Cedric hesitated for a moment, 'I wondered,' he tried not to show any judgement on his face.

They turned to the door as Meghan came in carrying her baggage.

'Here, girl, give me that load,' Cedric said reaching for her bundle.

'You have told Cedric then?'

'Sorry, Wulfstan, it was just a reaction,' Cedric said, annoyed with himself.

'Don't fret yourself, the news will be out soon enough. Come, let us take the horses out into the yard and I will see you on your way.' Wulfstan took Meghan in his arms and kissed her, then helped her into the saddle. 'Safe journey and Cedric make sure that Leofwine has considered the defence of our home, he may need your guidance.'

'I'm sure he is able enough, but I will lend my support,' assured Cedric, Wulfstan slapped the hindquarters of Cedric's horse, and they rode out through the gates for home.

Wulfstan seated himself on the well and massaged his chin thoughtfully for a while, then folded his arms.

'Ahhh,' he sighed. He needed to explain about Meghan to Aefre; she'd been preoccupied this morning and had never mentioned the kisses. She must have seen him at the wedding celebration, he thought, but she *would* mention it, he knew that.

I must tell her that I am to wed Meghan, but I will forgo mentioning the child, he chewed it over in his mind. He was not afraid to tell her, it might well ease *his* conscience. He had known people offload "The Truth" not to enrich, but to cause suffering, and make *them* feel more righteous, it was usually a "Truth" about others. *He* would carry this and save Aefre unnecessary misery. No, he would let that rest in its place for now.

'What price honour?' He said, pushing himself wearily from the well and walking towards the keep. He would go to see Aefre and find out if she had any orders for him, *and* he wanted to clear the air with regard to Meghan, as soon as he could. He understood only too well the pain of such, and he despised himself, for it was all-of-his-own making.

He knocked on her door; it opened, and both her maids were standing there. To his surprise, they left as soon as he entered, without a word from Aefre, she must have already spoken to them.

Aefre was seated and nodded to him.

'We are alone!'

'Yes… I have this moment been visited by Lord Hering.'

'*And?*' He could feel his blood immediately start to boil.

'He could not wait to inform me that you are to wed.'

'I imagine not. That fellow and I – will not have a long life together in this world.'

'Does he speak the truth?'

'He does, he is better informed than I, for I have only just this hour past made such arrangements. I have been promised to this girl for years, the match was agreed by our families. Such agreements are not only between kings and queens, may I sit?' Aefre gestured to the chair opposite to her. 'It appears that fate has ordered our lives, if not our hearts, aye, and perhaps our hearts too.'

'Was that the girl I saw you with at the celebrations?'

'It was.'

'She is very beautiful.'

'Yes… This changes nothing, I love you, I cannot bring myself to say those words to Meghan, that's her name, may the gods forgive me for the wrong I do her. I love you, and there will never be another for me. He rose from his chair and knelt at Aefre's knees and laid his head on her lap, she slid her fingers into his hair.

'Just hold me, Wulfstan,' he stood and lifted her from her chair, into his arms and held her quietly to his chest. 'I don't know how it can be, but life does not exist without you, I have even begged the gods, to my shame, that Æthelfrith does not return, how we are cursed by the gods or surely will be. I want to be *your* wife, to sleep with you, to bear your sons. Will we ever have a moment to ourselves?'

'You think that I do not want all that *you* want? We are stepping on to a path of no return and there is a wolf prowling desiring to gnaw at our souls. He has already been to visit you. If any tragedy should befall Æthelfrith, Hering will attempt to take the kingdom, I'm certain of it, he may do anyway. In the meantime, we have work, which at least allows us to be together and I will grasp such with both hands.'

'What work?'

'We must ride around your farms and see that they are defended and have plans if they are attacked. They must also see that their Queen is here and cares for them, but most of all – we will be together.'

'I will need clothes; I will be as quick as I can – suddenly, the day seems bright.'

'I'll send in your very discreet maids and go to organise men and horses.'

Chapter 17

Trapped

Wulfstan waited uneasily in the courtyard. The men chosen for the guard talked and laughed amongst themselves, happy to kill time until their new Queen honoured them with her presence.

Wulfstan had chosen a huscarl called Hrodulf to lead the men. He was of an age for such a responsibility and seemed respected by his fellow huscarls. The main reason for the choice was that Wulfstan had seen Hering lash him with his riding whip. As Hering walked away, Hrodulf had made a gesture, which was not one of undying love.

Wulfstan had yet to establish where loyalties lay. He knew he needed to get the warriors of the fortress on his side and stamp his authority as quickly as he could.

Wulfstan had made it known that Cedric would return soon and when he did, *he* would take charge and he *alone* would be obeyed. Anyone who challenged Cedric's right to lead would answer to him when he returned. In the meantime, Leofric, who had been recommended by Hrodulf, would be in charge. Wulfstan had told Leofric of his intended route and left orders if there was any threat a rider must be sent to him.

He was sure Hering would have his cronies in every quarter, and Wulfstan guessed they would be known by the men. It would take time, but he would weed them out.

There had been no sign of Hering; he must have thought it wise to keep well away from Wulfstan this morning.

Clearly, he'd taken the opportunity to go to Aefre when he was on the beach with Cedric and Meghan. No doubt, he was hoping to make trouble between him and Aefre, which meant he'd been watching him.

Wulfstan was concerned as to what he'd be up to while he and Aefre were gone. Their absence would be a gift to a devious schemer such as Hering.

'*Ealdorman*,' Aefre called as she came out through the door and he went to her; he bowed, and whispered, 'may I have a quick word with your maids, my Lady?'

Aefre looked bemused. Wulfstan went to them and drew them both close to him. Aefre couldn't hear what he was saying, whatever he said she could see them nodding, it was plain to her they were agreeing about something. Wulfstan smiled, and they curtseyed to him.

'And what was that about?' Aefre asked when he returned to her side.

'I merely asked Edith if she would walk with me when we returned.'

'You value not your head, Ealdorman,' she said smiling at his tease. 'I will ask Rowena as we ride.' Aefre was taking Rowena with her, for their journey could be for several days, and it would not be seemly for her to travel without a female companion.

'Here, let me assist you, my Queen,' and he swept Aefre off her feet and onto her pony, not in a fashion seemly for his queen, but in an action more suited to lovers.

He adjusted her stirrups for comfort and at the same time mischievously caressed her ankle. She leant down to him, 'have I told you how much I love you, you know how to tantalise a woman, Ealdorman Wulfstan?' He smiled and all but reached up and kissed her.

Once upon his mount, there was an instant change to his disposition, he was again the commander, the man of authority, and he signalled to Hrodulf to move off.

They would ride south along the wide beach for a couple of leagues and then turn west, inland.

When they came to the end of the long sandy beach further down the coast, they turned with the sun behind them and rode away from the sea towards the moors. By the late noon, they were on the high ground and stopped to look back. The northern coast of Bernicia was visible for leagues.

'It is a wondrous sight, Wulfstan and the fortress at Din Guyaroi is yet visible even from this great distance. No wonder you love this place.'

'Aye, all that I love is right here at this moment.'

She smiled, '*my* home at Eoforwic is in a great valley; it is called the Vale of Eoforwic. Though it is a beautiful fertile place, we are subject to flooding. It is quite flat, so we never have panoramas the like of this. This is a spectacular view, which makes one seem quite insignificant, good for the pride, I suspect, of you Bernicians,' she laughed.

'Might I remind you, good Queen, *you* are now a Bernician,' he said, poking her in her side with his finger, and she laughed all the more… 'Yes, I have always lived here, and still, the views cause me to stop and think. I can be out riding, never giving the scenery the slightest thought, then suddenly it catches me, and I'm captivated. Speaking of riding this has been a long day, are you tired?'

'A little, but at the same time invigorated,' and she breathed deeply and smiled.

'I think we will make camp for this night, yonder – in the lee of that hill.' He shouted to his leading huscarl, 'Hrodulf, we will camp over there. Have our scouts mentioned any sign of strangers to you? I'm sure there is some ground disturbance as if horses have passed this way not too long since.'

Hrodulf turned to him, and nodded, 'I've seen the prints, Lord. There have been horses this way sure enough. Thirty or so is my guess, but my scouts say there is naught to be seen of any strangers. We must hope they have moved on, whoever they were. I would have been more content if we'd seen them and understood their purpose.'

'Aye, me too, thirty's a large group to be riding without they have some trouble in mind. Perhaps we'll camp nearer to the wood, it will be more difficult to see us in the shadow of the trees. The high ground may be better to defend, but I'd rather keep out of view and avoid any trouble.'

'As you wish Lord, for what it's worth I'm of like mind.'

The party made their way to the edge of the wood where there was some cover and dismounted. Wulfstan reached up for Aefre and lowered her carefully to the ground, his eyes scanning their surroundings. He had not been a warrior for so long without developing an instinct for trouble, and he was uneasy.

'No fires Hrodulf, it's a warm night; we'll be warm enough. We have dried mete and bread with us, more than enough. I hope to reach our first village of Wandylaw by midday on the morrow. We will just have to be watchful. Make sure we have enough sentries.'

'Aye, Lord.'

'Are you concerned, Wulfstan?'

'Perhaps I am over sensitive because you are here Aefre, but I have reached my great age because of my senses. Often when there has appeared to be no danger, my senses have told me differently.' Wulfstan's manner was disturbing her.

'And do you sense danger here?' she asked nervously.

'We are a larger force than their number if the horse tracks are to be the measure of their true numbers. We will have to be watchful. Fasten my seax to your belt; I don't think it will be needed, but better safe than sorry,' he said passing it to her. 'Have you ever killed a man?'

'Never!'

'I didn't think so if you have to use it,' he pointed to the seax, 'don't think, just strike. Thinking can eat up the time between life and death. I will be ever by your side, and the huscarls will stand before you, that is what they are trained to do, but I think we will be safe, it seems quiet.' Much too quiet he thought, looking once more over the ground before them, there should be bird sounds, and there are none.

No sooner had Wulfstan spoken, then there was the most fearful screaming and crashing, as painted warriors rose like demons from the darkness of the tall bracken and charged towards the edge of the wood where they were gathered. No sign of any horses, they had been lying in wait. Most of Wulfstan's men were caught unaware as they were busily unpacking their belongings. Some hadn't even time to draw their weapons before they were slain. The attack was like lightning.

Wulfstan pushed Aefre and Rowena down behind a fallen tree and called men to him. The fighting was instant, vicious, shouting and grunting filled the air. He'd managed to grab his shield, as did some others and they were able to form some sort of defence. Hrodulf clearly knew his business and had picked good men. Although they had at first been overwhelmed, they were now holding their own, but for how long, they were clearly outnumbered.

'TO YOUR SIDE LORD,' Hrodulf shouted at Wulfstan as an axe-wielding Briton determined to cleave him in two. The stroke missed him by a whisker, so close he heard the blade swish by his ear. Wulfstan rolled over, and the axe head lodged itself in the trunk of the fallen tree that Aefre was hiding behind, landing just inches from her head, dislodging a large chunk of crumbling bark and flinging it into her lap. The impetus of the blow carried the man forward as he followed through with his swing. Wulfstan reacted instantly to the opportunity, driving Dream World up into the painted belly of the man. The man reached instinctively to the blade, grabbing it with his hands, swayed for a split second, and tumbled forward onto Wulfstan. Wulfstan pushed and wriggled to be free of the weight, scrambled to his feet, pressed his boot to the man's chest and withdrew his sword.

Another hand reached for Aefre, grabbed her by the hair, and dragged her from her hiding place.

She screamed and struggled, but the man wrapped his arm around her waist and lifted her from her feet, he was unaware of the seax in her hand. She drew the point of the razor shape blade along the full length of his forearm, opening the muscle to the bone. The man yelled and dropped her instantly as he instinctively gripped the wound, trying to staunch the bleeding, Aefre fell heavily to the ground. The blood poured from between the man's fingers. There was so much blood, she thought that she had been cut too; her clothes at her middle were saturated.

Wulfstan was on his feet in a flash, and he charged the fellow with his shield and bundled him to the ground, driving Dream World mercilessly through the fallen warrior's exposed throat.

'Make for the darkness of the forest with the women, Lord, we will hold them as long as we can,' Hrodulf shouted.

'Where's Rowena, Aefre?'

'Oh no, she's been taken.'

Wulfstan looked around, but she was nowhere to be seen.

'Come Aefre, we must go now.'

'*No*, we can't leave Rowena.'

'We must, or you will be taken too.' He grabbed her hand and dragged her forcibly after him. 'Run, we must get well clear before our men are overwhelmed.'

'But Rowena!'

He didn't give her time to think, he was pulling her as fast as she could run.

They ran until they could no longer hear the sound of the battle. Wulfstan leant forward, his hands resting on his knees and gasped for breath. His arm was on fire from dragging Aefre. Aefre fell back against a tree; she groaned and pressed her fingers into the pain in her side, she felt sick and dizzy.

'We will catch our breath for a second, and then we must get further away.'

'I can't, I just can't go another step.'

'Yes, you can. I will help you, come on now.'

'Not yet, please, a little longer.'

'No, we must keep going, come on,' and he took her hand once more and dragged her deeper into the forest.

She was staggering and stumbling, he knew that this was as far as she could go, she slipped and was unable to help herself and fell headlong into the mud, and he collapsed to his knees next to her, yet holding her hand.

'It's no good I'm finished...'

'All right, all right, we will hide here; it's too dark to go on anyway. They will not find us in the dark. Look,' he could do no more than move his head in the direction. 'There's a small hollow there; we'll lie in it and cover ourselves with dead branches and leaves. Take a minute to gather your breath first.'

Chapter 18

Hunted

Wulfstan struggled to his feet, 'Here, let me help you,'

'Not yet, I need some more time,' Aefre lay where she had fallen gasping and panting for breath. 'I'm exhausted, my whole body is trembling, I have never felt like this in my whole life.'

'Don't fret; I think we have put enough distance between us, and our attackers for now. I'm sure we will be safe here; it will give my brain time to grasp hold of some understanding of what's going on and what we should do come daylight. In the meantime, can you make your way over to that hollow?'

She looked up, 'yes.'

He helped her to her feet, and she limped unsteadily to where he'd pointed. She was in so much pain, she couldn't even stand up straight.

'I will lay my cloak onto the ground for us to lie on.' He did that and told Aefre to lie down.

'What about you?'

'I'll gather some branches and bracken fronds. Take your cloak off, we'll cover ourselves with it and then put the branches on top.' He dragged any forest debris that was near at hand to the edge of the hollow, then lay down next to Aefre, covered them with her cloak, reached from under it and pulled the sticks and large fronds of bracken over them.

'We should be safe, after all, why would they waste time hunting for two people? Unless they did not fall on us by chance.'

'What do you mean?'

'They were lying in wait for us, to do that they would have had to have knowledge of our route.'

'Who knew of it?'

'Only Leofric, I left him in charge at Din Guyaroi and made known to him our plans so he could reach us if needed.'

'Do you not trust him?'

'I don't know him, but Hrodulf said he was a good man and I trust him. I don't know the answer to all this, but this does not rest easy with me. Let's be still for now and try to rest,' and he pushed his arm around Aefre, and she snuggled into him.

'What of Rowena and the rest of the men? I can't bear to think what may happen to her, I pray she is dead.'

'When it is daylight, I will be able to make a better judgement. I need to go back to the battle site and see if I can discover anything which might help me understand.'

'Is that wise, they may be yet there?'

'Don't worry, I'll not be caught out a second time, but for now, let us sleep. Is there no kiss before we sleep?' She lifted her lips to his. 'I can't see a thing, and you are still beautiful.'

Aefre slept fitfully, but he could not sleep at all, he listened to every sound.

Aefre lifted her cloak from her face and felt for Wulfstan, he'd gone, panic shot through her, she sat up in terror.

'Good morning, I heard you stirring,' he looked down on her from above and smiled.

'Don't be afraid, I didn't want to disturb you. I've been looking around and listening, and there does not seem to be anything untoward. I've something to break your fast.' He past her a cloth full of blackberries, 'try them they are delicious, we from around here call them brambles.'

'I'm not hungry, I thought you'd gone.'

'No, you are stuck with this fellow I'm afraid,' and he leant down and kissed her. 'Try to eat those, we have not eaten since the day past, and if you were feeling like me, you would not have eaten enough to sustain a mouse.'

She sat up and reached for the berries, 'Ahhh, I'm so stiff; I will never be able to move this day. You can't imagine the pain in my muscles.'

'Poor Aefre, eat up and then I'll rub your legs. Once you get moving it will ease off.'

She did as she was bidden and ate the berries.

Once she'd eaten, he helped her to stand, and he rubbed her calf muscles.

She cried out as he rubbed, but he assured her that the warmth generated by him massaging would help.

'Does that feel better?'

'If I say no you might do it again, and I couldn't stand it, so the answer is yes, much better. Now – a *gentle* massage may have been a different story.'

He laughed and kissed her, 'At least it's helped your humour if nothing else. This is what we will do. We will skirt around the way we came, just in case our tracks are being followed, we don't want to walk into trouble. I will go ahead, and you will follow at a distance. When I'm sure it is safe to move forward, I will beckon you, and so we will go on. If there is any danger, you will lie down, cover yourself and not move until nightfall, and *then* only with great care. Is that clear?'

'Yes.'

'Have you my seax to hand?'

She felt at her side. 'Yes.'

'I'll go, wait until I signal for you to follow.'

Wulfstan was surprised how far they had run from where the action had taken place, it was further than he imagined, they must have run over two leagues. Eventually, he could see the moor beyond the edge of the forest, and by the look of the hill before him, he guessed that he was further west than where they'd been attacked.

He signalled to Aefre to take cover, and he crawled the two hundred or so paces to the tree line. He couldn't hear any voices, and there were some sheep grazing peacefully nearby, so he guessed that whoever they were, they had gone. He made his way cautiously back to Aefre and told her to stay where she was. He said that he was going to take a closer look at where they'd fought.

'Take care, Wulfstan.' He embraced her.

'I will, fear not,' and he released her and made his way to the site of the conflict. Before he reached it, he could see the dead, their mutilated bodies had been stripped of anything of worth. He didn't step into the open but crouched down just within the cover of the trees. There was a chance that men had been posted to watch for him. He counted the bodies, and there were at least ten missing the best he could make out, and no sign of Rowena.

'The ill-begotten earslings,' he said. He couldn't be sure of the numbers he counted, for there were also many of their dead, his men had fought well. He knew that there was money to be made from slaves and Rowena would fetch a rich price, so she may be safe. He could see the tracks left and wondered if they knew that he and Aefre had escaped.

His head was swimming with unanswered questions, if it had been planned, why had they not hunted for them.

By the time he returned to Aefre, she was distraught and leapt into his arms.

'I have never known fear like this in all my life.'

'I am well, they seem to have gone, I have a question for you Aefre. Think carefully, before you answer.'

'What question!'

'Do you want us to make our way back to Din Guyaroi, or… follow these Britons and see if any of our men live? It would be the wisest thing to make our way home...'

'I do not have to think; they fought without consideration of their own well-being and because of them we live. We will follow them.'

'Thank you my precious Aefre, you are all I thought, the lady who has my heart could do no other.'

'Then you did not need to ask.'

'I asked not for me, but for you, *you* needed to say the words. We will follow the tree line west, keeping in the shadows, and see how far it takes us and where to.'

They followed the edge of the forest for most of the day without sighting their enemy. Wulfstan could see Aefre was tiring she needed food and rest; they had only drunk once, from a stream, which ran through the forest.

Dusk was upon them when Wulfstan smelt the smoke from a fire. He pushed Aefre roughly to the ground behind a rock.

'Stay here,' he whispered, 'lie under your cloak as you did last night, and I will cover you.' She offered no argument, only nodded. He covered her and made his way silently in the direction of the smoke.

When he found the band of Britons, he was astounded that there were no guards. It unnerved him, and he lay for some time, listening and watching, fearful that he might stumble into guards he had missed.

There were no more than six of the Britons. He lay at the lip of the hollow, it was clear now why he'd not seen the light from the fire and only smelt it; their resting place was well hidden in what looked like an ancient quarry.

There were five prisoners, but he could not tell who they were. They were bound face down, tied to pegs driven into the ground, their arms and legs spread out. He caught sight of Rowena, she was suspended by her arms from the branch of a tree, her feet only just touched the ground; it must have been agony for her. Every so often, she would stumble, he guessed when cramp bit into her legs and all her weight was then supported by her wrists, and she'd cry out. Her captors would only turn to her and laugh.

Wulfstan's blood was boiling with anger, they would pay for this, suppose it cost him his life, but for now, he never moved a muscle, he just watched.

Where were the others? There were never so many bodies at the battle site to account for this shortfall of Britons. He heard a horse whinny and stared further to the right. That must be where they left their horses he thought, but there were now only horses sufficient for these fellows, as much as he could see. The number of the horses convinced him that the others were not here, but where were they, and for how long?

Wulfstan flexed his fists in frustration; he had to act now. He couldn't charge and challenge them, even if he were bold enough to take on six men, they had him at a disadvantage, because of their prisoners. They would likely suffer first for his bravado.

He decided that he would try to get to their horses, set them loose, that would divide the men. They would be forced to try and catch the animals, and they wouldn't have time to think about how they'd escaped.

He stared once more into the darkness to be sure there were no guards he'd missed. Taking advantage of the shadows, he crawled down to the horses. Their pen was ideal, it suited his purpose perfectly. All that contained them was a single rope tied to four trees making a square of sorts. He stood up behind one of the four trees, untied the rope, and laid it carefully to the ground so as not to disturb the horses while he was near to them. He crawled away to a safe distance and threw a stick at one of the horses, it squealed at the shock, reared and galloped from the pen, the rest followed.

The Britons to a man ran after them leaving their prisoners. This was better than Wulfstan could have dreamed of; he jumped up and dashed to his men cutting their bonds.

Saying to each as he cut them free, 'listen, do as I tell you, remain where you are, they will soon catch their horses and bring them back. When they sit once more by the fire, we will jump them at my signal, so watch me. I'll be nearby watching.' He left Rowena hanging but touched her as he passed. 'You will be free soon, be strong,' and he knelt in the shadows near to her and waited. It seemed like hours before they returned, arguing and cursing, he guessed, about whose fault it was that the horses had escaped. They were one short, where was the sixth man? Wulfstan strained his eyes, but he couldn't see him.

He must move now, he couldn't wait any longer in case the others returned; it had to be now. He rose quietly from his hiding place and sauntered towards the fire. He mumbled a friendly sounding greeting, not being able to speak a single word of their language and lifted his hand; his casual approach startled them. They only stared at him; he was almost within touching distance before they reacted.

As they stood, Wulfstan's men leapt up and rushed at the Britons, distracting them. In that split second Wulfstan removed one man's sword arm and another's innards, which spilt out like coiled snakes into his hands. The missing Briton must have been with the horses, realising that the prisoners had broken free and were now attacking his comrades and he rushed to help. The moment he arrived, he was struck square in the face with a burning log from the fire. Such was the force of the blow he was knocked off his feet. The others were overpowered before they had even touched their weapons.

'Slit their throats, we haven't time for them, get the horses saddled as quick as you can.' He turned, put his arm around Rowena's waist, sliced through the rope that held her, and he lowered her carefully to the ground. Wulfstan winced as he saw the fearful damage to her wrists. He picked her up, gently cradling her in his arms, and carried her to the horses. She never spoke.

'Quick, we've got to get clear of this place,' he lifted Rowena onto a horse and leapt up behind her.

'Which way, Lord?'

'Follow me,' and he galloped the short distance to where Aefre was hidden. He knew she would feel the ground vibrating from the pounding of their horses' hooves and be terrified, but to her credit, she never showed herself. He leapt from his horse and whispered her name before he uncovered her to lessen her shock. She was unable to still her trembling, he held her tightly to his chest, she couldn't even speak; her whole face was shaking.

'Be still Aefre, be still. Hrodulf, get up behind Rowena, I will ride with the Queen.' Hrodulf dismounted and jumped up behind Rowena, as he was commanded.

'Where to Lord?'

'We will head for the village of Wandylaw, where we intended to go and think again when we get there. It has seen plenty of trouble over the years, it's been there since the beginning of time. These horses can't go too far with us doubled up on their backs, it's too much to ask of them, but they'll make it to the village.'

Chapter 19

The Village

It was dawn when they drew near to the village and the unexpected arrival of mounted warriors brought panic amongst the waking villagers.

There was suddenly a furore of screaming, shouting, and men attempting to arm themselves. Wulfstan had a moment of despair for if they had been raiders, they would have wreaked hell and destruction upon the place.

He drew his men to a standstill just short of the village, dismounted, and walked on with his hands raised. A young boy emboldened by the hysteria ran to him with a spear.

'Put that up fellow before you hurt someone, I usually only offer this kindness once.'

An older man came to the side of the boy and pushed him, snatching the spear from him and giving him a token slap about the head.

He furrowed his brow and stared at Wulfstan, 'I know you, Lord,' he said bowing. 'I was at Catraeth when we thrashed the Gododdins, you gave me a gold torc, do you remember,' the man rolled up his sleeve and revealed the burnished gold armband.

Now Wulfstan stared at *him*, 'Ha, I remember, but your face was blacker that day, I didn't recognise you.'

'This is my pride, Lord; I *might* give it to this worthless wretch one day. Perhaps I should have sold it, but who has a torc like this?'

'Not me for sure,' Wulfstan smiled.

'Ah, but you have a fine helma, Lord.'

'That is true, it was a fair bargain.'

'My name is Hereweald, and this lackwit is my son, Osgar, perhaps the name of "Godspear" was ill-chosen,' he laughed and put his arm affectionately around his son's shoulder. 'This Lord, my dear son, is the great warrior I told you about.'

Osgar's eyes widened, 'You mean the Lord Wulfstan?'

'Aye, the very one,' his father added.

'Forgive me, Lord,' the young man said and bowed, 'I am as my father said a lackwit.'

Wulfstan laughed, 'Think of it this way Osgar, you were the only man in your village to be ready to face intruders. You too will be a great warrior like your father,' the young man visibly grew at Wulfstan's praise.

'What brings you to our humble village, Lord?'

'I come with King Æthelfrith's Queen, Queen Aefre, daughter of King Ælla. May we enter, and share mete, and I will tell all?'

Hereweald looked to the horses, saw Aefre and bowed. 'We are honoured, Lord, come to our longhouse and we will attend to your needs the best we are able.'

Wulfstan beckoned his men, and they came into the stockade. He went to Aefre and lowered her to the ground, she all but stumbled to her knees her legs were so weak. Wulfstan held her.

'My Lady,' Hereweald bowed once more. 'Are you hurt?'

'This is Hereweald, my Lady, he and I are old friends.' Hereweald smiled.

'We have been attacked not too many leagues from your village by Britons and many of our men were killed. Have you a tub and water where we might bathe? My maid is injured.'

'We only have one tub which we all uses,, my Lady, will that do?'

'That will do perfectly well, we will bathe before we eat.'

'Go to that roundhouse, my Lady and I will see that you have all that you need.'

'Ealdorman, would you carry Rowena to the house?'

Wulfstan nodded and reached up to Rowena and carefully took her down from Hrodulf's horse. 'You are safe now Rowena, your Lady will tend to you, don't be afraid.' He carried her into the roundhouse and gently laid her onto a framed cot.

'Thank you Wulfstan, I will see to her.'

Two girls arrived with a small tub, with some hot water and towels. They must have noticed the look on Aefre's face.

'It's all we has, my Lady.'

'It will serve our purpose well enough,' Aefre tried to sound convincing, Wulfstan smiled. 'Leave us Wulfstan, these girls will help me.'

Wulfstan saw Hereweald talking with Hrodulf when he emerged from the roundhouse.

'Is Hrodulf, telling you of our exploits?' he asked as he neared them.

'Aye, hellish, we have not seen a soul for days.'

'I'm surprised that you, a warrior, are so unprepared for trouble.'

'Aye, we have become lax that's true, but we never sees many strangers round here, and there's been no trouble since we chased the Gododdins at Catraeth. We're a bit off the beaten track to be noticed.'

'Well, things may be about to change.'

'So, your man here tells me.'

'My worry is what will happen when the renegades return to their camp, and they discover we've gone and their men dead, they may well follow our tracks. It would be easy enough for them if it were their wish. I think we must prepare, Hereweald. We need to be organised, you and Hrodulf should work together, and quickly, I will help too. These are mean and serious warriors.'

'We will start now, I'll have our women bring food to the men as they work, we can't sit and talk leisurely over mete,' Hereweald was rightly concerned.

'Did you learn anything while you fellows were prisoners?' Wulfstan asked Hrodulf.

'I couldn't understand a word they said, Lord. They dragged us behind their horses, Rowena too, poor girl, she stumbled and fell, but they dragged her anyway, she was sorely hurt. When we reached the camp we were tied, they argued for a while, they didn't seem sure what to do, they mounted and rode off leaving us with only those few guards.'

'Lord,' they all turned to Halth, one of Wulfstan's warriors.

'Have you something to add, Halth,' asked Wulfstan.

'Not much, I don't know the language either, but my father had been a slave of the Britons and knew some of their language. Not that he ever spoke it, but he always called my mother, "Banríon".'

'And?' Wulfstan was struggling to see any relevance.

'The word was a Briton word and meant, queen, I had the feeling that they thought Rowena was a queen. Not much help, I'm sorry Lord.'

'Mmm...' Wulfstan narrowed his eyes, 'that – may be of great help Halth.'

'In what way Lord?' asked Hrodulf.

'Let me ponder this, you be about your business, for now, making the village safe. That one word might explain much. Call me if you need me, but first I will ride around the outskirts of the village, I need to properly understand where we are, in relation to their camp. I will think on what you have told me Halth. Hrodulf send out scouts as soon as you can, see they have food and drink.'

Bread, pottage, and ale were brought to the men and they greedily cleaned their bowls and were thankful. Wulfstan went to the roundhouse where Aefre was and called, and she came out.

'What of Rowena?'

'She is distressed, but she has been bathed, and I am now trying to get her to eat something. She has been badly hurt from the way they treated her, but nothing beyond cuts and bruises, they did not molest her, it seemed they wanted to, but their leader forbade it. She can't tell me much because she couldn't understand them.'

'I understand something.'

'What?'

'I want to kiss you, and I don't care who sees me.'

'Be about your work, fool, or "I" will kiss you,' Aefre said and smiled.

Wulfstan playfully punched her jaw and left. As he mounted his horse, he heard Hrodulf giving out orders to the village men. He's a good man he thought, but he wished Cedric were with him.

Wulfstan rode to a low hill no more than a league from the village. It was well situated to give him the commanding view he wanted. He dismounted and sat on a rock. Looking back in the direction of the village he tried to memorise the landscape.

'Banríon', he said to himself, 'queen... they thought Rowena was a queen – or the Queen. If they had expected Aefre, they could easily assume she was Aefre. That might explain why she was not assaulted by those animals. They must not have noticed Aefre and I as we made our escape. I suppose we could have easily been overlooked in the turmoil of battle; I thought it strange that they made no attempt to chase us, especially if they had come to capture us in particular. They wanted a queen, and they had a queen, Rowena. She was of an age and similar in appearance to Aefre. There is more to this than a simple chance encounter, I'll stake my life on it.'

He stood and scanned the view before him once more, but he could not see anything to give him concern. Where could those other riders have gone. Surely, they should have returned to their camp by now. He patted his horse and mounted, nudged it with his heels and rode towards the village.

When he rode into the village, he noticed immediately there were guards in position, and men practising. Their animals had been brought near to the village, and no doubt, they would be brought into the stockade at nightfall.

Wulfstan rode over to Hrodulf, 'You have done well in a very short time, Hrodulf.'

'Aye, we are ready should they come looking for us. There are lookouts that will ride back and give us plenty of warning. What about getting back to Din Guyaroi Lord? We will be vulnerable, we can't take enough men from here to be safe, or that will leave the village at their mercy.'

'I will have to think on that, and my head needs to sleep. I will sleep in the doorway of the Queen and Rowena's roundhouse, but all must remain alert, they may come after dark.'

'If they do, we'll be ready, Lord.'

Chapter 20

Veil of Honour

It was dark by the time Wulfstan went to Aefre's roundhouse. He was tired, he had slept earlier, but since then, he'd never stopped his work, fearful to sleep because of the threat to them.

He went into the house as quietly as he could, closing the door and easing himself down on some skins near the entrance. Stripping off his woollen tunic and undershirt, he wearily slung them to his side and leaned back against the wattle and daub wall. He massaged the muscles in his arms and chest, yet tight from the battle; there were always wounds and aches of which he was unaware until later. Even serious injuries could be ignored in the excitement of the conflict. All warriors who had ever fought at the edge of death knew of the exhilaration, the intenseness. It was the aftermath that left the scars, on the body, yes, but far more long-lasting, in the head. He knew of men it had destroyed. To satisfy their hunger, they needed even more and more of the magic potion, more potent than any mushrooms. They became violent animals that could only ever be saved by death, and they longed and yearned for it.

He closed his eyes and thought of Aefre... *she* was – *his* – obsession, in touching distance, but not to be touched, a thin veil of honour separated them. The veil fluttered tantalisingly in the warm air surrounding his torment, daring him to rip it from its ephemeral threads. He wondered if what fuelled his passion was no different than the drug which drove the warrior in his need for ever greater soaring heights, and its ultimate reward would be the same... *death*.

At first, the darkness inside the longhouse seemed impenetrable, but he saw a shaft of moonlight, which shone through an opening in the wall and it touched   Aefre's face. It took several minutes before he could see her clearly when he did, he could see she was watching him.

She smiled, 'hold me,' she whispered.

He stared at her, she turned back the corner of the rugs covering her, she was naked, he could see the silhouette of her breasts touched by the glow from the embers of the dying fire, and then he went to her.

Her skin was warm and clung to his. Pushing back the hair from her brow he kissed her forehead, and whispered into her ear, 'I love you.'

'And *I* you.'

He lightly caressed her shoulder, and his thumb brushed her breast, which responded to his sensual touch. She moaned from a place deep within as he gently teased her swollen nipple with his tongue. She anxiously felt for his belt, and he eased himself free from his breeches, her hand felt the taut outline of his muscular thighs. *Slowly* he drew his fingertips down her spine to the curve of her waist, she responded eagerly, raising her hips – *and* – the two became one, eternity had engulfed them and the thin veil of honour – was torn in two. She moaned, and he tenderly laid his hand across her mouth for fear of waking Rowena, but Aefre struggled and groaned all the more.

Rowena *had* heard, but their secret was safe with her.

'No, please don't leave me,' Aefre grabbed his arm.

He leant forward and kissed her once more, 'let me go for mercy's sake, there is work for me. My men will be waking and will come for me. It may not go well if I am discovered in bed with their Queen.'

'I'll say you were protecting me.'

'And of course, they would believe their Queen,' he smiled. 'I must go you tantalising nymph.'

She released him, and he made to climb into his breeches, but he lost his balance and fell, crashing out the door and into the yard. He quickly scrambled back into the roundhouse, but it was too much for her to see him hopping around with one leg in and one half out of his breeches desperately trying to gain his balance. Aefre laughed uncontrollably, it was even too much for Rowena to maintain her discreet silence, and she laughed too.

'You miserable women, my toe is trapped in a seam.'

'Well, I can't help, I'm naked,' laughed Aefre.

'I will help him, my Lady.'

'No, you can't, *he's* naked too. Oh, let me see,' and Aefre reached from her covers, took hold of the leg of his breeches and gave it a sharp tug.

Wulfstan yelped, 'ahhhh, I think you've removed my toe.'

Aefre and Rowena laughed even more.

He stood, fastened his belt, and bundled the rest of his clothes under his arm leaving them, to dress outside in the morning light.

His eye caught Hrodulf walking towards him as he finished dressing.

'Are you well Lord, there seemed to be some disruption in your house.'

'You have no idea Hrodulf, I fell trying to dress in the dark, and I was no more than the morning's entertainment to our two ladies.'

'Ah.'

'Come, let's find some mete.'

'Over there, Lord, I have eaten,' Hrodulf said, pointing to a larger roundhouse.

Wulfstan was seated at a table next to Hereweald, Hereweald was telling him all that had been done.

'How long will this threat be upon us, Lord?'

'I don't know what to say about that, Hereweald. I don't really understand what's going on, but we must stay here until I'm sure that it's safe for the Queen to leave. Has there been any report of the Britons whereabouts from the scouts?'

'Not yet, Lord.'

'Where can they be, I wonder. Sooner or later, they will come back to their camp, that's a certainty. They might have gone west to fight against King Æthelfrith. If I knew that for sure, I would go to Din Guyaroi today. I don't so we will have to wait. They had prisoners, they were never intending to keep them tied for weeks, and there were too few guards to consider moving them.'

'Perhaps this day will tell us more,' Hereweald replied. He looked up and saw the Queen and Rowena, and stood, 'My Lady.'

'Ah, I think I am to be tormented so I will leave and see to my work.'

Both Aefre and Rowena laughed, 'Stay Ealdorman, we come to beg your forgiveness.'

'In that case, I will burden you a little longer with my company.' Aefre and Rowena took the seats offered.

'I will leave, Lord, my Lady.' Both Wulfstan and Aefre nodded.

'I will join you directly Hereweald. Now, what of you Rowena, you look more like your old self this morning,' he took her hand and examined her wrist. 'My dear girl, you have shown great bravery, you humble us all.'

'I am alive thanks to you and my Queen. You took great risks for us when you were free.'

'I think it is difficult to be truly free knowing you chose to neglect friends. Real freedom I have learned, is not the right to do what you like, but the power to do what you aught.'

'Your thoughts are greater than mine, Lord, but I will not forget what you gave up for me.'

Wulfstan was embarrassed by Rowena's gratitude and tried to make her laugh once more, 'You did not rush to help me in my hour of need this morning,' he smiled, and she laughed, as did Aefre.

'You are a good man I think Lord.'

'With that kindness, I will leave you, with your permission, my Lady.'

'If you must.' Now *he* bowed, laughing, and left them.

Chapter 21

Waiting

For two days, Wulfstan walked back and forth along the primitive defences, trying to understand what was in the mind of the renegades. He knew that eventually there would be some alarm sounded at Din Guyaroi when they did not return. It was almost five days since they had left. He had planned for such a time away, and that's what he'd told Leofric. They may allow two more days, but then they ought to be concerned.

Cedric should have returned to Din Guyaroi having taken Meghan home, perhaps he'd stayed for a day or two, but he had promised that he would return quickly with men. The whole question of the shortage of fighting men was a worry; if he took men from anywhere to strengthen one location, it inevitably left another vulnerable. That was his problem and why King Æthelfrith had left him in command, because he thought that he would be able to make the best use of what he had. Now Cedric would be faced with the same dilemma, but surely, he would come looking for them, if for no other reason than the Queen was with them.

Yet, there was the gnawing problem, that they had no knowledge as to the whereabouts of their erstwhile Gododdin captors. Wulfstan was sure that they must have returned to their camp by now and discovered that they'd escaped. Perhaps they had met with an unexpected conflict on their travels, and their numbers had been further reduced, or it was possible they could have *all* been killed or captured. All these thoughts swirled round and round in his head – and no answers.

The nights were spent in the arms of Aefre. Rowena discreetly left them each evening and returned to sleep once it was dark. Nothing was ever mentioned.

Both were aware that she knew, she would be a fool not to realise, and she was no fool. Aefre reassured Wulfstan that she trusted Rowena completely, as she did Edith. In their hearts, neither wanted to leave this place, but this was a dream that would end all too soon.

'Whatever will we do when Æthelfrith returns? The King is a good man, I can see that,' said Aefre shaking her head.

'I don't know, Aefre, I just don't know. Are we to be punished for loving? Is this a gift from Freya, the goddess of love who smiles on us, or from Lôgna, the Lord of mischief [18] and he laughs at us?'

'I *do* know there is no darkness in my heart. I am alive in your arms.'

'*I* am known to be an honourable man, respected, even by the King, he trusts me, and the lie is a hard load to carry, for I am anything but honourable.'

She was quiet for several moments, and stared at her fingers as she wrapped a loose thread around them, 'I am with child…'

'*No*… Æthelfrith's?'

'No, not Æthelfrith's my flux came the day after he left.'

'What are you saying, that it's my child? You cannot know such a thing. There has not been enough time for you to know.'

'*Trust me,* I know it in my heart, and I rejoice.'

'Never – you only imagine this, because that is what you want.'

'And would it disappoint you.'

'Aefre, please don't, why torment us with what cannot be, you know I have to marry, only a future in the Hellmouth awaits us.' He suddenly sat up and wrapped his arms around his knees. She watched him for a moment then sat up too and laid her head against his naked back.

'We never thought to have these days together, did we? We do not know what the future holds. Only the gods know that, but I do know that I will hold these days in my heart forever. To have known the complete love of a man, even for one moment, is the most special thing in life. It is a glimpse of the afterlife, and I do not see the afterlife as a place of warriors glorifying death, but of love and kindness.'

Wulfstan lay back, and she propped herself on her elbow, stared into his eyes and smiled.

He smiled too, 'There may be some warriors who will disagree, come here and kiss me.'

Aefre saw Wulfstan deep in conversation with Hrodulf. She could see by their faces it was of great importance, but she could not hear them. Hrodulf beckoned Halth, and he joined them; still they talked. Wulfstan looked to her but did not acknowledge her. Eventually, Hrodulf and Halth walked to where the horses were penned, and Wulfstan came towards her.

'What was that about, and why do I not want to know?'

'Step inside, and I will tell you.'

'Leave us, Rowena.' Rowena bowed and closed the door as she went out.

Wulfstan waited until the door was closed. 'Halth and I are going to ride to the Britons' camp.'

'No, I forbid it.'

He took her arms, 'Listen Aefre. I must know what is going on for the safety of us all.'

'Well, I'm coming too.'

'Aefre you are *not* coming, it might be dangerous, and it would be more of a risk to my life if I were constantly worrying about you, you would not want that.'

'Ooh, you think you are so clever. I forbid it, and that is an end to it.' Aefre's face was as stone, and she did not respond to his touch.

'I'm sorry Aefre, I must make decisions which are beyond *us*, for the safety of all of these people, and to make the best decisions I need to be informed.'

'But this is unfair, why must it be you?'

'Come here,' she relented, and he took her in his arms. 'I give you my word; I will be home by nightfall.' He was about to turn and go, but she held him.

'I'm not strong enough for all this, Wulfstan.'

'You are a Queen who will see me on my way without a single tear. I will walk out first, and you will follow when you have composed yourself.' She bowed her head in defeat and nodded.

On leaving the roundhouse, he saw Hrodulf and Halth with the ponies.

'These are the best ponies we have, Lord, better for hill work.' He heard Hereweald say as he walked towards them.

'Thank you Hereweald, they are fine animals,' as he spoke, he saw Aefre coming, Rowena joined her.

'Take care... Lord,' she managed to say when she reached them. Wulfstan saw Rowena take her hand. He nodded and rode out making for the Gododdin's camp.

'From which direction, for our safety, would you approach their camp Halth?' Wulfstan asked slowing their pace to a trot.

'For what it's worth I would come to their camp from the east. I would have thought them least likely to be riding *from* the east, that would have to mean they had been in the direction of our heartland and into greater danger.' Halth shrugged his shoulders, 'Just a guess.'

'Sound thought, you may be right. We will sweep round and come up from the east. Keep to the low ground, and we'll find what shadows we can. Not too fast so we can hear above our own noise.'

They rode east for some time, suddenly Halth twisted his pony, and it fell onto its side, and Wulfstan did likewise.

'What is it Halth?'

'Riders, Lord, look over there in that valley, maybe fifteen.'

'I see them; I don't think they've seen us. Is it them do you think?'

'Didn't get a good enough sighting.'

'If it is them, why in the name of hell, are they coming from that direction? Calm the ponies, I am going to crawl up that ridge to get a better look to be sure it is them.' Wulfstan passed him his rein and crawled quickly up the low ridge. He watched them until he was certain it was the Gododdins and was sure of their intention, then crawled back down to where Halth lay with the ponies.

'You did well there Halth, it is them right enough, we could have ridden straight into them.'

'So, what do you make of it, Lord, can you be sure they are the men we are after and not another group of raiders?'

'Well, they're Gododdins for sure by the look of their dress, and they are heading towards the camp where you were held. *Yes*, I'm pretty sure that's the fellows we are looking for.'

'Are you certain they're making for the camp? It could be a known place for their raiders to assemble.'

'Possibly, but they are making for their camp for sure. We will have to get closer to find out what they intend. We'll leave our mounts here and make our way on foot, let's hide them in that thicket.' He pointed to a dozen or so nearby trees. Once they'd secured their ponies, they ran along a narrow valley to the tree line and knelt to catch their breath.

'How far to their camp from here do you reckon Halth?'

'A league, no more.'

'That's my guess too, come on, keep low and quiet.' They walked more than ran, moving from tree to tree. As they drew near the camp, they heard shouting and lay down.

'Can you make out anything, Halth?' Wulfstan whispered.

'Not *a* thing.'

'Sounds like they are moving off, Halth, what do you think?'

'Aye, and not this way, thankfully.'

'We'll give them time to get clear then get closer to the camp and see if we can learn anything more.'

They waited for some time, even after it had gone quiet.

'What do you think?'

'I think they've gone, Lord.'

'Come on, let's get closer, but be careful.' The two slowly approached the camp; they could see that the raiders had gone for good, having taken all their belongings.

'By the look of their tracks, Lord, they are heading north-west, not towards the village.'

'Let's make our way back to our ponies and home. Whatever has been going on here, they look to have had enough and are now heading for their homeland. We won't do anything hasty. We'll remain on alert at the village, but I have a feeling we have seen the last of these fellows.'

Chapter 22

The Lyre Player

As soon as Wulfstan rode into the compound Rowena came to him, as did Hereweald and Hrodulf. Hrodulf took hold of the pony's bridle; Rowena was the first to speak.

'My Lady asks if you will go straight to her Lord, she is in the roundhouse.'

'Thank you, Rowena,' Wulfstan nodded. 'One moment men, I must attend on the Queen. Halth will tell you what we found out on our trip. I will return directly.'

They nodded, and Wulfstan walked steadily towards the roundhouse, Aefre would have been worrying herself into a state of panic. He knew that, and she would not have been able to come out to welcome him for fear of shaming herself.

As soon as he opened the door, Aefre leapt into his arms. 'Hold me, you have no idea how afraid I have been, I'm going mad. There is not a moment when you are not in my thoughts. I imagined every evil had befallen you.'

'Wōden was with us, Aefre. I'm sure if you had been in danger, I would have felt the same. Love is a strange beast, people crave it, but perhaps there is more peace without it. But not for me, there is no feeling like this moment in your arms.' He said as he lifted her chin and pressed his lips to hers.

'I can hardly stand I am so relieved, thank you Freya, *she* understands.'

'Let us join the others, there is good news, the Gododdins returned, we saw them, and they have left in the direction of their home.'

'What if it was a trick?'

'I doubt it, their number was down to fifteen, they would not risk an attack now, even if they wanted to.'

Aefre looked thoughtful, 'Good news, but this time together will be over.'

'Aye, we must talk to the others, come.'

He kissed her once more and gently caressed her cheek with the back of his hand. He opened the door for her, and she went to where the men were talking.

'Good news my Lady,' Hereweald said smiling as he saw her coming.

'Indeed, Hereweald.'

'You will be happy that you can now return to Din Guyaroi.'

'I will be sorry to leave you and your people, you have been generous, and kind to us, the King will hear of this.' She reached to her neck and withdrew an amber pendant on a golden rope torc, 'Please accept this as a gift for your wife Maga, it will look well against *your* fine torc, will it not?'

'My Queen, you are the one who is generous, we are forever your servants,' Hereweald knelt as he took the gift from Aefre.

'Set against our lives, it is a very small thing. You have shared all you have with us, and I can see you are not rich, I will make sure that you are reimbursed for your losses when we return your ponies.'

'Tonight, we will feast and dance, my Lady, if it would be your wish.'

'Indeed, it would, time for thanks to Wōden and Ēostre, [19] yes, and dancing and laughter.' She turned to Wulfstan; 'perhaps we may ride around this place before we go so that I might remember it better when we are once more at home.'

'Why not my Lady.'

There were ponies saddled, and Aefre's mood lightened, 'Will you need us to go with you, Lord?' asked Halth.

'No, we will not go far, you must rest today, you have worked hard, and I'm grateful for your support, these have been difficult days, Hrodulf.' Hrodulf nodded his appreciation of Wulfstan's praise.

Wulfstan lifted Aefre into the saddle, spoke to Hereweald, and his wife Maga, who'd come to thank Aefre for her gift. She could never in her life have hoped to own such a beautiful thing. It might have looked a little out of place alongside her worn humble clothing, but not next to her smile.

Wulfstan mounted, told Hrodulf they would return before dark, without fail.

'Take care Lord.'

Once out of sight of the village, Wulfstan reached for Aefre's hand, and she took hold of it.

'This is better for my heart than yesterday's fears. I wonder if the suffering then, is part of the joy now. The greater the joy, the greater the anguish, some other world balance set in place by the gods, to hold life together, what do you think?'

'I don't know… would be my answer, I am never quite balanced when I think of you. My toe yet hurts,' and he smiled. 'I might add, that professing undying love loses some credibility when you are laughing at another's misfortune.'

Aefre threw back her head and laughed at the picture of him hopping around the roundhouse.

'I cannot prevent a smile whenever I think of that night, it was so funny,' and she laughed once more.

'Look over there, by that stream, shall we sit there? I don't want to ride too far.' They rode to the stream through a flock of sheep, which scattered noisily before them.

They dismounted and tied their ponies to the branches of a willow tree, which gracefully reached down and stroked the surface of the still water affectionately with its feathery leaves.

'This is so beautiful and quiet, there's not a cloud in the sky,' she said shading her eyes with her hand as she looked up.

He stood behind her placing his fingers around her tiny waist, and lightly touched the fine hair on her neck with his lips. She shivered and reached over her shoulder to his face. Turning to face him, she felt to be covered in his love, and he drew her into his arms and kissed her.

'You smell of fresh air and warm sunshine,' he said as she rested her head on his chest, and he pressed his lips to her hair. 'Let's not go back, we'll stay here forever Aefre.'

'Now it's usually me who says things like that,' she said looking into his eyes smiling, and playfully bit his lip. 'We are both fools, that's the truth of it.'

He kissed her once more, released her, and laid his cloak on the ground for them to lie on. Stretching out he rested his head on his hands, and Aefre sat next to him with her back against a tree nibbling at a stalk of sweet grass.

'It's a beautiful day, and I'm happy, are *you* happy Wulfstan?'

'What do you think?' and she unhooked the silver clasps of her linen tunic and lay down beside him...

When they returned, the festivities were already underway, Aefre refused the place of honour, she would be as them this night. There was music and dancing, and she was as one with the village people.

'Never in my life have I done anything like this, there is so much innocent laughter amongst these people Wulfstan,' she impulsively kissed him, and the people cheered, fortunately, Wulfstan's shocked expression was real.

Towards the end, a beautiful young woman called Anie played a gentle love song on a simple home-made lyre, she had the voice of all innocence. She sang of her beloved who gave his life for her, and though she could not know him completely in this life, her heart longed for him, and she knew that one day they would be together forever.

They all listened in silence to the haunting voice, which floated on the stillness of the warm night. Wulfstan gazed at Aefre across the hushed reverence, saw the tears trickling down her cheeks, and squeezed her hand.

Chapter 23

Cedric

It seemed a long tiresome ride home to Din Guyaroi. Perhaps it was not home but merely the place where the King and Queen lived, Wulfstan wasn't sure where home was anymore. Was the place where he'd been brought up and lived with his father and brother since childhood, the place where his betrothed now waited for him, *home*? He didn't know; nothing seemed solid anymore. It was as if his life now floated on a mere whim of the gods.

It had been a difficult farewell, these humble villagers had become friends, something born out of a common purpose, even while they were mounted and ready to go, they yet lingered, talking, and laughing. Hereweald stood with his arm around his wife Maga and his son Osgar and laughed with them.

They may be poor thought Aefre, but they had riches she would never have, as she watched the three happy in each other's arms it seemed to poke fun at her. For the riches they had, was *everything* for which she longed.

A moment before they turned to go, Wulfstan loosened his belt and removed the sheath containing his seax. He beckoned Osgar to him and passed him the seax; the boy was clearly moved.

This was not just the gift of a fine seax, but it belonged to the great Wulfstan.

'Say naught son, but promise me this, that you will honour your father and mother all your days.'

'I promise, Lord.' Wulfstan nodded, and they rode off.

They rested at midday and ate what Hereweald and Maga had provided, but they spoke little. The men were happy; they had friends and family who would be concerned for them. It seemed that all he and Aefre had, were each other.

They returned by the same route they had left by some fifteen days past, was that all it was, fifteen days? To Wulfstan, it felt like it was a lifetime.

He could see some activity on the ramparts as they neared the fortress; they'd been seen. The small group made its way up the steep incline to the gates; Wulfstan could see Cedric waiting for them, arms folded and the most peculiar look on his face. He remembered that same look on his *father's* face when he's done something that left him speechless, something that was beyond a simple thrashing.

It was a strange reception, no cheering. People only stared, Cedric's face looked even more solemn as they came closer. Something was amiss. Aefre glanced towards Wulfstan, hoping he had some understanding. They rode to where Cedric stood.

'You have decided to return?' Cedric asked.

What an odd question, Wulfstan thought, it seemed somewhere between a question and an accusation.

'Yes, it's been a long time…' Wulfstan looked at Aefre, and then to Cedric, 'Do you not bow to your Queen, my friend?'

'We did not expect you home.'

'*Clearly*,' Wulfstan went to Aefre and lowered her from the saddle.

'Cedric, I ask you again do you not bow to your Queen?' Cedric gave a token bow that was verging on insolence. 'Cedric, there is something here I am not aware of, would you like to explain yourself.' The five mounted men with Wulfstan and Aefre looked equally bemused.

Hrodulf pushed his pony nearer to Cedric. 'Did you not hear your Lord's question, fellow,' he asked in a threatening tone. Wulfstan laid his hand on Hrodulf thigh to calm him; Cedric ignored Hrodulf.

'We were told that you had... run off with the Queen.'

'What! By whom.'

Hrodulf leapt from his horse and drew his sword and pointed it at Cedric's chest. 'Be careful what you say, fellow, your Queen, has been to the Hellmouth and back and we are in no mood to face your insults. I have slain men for less.'

'You can always try,' Cedric offered as a challenge.

'Enough of this, we will go inside, and you will explain to me, Cedric, what your contempt is about.' Aefre was speechless and simply allowed Wulfstan to steer her to the keep.

They sat around the large oak table in the King's chamber, the Queen at the head.

'Now Cedric, *explain* this disrespect to your Queen. *Hrodulf,* will you sit down, and give Cedric a chance to put in plain words what ails him. For though he might think so ill of *me*, I know *him* to be the bravest and most loyal warrior and there is clearly something amiss here.'

'Thank you, my friend,' Cedric said, managing to acknowledge Wulfstan's generosity.

'We are yet friends then, I thank the gods for that. Now, let me hear your voice Cedric, and speak plainly for my patience is not without limit.'

'Shortly after I returned from taking Meghan home, Lord Hering informed me that he had to inspect a farmstead, he took maybe... ten warriors with him.'

'Ha!' Hrodulf mocked at the mention of Lord Hering, whom he detested.

'Go on, Cedric,' Wulfstan scowled at Hrodulf's interruption.

'When he returned, he told us that he had been told by his spies that...' he cast his eyes down to the tabletop, 'you and the Queen had run off together.'

Wulfstan's fists were white with controlled fury. In a fearfully calm voice, he ordered that Lord Hering be brought to him.

'He's not here Lord,' Cedric told him.

'And, where is he?'

'He has ridden off with fifty men, fifty we can barely do without, to the west to inform the King of your... treachery.'

Wulfstan stood and smashed his fist into the palm of his hand. 'When did he go?'

'Five days past.'

'So, help me, I will have his head for this. The King faces an army – *possibly* – greater than his own forces, and now to add to his woes, he will soon believe that he is betrayed at his home. You tell Cedric the truth of this Hrodulf, for I am of a mind to ride after the ill-begotten snake in the grass and drag him back here as he did to my Lady's innocent maid Rowena.'

Hrodulf adjusted himself in his seat and cleared his throat, for his fury was none less than Wulfstan's.

'On the eve of the first day of our journey, we were about to make camp when we were attacked by Britons hiding in the deep bracken. They outnumbered us, and all but the number you see here were killed. My Lord and *your* Lord, Lord Wulfstan managed to escape with my Lady, and *our* Queen, to safety. We held back the renegades to give them time to make their escape; eventually, we were overwhelmed. We were taken prisoner and dragged behind their horses to their camp, not only us, but Rowena, and they hung her from a tree by her arms, show him, Rowena.'

She drew back her sleeves, and Cedric grimaced at the vicious weals and bruising to her wrists and arms. Rowena hung her head and was struggling to maintain her composure. Aefre rose from her chair and held Rowena in her embrace.

'That brave girl was in so much pain when our Lord and Lady came to rescue us, she was unable to stand. Yes, they came to rescue us. Though they were free, they risked their freedom for us, and – *I* – will not forget that. My life now belongs to them. We were shown more kindness and respect by poor ceorls than my Lord's so-called friends here in this place. They *shared* what little they had and asked for naught in return. We waited in fear of reprisal at their humble village, they were prepared to risk all for us without question. The attack never came; it is my belief… that the raiders came here to see that turd Hering, to seek his will and payment for their wickedness…' He looked at Wulfstan.

'That is my thought too Hrodulf, he probably ordered our deaths, then we would never have been able to dispute his claim.'

Cedric stared into the distance for some moments; even his breathing ceased, all that could be seen of life was the flexing of the muscles in his jaw. All watched him, he slowly stood and walked to where Aefre held Rowena, bowed his head, and fell on his knees before her.

'Forgive me, my Queen; I am a warrior who cannot live with shame. I have failed all that I hold dear,' and he drew his sword and passed it to Aefre. 'When I die, I will not die with my sword in my hand, I will cast it from me – for I will forever be unworthy.'

'Take your sword, Cedric, for we all carry shame, and I am not without fault. Therefore, I will not judge you, or be the hypocrite I am. Rise and take your seat once more at my table. Your honour is without blemish.'

I ask forgiveness of you all that I would set the word of that son of the god of mischief and wickedness, Lôgna, against all I know of my friend and sworn brother. When I next see him, I will destroy him, my oath on it.'

'What Hrodulf has spoken of is the truth, Cedric.'

'Aye, and more fool I forever thinking aught else.'

'You may go now and make known the truth to all who were deceived. I think the Queen may need rest.'

One by one they bowed and left the room, Cedric held the door and bowed to each as they passed through, even though they were ranked below him.

'I will speak with the Queen, Rowena; perhaps you could talk to Edith. I will call you when I leave.'

'Thank you, my Lady, for your kindness. I'm so sorry for the way you have been treated, people can be so unkind.'

Wulfstan touched her shoulder as she passed him. He sat down next to Aefre and took her hand. 'All is explained now Aefre, but we are yet in great danger, this is merely a *taste* of the wroth that awaits us,' he gave a long sigh. 'I will have to leave for your safety, who knows who saw what, and the repercussions do not bare thinking about.'

Aefre hung her head… 'I cannot think of a life without you.'

'I must marry Meghan. I will leave my estate in the hands of my brother, Leofwine, he is a fine man, and I will offer my sword arm to the King of Mercia.'

Aefre said nothing; tears filled her eyes and brimmed over in a steady flow and dripped from her chin. All the while, she moved her head *slowly* – from side to side, as if in denial. She tried to speak, but her lip trembled uncontrollably. Wulfstan stood, went behind her chair, and wrapped his arms around her, pressing his lips to her head, and she broke down and sobbed, frantically clinging to his arms.

'I – I – will ha-ha-ve – our – ch-ch-ild…' she stammered her words out in spasms, gasping for air.

'Awe, my dearest Aefre.' This is pitiful, where are you Freya, have you deserted us? Hide from me, torment me, but be merciful to my Aefre, he silently begged.

Chapter 24

The Dream

Wulfstan had made his farewells to Aefre, they were pathetically polite, and he rode in an ill frame of mind from the fortress. She was braver than he; he was certain of that. Their wretched lives were reversed; fate had colluded with every malevolent spirit of Wōden's pit to make them share the agony of each other's torment. Now it was *she* who had to think on *his* marriage, and he knew too well the pangs she would suffer.

His poor horse was made to pay for his anguish as he thrashed it mercilessly in the direction of his future.

What a jealous world we live in, he thought, as he lay in his bed staring up at the smoke-blackened rafters. I love Aefre, and she loves me, and no ordinary love it is.

He knew people married for numerous reasons. Practical reasons to provide and care for each other, so they were not alone, or to further themselves, as nobles generally did, but to love like them was the domain of fools.

Those who had never known the power of such love could well pour scorn on them and mock them. No doubt, *they* were judged and condemned, even though their love was not known, the words were already in the hearts of the accusers, and a mere spark would give them life.

I wish it could be different, why have the gods laid such upon *me*, I am not equal to this. He thought about Meghan, and how wounded she had been when he returned to the village, though she had defended him, she had been hurt.

She'd heard the rumours that he'd run away with the Queen. His brother Leofwine, to his credit, had spoken up for him too, assuring Meghan that it would not be so, but he knew how such rumours stuck like black tar to a cloth, and there would ever be niggling doubts.

He paused in his thoughts and squeezed his head between his hands, for he knew, though Hering's truths were malicious and determined lies, they were nearer to the truth than Wulfstan could bear to think on.

The gods had woven a hellish garment for him to wear upon his shoulders, where the liar speaks the truth, and the truth becomes the lie. What had they done other than fall in love?

He awoke, suddenly, it was yet dark, and his head was bathed in sweat. It was that moment where the dream of the night merges with the dream world of the day, and one's waking senses cannot separate the two.

He sat up trying to make some meaning of his surroundings, he shook his head attempting to shake free of the bony fingers of guilty sleep drawing him back into the world of nightmares. He'd seen Meghan in her wedding gown calling to him; she was on fire. There was a child too, and he was reaching for them, but he couldn't get to her, the child screamed, he could yet hear their voices as they reverberated around inside his skull. He shook his head once more trying to shake himself free from the confusion.

Cedric called to him across the roundhouse, and his voice helped him break free of the strands of the silken web.

'What is it Wulfstan, *Wulfstan*, you will wake the whole village!'

Wulfstan lay back on his bed panting like a dog, 'I have been in the Hellmouth of dreams, my friend and am thankful to hear your voice, a voice from this world.'

'I'm awake now, thanks to you and your dreams, too late for more sleep. I'm for finding some mete,' Cedric yawned, stretching and rubbing his eyes.

'Aye, then I will bathe and dress for my bride.'

It was Cedric's honour to attend to his Lord this day and ensure that he was presented to his bride in a fit and proper state. They had no trouble finding mete. Their slaves and bond-servants were already at work even though it was barely light, preparing for the great marriage feast of their Lord. Oxen were even at this hour on the spit, and Wulfstan guessed by the fine aroma, that they had been for some time.

Meghan lived in the next village, on Wulfstan's estate, and this was a great honour for her family that their daughter was marrying their Lord. On another day and another time Wulfstan would have been thankful, for Meghan loved him, he knew that, and she was a rare beauty – *but* – he loved another, and he took no pride in the deception. What in the name of Wōden and all his minions, could he do about it?

As they sat alone eating their most humble fare, Cedric laid his large hand on Wulfstan's shoulder. 'So, it is no different for you, my friend?' He asked sympathetically.

'No.' Wulfstan rested his chin on his cup of ale. 'No, it is no different, would that it was, I pray to Freya and hope that she might do something, she is deaf to me. I have even begged for death, aught to relieve me from this hell. Aye, hell, the word has become my close acquaintance and no doubt it is to be my home for the rest of my days.'

'You are man above men, most never have this struggle, for your fight is made all the worse because of the man you are. I know that your suffering would be naught so hellish, but for your honour.'

'Ha... honour you say, there is *none* less honourable than me, honour and lies are strange bedfellows are they not?'

'It was honour that brought you back to Din Guyaroi, and you came knowing the torment that was ahead. I am a man without honour next to you or my Queen, and I know the gods will see this too.'

Wulfstan smiled weakly at him, 'you are the kindest friend, come I must bathe, find me beautiful maidens to do the deed, no toothless hags.'

'That's more like it.' Cedric laughed.

Wulfstan waited at the village holy tree, in much the same way as Æthelfrith had waited for Aefre. He closed his eyes as the deadness took hold of him, he could not shake it from his limbs.

When he saw Meghan, he should have been thrilled, but in fact, Wulfstan trembled and was nearly sick. He was compelled to swallow down the bile for she was dressed exactly as she had been in his dream, even now he could see the tongues of fire leaping from her dress. He staggered and fell back against one of the holy stones, Cedric reached for him. Those watching laughed assuming he was suffering from a surfeit of ale, but his suffering was of a wholly darker nature.

He took Meghan's hand, and the Weofodthegn conducted the marriage rite in his timeless way, Meghan was passionately kissing him before he realised it was over.

She was happy, everyone was happy, but all he could think of was his nightmare, *and* Aefre, he knew she would be sitting alone, and all he longed for was to be with her.

'Ha, honourable,' he said to himself as he thought of Cedric's words.

They mounted their horses with Cedric by their side, he would take Meghan to Din Guyaroi where she would meet Aefre, that would be the challenge, better it was over and done with, he thought.

Wulfstan could see Aefre standing in the courtyard, with her maids, Rowena, and Edith; he noticed that Rowena took her hand. She had obviously been informed of their arrival.

The three riders rode to where she stood, and she smiled, but it was a smile that never touched her eyes.

Wulfstan wearily dismounted and reached up to Meghan, she laid her hands on his shoulders, and he lowered her to the ground.

Meghan curtseyed, 'My Lady.'

Wulfstan and Cedric bowed too, and Aefre acknowledged them with a dip of her head.

'It is a very beautiful bride my Lord Wulfstan has found,' Aefre said, again trying to smile.

'We have known each other since we were children, my Lady; it is I who am fortunate. To me, there is none more handsome, and I love him.'

'Yes, Lord Wulfstan told me. You will want to see your room. Would you take Lady Wulfstan to her room, Edith? I must make known to Lord Wulfstan the news.'

'Yes, my Lady.'

'I will see that your baggage is brought to your room, my Lady,' Cedric said very formally to Meghan.

Meghan squeezed Wulfstan's hand, she was fearful of this place it was so different from her small village.

'I will join you shortly, Edith will care for you, won't you, Edith?'

'I will Lord,' and she led Meghan to the keep.

'Come, Lord, we will go to my chamber there is news of the King.' She turned, and Wulfstan followed her. The guard opened the door as they neared and Aefre smiled at him, they walked through, and the door closed as if by magic.

Aefre turned to face Wulfstan, she wanted him to hold her, but she was not able to step towards him. 'Whatever did we do that was so wicked in our past lives that warrants all this pain at every turn Wulfstan?'

He shook his head, 'I don't know what to say Aefre. Meghan is the nicest, kindest person one could hope to meet, and she is my wife and I feel nothing. *This* is the person you love; I am the most wretched of people, a disgrace. I can fight giants, a dozen fearless warriors, and never flinch, but in this, I am but a helpless child.'

Aefre never moved apart from twisting her hands round and round each other, she only listened to him. Her face mirrored his hopelessness.

'But you have news, good news?'

'Yes, Æthelfrith sent riders, he has had a great victory at a place called, Degsastan. [20] Tragically his brother Theodbald was killed; Lord Hering fought there also.'

'That is tragic, Theodbald was a fine man, I liked him. To whom was the message sent?'

'To the King's *loyal subjects* at Din Guyaroi.'

'Mmm, not to the Queen.'

'No.'

'So that vile creature, Hering has done his worst. I must send Meghan back to her home; I should not have brought her. I will explain the best I can, it may be dangerous when Æthelfrith arrives, there could well be fighting, it would be wrong to have Meghan drawn into this.'

Neither had moved an inch since they entered the room as if fixed by fear to the spot. 'I just don't know what to do Wulfstan, I want you to hold me, but I'm afraid, I'm ashamed.'

'Ashamed that you love me, aye, ashamed to be in love, don't ask me, Aefre. I must go to Meghan now and explain to her what such news means for her.'

'Yes.'

He bowed and stared at her… shook his head despairingly and left.

Meghan was unpacking her baggage with Edith when Wulfstan entered, and she looked up and smiled.

'Leave us, Edith, I wish to speak to my wife.' Edith bowed and left them.

'How wonderful those words sound, "My wife",' and she reached up to him and kissed him.

'Sit down Meghan we must talk. The Queen has informed me that the King is on his way, we don't know exactly when he will return.'

'This is good news, is it not,' she narrowed her eyes and looked puzzled at his frown.

'Meghan, you know the lies that were spread by Lord Hering that I had run off with the Queen and how he tried to have us murdered, which is the truth, and there are many who will testify to it.'

'Yes, I know all this and never doubted you.'

'Yes, well the King does not yet know the truth and there may well be fighting when he returns. I would not have brought you here if I had known that the King was to return so soon.'

'What are you saying?'

'I want you to return to our home, where you will be safe.'

She stared at him, 'but a wife should be by her husband no matter what.'

'No, I will not risk your life. I will come for you, and we will go south to the kingdom of Mercia, I am known there by King Pybba, he will welcome me, he is a friend of King Æthelfrith and Bernicia.'

'*Mercia!* I don't even know where that is.'

'Don't be afraid, I will not have such a shadow, which I know these lies will cast, hanging over us or the King and Queen. There will be always those who wonder and whisper, people love intrigue at others expense. I will see that you are taken home to safety on the first of the morrow's light.'

'When will you come?'

'If I can make it right with the King, I will leave straight away and come for you. Be ready for me and explain all I have said to my beloved brother.'

Chapter 25

Retribution

Meghan was taken to their home by Hrodulf and Halth, Wulfstan had grown fond of them both since their time together at the village on the moors, and he knew she would be safe with them. He would have sent Cedric as he had before, but with the possibility of Æthelfrith returning any day, he wanted Cedric at Din Guyaroi.

Wulfstan had asked them if they would join him and Cedric when they went to Mercia, they said they would be honoured. He told them to stay and watch over Meghan, and he and Cedric would join them as soon as they were able.

Wulfstan and Aefre lay quietly together, it was dark; all he could hear was her breathing. She stirred, yawned, and kissed his chest. There was little light in the room, and he could barely see, but what light there was, was captured in her eyes, and he smiled at her.

'Our time is coming to an en...'

She pressed her finger to his lips, 'don't say it please, not now, not this night.'

However, what he had to say dwelt in his mind like an unwelcome guest at a feast. 'I must, it might be today that Æthelfrith returns, if not today, it will be the next day or the next. It will be soon now, and I will have to go, *if* Æthelfrith allows it.'

Aefre put her hand to her mouth and bit into it to prevent her tears.

They lay quietly, once she had composed herself, she said softly, 'I am pregnant, as I knew I would be, I have missed my flux.'

He shook his head slowly from side to side in despair. 'When will the child be born?'

'In the autumn,' she said touching her middle. She saw the agony on his pain creased face, 'Why has such an expression of our love to be clothed in the weeds of pain? Wulfstan, there is no joy without you in my life. Why has my whole life to be one of my turning from any hope of joy, I'm not brave. Why, why, why, why must it be me, why must anyone have to welcome pain as a friend and be thankful, where is such a thing written, tell me that? Pain is a sign that something is wrong, and by all that is right and just, *tell me* why *we* have been chosen to suffer such, and accept it, is this really what the gods intended, when they poured out this most precious gift to us?'

'Aefre, you always ask me questions as if I knew the answers to all mysteries when I know less now than I ever did.'

'I will have a child, your child, that should be ours to love, to share, a *part* of our love, but it will be a daily reminder of you, and I don't know how I will cope with such. I am just a breath of air for a while, not a god, a simple woman, here touch me,' and she set his hand to her breast. 'I feel – just like other women, cry like other women, laugh like other women, and hurt like other women.'

'I understand well enough how you feel for I have the same feelings. I know too that this life is a short thing, and one day you and I will be together forever, this is the *one thing* of which I am certain,' and he lifted her face to his and kissed her. 'When I go...' he had to pause, 'When I go, I will leave, my dearest Aefre, the only thing anyone leaves, and they are not earthly things, but love and memories, these things *no one* can take from us,' and he wrapped her in his arms and held her as if his life depended on it.

Riders galloped into the courtyard on steaming, anxious, excited horses, shouting, 'the King is near, prepare to receive the great King of Bernicia, victor over the Gaels. He will be here within the hour.'

The news spread quickly around the fortress. Wulfstan was with Aefre, 'Fear not, we will go down and wait for him. Dress in your most splendid clothes and be the Queen you are, that all might see.'

'You expect too much of me Wulfstan.'

'No, I know you to be no ordinary woman, you are my Aefre and my Queen,' and he held her and kissed her. 'I will go and find Cedric, and we will await the King's arrival.'

Cedric stood motionless by his horse, with Wulfstan next to him, Wulfstan kept glancing at him, but he never moved a muscle.

Aefre came from the keep, and she was every inch "The" Queen. Aefre was tall, but she seemed head and shoulders above all she passed, and all bowed, not so much to Aefre, but to the sight of this majestic superior being.

'My Queen,' Wulfstan bowed, and yet Cedric never moved. Aefre cast an eye to him but made no comment and stepped in front of them. They could now see and hear the army coming along the broad sandy beach from the south.

As they arrived at the foot of the hill on which the fortress stood, Æthelfrith's party broke away and made their way up the steep track to the stockade gates. Wulfstan reached forward and squeezed Aefre's shoulder, but she showed no response. Her heart was pounding fit to break free from her chest, but Wulfstan could not see that.

The small group of elite warriors waved and smiled at the adoring crowd lining the track. There was no doubting the surprise on Æthelfrith's face when Aefre and Wulfstan suddenly came into view. His surprise was equalled, if not even more profoundly, on the face of Lord Hering and his victor's smile disappeared instantly. Hering drew his horse sharply to a standstill, so sharply the horseman behind collided with him. In the blink of an eye, he spun his horse around and galloped off, the same way he'd but a moment since ridden in triumph. Cedric quietly mounted and trotted out of the gate past the King, he never even acknowledged him.

If Æthelfrith noticed he paid no heed, his eyes were riveted to his Queen. He slowed his massive charger and rode forward to them, Aefre curtseyed, and Wulfstan bowed. Æthelfrith hesitated for a moment. Clearly, this reception was not the one he'd expected, and he was at a loss as to what to do or say. He unhurriedly transferred his weight onto one stirrup, his saddle creaked and groaned at the readjustment of pressure, and he stepped to the ground.

'My Lord,' Aefre spoke first, breaking the tension, 'Welcome, a great victory I hear.'

Æthelfrith was still at a loss, 'I am surprised to see you.'

'And where else would your Queen be when her King returns from war? I notice that Lord Hering has suddenly decided to take his leave of us,' Aefre made play of leaning and looking past Æthelfrith to where Lord Hering have but a moment since been.

Æthelfrith looked even more confused and turned to look for Hering, obviously searching amongst his equally speechless men for the face of his cousin, he even stepped to the side to better his view. He turned once more to face them, the look of utter confusion on his face *almost* caused Wulfstan to smile.

Æthelfrith lowered his head and removed his helma, passing it to a servant, who bowed and took it from him.

Æthelfrith stared at them, pushed his fingers under his coif, and scratched his head.

'I am blessed to see you my Queen, and you my dear friend Lord Wulfstan. I have been the object of deceit it appears.'

'So, we hear Lord. We were attacked and nearly murdered, but for my Lord Wulfstan, and your brave huscarls, sadly many warriors were lost. I was hoping to talk to Lord Hering, but he appears to have decided to leave us with some urgency, something pressing no doubt.'

Æthelfrith turned once again to where Hering had been; and then back to Aefre, 'So it appears,' he smiled. 'Let us go to my chamber, we have much to talk of,' and he came forward to Aefre, embraced her, and kissed her. The relief was palpable, not only with Aefre and Wulfstan but with Æthelfrith also.

Suddenly he stopped, 'What am I thinking about, my thoughts are awash, I must send men to fetch our dear Lord Hering, I would speak with him.'

'I think Lord, that Cedric my huscarl, is at this moment attending to that work, but how available Lord Hering will be for conversation after his meeting with Cedric, I am not sure. We will have to wait and see. Cedric does not appreciate being taken for a fool.'

'Ahh, he can have been no more a fool than me.'

When they entered Æthelfrith's chamber, there was already food being laid out for him.

'This is all very fine Aefre, I have missed you; any news… he asked rather tentatively.'

'I am with child, my Lord.'

'Ha, I knew it, splendid,' he took her once more in his arms, lifted her from the floor, and kissed her passionately. 'What say you to that, Ealdorman?'

'Congratulations, my King.' He could hardly get the words to leave his lips they were so dry.

Aefre was unable to prevent a tear escaping; she cuffed it away quickly with her back of her hand, but Æthelfrith saw her.

'My dearest.'

'Forgive me, Lord, I am very emotional, it has all been a great strain.'

'No, it is I who is thoughtless, I only think of my own joy and myself. I was miserable beyond belief, but now I have a happiness which surpasses all.'

'Would you mind if I was rude and went to my chamber, Lord King? I have not felt well, with sickness, a common complaint I understand.'

'Not at all Aefre you must have all the care that can be given,' and he stood and took her hand. 'Here girl, see to your Queen.'

Aefre could not get to her room quick enough; once the door was closed, she fell into Rowena's arms and sobbed her heart out. Rowena held her tenderly stroking her hair.

'Whatever will I do, Lord Wulfstan is leaving.'

'What do you mean my Lady?'

'He is going away with his wife and never coming back,' Rowena could hardly make out a word Aefre said, but she didn't press her, she was content to hold her for now.

Wulfstan told Æthelfrith the tale of their time away, the attack, and Hering's subsequent meeting with the Britons.

They agreed that Hering must have ordered their deaths, and then ridden to Æthelfrith with his lies.

Æthelfrith told Wulfstan about the battle, how they had been greatly outnumbered, but Wōden had been with them and they had slaughtered the Gaels *and* their King.

Wulfstan told him how sorry he was to hear that his brother, Theodbald, had been killed.

'Yes… he fought bravely, all his men were killed too, sad, sad.'

Æthelfrith seemed to want to talk to Wulfstan whose head was screaming inside. Wulfstan told him that he would be leaving for Mercia with his new wife. The King looked surprised.

'You are married?'

'Indeed Lord, to my childhood sweetheart.'

'But why would you leave me, I need you.'

'Lord, you are no fool, and I want the best for you. I fear, that dirt sticks and I will not have people wondering about the truth, at your expense, or indeed my wife's. Enemies will want to believe Lord Hering's lies and may use them to cause divisions. I will not be a part of that.'

'Your leaving will be a great loss to my kingdom. You are a man of great honour, Ealdorman.'

'I think not Lord, as I have said, such lies will cause hurt to my wife.'

'That is true, I wonder if Cedric has caught up with that turd yet.' Æthelfrith slammed his fist down on the table, so fiercely the cups near the blow jumped. 'When will you go?'

'As soon as possible.'

Eventually, Wulfstan made the excuse that he must see that the fortress was secured for the night.

'May I just call on the Queen to offer my best wishes Lord? She looked fearfully unwell.'

'By all means, tell her I will bathe and come to her.'

'Yes Lord,' and he bowed and left. Once clear of the guard he leant against the stonewall gasping for breath. When his breathing had slowed, he wiped his face. Was he simply running away and deserting Aefre? He turned and pressed his brow to the rough stone. He began to tap his forehead against the wall; the taps became stronger until blood filled his eyes. When he wiped his sleeve across his brow, he was startled at the sight of all the blood. Shaking his head miserably, he dragged himself to Aefre's room.

He knocked; Rowena nervously opened the door and peered around the edge. Then she flung it back when she saw the blood on his face.

'Dear bride of Wōden, here let me help you, Lord,' Aefre looked up, gasped, and ran to him, fearing that he had fought with Æthelfrith.

'It is naught, I stumbled against the wall.'

'Here my Lady, water and cloth.'

It was enough to distract Aefre while she bathed his head.

'Leave it Aefre; I just needed to see you for a moment. Æthelfrith knows I have come, I told him I would see that you were well. He told me to tell you that he would bathe, and then he will come to you. Aefre, I must leave on the morrow or I will be your death. I had to hold you one more time,' and he took her in his arms and covered her in kisses, both their faces were now awash with blood and tears. He had been holding her off the floor; he set her to the ground and passed her hand to Rowena.

'Take her and care for her Rowena, for me,' he said, and he left.

Chapter 26

Final decision

Wulfstan had seen Æthelfrith briefly when he went to his bed after checking the night's guards. He had told him of his intention to leave on the morning's first light.

After his initial surprise, and on hearing Wulfstan's reasons, Æthelfrith wished him well and thanked him for caring for his queen and future heir to his kingdom. Wulfstan only bowed his head and said nothing. Æthelfrith slipped a large gold ring from his finger, took Wulfstan's hand, and gave it to him; he assured Wulfstan that he had a home forever with him and the Queen at Din Guyaroi.

Wulfstan could do no other than like this King, it was never his intention to hurt him, any more than it was Aefre's; fate had merely played a wicked trick upon them, which had brought suffering and heartache to all, no one was spared.

It was yet dark when Wulfstan and Cedric stepped out onto the courtyard from the keep.

As soon as Wulfstan lifted his head, he saw the gruesome sight. The staring eyes of the head stuck onto a spear in the centre of the courtyard, that all might see and be warned. Cedric made no comment as they walked past it to the stables; it was something personal to him, an oath fulfilled.

Neither spoke as they saddled their mounts and loaded their belongings onto a pack animal. It was a well-practised routine, and there was no real need for chatter.

Wulfstan fastened his cloak tightly around his shoulders. It was cold and damp, with eerie shadows, which appeared to move in the shrouded half-light of the morning mist. Cedric had not slept well and was tired, he grunted as he mounted his horse. Holding the reins, he placed his hands on the pommel of his saddle and waited patiently for Wulfstan.

Wulfstan placed his foot in the stirrup but did no more. He laid his head forward onto the leather skirt of the saddle and tapped his brow lightly against it, enough to reopen one of the wounds on his forehead. He lifted his head slightly and stared at the blood soaking into the leather, he felt nothing; he was dead to physical pain. His legs felt like lead, he didn't think he could lift himself onto his horse. Still, Cedric *patiently* watched him and said nothing. Wulfstan struggled into the saddle like an old man, and they moved off.

He never saw Aefre at the door of the keep, vainly *willing* him to look back. Her heart screamed to him, *"Take me with you"*, and she remembered their first kiss and how she'd willed him to turn back to her that day too. A gust of wind caught hold of her loose hair, sticking the strands to the tears on her face.

His brain was dead to all, and he rode out through the gates and from her life forever. She ran to the opening and watched him yet hoping… until he was no more.

They rode through the village and on up the long incline away from Din Guyaroi. Before them lay the large tidal bay, the tide was out, and it looked as dark and bleak as his future. At the summit, Wulfstan drew his horse to a standstill and stared ahead for some time. Cedric did no more than watch him. With a tug on his rein, he turned to look back to the fortress. Cedric could sense the aura of anguish emanating in waves from his dearest friend. He bowed his head not wanting to impose on this moment of tragedy. He was aware of the tears dripping from the end of Wulfstan's nose, which Wulfstan unconsciously wiped away with the back of his gloved hand.

Wulfstan never spoke; he merely stared into the distance for what seemed to Cedric like an eternity. It started to rain, Wulfstan wore no head covering and the water dripped from his curls until they began to lie flat to his head, and *yet* he never moved. It was the most pitiful, miserable sight Cedric had ever beheld.

Suddenly the moment was over, he'd said his goodbyes. He tugged his rein once again, his mount turned, and they rode off.

Their pace was erratic almost stopping and then galloping. All the while Cedric never spoke, the measure of his friendship at this moment was not to offer words of encouragement, or advice, or even reprimand, this was the most difficult of all friendship's different cloaks, to be content to watch a friend in torment, and just, "Be".

They didn't stop; midday came and went and still Wulfstan never uttered a sound. Cedric could see the village ahead; they would be there in half of the hour.

Cedric drew his horse alongside Wulfstan's and spoke for the first time.

'Can you do this my friend?' he asked softly.

Wulfstan lifted his head and looked at him as they slowed their horses to walking pace.

'I don't understand you! I am *Wulfstan* the *great* warrior, whose beauty, brilliance, skills are beyond ordinary men, my wealth, position, even my wife – *are* the envy of *all*. I am not to be numbered amongst normal men with their pathetic, infantile feelings; I am above common men. You, yourself have told me this, or have you so soon forgotten?'

Cedric was afraid as he spoke, the ice from his lips sent shivers down his spine.

'Come, we must press on before dark.'

Cedric shook his head in despair, and he nudged his horse to follow.

Chapter 27

The journey

They rode at a brisk pace into the village, and up to his fine longhouse. Wulfstan slid from his horse and paused, Cedric saw him take a deep breath as Meghan ran to him, and she was followed by his brother Leofwine, both were smiling.

Meghan leapt into his arms, and he hugged and kissed her, then he embraced Leofwine.

'My... I see signs of my son,' Wulfstan said smiling. Cedric couldn't believe this man; he was hiding his hell *from* all, for the sake of all.

Meghan was clearly delighted that he had noticed her swollen belly but caught sight of the cuts on his forehead and looked at them in horror. She reached up and gently pushed his hair from his brow.

'Wulfstan, whatever have you done, there is blood on your head and face?'

'Ahh, it is naught; A stonewall stood in my way as I determined to get here to my beautiful wife, no more. The rain must have softened the scabs and started it bleeding once again.'

'You fool, well come with me this instant. I will put some goose grease on it and bandage it.' She took his hand and led him into the longhouse.

Both his huscarls came to greet him, and he acknowledged them with a nod of his head.

'Our King's home safe from the war Lord – *did* – all go well?' asked Hrodulf hesitantly as he caught sight of the blood.

'He *fell* into a wall, Hrodulf, so I'm told.' smiled Meghan.

'Ah... dangerous things, falls.' Halth said, deciding that he would not pursue the conversation; he looked at Hrodulf and shrugged his shoulders as they watched Meghan lead Wulfstan by the hand to the longhouse.

'Sit there,' Meghan pushed him into a chair while she cut some cloth for bandages.

Leofwine followed them into the longhouse and laid his hand on Wulfstan's shoulder. 'What's all this I hear about you going to Mercia? Surely that cannot be true.'

'Aye it's true my dear brother, I want to get away from all the rumours and sly looks of doubt.'

'But no one believes what was said of you and the Queen, we all know they were vicious lies. I would never believe such a thing of you, my brother. You of all people are the example for us to live our lives by.'

'You are a good brother, but time will pass, and the stories will re-emerge. I will offend someone, and they will be only too pleased to resurrect the tales once more. *No* – I cannot stay – people will get hurt. I don't want that for Meghan, *or* my King and Queen. It is for the best that we make a clean start in Mercia.' Wulfstan was struggling and had to clear his throat, he couldn't look at Leofwine. He knew he couldn't tell him of his real fears, as much as he deserved to be told. They'd never had any secrets between them before.

'But what of your home, all that need you here?'

'I have a brother who is equal to any demands of this estate and I know he loves this place and the people,' Wulfstan smiled at Leofwine.

'But you are the Lord, not me.'

'Not anymore, I will leave, if not on the morrow, then the next day. It will be a long journey south, and Meghan is with child, we must go sooner, rather than later, for the babe's safety *and* to ease Meghan's discomfort.'

'My dear brother is there never a time when you do not think of others, you shame me.'

'Leofwine, you could not be more wrong about me, I am the most wretched of men.' Leofwine looked at him in astonishment, there was no one to compare to his brother, who was his idol and always had been. Meghan returned before he could further the conversation.

Wulfstan took her by the waist, 'what is this nonsense about bandages when I have rushed here to see you.' Meghan laughed; it was everything to have him with her for good. 'Have you told your family that we are leaving?'

'Yes.'

'And how did they take it?'

'They were brave but sad, sorry that they may never see their first grandchild.'

'Aye, that is a sorrow, I can see that. When we are settled, they must come to live in Mercia. Tell them that it is a fine rich kingdom and I will make us rich.'

'I am already rich Wulfstan; I have the person I love and the first of many children in my belly. I will speak to my father.'

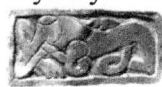

'It is wonderful to be in your arms, are you happy to be here with me?'

'What do you think?'

'It's just that I am not like the people you mix with now, you are the friend of kings and queens, all men look up to you. I'm a simple country girl with rough manners, I may shame you.'

Wulfstan's heart was touched by Meghan's humility, 'Meghan, people are no different wherever I go. There are rich fools as well as poor, foolishness, rudeness, ignorance, meanness of spirit are not the sole property of the poor and lowly, believe me, Wōden has distributed such gifts freely amongst all men *and* women alike.'

'Even your thoughts are above mine.'

'My dear wife, I will be proud of you, whichever company I find myself in, never will I be ashamed of you.'

'Thank you Wulfstan, I do love you… you do love me?'

'Of course, I do,' try as he might he simply could not say the words.

Wulfstan awoke early; it was yet dark, there were only flickers of the new day, which touched the rooftops, and the morning mist sparkled as the fresh day's light brushed against it.

He caressed the frame of the door where a thousand hands had worn it smooth, as lives had entered and left. All he'd known from a life past had touched this place.

He remembered too, another door and another girl in bed, she'd laughed herself into tears that day when he had fallen through a door much like this one.

'Wulfstan,' he turned to the whisper.

'Ah, Meghan, you are awake.'

'Yes, lie with me, it is yet early,' he turned and knelt by her and kissed her.

'I have a favour to ask of you, Meghan,'

'All you have to do is ask…'

'I know that I have only just returned,' she was a little nervous, what was he saying. 'Would you mind if I rode alone around my home, once more before we go south? I want us to leave on the morrow, and I don't know when, if ever, I will return.'

She breathed a sigh of relief, 'I understand fine, you must do as you wish.' He kissed her once more.

'I will ready myself and go, thank you.'

'What about mete?'

'I will grab something never fear.' He hurriedly slipped on his clothes, kissed her once more and left.

He rode into the hilltops overlooking his home and dismounted. He'd always believed that this summit, which had views that reached as far as the eye could see all the way to the coast and Din Guyaroi, was where the gods lived so they could watch all their minions go about their daily chores.

He rested his head wearily on his knees and massaged his stomach. He was unable to rid himself of the constant feeling of being full. He threw the mete he'd brought to the birds in despair; it was no use to him he simply could not swallow it.

'Are you listening Freya? I will rejoice in my suffering, if you tell me that the more I suffer, the less Aefre suffers. Give it all to *me*, let that be your most precious gift. May she forget me and know only happiness, do this for me Freya, I beg you.' He lifted his head and stared into the distance. He knew that Aefre was there, in that tiny speck he could barely make out on the coast.

It was still light when he stepped down from his horse, and Meghan came to him.

'Mother and Father want to see you before we go on the morrow.' He took her in his arms.

'Of course, shall we go now?'

'What about mete?'

'Fear not I have eaten, no doubt your mother will have food for us, from what I remember of her,' Meghan smiled. 'Shall we walk?'

'Yes, I would like that.'

It was very difficult, there were many tears; it seemed wherever he was, people shed tears. That was who he was, his gift from the gods, the purveyor of tears.

Meghan's mother *had* packed a bag of food; he glanced at the bags and asked her mother if Meghan would be able to carry them home, they looked heavy.

Her mother slapped him and laughed saying, 'that's why women marry, so they have someone to carry their load.'

Morning came soon enough, and they said their goodbyes. Wulfstan patted the horses Leofwine had chosen for them, Wulfstan nodded to him, he had obviously chosen the very best mounts from their stable. Leofwine kissed Meghan and helped her up onto her mare. Once they were all mounted, Wulfstan cast his eye to the other horses just to be sure that they were secured. They had extra horses so they could change; there was ever the risk that an animal could go lame. The ponies carrying their belongings were tied together and strung out in a line behind them. They turned for one final look at their past life and then moved off on the long journey south.

Wulfstan asked how Meghan felt as their home disappeared from view. 'At this moment, *excited*,' she said. 'No doubt I will feel differently later, but at this point, I'm thrilled at the thought of discovering new places and meeting new people. I have never travelled more than a few leagues from our home in all my life.'

It was three days before they came to the border of Mercia. They had seen very few people, Wulfstan steered clear of settlements, as there was ever a danger that villages would feel threatened and attack them.

Wulfstan was making for their capital of Taemwerh [21] on the River Teme. It was his intention to find the river and follow it south. He knew that it would take him straight to Taemwerh. He'd travelled that way previously, so he had some familiarity with the route.

Briton
Circa 600 AD
Lothian
Strathclyde
Galloway
Bernicia
Northumbrians
Deira
Humber Estuary
Lindsey
Britons
Mercians
Middle Angles
South Angles
North Folk
East Angles
South Folk
Hwicce
East Saxons
Middle Saxons
Surrey
West Saxons
Kent
South Saxons
ENGLISH CHANNEL

Chapter 28

Mercia

Wulfstan pointed to the highlights on the water in the distance. 'There is the River Teme ahead of us Meghan, perhaps one more day and we will be in

Taemwerh our new home, in truth, what you see is the Dove, but it flows into the Teme. We will rest in a village on the Dove called Ilam, not far, I have stayed there before, I am known.'

'Will we be safe, Wulfstan?'

'Nowhere is safe Meghan, is that not so Cedric?'

'It is as you say, Lord.'

'What do you say, Hrodulf, or you Halth?'

'There will never be safety as long as the Britons want their land back and they are not far from here, it's the same as in Bernicia. All land to the west belongs to the Britons.'

'There you have it from the lips of Hrodulf, one who knows, *but* you should not be afraid, "Why" because they do not have any warriors comparable to the ones who ride with you,' and they laughed, 'we slay Britons by the score.'

'*But* Mercia is a rich land, King Pybba is known for his wealth, *you* told me so. Surely that is both good *and* bad, to my simple mind it makes it a place to be envied by the Britons.'

'You speak truly Meghan, that's why there are strong ties between King Pybba and King Æthelfrith, they know they need to be as one to resist the Britons.'

'Perhaps we should press on towards the village Lord, for safety's sake,' Halth suggested, 'before nightfall, my backside is in need of some rest.'

'Aye, ride ahead Halth, see what you can see.'

They watched Halth go then followed at a steady trot. It wasn't long before they saw Halth returning and they drew to a halt to wait for him. He rode around them then came up alongside Wulfstan.

'I didn't see the village, I didn't get that far, I could smell death, Lord burned flesh. My guess is that they have been raided within the last day or so.'

'What do you think, men?' There were several moments of silence amongst the warriors as they considered the best course of action.

'Could you hear any noise, Halth?' asked Cedric.

'No, it was only the smell.'

'Mmm, we'd better take a look but be watchful; Meghan ride between us, if we are attacked don't be separated from us and lie flat to your mount, make yourself small. Give me your rein I will tie it to my saddle that will help keep you next to me. If they have left, it's probably the safest place to be, where *they* have recently been. Are you clear about what I've said, Meghan?'

'Yes.'

'Are we agreed?' He asked, turning to his three huscarls.

'Agreed,' they said as one.

On nearing they could see that the village had indeed been raided and burned, the dead littered the ground, some charred beyond recognition. Meghan lifted her shawl to cover her mouth and nose; the smell was hellish.

'By Wōden's breath, women and children have been burned to a cinder,' she said gasping at the sickening stench of burned human flesh.

'Aye, the ones who are not here may have worse to face. We will make this known to King Pybba if he does not already know.' Wulfstan dismounted to look amongst the ashes to see if any had escaped, but there was no one. 'Come; let's get from the place. Any who were not killed will have been taken to sell for slaves,' he said springing onto his saddle. 'Not too quickly, keep your ears open.'

They never saw a living soul until they reached the outskirts of Taemwerh and safety. Wulfstan guided them through the muddy streets towards Pybba's palace.

'Not quite the fortress of Din Guyaroi, my Lady.'

'I'm afraid not, Hrodulf, we must hope that such is not needed,' responded Meghan.

At the entrance, they were challenged by guards brandishing spears.

'I am Ealdorman Wulfstan from Bernicia, a friend of King Pybba, tell him we wish to see him.'

The guards looked to one another, they hesitated; one nodded to the other, and he went inside. The guard returned quickly and bowed, 'the King will see you, Lord, he has ordered me to take you to him.'

Wulfstan signalled to his men, they dismounted, and he helped Meghan from her saddle. 'Don't be afraid Meghan, I'm known as I have told you – and remember who you are, a great Lady from Bernicia,' she smiled.

'I'm no great Lady!'

'Indeed, you are, take my arm.'

The King was seated at the end of his large impressively decorated hall. There were lavish wall hangings on every surface.

He stood as they neared, stretched out his arms in a gesture of welcome, and smiled.

'Lord Wulfstan, our friend from Bernicia.'

They all bowed, 'Too long since we have seen you, Lord,' Wulfstan said embracing the King.

'And you bring a lady and friends.'

'This is my wife, Lady Meghan, Lord.'

'My Lady,' the King said, and Meghan bowed once more.

'And my huscarls, Cedric, Halth and Hrodulf. The finest any Lord could wish for.'

'You are all welcome in my court. How is my good friend King Æthelfrith? News of his great victories have reached my ears.'

'He is well and sends greetings and thanks you for your continuing friendship.'

Pybba beckoned servants, 'see mete is set before my guests. Be seated and tell me what brings you here to Mercia. I'm always at the service of our friends from the north.'

Food was quickly set before them, and Wulfstan told King Pybba of his reason for leaving Bernicia. King Pybba listened intently to all Wulfstan said. He had heard the stories, any leader who hoped to survive made sure he knew what was happening in neighbouring kingdoms. He didn't make it known that he was already in possession of such knowledge. A Queen running off with a noble was essential information; it could well have affected the stability of Bernicia and in turn Mercia. He was impressed that Wulfstan had told him the truth, for it was a difficult thing.

'I have always work for men such as you, the Britons are ravaging the border villages of my kingdom.'

Wulfstan told him of what they'd seen at Ilam.

'WHAT! I did not know about this latest outrage, it must have only just happened. We are constantly subjected to these attacks,' and he slapped his palm on the table. 'I must send warriors to avenge this insult. It cannot go unpunished, or I will be seen to be weak. It is the right of subjects to expect protection from their Lord. If I can't keep my people safe, how can I ask them for their loyalty?' King Pybba stood, knocking his chair over and prowled back and forth, giving full vent to his rage. '*Earslings*,' he shouted, 'they will suffer ten times for anything they do to me.'

'King Æthelfrith has been faced with the same dilemma, but he did not just return raid for raid.' King Pybba ceased his shouting and listened to Wulfstan. 'He attacked their rulers and destroyed the King of the Gododdins who is no more, and neither is the King of the Gaels.'

Pybba tugged at his beard all the while Wulfstan talked. 'We will speak more on this Ealdorman, but for now, I will find a place for you, your Lady and your men. I am fortunate that someone of your distinguished reputation has decided to make his home with us. This makes the links even stronger between our two kingdoms.'

King Pybba was generous to them; he gave them a fine longhouse and slaves. Meghan had been delivered of a son, and they had called him Leofwine, after Wulfstan's brother. It was difficult for Meghan, Wulfstan knew she missed her mother and father, but she never complained.

He had led several raids into the Britons' heartland since the burning of Ilam; there had been no reported attacks on Mercia.

Wulfstan leant against the doorframe and looked up at the sky. It seemed to be touching the rooftops it was so low, the rain was relentless, mud and filth everywhere. He watched those who ventured from their dwellings scamper quickly for cover. The last leaves, which had yet clung to life were being blown from the trees and lay scattered in soggy heaps.

It all had a different significance to him, it was autumn, and that thought drew the chill of winter into his bones. He knew that Aefre would be near her time too if she had not already given birth. Their child, his child, would be adored by another.

He could only guess at her suffering, and he touched the scars on his head. They had never properly healed, perhaps he would not let them; he was forever touching them and picking at them.

Wulfstan hoped that he was kind to Meghan, he did try, strange he thought, I never needed to think like that about Aefre What I felt for her came from my heart, not my head. He felt as miserable as the weather. There would be no raiding this day; he knew that there was other work, even for warriors at this time of year. There were the long winter months ahead, which touched Britons and Saxons alike. It must be prepared for, or there would be deaths, and that was a battle common to all.

'What are you thinking about, Wulfstan? Let me guess… Din Guyaroi and…' he held his breath at what she was about to say. 'The fresh sea breezes.'

He breathed again, 'aye, I miss the sea, don't you?' He turned to her, she passed his son, Leofwine, to him, and he smiled.

'You forget that I did not spend so much time there as you. I miss my family, but you know that. Perhaps we could return for a while?'

'Aye, in the spring,' but he knew he never would. 'Has this fellow been out in the rain, my hand is very wet?' He laughed.

'Give him to me, I will change him.'

'I must make the most of this opportunity and take Dream World to the smith for him to sharpen.'

Chapter 29

The wooden sword

Throughout the winter months, King Pybba had met many times with Wulfstan, and his Mercian leaders; this night was no different.

It had been a harsh winter. Some of the elderly, no longer able to fend for themselves, had perished. Meghan said to Wulfstan that perhaps they had merely given up, life was just too much of a trial. He knew she was thinking of her parents in Bernicia.

He had reminded her that *they* were not alone; she had a sister Ealfe and her brother Ælfweard, and they would see that they were taken care of when they were no longer able to care for themselves.

She had nodded, but she nevertheless longed to see them, if they were yet alive, they'd heard nothing from Bernicia since they'd left. Wulfstan forever promised that they would go home to see them, but he was always too busy.

He had become as influential with King Pybba as he'd been with King Æthelfrith, that was simply who he was. She had always known that he was no ordinary man; perhaps that's why he was so attractive, he stood out. He always drew people's attention, she often saw women watching him, and she knew they desired him. He was handsome, there was no question about that, even with his scarred head and twisted nose. He had tanned skin; even in winter, when everyone else looked pale and sickly, still he looked the picture of health.

His eyes were the warmest brown. He had thick jet-black curly hair; most women would have given their right arm to have such hair. To her, he was a god, and what forever endeared him to her, was that he didn't seem to realise how extraordinary he was. He ever treated people as if *they* were the special ones, even servants. He knew them all by name and regarded them with dignity as if they were actually human beings, not simple things whose sole purpose for existing was for his use and then discarded when they were no longer needed. She knew servants and slaves were often flogged for the most trivial of offences, but *never* in Wulfstan's house. It was no wonder that his men would die for him without a second thought. Servants and slaves willingly rushed to attend to his every whim... *and* he was *her* husband and father of her child.

The men gathered around King Pybba's large oak table looking at the rough sketches of the kingdom of Powys. Wulfstan didn't know the place, so was content to allow those who allegedly did to argue about the accuracy of their maps, and argue they did, for opinions differed greatly.

It was cold, the winter's snow yet lingered, though it *was* thawing. Consequently, there was mud and filth everywhere, it was almost impossible to keep anything clean.

All gathered around the table were wrapped in their winter furs to ward off the cold and damp, but this night they were not needed, for around this table – the temperature was anything but cold. In fact, it was hot, *very hot*, at one point, tempers were heated to such a pitch that seaxs were drawn and King Pybba had to shout to restore order, commanding that they be seated. After a brief hiatus of glaring eyes, they begrudgingly obeyed him and sulkily returned to their seats. Wulfstan had never moved and said little, he was content to sit to one side and be entertained.

Eventually, it was settled that they would take a large army to Pengwern, the main town of Powys, and finish once and for all, their constant tormentor, King Brochwel.

It was agreed that they'd march before the spring, it would be difficult underfoot, they all knew that, but it would give them the advantage of surprise. Such timing of an attack would be unexpected, and King Brochwel would not have the opportunity to rally support from neighbouring Briton Kings.

The subsequent weeks were hectic; everyday implements were being turned into weapons. It was the same as it had always been before every battle Wulfstan had been involved in since he was a boy. He'd fought for the first time with his father, Wulf, against their old enemy, the Gododdins, when he was only fifteen. He was no longer afraid at the thought of death; fear was a forgotten friend to him since he'd left Aefre.

There were constant border battles when he was a fledgling warrior. He remembered being terrified but fearing to show it in front of the older warriors and shaming his father. His father knew, and had wrapped his arm around him and winked, making sure he was kept away from the main fighting, he didn't realise that at the time, but he did now.

He wondered if King Æthelfrith would teach *his* son, as *he* would have, showing him all that he had learned from his father. It was a hard thing, to think of someone else tutoring your son and him learning another's values. Then he thought, perhaps it was King Æthelfrith, who had the more admirable qualities. Wulfstan hung his head, and his knuckles turned white as he squeezed his clenched fists at the ache he felt, he shook his head and cursed.

'How can I live on like this? I can't keep going with this pretence. Surely, the pain will ease sometime. Dear Wōden and all your minions, help *me* please.' he whispered under his breath.

He didn't know if Aefre had a son or a daughter, he knew nothing, that was the truth of it, but his thoughts wouldn't stop at the "Not knowing", they just went around and around in his head.

Leofwine was two now, walking and saying a few words, "Da – Da" was his first, he was sure that was down to Meghan's persistence, but nevertheless, it pleased him.

The day came soon enough for them to leave, horses were milling around, churning up the wet ground making it worse than it already was.

Wulfstan went once more into his longhouse to say farewell and give Leofwine a wooden sword he'd made for him. He kissed Meghan as she clung to Leofwine; he wriggled and squirmed in her arms determined to go with his father. Wulfstan wanted to tell her he loved her, but he couldn't. He told her how beautiful she was and how fortunate he was to have her for his wife, but he couldn't say the words she most wanted to hear. Perhaps he loved her too much to speak such intimacies that were not the truth, not as she wanted them to be anyway.

'Wulfstan, take care, as I say the words, they sound foolish to my ear for I know you will always be where the thickest of the fighting is. If it be possible, please remember you have a family who love and need you *and* to speed your return know that I am with child once more.'

All he could do was stare into her face, before he could reply Cedric came in through the door to fetch him; 'We are ready Wulfstan.'

'Take care of him for me Cedric.'

'Fear not Meghan, the devils take care of their own,' and he smiled.

Wulfstan hugged her once more and had to prize loose her grip, so tightly did she hold him.

She stood in the doorway and waved, took hold of Leofwine's tiny hand, and caused him to wave too, but he was having none of it, he wanted to be with his father.

As they rode to the edge of the village, Cedric turned to him, 'You never seem fearful when we go to war, do you, my friend.'

Wulfstan didn't respond immediately... 'That is no mystery; you fear death because you hope to live, whereas I do not fear death, because I hope to die.'

Cedric didn't reply and wished he hadn't asked. He forever hoped that things had changed with time. Wulfstan had never once mentioned Aefre; *but* clearly, time had changed nothing. Cedric cast his eyes to his hands resting on his saddle, and they rode on in silence.

They would only camp one night, the plan was to ride through the next night and strike quickly before daylight when an attack would be least expected.

The final decisions were made as the leaders were seated eating their dried meat. There were to be no cooking fires or lights of any sort that may give notice of their intention to nearby Britons, and they called to Wōden that they might not stumble into any of their raiding parties, but that was unlikely this early in the year. They had taken all the able men with them in the certainty of it.

Wulfstan and his three faithful huscarls were given the task of scouting ahead before the assault at daybreak. As soon as they returned with their information, the warriors made their way silently to their positions. The town was in a valley, and they completely surrounded it.

There was a moment of utter silence, men holding their breath. Nervous flexing fingers gripped spears and swords – the signal was given, and all hell was let loose as screaming warriors ran like painted demons to the wooden walls. The poor hapless guards didn't even have time to close the gates before they were overrun and slaughtered.

It was all Wulfstan imagined that the view through the Hellmouth would be. He saw one woman cleaved down the centre of her spine by an axe as she turned to protect her child. He hated this type of bloodshed; it was not a battle of noble warriors facing each other across a field, certain of glory and honour in the afterlife. This was a war against families, women, children and old men who had no hope of defending themselves, some were merely beaten to death if it breathed it died. The killing went on even after they had clearly defeated the miserable defenders. The wantonness of it all was pressed into his gut, and he was sickened when he saw a warrior needlessly remove the head of a small barking dog tied to a post, for no other reason than the sheer need for more brutality.

He heard that King Brochwel, his wife and all his sons had been butchered. The first he knew of it, was when he saw the King's mutilated body being dragged through the streets behind a galloping horse. At least they said it was the King, no one would know, he was unrecognisable, merely a bloody lump of meat.

There would be some who'd escaped, perhaps, but it would be a long time before the Britons would again challenge King Pybba.

The town was sacked, anything of value was taken; even Wulfstan had gold in his bags as they rode away from the burning pyre. He didn't know why he'd bothered, he no longer cared about gold, *a habit* he supposed.

Cedric, Hrodulf, and Wulfstan rode side by side, but there was *no* Halth. He had been stabbed in his leg, not by a warrior, but a mere youth who'd caught him from behind. The blow must have severed a main artery for blood poured from the wound, and they could not stem it. Hrodulf held him in his arms while his life pumped from him. The youth would never boast of his kill, for Cedric had near cut him in half with a single stroke.

When they approached Wulfstan's manor, on the outskirts of the town he stared in horror, flames were leaping from the roof of the longhouse. There was just one moment of disbelief, and the three dug their heels into their mounts and rode the already weary beasts without regard for their lives. Wulfstan flogged his horse to its death; it staggered and collapsed throwing him as he entered the yard.

He rolled over and over and came to his feet with his sword Dream World in his hand. There were maybe eight raiders. Wulfstan had slain three before he'd moved from the spot.

There were dead retainers laid in the yard who'd made some attempt to fight off the raiders, and with some success, but they had been ultimately overwhelmed, it was inevitable. No one had expected this they'd thought that they were safe from raids. He heard screams from within, the heat was ferocious; he dipped his cloak in a barrel of rainwater and covered his head, a baby cried. He kicked at the door, and it broke open, but the fire exploded from the opening into his face, throwing him onto his back.

Someone leapt onto him, and he drew his seax and ripped him from his groin to his ribs. He pushed himself free and covered his head once more with his cloak, Cedric grabbed him, and so did Hrodulf.

'IT'S NO GOOD WULFSTAN, it's no good,' Cedric yelled.

'Let me go you earslings, I'll gut you both for this.'

The beams began to crash to the ground in showers of sparks; there were no screams now. The longhouse was falling apart.

'I will never forgive you for this, never.' He snarled at Cedric and Hrodulf, 'Get out of my sight the pair of you.'

'There is one prisoner, Lord,' Cedric pointed to a dazed terrified man lying on the ground fearing to move.

Wulfstan walked to him, grabbed him by his collar, and dragged him from view.

Neither of the two seasoned warriors had ever heard screaming the like of that prisoner. Hrodulf stared at Cedric... 'I hear him, and care not, let the murderer wear the colour of his trade,'

But the screams would live with them long after this night. They went on until daybreak when Wulfstan returned covered in blood.

It was evening before they were able to recover the charred remains because of the searing heat in the embers. There were four bodies in all. Wulfstan carried out the rigid blacked remains of what was left, Meghan first and then Leofwine. The remnants of his wooden sword were burned to his hand, Meghan had obviously lain on top of him to try to protect him.

They buried the rest of the bodies in separate graves, but the bodies of his wife and son they lay in the same grave wrapped in Wulfstan's cloak. Cedric kept looking at Wulfstan, but there were no tears until he placed them tenderly into the shallow grave, and he remembered his terrifying nightmare the night before they married, when he'd seen Meghan on fire. The gods had tried to tell him, but he'd never listened. He stepped back, fell to his knees, and wept saying softly, 'I love you, Meghan.'

Cedric and Hrodulf walked away and waited by their horses so that Wulfstan might have these last few moments alone with his wife and son.

They retrieved one of the raiders mounts to replace Wulfstan's dead horse. Cedric sat on his hunkers and Hrodulf laid his hand on his shoulder.

'Have you known Lady Meghan for many years, Cedric?' asked Hrodulf.

'Aye, we were all children together, I was a couple of years older and always watched out for her. I loved her, everyone did, but she only ever had eyes for Wulfstan, and he for her, so it was at one time.'

'I liked her too, and the little lad, he was always full of mischief.'

'Aye… how he will cope with this on top of everything else beggars' belief, he will need us now like never before, guilt is an exacting master.'

'He has no guilt he did all he could,' said Hrodulf.

'You might think so, but he will not see it like that, that I do know.'

'Whatever he sees as his failings, I will be there – I owe him my life, once he could have left me to die, but he did not. I will suffer all the anger and hurt he doles out, and yet I will be in his debt. He's the finest Lord I've ever had.'

Wulfstan carefully covered his wife and son and lifted some flat stone slabs from a nearby path, to lie onto the small mound. They were heavy, and he struggled, but he would not ask for help from Cedric or Hrodulf, he hated them; they should have let him die too.

He had nothing, nothing now, but yet the gods did not seem to want to release him from their grasp. No, he was solely to exist for *their* entertainment, how they must be laughing at his hell.

No matter what he did he was not touched, weapons turned from him, and he was heralded as the greatest of warriors. He glanced at his sword, perhaps it was a cursed sword; a gift from the gods and his head was in the helma of the damned.

He stared at the pathetic few graves of his servants, and to the one that marked the brief life of his son and most loving wife. He gasped for air while he tried to steady the muscle spasms in his throat and chest, sobbing afresh. He wiped his face smearing it with the dirt from his hands and walked to the horses. Cedric passed him the reins; he snatched them from him, mounted, and galloped off without them.

Chapter 30

Din Guyaroi

King Pybba was seated and beckoned Wulfstan forward, 'be at your ease Ealdorman,' and he pointed to a chair.

'I will stand if I may, Lord.'

'You may not, sit down!'

Wulfstan insolently dragged the chair from the table and did, rather sullenly, as he was bidden.

'Ealdorman, I know of your suffering, to lose a son and a wife in any way, never mind the way *your* family was taken, is a hellish thing. For that reason, I will ignore your impertinent manner.'

'There are plenty of women to give brats, what care I, to lose one.'

'Take it from me, Ealdorman, I have lived longer than you, and I have found that it is the ones who do not shed tears that hurt the most.'

'I don't understand you, my Lord.'

'I think you understand me fine well,' the King replied, lightly bouncing the tip of his seax on the tabletop.

'You sent for me, my Lord; can I be of service?'

'I like you Wulfstan, you have served me well – at *great* personal cost,' Wulfstan listened without doing more than flex the muscles in his jaw. 'I have work for you, and work which may benefit us both,' the King paused, stabbed an apple in a bowl with the point of his seax, and began to peel it. 'I want you and your huscarl, Cedric, to go to Din Guyaroi as my envoys.'

Wulfstan only stared at him, he was unable to speak, 'Would we not better serve you here, Lord.'

'I always need your service, Ealdorman, but in this case, you will serve me best by going to Din Guyaroi to organise a meeting between your King Æthelfrith and me. We are friends and allies, now I want our relationship to be further enriched by trade, to that end I wish to meet with him.'

Wulfstan was trying to listen, but his brain had become clouded. King Pybba was watching him, trying to gauge his manner.

'Will you do this for me?'

'I will do as you wish Lord.'

'Very well, we will talk further, and I will give you my message. I want you to go as soon as you are able.'

Wulfstan rose from his chair and walked unsteadily from the room. King Pybba watched him go and frowned.

Once outside, Wulfstan slid down against the wall of the longhouse and sat for some time, trying to think on all the implications of such a visit. He would inevitably see Aefre and his child. What if she'd had more children, what if she did not love him now, what if she did, what if, what if, his head was spinning.

Cedric saw him, they'd never spoken since the fire, but he spoke now at the odd sight of his friend sitting on the ground with the strangest expression on his face. He had the appearance of a lunatic begging on the street.

'Are you well, Lord?'

'Well, yes, well. Ah, Cedric, we are to travel north to Din Guyaroi as soon as we are able. King Pybba has a message for King Æthelfrith, and we are to deliver it.' Wulfstan spoke to him as if they'd never been estranged. Cedric was yet not sure he was well; there was an unsettling vacancy about him.

'Yes, organise for such a journey Cedric.'

'Might I help you to your feet, Lord,' Wulfstan suddenly looked around, and seemed to take stock of his position and looked again at Cedric.

'You have work, be about it,' he ordered sharply. Cedric guessed that he'd been shaken loose from whatever malady had gripped him, the moment passed, and now he recalled the division between them.

They rode north on exactly the same route that they travelled south three years before. Wulfstan spoke little and Cedric was content to leave it at that. It was clear that their relationship was yet difficult; he could sense the hostility, though they spoke little.

Making no mention of it they swept well clear of the burnt village of Ilam where they had passed through on the way south. However, it must have been in Wulfstan's mind, for sure, it was in Cedric's. Wulfstan had lost a wife and child, but Cedric had lost a childhood friend, their death was no small thing to him, he was hurting too.

When they veered away from the banks of the River Dove on a more direct northerly path, Wulfstan inexplicably drew his mount to a standstill. Cedric did likewise, stopping, a length behind him. Wulfstan turned slightly and waved Cedric to come alongside him, still he didn't speak. Cedric could tell Wulfstan wanted too, but he knew he was struggling to find the words.

'I'm sorry that I offended you on our return from Powys Lord, it was never my intention.' Cedric couldn't bring himself to mention the death of Meghan. He'd suddenly realised that being so concerned for Wulfstan, he'd actually not given his own grief enough consideration. Being here with Wulfstan and having to face up to it, upset him greatly.

Wulfstan looked to him and lifted his leg across the saddle, the leather creaked, and he stepped to the ground, reached up his hand to Cedric who also dismounted.

Wulfstan cleared his throat, he was struggling, he looked at his foot and tapped a clump of grass with his toe, 'I'm sorry Cedric for the way I've treated you. It was shameful; I know that you loved...' he cleared his throat once more, 'loved... *Meghan* too.'

'Aye, that was a hellish day.' Cedric stepped forward and they embraced.

'I love you like a brother, you are the one friend I needed like no other at that moment, and I pushed you away.'

'Did I not tell you that nothing would ever separate me from you again? Unless it was *your* wish, I meant it.'

Both battle hardened men had tears on their cheeks.

'There is a fallen tree yonder, let us sit there Cedric, if you will make do with the company of a sorry fool.'

They ambled over to the tree, tied their reins to the branches, and were seated.

'My life has turned into a… difficult place to be, my friend. I was never fair to Meghan, I tried. Wōden and Freya both know that to be the truth.'

'I know it too. Has your feeling never changed for Aefre?'

'Not one bit, nothing has changed. I am afraid, not of death, remember you asked me before Powys?'

'Aye, I remember, I knew then how it was.'

'I fear meeting her, Pybba had no idea what he asked. I will never again leave Din Guyaroi, I know it in my blood.'

'You don't know, perhaps Aefre will have moved on.'

'No, that will not have happened. My dear friend, unless you have been touched by such love, you cannot know its power. What we feel for each other, is no fleeting passion, believe me. I wish it were, even if it was just me who felt this way and Aefre had moved on, *but* I know she will not. Even though we have been separated for three years, I know she will feel for me as ardently as I for her.'

'I'm so sorry, my dearest friend'

'Aye, and there is more,'

'More!'

'Aye, more, and I tell you this because of the regard I have for you… Aefre's first child… is mine.'

Cedric never spoke for some moments.

'I wondered.'

'Well now you know. I pray that she is well; one never knows what suffering childbirth brings. It may be a girl, she always said it would be a boy, but all her wanting will not make is so. I do not know any more than she could have. Life has taught me the cruel truth that the gods pay little heed to our wants. Will you do this thing for me, Cedric?'

'Anything my friend.'

'Will you see that my Ulfberht is given to Aefre's child, even if it is a daughter, perhaps she in turn will have a son one day and...' He lowered his head once more and his voice shook, 'Tell the child the truth someday about its mother and me. I know this is a great deal to ask and it will take great wisdom, but surely all our love cannot have been for nothing. I will not have any more children now.' Tears filled his bloodshot eyes; his face was that of a beaten man, furrowed and haggard. He wiped a drip from his nose with the back of his gloved hand and cleared his throat once again; Cedric laid his arm around his shoulder.

'I will do my best for such a child, but who of us knows what the future holds, only the gods?'

'Aye, the gods know all, they told me about Meghan.'

Cedric didn't know what he meant but let that go for now. He could see his friend had all that he could cope with tearing in his head at this moment.

'Well, I'm for staying here for the night, we've made good time and I'm tired.' Cedric said trying to move on and lighten their mood.

Wulfstan lifted his head and smiled, 'Aye, do you think it's safe for a fire?'

'I think so, we'll move into the forest, and damp it down before we sleep.'

The two laid out their saddle blankets, sat back against their saddles, and talked like the old friends they were.

'Do you remember riding off onto the moors, and spending nights like this when we were boys?' Wulfstan asked him.

'Indeed… the four of us, aye, happy days were they not? I hope we'll get a chance to see Leofwine and the others.'

'I'm sure we will, I have missed my little brother.'

They both felt better and stronger when they mounted and rode off the following morning. Wulfstan felt able to talk about his fears of meeting Aefre and King Æthelfrith. That uncertainty dogged them both for the next day, and never more than when the great fortress of Din Guyaroi came into view as they rounded the sandy headland.

They would have been spotted, they were sure of that, but their identity would be in doubt.

They rode up the track to the gates, nothing had changed… then he saw her… She had been riding and was dismounting, she passed her reins to a boy then turned, and she saw him… Aefre froze, he walked his horse to where she stood, leapt from the saddle, and bowed.

'My Lady.'

Cedric dismounted and bowed too.

She did no more than shake her head slowly from side to side, and closed her eyes, as if she was unable to comprehend what was before her.

'Is the King here, I have been sent by King Pybba?'

Aefre stared at him yet shaking her head. He wasn't sure what the gesture meant, *or*, if she'd *even* heard him.

'May we go inside my Lady?'

'Err… yes, yes, by all means!'

'Cedric will you see to our mounts whilst I go with the Queen?'

'Indeed, Lord,' and Cedric bowed. Wulfstan motioned with a sweep of his hand towards the keep entrance and Aefre walked before him. A guard opened the door and bowed closing it behind them. It was dark in the vestibule having stepped from the bright sunlight.

Aefre leant against the wall, 'Wulfstan, is it *really* you?'

'It is really me, the very same, and my heart has never changed, I love you and I forever will.'

'Shush, come to my rooms,' she stepped towards him, then thought better of it and turned, walking quickly up the stairs, he followed. Once more, a guard opened the door before her, and they entered.

Rowena looked up and beamed, 'My Lord, this is a great joy to see you, we have missed you sorely, if I may be so bold.'

'And I you.'

'We will leave you, no doubt you and the Queen will have much to talk of,' she smiled and bowed, 'I will see that you are not disturbed my Lady,' and left them.

'Wulfstan!' Aefre flung her cape to the floor and all but leapt into his arms. 'I love you, I love you,' she wanted to merge with him she could not get close enough. Their kisses were heady and passionate, 'How I have dreamed of this moment, a thousand, thousand times.'

'*And*, I have not?' He smiled.

'Come, I have something to show you, no, a moment,' she went to the door, and he heard her speak to Rowena, who must have been waiting outside. Aefre closed the door and leaned back against it smiling and laughing, 'I am so happy this moment I could die.'

'*What* – and me only this minute arrived.'

She had never moved when there was a knock on the door. 'Close your eyes!' he did as he was bidden, and she opened the door. 'Now, open them…'

He didn't need to be told, she held their son. 'Aefre, he has my eyes,' and she kissed his round cheek and he smiled.

Aefre went to Wulfstan and whispered as she held out her son for him to take hold of, 'Oswald this is your father,' – but Oswald clung to her.

'Don't frighten him, he's shy, I'm a stranger,' Aefre looked deflated. 'We will get to know each other and be great friends.'

'I'm sure of it.'

For no reason, Oswald had a change of heart and inexplicably reached for his father. Wulfstan took him in his arms and lifted him above his head, and Oswald giggled.

'I will give him back to his nurse for now. He sleeps in the forenoon. I so longed for this moment when he met you, you cannot imagine how precious it is to see you together.' She opened the door and passed him out to waiting hands.

'Did you like him?'

'Who would not?'

'Wulfstan my head is spinning with excitement; I have so much to say and ask. I will send for food and wine, we will not leave here, Æthelfrith has been gone for three days with your brother; he has become a friend of Æthelfrith, and they spend much time together.'

Chapter 31

Friend of a King

It was daybreak, it took a moment for Wulfstan to collect himself; he flexed his fingers. Aefre stretched, yawned, and smiled at him. 'My arm sleeps woman.'

'I'm sorry.' She moved her head and smiled. 'What can I say, when I went for a ride this day past, I never imagined this, thank you Freya. Please don't ever leave me Wulfstan, we will be together someday, I would rather die than be separated again. This is hell, for you have a wife and I even cry for her, she is a good person, Leofwine has told me of her. She is good, but I am wicked, that's the truth of it.' Wulfstan was serious now, Aefre noticed the change, 'You see, I have upset you, forgive me.'

'No, it's not that. You are not wicked Aefre, it's the gods that decide our paths, and natures. Do you remember saying to me that we can't fight against the will of the gods because we wish for different lives? I never loved Meghan, as I love you. I am ashamed to say that although I tried it just would not happen. We had a son.' She heard the past tense but was content to wait. 'She died in a fire along with my son, Leofwine.'

'My, dear beloved, what can I say?' She slipped her legs from the bed and buried her face in her hands.

'It's not your fault, Aefre. Meghan was happy, we had a good life, and it hurt me when she was killed. It was awful; my home was raided when I was away. It happened just moments before I arrived home. I tried to save her, but I was too late.' He lifted his arm to show her the scars from the burns.

She turned back to him and lightly touched the puckered skin. 'How awful, does is hurt?'

'No, not really now, perhaps if I catch it.'

She tenderly kissed his cheek, and he smiled sadly.

'Can we leave that where it belongs, in the past, Aefre? It was not because of our love that she died, and I'm *here* with you, and *now* is all that I have – *now* is all any of us have. We can dream about the past or the future, but all we ever actually have is now, this moment.'

'I love you and I can't change that, nothing can. If *now* is all we have, I will take that "Now".'

'Let not the past, steal our – today.'

'Shall we walk on the beach *today*, that always clears my head?'

They laughed as they walked, it was difficult not to touch, but they resisted, for there were eyes everywhere. They were so happy they laughed even *at* the watching eyes; or perhaps it was because of them.

When they returned to the fortress, they were invigorated by their walk, knowing that they'd soon be once more alone in the privacy of Aefre's room.

The moment they stepped through the gates, they froze in their tracks, and despair descended upon them like a cloud, for they saw Æthelfrith had returned. He was yet mounted as they walked into the courtyard.

'*No*,' Aefre gasped despondently, 'he was not to come home yet! This is not fair.'

The King saw them and smiled. '*Wulfstan*,' he called, 'I have this moment been told of your return, welcome.'

Wulfstan bowed, 'I bring greetings to you from your friend King Pybba.'

'I hope the Queen has been taking good care of you.'

'Indeed, Lord we have had much to tell each other of our lives since we last met.'

'And how is *your* good Lady?'

Wulfstan looked down and cleared his throat… 'She was killed my Lord…'

Æthelfrith only stared; he was genuinely lost for words. 'I am *so* sorry, my friend.'

Leofwine slid from his horse and embraced his brother. Wulfstan wasn't sure if the embrace was for Leofwine's comfort or his. He knew how much Meghan had meant to him, she was like a sister and this news would be a hellish shock.

'We must talk, brother.'

'Indeed, we will, I have missed you. I will want to go to see Meghan's mother and father, before I return to Mercia.'

Every word he spoke seemed like dust blowing on the wind. He knew he was *never* returning to Mercia. On his way here, he had imagined that he would be able to leave Aefre, *but* he knew now, he would not.

'Come Aefre, we'll leave our guest to ready himself for mete.'

'Thank you, my Lord,' Wulfstan bowed.

Aefre looked as if her world had at this moment fallen apart, and she trembled like a frightened deer before the hunter's arrow, frozen to the spot by fear, waiting for death to penetrate her heart,.

Æthelfrith dismounted and took her hand and they walked into the keep. The two brothers followed them.

At the night's mete, Aefre could not take her eyes from Wulfstan who was seated next to his brother; she struggled to eat and jumped every time someone spoke to her. Wulfstan saw it *if* no one else did... she was never going to be able to maintain the pretence; it was too much for her. He should never have returned; this could only ever have one outcome, he knew that now.

Chapter 32

Betrayal

Wulfstan was at that moment about to enter his room when he heard light footsteps; he looked up.
'*Aefre!*'
'Wulfstan!' She gasped.
'Whatever are you doing here?'

'I had to see you, I just had to.'

'This is foolishness, what if anyone saw you. Quick – into my room.' He opened his door and she stepped in, he glanced back and forth along the passage hoping that they had not been seen, and followed her in.

'Wulfstan, hold me, I'm afraid.' He wrapped her into his arms and kissed her. 'Your brother asked if I remembered the stories of Lord Hering, I said I didn't understand his meaning and he walked off. The way he spoke sent cold shivers down my spine, I thought I should tell you.'

'I will speak to him, it will be nothing.'

'Please don't go again, I have lived in hell without you. Æthelfrith has been kind; ever concerned for me; no matter how I tried he could see how unhappy I was. He does not deserve a wife such as me. I simply can't smile, not even when I hold our son, Oswald.'

'He is beautiful,' Wulfstan smiled sadly.

'Æthelfrith thinks that he belongs to him and loves him dearly, and yet I am in agony to see them together. Oswald asks for his father, all he wants is to be with him. You can't imagine how much that tortures me, Wulfstan. I wanted *you* to hold him, and when you took him in your arms this day past, and he smiled, I nearly cried out with joy. By all the gods, I am condemned to the hellmouth, I'm food for the dragon and he tears daily at my flesh…'

'My dearest Aefre, do you think I am spared? I too live each day in the hellmouth of guilt, as you know my wife and son were burned to death, and yet my heart *still* yearns for you, just to touch you, the longing has *never* left me for a single moment…' And he hungrily pressed his lips to hers.

Suddenly the door was flung open, crashing against the wall, *and* Leofwine stood in the opening.

'I followed this, this Queen of deceit,' and he spat scornfully on the floor. 'I was suspicious; I saw your eyes when she was near and her eyes which never left off looking at you. I didn't want to believe it, I just didn't, but now I see it was true. All Lord Hering said was the truth.' Leofwine snarled with utter disdain, stepped from the door opening, and walked off.

'Stay here Aefre, I will go to him.'

'It's too late.'

'*No*, he will listen.' He ran out and after his brother. Aefre closed the door and fell back against it; she was trembling like a leaf. Wulfstan quickly caught up with Leofwine, grabbed his shoulder, and pushed him back against the wall.

'Listen, Leofwine, you don't understand.'

'Don't take me for any more of a fool than you already have.'

'Listen!'

'*No*... I *worshipped* you, I only ever wanted to be like you, the great warrior that all looked to. I sang your praises, I spoke up for you when the rumours spread that you had run off with the Queen, no, not my brother I said, there is none more honourable. Now... I despise you, you disgust me, you are no longer part of our family, I disown you. I will take this shame to the King and try to gain back some honour for my family. You are forever an outcast. Now let me go or kill me in this dark place, that's where you do your work, you and your whore.'

Wulfstan stepped back and hung his head. 'What can I say brother, know that whatever happens you have my forgiveness.' Leofwine struggled but Wulfstan held him fast. 'You may pour scorn on that for now, but I know you will *need* to hear these words in your head, believe me. For you are about to set your foot to a path of regret.'

Leofwine pushed Wulfstan away from him with both hands, snorted his derision, and walked away. Wulfstan watched him go; his heart was broken. He shook his head and quickly ran back to his room and called, 'Aefre, it's me, open the door, quickly.

'Wulfstan!'

'We have no time to talk, Leofwine is making for the King to tell all; we must escape.'

'Our son?'

'He will be safe, we must get away from the fort now, there is not a moment to waste, come now just as you are.'

He took her hand and they ran like the wind as if Wōden's hounds from hell were snapping at their heels, down the stairs and into the courtyard to where two soldiers were standing by their horses. Wulfstan pushed them out of his way, lifted Aefre into the saddle of one, and swung up onto the other mount.

'What is it Lord, can we help?'

'Get out of my way,' Wulfstan shouted and pushed the man in the chest with the sole of his boot. The poor confused soldier fell back onto a pile of logs. 'Follow me, Aefre, we have only moments.'

They galloped through the gates and down the hill; the horses slipped and skidded as they turned sharply west. 'We'll make for the forest over towards the village of Ella's sons,' [23] he shouted back over his shoulder. He knew Aefre was a good rider and she would keep up with him. Their mounts pounded across the fields throwing up great clods of earth and mud into the air, grunting and snorting at their pace.

Wulfstan looked back towards the fortress. There were no signs of pursuers, not yet. They would come; he knew that. He wondered if perhaps Leofwine would not be believed at first, perhaps the King did not want to be made a fool of a second time, but he would know the truth soon enough.

He glanced once more over his shoulder and saw Aefre falling behind; he slowed his pace and waited until she caught up.

'It's not good Wulfstan, this mare's gone lame.'

She didn't need to say it. He could see the poor beast was struggling. 'Fear not, we have almost reached the cover of the forest and I can see that there are no followers, *yet*. We will rest here then walk the short way to the trees it's getting dark. *"The dark place, that's where you do your work"*. His brother's words ripped mercilessly into him once more tearing at his heart.

He helped Aefre down and took her in his arms. There were no tears now. This was a woman who had learned to suffer in silent torment. Whatever beating her heart had been subjected too, she had retained her dignity.

'I have never loved you more than I do at this moment, this is eternity, and there is no world beyond this moment, just you and me.'

'I know it Wulfstan – this – is not the end, it is the beginning of forever for us.' Wulfstan had to turn away. He couldn't look into her eyes; he stared over his shoulder towards Din Guyaroi.

The night was upon them and yet there was no sign of the hunters, but he knew they would come, yes they would come.

'Have you caught your breath,' she nodded. 'Then we will walk on to the forest.' He could see her mount was finished. He removed its saddle, hid it, covering it with branches, slapped the horse's rump and it hobbled off.

'She will make her way home to Din Guyaroi and they will see her and know our condition.'

'Aye…' he replied despondently.

It was much darker once they were among the trees; he tied the bridle of his horse to a branch and laid his cloak onto the leafy ground.

'We will rest here until first light and we will make our way through the forest.'

'And, then what, Wulfstan?'

'We will travel first west and turn south.' He knew there was nowhere to go, all would fear bringing upon their heads the wrath of the mighty King of Bernicia. They were now lepers to be repulsed, he knew that, and he knew that Aefre knew it too, in spite of his hopeful plans.

He leant against a giant oak and wrapped the edge of his cloak around Aefre as she pressed into him. It was almost as if, she believed if she clung tightly, they would become one spirit and confuse the gods who hated them and their love.

As he stared into the canopy above his head, he thought of all the symbolism of the oak tree and all it meant to their gods. It was worshipped for its endurance, longevity, its strength, and steadfastness, the "Pride and glory of the forest", the holy tree, the tree of life. Its strong roots penetrate deep into the underworld as its branches soared to the sky.

He thought of their love and its roots and branches, it was like this tree. He knew they were never leaving this spot and the tears flowed silently down his face onto her hair. He thought she slept, but she did not, and his tears trickled down onto her cheek and flowed into hers. Their tears were one, as they were one, and that could not be taken from them.

It was before the first light; he heard the dogs and he knew it would soon be over. Aefre stirred, he stood and raised her to her feet.

Chapter 33

The Price of Honour

As she stood, suddenly he remembered her sitting alone on a windy hilltop leaning against a cairn. He had taken her hand that day too, that day – the die was cast, or perhaps the gods had already brewed their potion before they were born, in waiting for the first moment their eyes met, and their eternity was sealed.

Aefre winced as she stood; her legs were cold and stiff. They heard the dogs coming for them and Wulfstan drew Dream World. What little light there was, was drawn to this perfect blade, and it shone as if the action of drawing it from the darkness of its sheath brought it magically to life.

Suddenly there were riders before them, thankfully Wulfstan could see the dogs were on rope leashes, but they strained and tugged to be free and upon their quarry. They hung from their collars, their front legs in the air with long strands of saliva drooling from foaming fangs.

Aefre clung to his arm, 'I love you; every moment was worth this, *forever*,' she spoke quickly for fear she did not have time to say the words just *one* more time. The words that were *forever* on her heart, clamouring to be free, the words that said all she was.

Wulfstan turned to her and pressed his lips to her forehead; let them see now, this was the truth and he'd *never* been ashamed of this love. It was not some murky thing of lust; it was only *ever* hidden for the sake of others.

'I love you, and we will be together always, bless you, I love you, I love you.'

Leofwine dismounted and looked up at King Æthelfrith. '*Unleash the hounds*; let them have them, the traitors. A quick death is too good for them,' he was frantic, possessed.

Wulfstan's throat was restricted, at the sound of revulsion in his beloved brother's voice, he couldn't swallow, anyone but his brother. He had cared for him for as long as he could remember, picked him up when he'd fallen, loved him, wiped away his tears, anyone but him, no sword could cut so deep a wound as those words.

He gently moved Aefre behind him, between him and the oak tree.

'*NO!*' Æthelfrith shouted firmly in response to Leofwine's cry for vengeance.

Bowmen slipped their bows from their shoulders and nocked their arrows.

Aefre screamed and pushed in front of Wulfstan.

'No…' The arrow went straight through her neck. She gurgled and felt to her throat, the blood seeped from between her fingers, as she gasped for breath. She slumped to her knees twisting her head as she fell, to look once more into his eyes. Her lips moved as she tried to speak, but there was no sound, only blood bubbled from between her lips, and she lay down onto the soft bed of leaves prepared for her.

Wulfstan knelt by her and kissed her cheek and she gradually closed her eyes. He turned and glanced at Æthelfrith who merely lowered his head. Leofwine ran at his brother his sword raised.

'NO LEOFWINE,' shouted Wulfstan – 'not you – brother.'

'*I HATE YOU*!' Leofwine yelled.

Wulfstan quickly pushed himself to his feet and parried Leofwine's blow. Leofwine recovered and swung his sword once more. Wulfstan could see there was no other way and he did no more than lower the tip of his sword to the ground… It was too late for his brother to draw back, his blade bit deep into Wulfstan's neck, and his head slumped to the side. His fingers relaxed, Dream World slipped from his hand, and he slowly folded face down next to Aefre. His nails desperately clawed at the earth as he reached for her hand and stilled as their fingers touched…

Cedric walked forward and threw Leofwine to the ground.

'Leofwine you are a miserable desolate creature, your *brother* never even *tried* to defend himself,' Cedric sobbed. 'THIS MAN – my dearest, dearest friend,' he turned and shouted to all present, 'had more honour than any man I have ever known, and – he paid "The Price of honour."

There was a sudden gust of wind, and the oak leaves they lay amongst were blown over them, it was as if the mighty tree of eternity was claiming His own.
Cedric reached down and picked up the Ulfberht, the sword from the world of dreams, he would see that it was given to their son.

To be continued

Author's Notes

King Æthelfrith

In 615, the Bernician capital Din Guyaroi, was renamed Bebbanburgh in honour of Bebba, Æthelfrith's new wife. The name meant the fort of Bebba, but it would gradually come to be pronounced Bamburgh.

This was perhaps one of many Celtic place names that were replaced by Anglo-Saxon names in this period and may reflect the gradual replacement of Celtic with Anglo-Saxon speech. It seemed that the native Celts were no longer the major threat to the expansion of the Angles and Æthelfrith for one was now preoccupied with defeating his Anglican rival.

Later in 615 A.D, he ousted King Cearl from the Kingdom of Mercia and took virtual control of the midland kingdom, although he employed a Mercian to look after Northumbrian interests here. Edwin, Æthelfrith's major Northumbrian rival fled from Mercia and took refuge with the King of East Anglia. Edwin was still a threat to Æthelfrith, but a seemingly more distant one and it seemed there would be no end to Æthelfrith's expansion. In 615, Æthelfrith defeated the Welsh in battle at Chester and once again seized Cumbria, bringing it firmly under Northumbrian rule. It was a significant event as it isolated the Britons of North Wales from those of Strathclyde and the Lothians, although that is not to say that the Britons were exterminated in the District of the Lakes.

However, Æthelfrith's expansion would not remain unchecked forever. In 616, he finally met his end in battle against Raedwald, King of East Anglia, at Bawtry on the River

Idle. This site lies close to the present borders of Yorkshire, Nottinghamshire, and Lincolnshire. In Æthelfrith's time, this area lay on the southern reaches of Northumbria, a dangerous marshy region close to the border with Lindsey and easily accessible from the East Anglican kingdom.

Oswald

Æthelfrith's son *"Oswald"* born 604 A.D, was King of Northumbria until his death on the 5th August 642. He was later venerated as a saint.

Oswald became the most powerful ruler in Britain. After some years in power in Bernicia, he also became king of Deira, and thus was the first to rule both kingdoms, which would come to be considered the constituent kingdoms of Northumbria.

Bede writes of his unparalleled *honour* and saintly Kingship, a man who walked in the steps of his father, a man *who* loved.

Lord Hering

Hering, son of Hussa (late 6th century-early 7th century) was a Bernician prince. He was the son of Hussa, king of Bernicia from 585 to 592 or 593. After Hussa's death, the kingdom went to Æthelfrith, Hering's cousin.

During the first half of Æthelfrith's reign, Hering fled to Dal, (a Gaelic kingdom that included parts of western Scotland and north-eastern Ulster in Ireland) where he was given refuge by their king, Aedan mac Gabrain.

In 603, Hering led a part of a Dalriadan army to attack Bernicia but was defeated at the Degsastan by Æthelfrith: the Anglo Chronicle (manuscript E, year 603) mentions Hering's participation, although Bede does not. Hering's ultimate fate is unknown, *apart that is, unless you have read this novel.*

Book 2

Warrior ~ King ~ Saint

Oswald

Chapter 1

Escape

Pungent, dirty brown and white foam blew from the withers of the exhausted ponies as they thundered west. Their nostrils flared as they galloped, desperate to fill their burning lungs and bring relief to their aching muscles.

'*Cedric,*' a young boy called to his friend as he drew near to him. 'We will have to rest soon, if not for Mother's sake, then for these poor animals.'

'I know Lord, I know…' Cedric conceded on hearing his own thoughts given flesh. '*Hrodulf,*' he in turn shouted to the rider before him. The warrior turned without breaking pace. 'We will stop at that thicket yonder.'

'I see it…' Hrodulf shouted back over his shoulder, at the same time adjusting the direction of his mount towards the wooded rise of silver birch. The rest followed, their horses stumbled and staggered the last few elnes [1] to the edge of the tree line and stopped. Cedric slid despondently from his hot saddle, which creaked and groaned in sympathy. He paused, straightened, and stretched, pressing his hands into the small of his aching back, rubbed his leg and then went to the side of Queen Acha.

'My Lady,' he said bowing and offering his hand to her.

'Is it *safe* to stop here, Cedric?' she asked hesitantly, and glanced at Queen Bebba, without responding to the proffered hand.

Cedric thought how tired she looked, and not just from the unrelenting pace of the journey. The last years had been thorny for her. 'We have little choice, I fear, my Lady; our ponies can go no further unless they are rested. I can't see any pursuers and we have a clear view from this place. I'm confident that we are safe for the time being. We will only stay here until we, and our mounts, have had time to be refreshed and regain some strength. They are wiry little animals they will soon recover. Fear not my Lady, we'll make it to Ad Gefrin [2] and safety before nightfall.'

'If you say so Cedric, we will be guided by you,' she replied and only now leant forward so that the old warrior could take her by the waist and help her from her saddle. Though she was well able to ride, the pace had been frantic as they fled from her brother Edwin's forces heading north towards her home of Din

Guyaroi, [3] or *Bebbanburg* [4] as some now called it, since Æthelfrith had taken his new wife Queen Bebba. Cedric and Queen Bebba were respectful to each other, but no more. He thought she was haughty and a schemer, ever trying to assert her will over Queen Acha who was gentle, like her sister Aefre, whom Cedric had loved.

His plan was to stay a night or so at Ad Gefrin, rest, take stock, and make sound preparation for the long journey ahead. He was sure King Edwin wouldn't waste his time following them as soon as his forces reached Din Guyaroi. Cedric's home would forever be Din Guyaroi to him, never Bebbanburg. The plan was then to head west to the Court of the Dalriadan [21] King, Eochaid Buide, the relative of Queen Bebba, and hope that he'd look favourably on them *all*.

Æthelfrith had spent many years suppressing the northern kingdoms; King Eochaid's amongst them, and now

Æthelfrith's family would be seeking refuge with him. Cedric knew what he would do if he were Eochaid and who could blame him. Queen Bebba insisted that this was their only option and Cedric had reluctantly agreed, even though he knew that it would be difficult for Queen Acha. He would see that no harm came to her and he had made that known to Queen Bebba in no uncertain terms. He was a warrior who had earned his right to be heard and taken note of and was not in any frame of mind to be intimidated by a woman, Queen or not.

His view of kings and queens had changed forever that day when he'd knelt by the side of his dead friend Wulfstan, even *King* Æthelfrith had not challenged him after that, not because he feared Cedric, their relationship was more complex than could possibly be summed up in one word. Cedric spoke to Æthelfrith, not as his King, but his equal, all fear of man had died that day his friend, and the woman he'd loved had been murdered. His friend had set honour before any earthly title and had died for it, now Cedric saw the world through his friend's eyes.

Cedric turned to help Queen Bebba from her horse, but she had already dismounted and was speaking to Prince Eanfrith.

The news of the death of the husband of the two Queens, King Æthelfrith, had reached them but a day past. The shock had struck panic and horror into the hearts of those left at the fortress of Din Guyaroi, fearing the forces of King Edwin.

Æthelfrith's power had rested on his military achievements. His success had now ended emphatically, at the hands of the exiled King Edwin of Deira, who, with the support of King Rædwald of the East Angles, had defeated and killed him in battle at Bawtry by the River Idle in the kingdom of the East Angles.

At first, those left at Din Guyaroi, couldn't or wouldn't believe that the great warrior could have possibly been defeated, but as more and more rumours of the large army coming north began to filter into the fortress, they were forced to believe the unbelievable.

Cedric had been left in command by Æthelfrith. Both knew that the fortress was undermanned. Æthelfrith had taken most of the warriors to face his wife's brother, never imagining the outcome. Cedric was certain he had taken the only option possible for the safety of the Leodwalding line. [5] He knew if they were ever to hope to get their kingdom back, they needed to be separated from King Edwin. Otherwise, they would have been part of all manner of family intrigues and possibly been murdered.

Cedric bowed to the two Queens, then glanced around at the faces of the Bebbanburg royal family, *eight*, he mentally calculated. Five were the progeny of Acha, and there was

Eanfrith, Æthelfrith's son from his first marriage, who was twenty-six now. Oswiu and Æbbe were Queen Bebba's children. Cedric smiled warmly at Æbbe, she was a special child and he had a soft spot for her. Edric she always called him, she had a habit of shortening names.

Cedric's eyes lingered for a moment longer on Æthelfrith's second child Oswald, who called Acha – Mother. This prince held a place in Cedric's heart, which was his and his alone. Prince Oswald was eleven now, and he was the *double* of his father in every way, even topped off with his black curly hair, *except* that is – for his eyes, they were the gentle soft brown of his mother's and just one glance could warm the coldest heart. His father's eyes had been piercing blue, they could look straight into a man's soul, but Oswald's were the complete opposite they were tender and forgiving.

Oswald would forever be the apple of Cedric's eye; he could not love him more if he had been his *own* son. To Cedric, he was perfect in every way, both physically and in his nature. Their eyes met and a smile touched their lips. What was between them passed in that smile, Cedric acknowledged the moment with the slightest nod of his head. He knew he had been more of a father to the boy than Æthelfrith ever had. Æthelfrith was ever too busy being king and he'd left Oswald in his care, *which* was what the gods had always intended. He was a child touched by the gods; Cedric had no doubt of that.

Even though much time had passed – the pain was yet fresh in Cedric's heart, as fresh as the first day he'd lost his friend.

Leofwine, Wulfstan's brother, had hanged himself only days after Wulfstan and Aefre's murder. Cedric guessed that he couldn't live with the betrayal of his own kin, his brother, who had loved and cared for him since childhood. Once he'd come to his senses and realised what a wicked thing he'd done, it was too much for him.

Cedric had found him hanging in the stables, but someone else had had to cut him down, Cedric couldn't touch him, even when he was dead. Cedric was filled with disgust. He had never spoken a word to Leofwine after the murder. His utter contempt for his treachery burned like molten lead through his veins and did yet.

Cedric had once judged his friend Wulfstan and couldn't forgive himself; there was no way he would ever forgive Leofwine for such a despicable act, he would rather rot for eternity in the Hell Mouth.

In Cedric's eyes, Wulfstan was nobler than any man he'd ever known; Wulfstan had understood that his brother, Leofwine, would despise himself once he realised what he'd done, and Wulfstan had told him that he had forgiven him even *before* his act of treachery. Wulfstan knew *full well* – that Leofwine was about to betray him and Aefre, and it would cost them their lives, but such was the nobleness of the friend Cedric loved – that he would forgive *even* their betrayer.

Cedric shook his head at the memory, and he trembled as the pain of that day tore through his limbs afresh – he could *never* understand such forgiveness. Cedric remembered yet his unabating fury at Leofwine. If the moment had presented itself, he would have done the work of the rope on Leofwine's neck and strangled him with his bare hands – aye – and gladly.

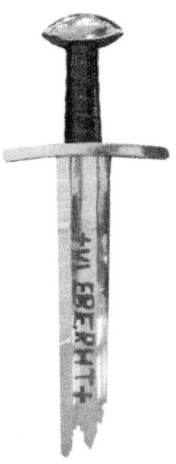

Chapter 2

The Gift

Cedric flicked his head, discreetly beckoning Oswald to his side as he seated himself on the trunk of a fallen tree.

Oswald acknowledged his bidding with a slight nod. As he walked towards his friend and mentor, he noticed a rolled bundle across Cedric's knee, tied with leather laces.

Oswald sat down next to Cedric, he didn't say anything, it was plain to him that Cedric was deep in thought and *he* was content to be still and wait for him to speak. He glanced at the bundle Cedric was holding tightly on his knee. Oswald watched as his fingers repeatedly tightened and relaxed their grip on the bundle. All the while, Cedric stared into a nowhere land, in another time and place.

Whatever was before Cedric's eyes at this moment, Oswald, as young as he was, could tell Cedric was looking into the labyrinth of secret places in his mind, into the veiled world of dreams. It was clearly a memory or a defining moment from long ago. By the look of the deep furrows on his friend's brow, it was a cheerless, aching sight; a moment of torment yet to find a place of peace and rest.

Cedric was a man of few words; he always believed that, when all was said and done, it was a person's life, which defined him, not his words. Cedric was never one for idle chatter or gossip and he had no time for those who lived out their lives in that mire. Whatever was troubling his friend, Oswald had the unsettling feeling that *he* was a part of it.

Oswald yet waited patiently, leaning forward with his arms rested on his knees. After several long minutes, Cedric cleared his throat, straightened his back, and from under thick bushy eyebrows, he slowly scanned the group of weary travellers. Most were seated quietly, probably fearfully contemplating the sudden uncertain interruption to their lives.

Cedric coughed once more and gradually began to speak. 'Mmmm, you must be wondering why I beckoned you to my side, my Prince…'

'I assumed that you had something of some importance to say to me, something private perhaps. By the goodwill of the gods, I hope that I have not given offence to you in some way.'

'No – you have not wronged me lad, but I have something to say, right enough, then again, at this moment what I have is more something to give.' He began to slowly loosen the leather laces of the package resting on his knee. Oswald looked on, with more and more curiosity. Once Cedric had loosened the binding, he went on to unwrap the oily cloth covering to reveal a magnificent sword, Oswald's eyes widened in amazement.

'By Wōden's beard, I've *never* seen such a sword, Cedric. One would only need a glance to know that what is before me is no ordinary sword. Where has it come from? You've never shown me this before.'

'If you are asking where it was given birth, that I cannot tell, for I never knew, perhaps it was a gift from the gods. I do know how it comes to be here on my knee. It was taken from a dead warrior at the battle of Catraeth. The Gododdin came at your father from behind and was about to cleave him in two with a mighty war axe, but your father was too quick for him. In one masterly movement, he spun around and sliced into the warrior's hamstrings just below his mail, the fellow folded into a heap and your father mercifully sent him to his gods.'

'My father, you say? He was the greatest of warriors,' Oswald declared proudly.

'… Aye… *your* father, he was the greatest warrior I have ever seen. None could stand against him.' Cedric glanced away from Oswald's eyes to the sword on his lap.

'What does that word mean,' Oswald asked pointing to the letters on the sword blade but fearing to touch the mysterious weapon. 'Is it the name of a god? Perhaps the Christ God, look at the crosses at either end of the word.'

'Maybe,' responded Cedric, '*Ulfberht*,' [22] he spoke out the word as he ran the tip of his finger over the embossed letters. 'Though I know naught of the Christian God and never wish to, His followers eat bits of Him is the little I've heard, so there can't be much left now,' Cedric gave a muted chuckle. 'He'll not be much of a challenge to Wōden with half of Him missing,' Oswald smiled too at Cedric's jest. 'What I do know for sure, this is the finest sword I have ever seen, or held.'

'Who did it, or who does it belong to now?'

Cedric hesitated for some time... 'Your father took it and made it his, I was commissioned on his death to make sure it was given to you.'

'Me!'

'If it was my father's it is mine by right.' The voice of Prince Eanfrith came jarringly from behind, soiling this personal moment. Oswald turned to his brother, but Cedric without lifting his head growled.

'When you speak to me *Earsling* – you had better kneel before me, with your head bowed, if you value your life.'

'I – am now your *King*, it is you who will now bow to me.'

There was a moment of deafening silence. 'King or no king, if you are yet standing there when I take my next breath you will have taken your *last* breath. Do you hear me, *boy*?' Cedric said in a fearfully calm voice, but a voice that had the force to burst onto the moment like a jagged shaft of lightning. The energy was more than Eanfrith could stand against and he turned and slunk off muttering to himself. He knew well enough that Cedric might only be a huscarl, but for some unknown reason he held a mysterious position of authority, and no one ever understood why. There was not one, who would dare question him, not even his father King Æthelfrith, who was the greatest warrior of the age.

The two were quiet now, while the sudden squall of emotions stilled. Oswald stared at his hands more than a little embarrassed by the interchange. Eanfrith had in fact spoken correctly, in truth, he was their father's eldest and what had belonged to their father was by right his, but *he* was not about to correct Cedric at this moment.

'There is much you do not understand, my Prince. An apple may be red on one side and green on the other, one man sees it as green the other sees it as red. Who tells the truth of it? The truth can be more than we see. I have told you this is your father's sword and it is so; let that be enough for now,' with that odd assertion Cedric passed the sword reverently to Oswald.

Oswald lifted it, felt its balance and then made a play with it slicing through the air. 'This is as you say, like no other sword I have ever felt, my friend. Is it magic?'

'Perhaps it is, it is a sword of honour. It belonged to the most honourable man I have ever known.'

'My father!'

'Aye – *your* father, he called it "Dream World". Ask me no more this day, for what truth I know is mine to know... *for* now.

Treasure his gift to you for I fear that today, young as you are, you have become a man, and boy or man, I know you, Prince of Bernicia, will never dishonour your father's trust.'

Oswald stood, slipped his own sword from its frog and replaced it with the
Ulfberht. 'What can I say Cedric, I have this precious gift and I will *never* be able to thank my father in person.'

Cedric now rose, faced Oswald and laid his gnarled hand on the boy's shoulder. 'Aye, that is a hard thing, my son – for me too.'

'Why ever would Father give this prized gift to me above any of his other sons? I cannot but help feel for Eanfrith's hurt.'

'As I have said, for now, I will hold my peace. Truths have their season to be told and this is yet winter. When the warmer days come and the time is right, you will know all, I promise you that.'

Oswald frowned at the double talk, but accepted what Cedric said without argument. He knew Cedric to be the bravest and wisest of men – that *truth* – he had *already* harvested.

'But for what comfort it is my son, I know your father would have been proud of you…' Cedric hesitated… 'As *I* am,' and he embraced Oswald.

As Cedric held him, Oswald whispered into his chest, 'I love you my friend.'

Chapter 3

Ad Gefrin

As they rode nearer to Ad Gefrin, Oswald was surprised at the size of the hill fort. It was several years since he'd been there. It was his place of birth and much of his early life had been spent at the palace. He remembered it as being large but thought that might only be the memory of a child.

Now he saw it was actually even bigger than he remembered.

It was not a fort in the military sense, though it had two timber palisade walls around the perimeter, one inside the other. It was more of a royal palace, a meeting and trading centre for all the local tribes and villages. He remembered that there were four enormous halls, it even had an amphitheatre, and on reflection, he thought that it must have held at least three hundred people or more.

The gates were opened as they neared, and the party rode in to be welcomed by anxious slaves and servants rushing hither and thither. Oswald watched Cedric who took a moment to dismount. He leant forward onto the up-stand of his saddle and looked around. Oswald smiled, Cedric never rushed, he was always a man of steady decisions and once he's made up his mind, look out if you stood in his way. To Oswald, Cedric was a hero, he admired everything about him, and he would learn all he could from him, whilst he was here.

Oswald abruptly clenched his rein tightly at the thought of the inevitability of one day losing his friend. His pony suddenly rebelled at the tightness of the rein, Oswald was conscious of Cedric's eyes upon him and he relaxed his hold and the pony steadied once more. Oswald slipped from the saddle; Cedric was the last to dismount.

Prince Eanfrith was already speaking to someone who appeared to be a man of some note, no doubt asserting his newfound position in the Leodwalding family. Oswald smiled, for he knew how little any title meant at this moment. Cedric's voice was the only voice of importance and Eanfrith would do well to take hold of that truth, and quickly. Oswald knew that Cedric did not suffer fools, not that Eanfrith was a fool, not by any means, but he was no leader either, people were not attracted to him. Whatever the indefinable quality was that drew men to follow and die for another, Eanfrith was not blessed, (or cursed) with such a gift. No matter how Eanfrith wanted men's respect, men never looked to him, in fact, Oswald knew the harder he tried the more he was disliked and that saddened him, for like it or not, Eanfrith was in truth, now the head of the Leodwalding family.

Oswald was distracted from his thoughts at the sound of Cedric's voice, 'To me Torem.' Oswald watched as the man talking to Eanfrith bowed to him and went to Cedric and they embraced, plainly he was well known to Cedric. Cedric turned to Oswald and beckoned him to come too. When Oswald neared, Cedric introduced Torem as an old friend of many years. 'This is the headman, Torem, he has served your family faithfully all his life, Torem this young fellow is Prince Oswald of Bernicia,' Torem bowed and smiled.

'I remember you as a small boy, you have grown since we last met, Lord.' Oswald nodded politely, but he was distracted, he'd glanced at Eanfrith. He could see that he was furious at what he would interpret as a snub by Cedric, but Oswald knew that would not be Cedric's intention, he simply didn't function like that.

Cedric was blunt, a man of action not one for the social niceties, he didn't care whether he was liked or not, he didn't seek position or approval of men, or even Queens come to that. Oswald tried to concentrate on what Torem was saying, but he was more concerned as to what Eanfrith was talking to Queen Bebba about. He wondered if their mutterings were their shared disapproval of their head huscarl, not that their displeasure would trouble Cedric in the slightest, nevertheless, what their thoughts and whisperings were about troubled Oswald. He was sure that Cedric lacked wisdom when dealing with Eanfrith.

Even at his young age, *Oswald* could see that Eanfrith was a young wolf on the prowl, determined to assert himself, and would not forever tolerate those who challenged him. He could well nip at Cedric's heels until he brought him down and Cedric would do well, not to unnecessarily provoke him.

It was by no means certain that Eanfrith would be given the mantle of his father, after all, Æthelfrith had not been the direct heir to King Hussa, yet he was made king much to the chagrin of Hussa's son Hering. Eanfrith would yet need to be elected by the Witan. Then there was Queen Bebba; she was cunning, *and* Cedric was entering their homeland where he would not have the unchallenged power, he had enjoyed at Bebbanburg.

A voice broke into the moment, 'Edric,' Princess Æbbe was tugging at Cedric's sword sheath, he looked down and smiled, Æbbe could always draw a smile from Cedric, one of the few who could, Oswald had to concede. Cedric reached down and picked up the child, he even kissed her, and she wrapped her arms around his neck.

Cedric turned his attention once more to Torem and made known to him, the predicament in which they now found themselves. Torem was visibly shocked, like everyone else he could not believe that the great King Æthelfrith could, not only be defeated, but also killed. Cedric told him that they would be here no more than two days, but first, he needed to find places for the family to sleep and then he was to return to him, and he would be given further instruction. Torem bowed and called two men to assist.

Cedric knew they would be safe for a short while, but he also knew they needed to make haste, and be on the way west as quickly as possible. Any small-time advantage they had must not be squandered. The now *King* Edwin would come soon enough to stamp his mark on his new kingdom and this palace was a central part of that kingdom.

Oswald saw the royal family being led into the largest of the halls. He remembered it had partitions at either end, which divided the whole area into three. He imagined that Torem would make the most of the two rooms at either end of the hall and see that the queens were separated by the length of the hall, not that Cedric would give such consideration the slightest thought. He did not have time for petty power struggles, as he saw such behaviour.

The safety of these royal athelings [6] was his concern, and all that was to happen now would happen at his command. The Leodwalding line would not die out because of his neglect.

'Do you need me Cedric? For if you do not, I will go to Mother and see that she has all that she needs. I'm worried about, her she does not look well.'

'You do as you must, Lord. Return to me as soon as you are at peace,' Cedric and Torem bowed to Oswald and he went to seek out his mother. Oswald paused for a moment when he entered the hall, simply to gaze at the size of the space. It was the biggest hall he'd ever been in, there were doorways in each wall. The roof beams were enormous, oak, he guessed, all brightly painted in yellows, greens and reds with serpents and dragons from the underworld. The wattle and daub walls were whitened, and they had been painted with hunting scenes. At the far end, there was a raised floor no doubt, where his father and mother would have sat. He wondered, for a moment, if he would be asked to sit there now. He knew Eanfrith would take the centre seat, his mother *and* Queen Bebba would sit either side of him perhaps even Cedric might sit at the high table, but he doubted it, being on show was not Cedric's way.

The whole sight before him was quite magnificent, much bigger than their hall at Bebbanburg, but then they were more limited for space on top of the rock. Moreover, there were another two halls almost as big as this, what a place of entertainment and laughter it must have been, but not now, not today.

Oswald shook his head and returned to his purpose for being there and went to find his mother. She was lying on her bed when he found her and his younger brothers Osguid and Oswudu were there too.

'Where are Oslac, Oslaph and Offa?'

'Fear not son, they are with servants,' Oswald's mother said reassuringly.

'Is there anything I can do for you Mother?' Oswald was concerned, for she did not look well at all.

'No son, you help Cedric. I need to rest and straighten my back after all that riding, no more than that, I'm not as young as you,' and she smiled. 'We will need to move on, we can't stay here too long,' she reached up and drew Oswald near to her. 'Stay close to Cedric whatever happens, Oswald.'

Oswald nodded in acknowledgement of her concerned advice. There was a strange intensity in her voice, but he said nothing, he bent down and kissed her, then turned to his brothers. 'You two find our brothers and make sure they come to no harm. I will be with Cedric, Hrodulf and Eanfrith if I am needed. Go now and let Mother rest.'

The next days were spent sourcing all their needs, which could be taken with them, such as ponies, clothing, some food, and tents. There would also be the sharpening and repairing of weapons, all that they would need for the long journey west and the possibility of any subsequent conflict.

In the midst of it all, was Cedric. He, Torem and Hrodulf never seemed to stop. There had been no feast so the question of who sat where never arose.

The few warriors who were at the fort would go with them, as would any who feared the arrival of King Edwin's men. There was some talk of firing the place, but it was decided that it might slow down any pursuers if it was seen to be intact. They may suspect a strong defence of some sort and any time gained would be to their advantage.

It was summer so they could at least hope for good weather and every league west meant greater safety from Edwin. Cedric had been convinced by Eanfrith and Queen Bebba that King Eochaid Buide and his Dalriadan court, at Dunadd would welcome them.

When the last of the travellers walked out of the gate, it was drawn shut and they headed off down the far side of the hill from the now ghostly fort, with the morning sun at their side.

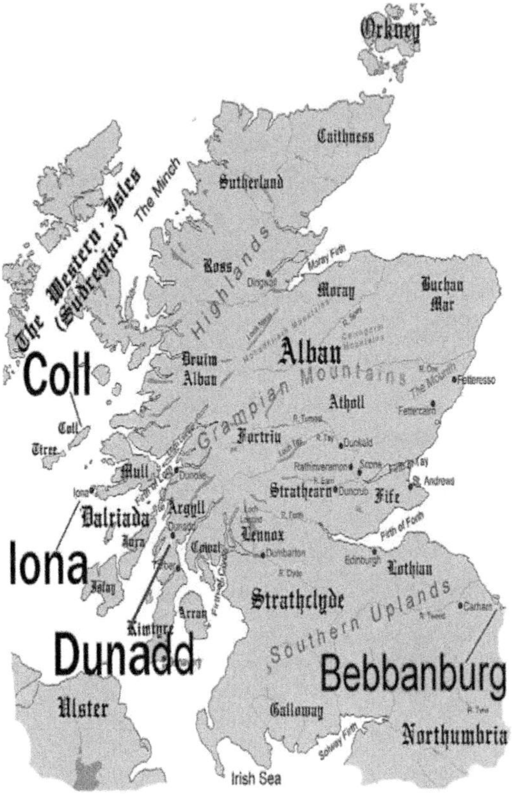
Orkney
Caithness
Sutherland
The Western Isles
(Sudreyjar)
The Minch
Ross
Highlands
Moray Firth
Moray
Buchan
Mar
Alban
Druim
Alban
Coll
Grampian Mountains
The Mounth
Fetteresso
Atholl
Fettercairn
Coll
Tiree
Fortriu
Dunkeld
Mull
Scone
St. Andrews
Iona
Strathearn
Fife
Dalriada
Argyll
Firth of Forth
Lennox
Jura
Cowal
Dumbarton
Edinburgh
Lothian
Iona
Islay
Strathclyde
Southern Uplands
Carham
Arran
Kintyre
Dunadd
Bebbanburg
Ulster
Galloway
Solway Firth
Northumbria
Irish Sea

Chapter 4

North West

The only one, with any knowledge of the way to get to Dunadd was Queen Bebba, they all knew that it was Northwest of Bebbanburg, or Din Guyaroi as Cedric insisted in calling their home, but no more than that was known.

Their intention was to ride north until they reached the River Abhainn Dubh, [7] the most northerly edge of Æthelfrith's Bernician kingdom, then they would follow the river west past the Roman's most northerly wall, not the one Oswald knew, this wall was much further north, until they reached the western sea.

By the guiding hand of Wōden, they would turn north once more and follow the coast until they reached the kingdom of King Eochaid Buide. With a fair wind, it was thought that the journey would take five or six days. There were families with children walking with them and that would slow them down. They knew it would be dangerous, they might be troubled by all manner of threats; none more worrying than the tribal raiders they might have to face. There were many unfriendly Britons where they were headed, but they had experienced warriors and huscarls with them, they would not be taken easily.

As Cedric contemplated all they might be faced with, he was momentarily distracted as he glanced at Oswald on his pony, riding straight-backed with his hand proudly on the pommel of his new sword, in every way he was an atheling. What set him apart, other than his looks, for he was the most handsome of young men with his tanned face and a thick mass of curly hair, was how he treated people. He genuinely cared about those lower than himself, even now as they rode, he had the small child of one of the slave girls sitting before him on his pony. He was special, Cedric knew that, and he had pleaded to Wōden to not take him to the "Great Hall" until he'd seen Oswald safe into manhood. Cedric knew Oswald's father and mother would have been proud of him too. He begged the gods that they would tell him the right moment to make such knowledge of his parentage known to him.

It was the afternoon of the third day; they had been travelling for an hour or so since they had rested and eaten. Oswald nudged his pony from his designated place in the line to Cedric's side.

'We are being followed, Cedric. Look on that ridge to our right, through the pines. I can just make them out,' Oswald said discreetly to Cedric.

'Aye, I see them, Gododdins by the look of their garb. What number do you reckon, son?'

'Twenty, at least, that I can see, possibly more,' Oswald answered, turning to the sound of another rider and seeing Eanfrith coming to them.

'Aye, I'd guess the same,' Cedric said agreeing with Oswald's assessment.

'Is there some problem, Cedric, why have we slowed down?' Eanfrith asked with some irritation. 'Oswald, return to your position.'

'Stay with me, son, I need your eyes…'

Oswald looked at his brother, distressed by the awkwardness he always felt when he was the third party between Cedric and Eanfrith. Cedric always gave the impression he didn't like Eanfrith, but Oswald knew Cedric didn't care either way, what annoyed

Cedric was anyone over-concerned with his or her social position. He related to people on merit, not any birthright. However, Cedric's challenge to Eanfrith's command passed without further comment.

'There are some riders on the ridge, to our right, behind the trees, Eanfrith. DON'T stare,' Oswald said more forcefully than he intended as Eanfrith was about to turn his head and look.

'What riders? I haven't seen any riders, you are imagining it,' Eanfrith replied.

'It's not imagined,' Cedric said in a tone that dared Eanfrith to contradict him.

'If it is so, I'll send men to see them off,' Eanfrith said trying to regain some command of the situation.

'Aye, and risk life unnecessarily. You will do no such thing; we know not their number. There may be more men out of sight. We will wait and watch. For now, *Lord* Eanfrith, ride along our line and see that we close up. Do it without attracting attention, if they think they have the advantage of surprise, we will make – that thought *our* advantage.'

Referring to Eanfrith as *Lord* was sufficient to placate him for now, and he turned his pony and did as he was bidden.

Cedric turned casually and beckoned

Hrodulf, with a nearly imperceptible flick of his head and Hrodulf rode slowly up to them.

'You see them, Hrodulf.'

'Aye, I see them.'

'We will make for that bank yonder afore the river, there is a level sandy place betwixt it and the riverbank, probably made when the river was in spate. We'll need to be careful it might be soft. We'll rest there and wait, with the bank afore us, and the river at the back of us, it'll limit their attacking options. Ride back and ready our warriors for any attack, *no* fuss, Hrodulf.'

Hrodulf turned and made his way to do as he'd been told. Oswald smiled as he watched Hrodulf go about his business. The link he had with Cedric was uncanny, even spiritual. They both thought as one and woe betide anyone who stood against them. Hrodulf was every bit as wily as his old friend Cedric, what they had lost in physical prowess over the years, time having done her relentless work, nibbling slowly away at eyesight, muscles and joints, turning young warriors into old, they more than made up for in experience. The pair had faced every manner of adversary over their years *and* lived to tell the tale, that was enough said.

Oswald knew how fortunate he was to be alongside such warriors, and he would watch and learn from them. He saw Eanfrith returning and braced himself for the next moment of confrontation, he wished

Eanfrith could recognise the value of having such experienced men around him and cease forever the constant need to assert himself. Cedric was never going to be cowed by any man merely because of who he was.

Oswald remembered asking Cedric if he was ever afraid of anything. He'd thought for some time before he answered, then he said, 'I remember your father saying to me once, before we went to fight the Britons in the kingdom of Powys, west of Mercia, "*You* fear the battle, Cedric, because you hope to live, *I* do not fear the battle because I *hope* to die".'

Oswald frowned as he thought on the conversation. It troubled him then, as it did now. He supposed that Cedric could have meant that his father looked forward to going to dwell with the gods, in the hall of warriors, but something in the way he spoke had undertones of a wholly darker nature.

No more than the undertones of the *current* dilemma, which Oswald focused on once again as Eanfrith returned.

'I have done as you instructed Cedric. What shall I do now?' Oswald breathed a sigh of relief at Eanfrith's welcome deference to Cedric.

'Go to the Queens, your brothers and sister, see that they are protected, and follow us to that riverbank yonder, you see it?'

'Yes.'

'Then have them dismount and take shelter behind it but do it casually as if we are merely stopping for a rest.'

Eanfrith nodded, turned and trotted back to the family. Perhaps this is a new Eanfrith thought Oswald, "*Hopefully*", feeling greatly relieved that another moment of tension had passed them by without confrontation.

No sooner had they dismounted than the Gododdins broke from the cover of the Scotch Pines and charged at them on foot, yelling fearful ear-piercing war cries. They must have noticed the secure position that Cedric had chosen to stop and decided to attack quickly before they had time to establish themselves.

Little did they know that Cedric's warriors and huscarls were already prepared for the conflict, even now, men were linking their shields to form an impenetrable wooden wall. There was the familiar crash of the metal edges of the large painted lime-wood shields, as they locked together. The screaming Gododdins faltered only for a split second, perhaps surprised by the speed that the shield wall had been assembled before them, but they were committed now and continued unabated.

Oswald stood behind Cedric as he'd been told. He was too young to stand in the shield wall itself, even if he wanted to. Only the strongest and most experienced warriors had that honour. He knew that the men in the wall needed support. For those standing behind the wall, there was vital employment, which added to the overall effectiveness of the defence. There was important work for the young, would-be warriors, such as clearing the dead from amongst their feet, or chopping and grabbing at spears that penetrated the wall, as the barricade forged forward.

At the moment of contact, when the two forces came together, the withering shock to the limbs of those in the wall tore through their knotted muscles down their torsos and legs into their feet, hopefully solidly set into the earth, ready to resist the force. The noise was deafening, both sides grunted as one, as the sudden impact forced the air from their lungs.

There was an almost imperceptible hiatus, then more grunts, which were now punctuated by screams as the lethal sharp edges of axe or sword made contact with flesh and bone. The warriors were being bathed in blood sprayed from severed limbs. At first, the Bernicians were outnumbered, but within seconds, the numbers were even. The shieldwall had done its work and held without losing a single man. Now the

Bernicians were pushing forward, the Gododdins were on the back foot trying to resist the energy of the combined force of men linked together. Some of them were tumbling over the bodies of those who had already fallen as they tried to link their shields to offer some credible resistance to this human wall of death, coming remorselessly on to them. It was too late; they had been totally taken aback, thinking they had the irresistible advantage of surprise.

Cedric and Hrodulf were now driving the wall forward at a pace, hacking and slicing as they pushed, which was simply overwhelming the young inexperienced attackers. The handful that were left standing now turned and ran back to the tree line.

'HOLD,' yelled Cedric and the wall came to a sweating, cursing standstill. Oswald knew Cedric would not give chase in case it was a feint, a ploy, to entrap them, but no, he could see those who'd escaped, mounting their ponies and riding off. The wall now broke, and the warriors hacked to death those not already dead. This was the ugly side of victory, which Oswald hated, but he knew that to leave the dying to be tormented by their suffering was far crueller.

'Collect up anything of use, we will take the weapons with us, those dead holding their swords or axes, render them so that they are useless then bury them with the fallen so they might enter the Hell Mouth as noble warriors.'

'They might be *Christians* Cedric,' Oswald said, a little unsure what was the right thing to do.

'Then they will be in for a pleasant surprise when they wake up where people are enjoying themselves, instead of finding that they are with their miserable priest-monks, praying to their miserable half eaten god.' That was Cedric's response to Oswald's show of concern, and Cedric laughed, as did those around him. Once the laughter had passed, (Cedric wasn't known for his spontaneous humour, but his description of the Christian afterlife had clearly amused him) he wiped his eyes, put his arm around Oswald and turned to Torem.

'There must be ponies in the wood up there, which belonged to these fellows, fetch them Torem, but take some of these young warriors with you, and watch your back, do you hear?'

'Fear not Cedric, I like life too much, you watch out for your own hide, and I'll watch out for mine,' he replied throwing a lump of dried horse dung at him and laughing, Cedric ducked and laughed too.

They watched Torem go then Oswald and Cedric went down to the river, Cedric yet with his arm around the shoulder of Oswald, to wash the blood from his hands and face the best he could. 'You did well young Oswald of Bernicia, it is important work behind the shieldwall, it can make all the difference in a battle, I'm proud of you, son.'

Oswald always grew a hand's width whenever Cedric praised him; Cedric had that effect on people.

Once Cedric had washed, he made his way to where the queens were sheltered, to reassure them. Cedric quickly explained to the family what he intended to do. They would move off, ford the river as soon as that was possible and travel west on the northern side for it was likely that those who'd escaped the day's conflict would bring others to avenge their defeat. With the help of Hrodulf and Torem, Cedric assembled the travellers and they moved off as quickly as they could, to get clear of the battle site. Once mounted Cedric rode back and forth along the line encouraging and praising his warriors, he seemed in high spirits.

Like all warriors, Cedric was mystically empowered after a battle; so, exhilarating was the aftertaste of the conflict. Oswald knew warriors needed that moment of intense excitement, which could only be found on the cusp of life and death. However, for Cedric, underlying and tainting this encounter, was his fear for the Bernician athelings; time was not on their side.

By the time they found a crossing, it was dusk, and he was insistent that they crossed over before nightfall. Cedric sent warriors over the crossing ahead of them and waited uneasily for their signal to enter the water and cross over.

Eventually, they returned to the far bank, Hrodulf waved and beckoned the main party, now they were sure that it was safe. Cedric was last to cross, he made certain that all were safely to the other side, he took one last look back over the road they'd travelled then nudged his pony forward into the cold, fast flowing, brackish water.

They camped on a derelict farm holding that night, Oswald slept lightly, as most of them did. Every time he stirred and glanced over to where Cedric had laid out his bed rug, he saw that Cedric was awake walking back and forth along the perimeter of the camp, stopping every few steps to stare out into the darkness.

They were well beyond the kingdom of Bernicia now; every step was measured in the pounding heartbeats of the warriors. They knew that they could be attacked and overwhelmed at any moment. Though they were able men, their numbers were few, too few to venture into an enemy's heartland with impunity.

When they neared Dunadd, the plan was that they would send a rider to meet King Eochaid Buide at the Dalriadan court; perhaps Prince Eanfrith himself would go because of his mother's connection to King Eochaid. Queen Bebba had a ring he would recognise, and the rider would give it to him.

Cedric tried, but he could not convince himself that this was a wise plan, but he could not think of a better one. Even if the royal family were saved, because of their kinship, King Eochaid Buide might still have the men murdered for his own safety. Cedric thought that he would be happy just to know the family were safe, his life was theirs so what did it matter.

Oswald was pleased to see his mother Queen Acha looking better, she hadn't looked well of late, some malady of her gut, he'd been told. Eanfrith had been kind to her, for she had been his mother too since he was, thirteen or so, Oswald reckoned. He wasn't quite sure when his father and mother were married, he must ask her or Cedric, he'd never thought about it before.

There would be no fires this night, but it was a warm night, so it was no hardship to them.

Chapter 5

Dunadd

The Bernicians were now on the borders of Dalriada, and so were at this moment in even greater danger from attack. Cedric decided that they would camp in a large rocky outcrop on the side of a valley. They would not be easily seen and yet they would have a good view of the surrounding vicinity. He knew that it was far from perfect as a defensive position, but they would have to make the best of it.

Oswald was thankful that there had not been any more conflict between Cedric and Eanfrith.

When Eanfrith had announced that he would be the one to approach King Eochaid Buide, at the Dalriadan court, Cedric said nothing. Hrodulf would go with him and two more huscarls; the two queens and their children would wait where they were. Queen Bebba told Cedric that it was less than a day's ride to the hill fort of Dunadd. If Wōden were with them, Eanfrith would return before nightfall.

'Take care Hrodulf,' Cedric said quietly to him, 'and keep a tight rein on the young hothead. As much as he annoys me, he is brave enough to do this. It's his arrogance, which is his downfall. Talk to him on the way, try to steady his natural tendency to act rashly, so that he doesn't end up without his stupid head.'

'Fear not Cedric, I will watch out for him, we will be back before nightfall.' With that, Eanfrith gave the order to move off.

They watched the small group ride away and Cedric turned to Oswald. 'That's it for now, young Oswald, all we can do is wait and hope that the gods are on our side.'

'Do you think that King Eochaid Buide will look favourably on us, Cedric?'

'Queen Bebba seems certain that he will, I'm sure she knows best.' Cedric was trying to reassure his young prince, and he hoped that he sounded more confident than he felt. It was out of his hands now and solely down to the benevolence of the gods.

Cedric leant casually against a large pine, chewing on a stalk of grass, and staring in the direction of Dunadd. He'd been standing alone for most of the day. It was mid-afternoon when he suddenly pushed himself from the tree trunk and stood erect with his hand mindlessly flexing around the pommel of his sword.

'Ready yourselves men,' he turned and called to the warriors relaxing around the camp. He had spotted riders, he couldn't yet be certain if it was Eanfrith or not, there were about twenty in total, both Oswald and Torem came to his side.

'Is it Eanfrith?' asked Oswald.

'You tell *me*, I can't make any of them out, but they've turned this way and are definitely coming towards our position.'

'YES, it's Eanfrith and our men.'

'Is Hrodulf with them?'

'Yes, and others, I do not recognise, there seems to be a boy with them.'

'A *boy*!'

They watched intently as the riders drew ever closer. There was indeed a young boy with them much the same age as Oswald.

The group stopped half a league short of the forest. Eanfrith and the boy separated from the group and rode on towards them.

'*Eanfrith*,' Oswald called with genuine delight at seeing his brother, safely returned.

'Oswald, Cedric,' Cedric gave a curt nod of his head. 'This is Prince Domnall Brecc, son of the great King Eochaid. King Eochaid has sent his son, Prince Domnall, in good faith, to show that we are welcome, and need have no fear.'

Queen Bebba now approached them, Eanfrith glanced to her and smiled, 'King Eochaid looks forward to seeing you once more, my Lady.'

She smiled too, 'Thank you Eanfrith. You are a fine young man now, Prince Domnall, do you remember me?'

The boy smiled and spoke for the first time, bowing, 'I'm sorry, I do not, but I know *of* you, you must be Queen Bebba. My father has spoken of you often, clearly, he thinks highly of you, he sends his greetings to you and all the Bernician family.'

Queen Bebba was clearly delighted; she reached up and affectionately squeezed his hand.

'You have done well, Lord Eanfrith,' Cedric said with some generosity of spirit.

'Thank you, Cedric, King Eochaid is expecting us to return before dark, so we will need to make haste, are we ready to go?'

'Yes, we did not unpack the animals, all we need to do is mount up and follow you.' With that Cedric gestured and those waiting, mounted. Eanfrith turned his pony and took the lead followed by Prince Domnall.

Cedric was quite happy to drop behind; first, to be sure Queen Acha was not too fearful. Once he was satisfied that she was at peace he went to speak to Hrodulf.

'What did you make of this King Eochaid, Hrodulf?'

'He seemed very friendly, I liked him, he's well past the flush of youth, maybe… in his early thirties, is my guess. He has a head of long thick fair hair, hence his name, Eochaid *Buide*. The lad's only ten,' Hrodulf nodded in the direction of Prince Domnall Brecc. 'I asked him his age as we rode here. I thought it an opportunity to learn what I could. He speaks Saxon well enough. He has a sister; she's eleven and has the makings of a fine beauty. The lad's called Domnall Brecc, because of his freckles, so he told me.'

'Aye, he has a rare ginger mop right enough,' smiled Cedric.

The conversation with Hrodulf put Cedric at ease. Perhaps all that Queen Bebba said would be, is exactly how it was, thanks be to the gods.

It was dark by the time they reached the hill fort of Dunadd, [10] but it was clear to Oswald that it was more of a fort than Ad Gefrin. There were fortified earth mounds within the stockade with many dwellings and places of work. The earthen mounds were at one end, there were several, one on top of the other, with deep ditches around each mound. At the summit, there was a large flat area with a longhouse and several smaller buildings. They rode onto the first raised area and stopped; Oswald assumed that at the top was the dwelling place of King Eochaid. It was not unlike Bebbanburg, a rocky hill set in the earth, a place that stood out in the landscape. A position well suited to give visible status and authority to any king.

They dismounted and servants took their ponies. As they were led on foot, up the steep inclines, and through the narrow entrances to each level, Oswald took his mother's arm and she smiled at his kindness. There were three raised mounds in all. At the top, they were taken into the large imposing longhouse. Cedric was the last to enter. There were several people seated at a long table at the far end of the hall, on a raised platform. All this seemed familiar to Oswald; it was much the same as any other longhouse.

Oswald assumed the man seated at the long table was King Eochaid, who, on seeing them enter, rose to his feet, stepped from the platform and came towards them, his arms outstretched in welcome.

The two Queens were greeted warmly. He embraced Queen Bebba first, then he bowed to Queen Acha and embraced her too, with equal kindness, and then he embraced Eanfrith.

Oswald thought him a very pleasant individual although he was struggling to make out much of what he said. One by one, Æthelfrith's family were introduced to the King and they each in turn bowed. There was a slender very beautiful young girl standing on the dais, who caught Oswald's eye, and they exchanged smiles, he thought that she must be the princess that he'd heard Hrodulf mention to Cedric.

The Queens were seated on the dais next to King Eochaid, and his son. Oswald, his brothers and sister were seated just below them, but still in a place of honour. He sat next to Offa with his other siblings between him and Oswiu. Each time Oswald glanced up at the princess, she smiled at him. He thought, if this was to be the welcome, they were to receive he was feeling very welcomed indeed.

However, he doubted that Cedric felt the same. He was seated next to one of their priest-monks, and, if his facial expression was to be the measure, he didn't seem to be enjoying the experience. Oswald couldn't help noticing the priest monk's unusual bald head. He was compelled to smile at Cedric's obvious discomfort.

The mete was better than they had had for days, but not what he'd describe as a feast and there were foods of which he was unfamiliar. He was sure if they had been expected, King Eochaid would have done more to impress them.

After they'd eaten, while he was speaking to Oswiu, a hand tapped his shoulder and he turned to the smiling face of the princess from the high table.

She bowed and he responded in like manner. She was obviously offering a welcome of some sort, but his knowledge of her language was limited to the few words he'd learned from Queen Bebba on the journey here. He established that her name was Helen, an unfamiliar name to him; it did not trip off his tongue easily. He hoped that she understood that he was called Oswald, the second son of the famed King Æthelfrith of Bernicia. All the while he tried to talk to her, she smiled. She actually spoke more of his Saxon than the miserable few words he'd managed to speak of her Hibernian, if that's what it was. She said that she'd been taught by their holy people and that *they* were all learned men.

Whatever language it was, it was pleasing to the ear, soft and easy to listen to, almost musical. The pleasant few moments were interrupted by Cedric, Oswald introduced Princess Helen to him, and he smiled and bowed. Cedric told him that he was going to be shown where his men were to stay, by a Briton warrior of some authority and asked if Oswald was content to wait in the hall until he returned. The Princess said she would show Prince Oswald where he and his family were to sleep. Cedric hesitated for a moment, bowed, and left.

The Princess took Oswald's hand and led him out of the hall to another building, which was being cleared. She showed him where Queen Bebba would be housed and yet another roundhouse where Queen Acha and *her* servants would sleep.

Oswald asked her where her mother, the Queen, was. The smile slipped slowly from her face, she lowered her eyes, and there was a moment before she spoke. Eventually, she said in a soft whisper that her mother had died when her brother Prince Domnall was born.

'I can barely remember her. My one lasting memory of her is the warm comfort of snuggling into her hair.'

Oswald told her how sorry he was, Helen said that her father had told her this day that his mother was also dead, killed when he was a baby.

Oswald drew his head back, stunned; unsure he'd understood her. It was now his turn to be slow to respond.

'No, no – my mother is not dead she is Queen Acha. You must mean my *half*-brother Eanfrith, *his* mother is dead.'

'Oh... no, not Prince Eanfrith, his mother was well known to my father, she died many years ago. I was told your mother was Queen Aefre, Queen Acha's sister and she was killed in some fearful accident.'

Oswald could only stare vacantly at her; he didn't know what to say. *Slowly* – little scraps of things that had been said over the years took on a completely different shade, and shape... he was speechless. He'd never heard of a Queen called Aefre, what was this girl saying? Aefre, Aefre, he'd never even heard the name. Then somewhere in the fog of the past, he recalled a servant called Rowena, *yes*... Rowena, that was her name. She was always especially kind to him, yes Rowena, he remembered her now. She was combing his hair and said that the comb was very special to her; it had belonged to her Lady Aefre whom she had loved... yes, he was sure that was the name, Aefre.

'*Aefre*,' he spoke the name out loud.

'Perhaps, I misunderstood, or my father was mistaken,' she suggested gently, seeing the distress suddenly transforming Oswald's face.

'I'm sorry if I have caused you some pain, Oswald.'

Oswald hadn't heard her.

'I'm *sorry* Prince Oswald,' she said once more.

'Oh... yes, yes, no, it's nothing don't be troubled, a trivial misunderstanding.'

It was black dark now, though the hilltop was well supplied with flaming torches, it was yet difficult to see, as if the darkness swallowed up the light, and with it, all he believed was his past.

Oswald needed to find Cedric; his head was in turmoil, he couldn't think straight. This innocent young princess had unsettled him more than she could ever imagine. He asked her if she knew where Cedric might be, she pointed to one of the larger roundhouses, and he thanked her for her kindness, in making their new home known to him. He said he would walk back to the main hall with her and then go to his friend; she nodded yet feeling that she had without intention, hurt this gentle young prince.

Chapter 6

Revelation

Oswald literally stumbled into the roundhouse where Princess Helen had told him Cedric would be. He leant against one of the posts supporting the rafters, pressed his head back against the rough wood, closed his eyes, and tried to collect himself. Princess Helen's revelation had disturbed him to the point that he could hardly function; he could barely put one foot in front of the other, never mind think.

Cedric didn't see him at first; *he* was talking to a Dalriadan warrior, a Briton from the southern kingdom of Pengwern. A Wealas [11] man called Daffyd whose arms were beautifully decorated with lavishly coloured tattoos of twisted serpents and animals from the underworld, worked into eternal knots. [14] Cedric had never seen such fine workmanship and was fascinated. When he glanced up, he caught sight of Oswald and he was immediately alarmed by the look of utter anguish on his face.

That was the end of any social pleasantry for Cedric. His conversation with Daffyd ended abruptly, it was no longer possible for him to continue talking to the Briton; he was too distracted by his concern for Oswald. He offered his paltry excuses to Daffyd and made his way *fearfully* to where Oswald was slumped awkwardly against the roundhouse frame. Cedric's hand gripped the pommel of his sword and his eyes scanned his surroundings for any sign of threat as he neared Oswald.

Oswald was clearly distressed, Cedric glanced to the entrance; he'd not heard any disruption outside. Oswald didn't appear injured in any way and yet he was obviously disturbed. Oswald seemed to be unaware that Cedric was now standing in front of him. Cedric laid his hand lightly on his shoulder.

'What has happened, son? Are you hurt?' Oswald's eyes gradually rose to meet Cedric's and he slowly shook his head. 'I don't rightly know.'

'What do you mean? Speak plainly boy, not in riddles.' This sort of confused speech was not how Cedric's thought world worked.

Cedric was a man of clear thought, a decision maker; he didn't spend his days in tortured anguish over relationships, like some lovesick scop [12]. He did what he thought was right and honourable and that was that, take it or leave it. Either he liked a person, or he didn't and expected no more from anyone else, *but*... it was so different when it came to Oswald. Their relationship contradicted everything that was Cedric, and he was rendered maddeningly helpless before it.

Oswald did no more than slowly shake his head at Cedric's question.

'Come boy, we will sit by that pile of skins yonder,' Cedric said in a whisper, taking Oswald's arm, and leading him into the darkness, where he bade him sit. 'You were smiling, a young man very pleased when I left you, but a short while since. This is not the face of a man flattered by the attention of a beautiful young princess,' Cedric said, floundering out of his depth, and attempting to lighten the moment, *without success*. 'Do you wish to tell me what ails you, or do you desire your own company, I will afford you either?' His voice now had more than a hint of irritation.

Oswald again shook his head despondently and Cedric made to rise, but Oswald gently laid his hand on his arm, Cedric hesitated and relaxed once more onto the ground.

'I don't know what to say, Cedric... The *princess* – told me the strangest tale and I know not the truth of it, but it had the echo of things past and stirred up scraps of half-memories which were sleeping, ready for such a moment to awaken.'

'Mmm... you are yet speaking in riddles I ask again, *speak plainly boy*,' Cedric asserted, perturbed, and unsettled by the tone of Oswald's voice. 'Do you want to share these awakened memories or not, if you wish me to offer some help, speak clearly? Perhaps I can cast some light on what ails you.'

Oswald stared at Cedric for some time as if daring himself to open the secret box and find out what was inside…

'Who… was… my *mother*, Cedric?'

Cedric felt the blood draining from his head down his spine, out through his backside and into the dirt floor, and was mightily thankful he was at this moment seated. The roundhouse was suddenly a spinning empty space, a void, a timeless hole; the only sound was the pounding pulse in his head. Before he could even attempt to answer Oswald's question, Oswald spoke once more.

'The princess said my mother was called Aefre, and she'd been killed when I was a baby, what do you know of the truth of this?'

The only movement on Cedric's expressionless face was his flexing jaw muscles. He was struck dumb; no words would form on his tongue. Oswald was staring at him now. Cedric could only look at Oswald out of the corner of his eye. He ran his dried-out tongue over his parched lips and cleared his throat, in a vain attempt to give life to some response, *and* still Oswald stared at him.

Anything but this, whatever could he say… this was the question he ever feared, what – *should* – he say? Cedric knew he would swear and lie his way into the Hell Mouth for this boy, aye and willingly, but could he lie – *to* – him?

What *was* the truth? Oswald was a bastard and would be an outcast, no place for him in the royal family. The world would cast him into the outer darkness of the wandering spirits who had nowhere to rest their heads. He'd be no more than a shallow breath in the never-ending story of memories past.

Cedric was sure that no one knew the true story, suspected, yes. He was only too aware of the gossip that had been spread far and wide by the toad of toads, Lord Hering. Cedric had removed the head of that earsling and affixed it onto a spear shaft driven into the middle of the courtyard at Din Guyaroi, so that all might see the end that honour served out to traitors. The *rumour* had been mete and drink to those who yearned to undermine King Æthelfrith.

Cedric would have rubbished such a story, and had many times, but this was different. Was he to taint this precious relationship with lies? He filled his lungs and breathed out slowly, just as he would when facing any giant.

'…The princess…' he cleared his throat once more, 'speaks the truth…' the words fell from his lips like rotten clay. Oswald never flinched. 'Your birth mother… was the sister of Queen Acha. She was called by the name of Aefre and married to King Æthelfrith… *but* she was in love with your father and had been from the moment they met.'

'*My father* what do you mean? King Æthelfrith was – is my father.'

'I'm sorry son, but your real *father* was my Lord and friend, though I was never worthy of his friendship. He was so far above me in every way. He was Lord Wulfstan, the bravest and most noble warrior there ever was, or ever will be. An example to all and loved by all, but none more than me, save your mother.'

'I don't understand, Cedric. "*The* great Wulfstan", all talk of him, but King Æthelfrith always treated me as his son, and I called *him* Father.'

Cedric was again quiet for some moments; he hung his head and rubbed his face with his hand.

'I alone know the truth of this, others may have suspected, but none spoke of their suspicions for fear of what I may do to them. In that, they were wise, for I would have sent them straight to the Hell Mouth if they had uttered a single word of their doubts.'

Oswald hardly breathed as Cedric spoke.

'King Æthelfrith chose to believe you were his son, if he ever suspected differently, I know not, for no such doubts were ever breathed or made known to me, and I was content with that.'

'But what happened to them, this Aefre, and this Wulfstan?'

'Their love was such a love that is given by the gods to only a very few. A love which is not quenched by death, an eternal love, the like of which I have never seen before or since. They were betrayed by a man, with the name of all that is wicked, and then murdered. Neither offered any defence and died in each other's arms, robbed of life by the hand of treachery. Your father's last words were for you and you now hold fast to his hand when you grip his sword. There was his helma too, the most beautiful helma you could ever imagine. I have never seen it's like afore or since. It was made to look like a fearsome face, it had two golden winged dragons over the crown, their wings formed the eyebrows of the helma, and they were mounted with blood red garnets. The cheeks and the face guard were engraved with mystical scenes. Aye… it was terrible thing to behold. On seeing it, men trembled with fear, for they thought that they were faced with a warrior from the spirit world. King Æthelfrith took it after your father's death, but I kept your father's sword, it was his dying command, that it should be given to you and that I have done. King Rædwald no doubt has the helma [20] now, the ill-begotten spawn. Might it be affixed to his head forever in the spirit world where all that is unworthy dwells.' Cedric turned to Oswald, saw the tears streaming down his face and he drew him into his arms. Neither spoke for several minutes.

'Does my mother know of this?' Oswald asked drawing his forearm across his eyes to wipe away the tears.

'I don't know what she knows except that you are not hers, but her sister, Queen Aefre's child. I think that your real mother's maid knew the truth of it, they were very close, but she never talked of it. She is dead now, she was a brave loyal woman. I fancy that she suffered some lasting injury when she was captured by the Gododdins who dragged her behind their horses, then hung her by her wrist. Your mother and father risked all to rescue her. Hrodulf will tell you of their bravery, he was there, and he too owes his life to them. They were not like the rest of us, all who knew them would die for them, aye and willingly.'

'Was this maid called Rowena?'

Cedric was for a moment startled by Oswald's knowledge, 'Aye, *Rowena*, that was her name. She nursed you when you were young, until she died. I do know that Queen Acha, whom you know as mother, has loved you as her own, and I'm forever thankful for that. She is a good woman and a good mother.'

Both Cedric and Oswald now sat silently with their heads hung between raised knees.

'Why have you never told me this before, Cedric, I had the right to know?'

Cedric raised his head, narrowed his eyes and stared across the smoky air of the roundhouse.

'Aye… no doubt you had, and I would have told you, believe me, but there has been enough pain wrapped up in this tale to last a hundred lifetimes and more. Try to understand that these people that we're speaking of, are merely names to you at this moment, yes, by the gods, important names I grant you, but only names nevertheless, *but* they were real living breathing people whom *I* knew and loved. You can never hear your father's voice, or your mother's laughter, *I can,* and I carry the pain and guilt every day.'

'Why do *you* carry any guilt? Any such guilt that there was, was surely not yours to bear.'

'You think not do you? If I hadn't been such a blind fool, I could have done something to save your mother and father, they need not have died and that is a hellish load for a man the likes of me to carry, believe me, son.'

'Is that really what you believe? Is it not the gods in the end, who decide whether we live or die? That's what *you* would say to me, or do the gods have different ways when it comes to you? If they were truly my mother and father, as you say, in their name I absolve you of any guilt.'

Cedric lifted his head and stared at Oswald for some moments, tears filled his eyes, and he leant forward, reached out his trembling hand, and touched Oswald's knee. Oswald had never seen this side of Cedric and it humbled him to see this great man, whom he loved, so broken.

They sat in silence for some time until Oswald whispered, 'I want you to tell me everything about these two people Cedric; perhaps you are the only person who can.'

'Aye, perhaps I am,' he answered in a sad uneven voice.

'But not now, I must walk in the dark alone and think on all that has been made known to me. Thank you, Cedric, do not chastise yourself for any neglect. This changes nothing between us, if *anything*, the bond has tightened.'

'Aye, I know son, I am bound to you for life, naught but death will separate my heart from yours,' Cedric formed a sad smile on his lips and gave a sharp nod of his head.

Oswald stood and walked from the roundhouse leaving Cedric sitting in the shadows, staring blindly up to the rafters.

Iona Cathedral

Chapter 7

A Future Decided

Oswald had slept little over the last few days and this night was no different. Whenever he glanced over to his brothers, they were sleeping; all was quiet. The only light was the glow from the dying embers of the fire, and it touched the edges of their sleeping faces.

Time and again, fear swept over him in waves of uncertainty. Those around him were uncertain about their future, but *he* wasn't even certain about the past. All he had ever known and believed to be true about himself had been turned upside down.

He stared at Oswiu, who lay nearby him, of all his brothers, Oswald always felt closest to him, though he was almost seven years Oswald's junior. Perhaps it was because he'd always looked after Oswiu, he had cared for him since he'd been a toddler; they'd always had some deeper connection. However, these were – *not* – his brothers, not even his *half-brothers*, he was in *no way* linked by blood to anything of King Æthelfrith, whom he'd always known as Father.

If what Cedric had told him was the truth, his mother was his aunt and the man now on the throne of Bernicia, King Edwin who was his uncle, was more his relative than those he'd always known as his nearest kin. He had no birthrights within this family who were sleeping so soundly around him. He could even be seen as a threat, a danger, as the nephew of the usurper Edwin. Eanfrith of all his brothers would probably hate him. He never had a close to Eanfrith who was now, at the very least, "Head" of the family.

Oswald knew that over the years, they had done no more than tolerate each other. He had always thought Eanfrith a very plain man, lacking any colour, and with not much imagination, they had little in common. Eanfrith was forever obsessed with people respecting him and acknowledging who he was, but this obsession had the opposite effect on people, and they respected him less.

Oswald stared once more into the gloom of the smoke-blackened rafters and sighed; perhaps Cedric was mistaken. He couldn't know for a fact that he was not the son of King Æthelfrith. Oswald knew that Cedric would never intentionally lie to him, *no*, for Cedric to lie to him was inconceivable. It was obvious how much it had cost Cedric to make such a thing known to him, but he *might* have been mistaken. Because Cedric believed it to be the truth, it did not mean that it was the truth. Would it now be right to make such known to all, and cause hurt to those he loved by telling this uncertain truth? On the other hand, was he saying this to himself as a way of merely pouring salve on his conscience, if he kept this information secret? If he kept the secret, his life would suffer no disruption and he would retain his position without question, but could he live with such a lie? This was impossible, he would have to talk to Cedric once more and tell him how confused he was and seek his advice about what he should do.

Since Cedric had made this nightmare known to Oswald, it had not been mentioned again, but their times together had become strained.

Oswald thought, perhaps this was why Cedric had said naught to me all these years, he had known what turmoil such knowledge would cause in my thought world and he wanted to spare me.

Oswald awoke to the noise and chatter of his brothers rising to the new day, whilst *he* felt as if he had only just fallen asleep. The very last thing he needed this day was his sister Æbbe jumping on him.

'Cuddle, Swald,' she giggled.

'Why are you not with your mother?' He asked her, rubbing his eyes.

'I wanted to see you.'

'Well, aren't *I* the blessed one,' he said unconvincingly, whilst hugging and kissing her. 'Leave me, you child of Eostre [13] and I will wash and ready myself, then I will see you in the main hall when we eat. Off you go.' With that, Æbbe jumped up and ran out the door. Oswald sat up yawned and stretched then promptly fell back on his bed.

'Cedric came in earlier to see you, but you were yet asleep,' Oswiu called across to him as he was leaving the roundhouse.

'Did he say what he wanted?' asked Oswald raising himself onto his elbows.

'No, he said that he would see you in the hall when you went for the morning's mete.'

Oswald raised himself, and went to the half barrel filled with water for them to wash in. He submerged his head in the cold water, withdrew it, shook it vigorously, like a dog coming out of a river, and dried his face on a cloth. He was startled as a hand slipped round his shoulder and he spontaneously shivered.

'Cedric – you surprised me. I was told that you would be in the hall.'

'Yes, I was, but I was unable to settle and came once more to see if you'd yet stirred. I am concerned. We have been avoiding the things which are on our minds.'

'I know, I'm sorry, but I need time to let all you have made known to me take a proper place in my life. Unless that is, you have something else pressing of which you wish to speak.'

'No, nothing that will change what I have already said, as long as you know that I am here for you – if you want to ask me questions.'

'Forgive me Cedric. It's not that I am avoiding you in any way; it's simply that I do not know what I should, or want, to know. This might take some time to find a place of rest in my head – before I can have any clear questions.'

'I always knew what confusion it would bring, that said, let it be no obstacle between us. Come, join me in the hall, if it is your wish.'

Oswald nodded, 'Thank you, Cedric, as always, I know your friendship and counsel to be sound,' and Cedric wrapped his arm around Oswald's shoulder, and they made their way to the hall.

Oswald knew that he was late, the hall was full, but they found a place to sit, some had already eaten and were leaving. The settlement was even now busy with the day's work.

As soon as Æbbe saw him, she ran to him and climbed onto his lap. Whilst Oswald and Cedric were eating, a servant came to them, bowed and informed Oswald that King Eochaid Buide wanted to speak with him.

'Now?'

'Yes, Lord.' Oswald turned to Cedric; Cedric could only lift his hands and shrug. Oswald set Æbbe onto the ground, rose from his bench and followed the servant.

King Eochaid Buide smiled as Oswald approached. Queen Acha, Queen Bebba, Prince Domnall, Eanfrith and Helen were sitting with him; Oswald noticed Eanfrith's severe countenance. The King gestured with a sweep of his hand for Oswald to be seated; Oswald bowed and took the seat offered. King Eochaid Buide looked to Queen Bebba.

'The King has asked me to speak for him, his grasp of Saxon is limited.' Oswald nodded to the King. 'The King wants you to go to an island nearby to learn from the monks who live there. They will teach you to read, write, and speak Hibernian so that you will be more able to converse with him, and his people.'

Oswald was silent as he thought about what she said. What did she mean, go to an island, was that to live there, *forever*?

Queen Bebba waited a moment for Oswald to respond, then, continued, 'You will not be alone, Eanfrith and Oswiu will go too, as will your other brothers when they are older, we spoke to them before you came into the hall. The King thinks such learning is vitally important for all young athelings.'

'Will *you* come with us Mother?' Oswald asked Queen Acha.

She shook her head and Queen Bebba answered for her. 'No, they do not allow any women on the island, but your mother, the Queen will be nearby on the island of Coll, it's not far from the island of Iona, where you will be, so you will be able to visit her often.'

'Is this your wish, Mother?'

At last, his mother did speak, 'I think that it will be for the best Oswald. I will have my own people with me on the island and will be independent, it is very considerate of the King to think about my feelings, and as Queen Bebba says, you will be able to come often to see me.'

'What of Cedric?'

'He will go with me, and be my lead huscarl, as he has always been.'

'If it is your wish Mother, I will do as you advise.'

Queen Bebba, then spoke to King Eochaid Buide and he smiled at Oswald.
Oswald supposed that she was telling King Eochaid what he had said.

'You will learn much,' the King offered, speaking in his faltering Saxon.

'The King has told me that you may do as you wish while you are in Dunadd. He hopes that you like your new home, for he says it will be your home for as long as you need it to be. *Eanfrith*,' Queen Bebba said turning to Eanfrith, 'you might think it necessary to talk with your brother, perhaps you could walk with Oswald and reassure him.'

Eanfrith stood up and beckoned Oswald as he stepped abruptly from the raised platform. Oswald glanced once more at Queen Acha and then followed Eanfrith who was clearly not enthralled by the proposals for their future.

As they walked from the hall Oswald could see Cedric watching, and didn't want to leave without speaking to him.

'One moment, Eanfrith,' Oswald said tugging on Eanfrith's sleeve. 'I must speak to Cedric and tell him what was said to us by the King.' Cedric watched suspiciously as they came to him. Oswald sat next to him in the place he had moments since vacated, fortunately, Æbbe had run off to lavish her attention on someone more disposed to entertain her.

'What has been said then?' Cedric asked with some reservation.

Oswald repeated what he'd been told. Cedric looked to Eanfrith for confirmation and he nodded his agreement.

'When will these things happen?' Cedric asked Eanfrith.

'As soon as possible, two, three days perhaps,' Eanfrith answered with undisguised agitation.

'I can see benefits to learning the things that these people know, Cedric. What is there to lose and much to gain?'

'Mmm,' was all Cedric would say.

Eanfrith and Oswald walked in silence for some time before Oswald had cleared a place in his mind and was able to say what had assembled in the space. 'Perhaps this is a good thing, Eanfrith.'

'You're a fool, they want to make us be and think like them, then they will use us for their own ends.'

Oswald was surprised at Eanfrith's tone, 'I thought that you had *agreed* to do this!'

'I had no choice, but I will never be like them.'

'But these are your relatives.'

'I am a Bernician and a King, *that* comes first. I will not be robbed of my inheritance. As soon as I can I will drive the usurper, *your* mother's brother, from my kingdom.'

Oswald was confused now; Eanfrith was all but making him chose between him and his mother. They continued on in silence, walking around the timber stockade until they returned to where they'd started, having said very little of consequence. Whatever Eanfrith said, Oswald was determined that he would make as much as he could from the opportunity, besides he was curious about this god that his followers ate. He wondered if it was a bit like holding his father's sword. His father was in the sword and by holding it he became in some mystical way, an extension of his father. Perhaps this god eating was more symbolic, and it made those who did this, figuratively part of their god.

'I will leave you now Oswald, I need to make myself known to the smith, think on what we have said. Don't forget who you are, or who I am, remember I am your king, *not* King Eochaid Buide.'

Who *am I*? I no longer know... Oswald thought to himself... I will go to this island and learn all I can from these monks. I will make it my strength, not my weakness.

'*Prince Oswald!*' a voice suddenly forced its way unceremoniously into his world of thought.

Oswald instinctively looked up and smiled as he saw Princess Helen coming towards him.

'Hello,' he replied smiling, 'I'm sorry, I was deep in thought.

'You are always thinking, I leave such an occupation to my elders, come, would you like to ride outside the fort? I will show you some of my favourite places. If you are leaving for a while, I would like you to remember me, *perhaps* "Some time", when you are not so busy with your thinking,' she laughed and poked him with her finger, making Oswald laugh too. She was one of those people who brought laughter with her wherever she went. There was something clean and innocent about her, he thought and smiled.

'I'm sure I will remember you. Will it be *safe* to ride alone outside the fort?'

'Oh, we will not go far from the fort, Father would be furious.'

'In that case, I would like that very much.'

The princess took him to the stables and two ponies were saddled for them.

They gently walked their ponies and talked without losing sight of the fort, Oswald made sure of that.

'Helen is a name I am unfamiliar with, Princess.'

She smiled, '...we have many traders who come here from far-off lands to sell their wares. My brooch,' she pointed to the beautiful silver pennanular brooch securing her cloak. 'These stones are called garnets and they come from a land that is so far away, it is in another world.'

'I wonder where that is? Your brooch is very beautiful.'

'Thank you, I think so too. My father bought it for my mother, from a trader who told a wonderful story of a beautiful young princess from his land, called Helen. She was so beautiful that all men wanted her for their wife. It is a very complicated story with much intrigue, but she was kidnapped and held in a fort made of stone, even bigger than Dunadd. The bit I like best is where those who came to rescue her pretend to leave and hid in the belly of a great wooden horse they'd made. The people dragged the horse into their fort, they didn't know about the warriors inside. At night, the warriors came out of the wooden horse, conquered the fort and rescued Helen.'

'And what happened to her in the end?'

'It was a sad end, I'm afraid. She went to live with someone she thought a friend, a woman called Polyxo.' Oswald drew back his head at the odd name.

'I have never heard of that name either, it's not so easy to say as Helen.'

'The story is filled with strange names from this far-off land,' Helen laughed. 'This woman Polyxo, actually hated Helen, blaming her for the death of her husband who had been killed in the wars, and she wanted revenge, to that end she pretended to like Helen. One night when Helen was bathing, she was tricked by the woman, taken and hanged.'

'That is indeed a sad tale, may the gods have prepared a life of only happiness for *you*, Helen.'

'Ha, my mother loved the story and she liked the name Helen so much, she made it my name. Perhaps the trader will come again this year and he will tell it once more.'

'Do you know, I *will* miss you, Princess Helen.'

Chapter 8

Journey to Iona

It was a fresh autumn morning as they made their way to the shore and the four awaiting boats; someone said they were called curraghs. [15] On nearing the craft, Oswald was somewhat concerned, for they appeared very flimsy indeed.

At first glance, they seemed to be no more than a light wooden frame covered with either cloth or skins and coated with tar. They had one mast with a large square sail, and on the side, there were places for oars, but even the oars looked too feeble for their purpose. Men were waiting by the boats each holding an oar upright at his side. Oswald reckoned they were not quite twice the height of a man in their length.

Never before had Oswald noticed any clear expression of fear on Cedric's face, but there was today as he stared at these boats. So much so, that Oswald was distracted from his own apprehension.

Eanfrith, Oswiu and Oswald would travel together with some of Queen Acha's household; the boat would leave *them* on Iona and take the *rest* on to the island of Coll with his mother.

King Eochaid Buide, his children and some warriors, one of whom was Daffyd, had come with them to see them on their way. Cedric had quite taken to the warrior; he was even now talking and *laughing* with him, as if they had been friends for years. No doubt, Cedric was seeking confirmation from him that these craft, were indeed seaworthy.

Meanwhile, the men from the boats were carefully stowing their belongings on the little craft, under the supervision of Torem. 'I wish I were coming with you, Prince Oswald,' Helen said looking genuinely sorry that she was going to be left behind.

'Awe, that is kind of you Princess,' and Oswald hugged her. 'Sadly, they do not allow women on the island.'

'Do you think that such a thing is right?'

'Well… I don't know, you Christians seem to think of women differently. It seems odd to us. We don't think women are lower in some way to men,' he said facing her, his hands resting on her shoulders and looking sympathetically into her eyes.

'I'm going to marry you, Prince Oswald of Bernicia...' she unexpectedly blurted out.

Oswald's eyes widened, with total incredulity. At the great age of twelve, marriage was not at the forefront of his thoughts this day. Her face froze, embarrassed that she had bared her heart to him. She had even surprised herself and now felt foolish; *he* clearly did not feel the same. Oswald saw her eyes fill with tears; she was about to cry.

'If I was to have you for a wife, I should think myself very fortunate indeed, you honour me, if it is your wish then it is mine too,' he quickly added, and her tears slowly turned to smiles, as if the sun had unexpectedly appeared from behind a cloud heralding a summer's day. She kissed him on his cheek and hugged him once more.

Oswald slowly released his hold on the princess and went to where his mother and friends from Bernicia were gathered. He embraced Hrodulf and Cedric and thanked them both, certain that they would care for his mother.

'Please don't say anything to my mother about our recent conversation, I don't want to hurt her,' he whispered to Cedric as he held him. Cedric responded by briefly tightening his grip signifying that he understood. Finally, Oswald held his mother who was unable to prevent her tears.

'I will miss you son, do take care of young Oswiu, he is so young to be on his own, and I'm fond of him.'

'I will Mother, and he will not be on his own, I will be with him. You know how close we are, you can reassure his mother. I have told her not to worry and promised to care for him.'

She kissed him and held him, reluctant to let him go.

'Thank you, son, you have always been a good boy and I have forever loved you as my own, have I not?'

So, what Cedric had told him was now confirmed, was that what she had meant, be it unintentionally?

'Yes, I could ask no more from any mother,' and with those parting words he kissed her once more, prised himself free of her, and walked into the water to the curragh.

With a little help, Oswald clambered gingerly over the side of the boat, fearing that he might put his foot through the rather flimsy looking skin. He felt the structure flex even as he took his place on the wooden thwart. [16] The curragh rose and fell most unsettlingly as the waves rolled up onto the white sandy beach.

In many ways, this was not unlike the beach at Bebbanburg. He'd always thought that the coast and beaches of his home were the finest and could not be bettered, but he had to concede, that this beach, though smaller, was almost the equal of the beautiful long stretches of golden sand between the sea and the fort of Bebbanburg.

Suddenly there was a violent jerked as the little boat was pushed free from the grip of the sand, Oswald was caught off-guard, and almost tumbled back over from his seat. At the command, "PULL", the oars fought as one to overcome the momentum of the incoming swell. *Gradually* – with a final fused dip of the paddles, they were rewarded with their freedom, and the little craft glided across the water like a bird floating on a breath of air, and into their future.

Oswald became quickly aware of the ingenuity of this ever-flexing marvel. He could see how it in fact twisted and bowed in perfect harmony with the rise and fall of the swell, as if it had a living rapport with the ocean. He actually felt much safer on this little boat than he had when he'd travelled on bigger boats with his father, Æthelfrith, to the islands off the coast of

Bebbanburg. Alas, as he glanced at Eanfrith, *his* face told a different story.

As the large square sail was being unfurled, it rebelled for a moment then billowed contentedly as it surrendered its will to the unrelenting persuasion of the wind.

Oswald turned to look back at the shore, which was now disappearing surprisingly quickly into the distance. Already those left behind were turning from people into merely unrecognisable shapes, but he could yet see one small arm waving, and responded likewise until he could see it no longer.

He had been told that they would not reach Iona until the evening; it was about fourteen leagues travel. They had first to negotiate between two islands off the mainland before they were on the open sea. Oswald thanked the sea gods that they were at peace this day. Calm as it was, his head felt a little unsteady, as did his gut.

He hoped too that his mother and Cedric would be safe. Their intention, he'd been told, was to beach and make camp for the night on the island of Muile, [17] continuing their journey next day. They would have another half day's sailing to the island of Coll. It would be unnecessarily dangerous to travel through the night and it was pointless to take such risk. Oswald wished that Cedric had come with *him* and stayed the night on Iona before they went on, but women were forbidden on the island and he would not leave Queen Acha.

Oswald thought that was true, but he suspected that Cedric didn't want to be anywhere near the monk priests and was only too happy to have his *duty* as an excuse for forgoing that option.

There was shouting and waving of farewells as the boats separated. Acha might not be his birth mother, but she was the only mother he'd ever known, and he knew this would be no small thing to her. Oswald watched her sitting quietly at the rear of the craft; Cedric was standing next to her.

Oswald stared for some time even after the boats, with all he knew, disappeared into the haze. It was quiet now; all he could hear was the gentle ripple of the sea as the boat sliced its way through the water and the occasional flap of the sail, fleetingly luffing as it lost the wind.

The warriors on Oswald's craft would be taken on to Coll after the three princes had been delivered to their new home.

It was yet light when the island came into view – they had made good time. Oswald was mesmerised by the crystal-clear water, he could almost see down to the seabed. They were cutting through shoals of tiny fish, which swam off in every direction.

Ahead of them was the rocky coastline of Iona. The curragh, adjusted its final tack making towards a small sandy inlet, ideally suited for beaching their craft safely.

Set back from the shoreline, he could see what he supposed was to be their new home.

It consisted of a small group of stone buildings; one was much larger than the rest, Oswald guessed that it was the temple of their gods. He assumed that they had chosen stone to build with instead of wood, because of the lack of trees. He could not see a single tree on the island, but there was stone aplenty.

As they neared the beach, two men quickly rose from their places, and in a well-practised manoeuvre, took in the sail, neatly wrapping and binding it to the crossbeam, and the small craft glided gently up the sand, then nestled peacefully onto its side.

Two other men leapt over the bow of the boat with ropes, and skilfully tied the boat to posts dug into the ground, no doubt for that very purpose.

The headman ordered them to disembark and make their way up to the "Monastery" as they called it, saying his men would see that their baggage was carried there for them.

Eanfrith look strangely subdued, not his normal ebullient self, but then Oswald knew what Eanfrith was like; he was never confident when he was amongst strangers. He felt sorry for him at this moment. As Cedric had once said; anyone with the constant need to be assertive; was not a secure person. Oswald knew that for now *he* would have to take the lead *without* making Eanfrith feel threatened, but he was used to doing that, so it would be no hardship.

This holy place was obviously yet in a state of ongoing construction even after sixty years. There were buildings that he supposed were where the priest-monks lived.

They were taken to the larger of the dwellings. Oswald saw one of the priest-monks, an elderly shabbily dressed man with short unkempt hair, and a big cross on his chest, with an equally big smile on his face. He was standing at the door to welcome them, surprisingly, in their own native tongue.

'Welcome, welcome, young Princes come inside, and we will find mete for you. I am the Abbot Fergno,' he said, and he bowed humbly to them.

The hall was poorly lit; it took a moment for their eyes to adjust to the gloom. Oswald could see that it was a clean but drab place totally lacking in colour.

'Be seated,' said the Abbot smiling

Eanfrith was quiet, as was Oswald, for he suddenly felt to be a long way from Bebbanburg, Oswiu pressed closely to Oswald and Oswald put his arm around him.

The three took the places offered at the long table and the Abbot sat down opposite them.

Young men in plain, coarse, woven, drab robes, which were perfectly suited to their surroundings, came with wooden bowls and platters, filled with fish, beans and small loaves of fresh bread. It was plain fare, but welcome mete for they had eaten little since they'd left Dunadd that morning. There was drink too, a strange sweet drink, the Abbot said was called mead, and was made from honey. He told the princes that they kept honeybees here on the island; and caring for the bees was one of the many skills the young monks learned, as part of their devotions to God.

'We believe that one's whole life should be an offering to God. He is interested in every little thing we do; therefore, we should do *everything* as if we were doing it just for Him.'

Oswald thought the Abbot's god was easily pleased, if keeping bees was a devotion to him. Everyone knew that it was great deeds of valour, which pleased their Saxon gods, *not* humble bee keeping. No wonder the followers of this Christian god were always being killed by the Saxons.

The Abbot went on to tell them that they tried to make and grow all they needed, here on the island. Their greatest need was timber for their building work. Oswald had already noticed there were no trees on the island, or none to speak of, so of course all their timber would have to be ferried from the mainland.

'Tell me first, what are we to call you handsome young men? I was given a note of the names of those who were coming, but I do not know to which face to affix each name. I love to know people's names,' he said smiling at each of them. 'Names are so important; they denote us as unique individuals, a *single* word which identifies us, and to some extent defines us. What a special thing. For example, one of you is called Oswald, so I'm informed,' he looked at each enquiringly and smiled. '"Os", means god, and "Wald", comes from the Saxon word, "Weald" which means, *rules*. Therefore, "Oswald" means *God Rules*. A fine name that is a statement every time it is spoken, perhaps you do not share my amusement?' he said smiling once more.

They all stared at this strange man. 'I am Oswald,' Oswald said feeling proud that it was his name, 'this is Prince Eanfrith, now the Lord of Bebbanburg, and the youngest of us is Prince Oswiu,' he said placing a comforting arm round Oswiu.

'I am honoured to meet you all. You are here to study and learn so I'm told.'

'Our god is Wōden, not your half-eaten god. We do not eat *our* gods,' Eanfrith asserted with all the bravado he could muster.

The Abbot turned to him and smiled, nothing seemed to fluster this man. He was most annoyingly serene.

'You are a devout man, I take it Lord?'

'What do you mean, devout?'

'Simply that you follow your god with commitment and sincerity.'

Eanfrith looked flustered, 'we have *many* gods. You only have three gods, and you eat them. You see, I know all there is to know about your gods.'

'Ah, you are clearly a very clever young man for I am still learning, but I am old and slow to learn, you will need to be patient with me I'm afraid. I will be interested to hear about all these gods of yours. I am always eager to learn, it helps me to understand, and understanding helps me govern wisely. I hope in time to share with you what *I* have learned and that you will share with me what *you* have learned, and we will walk together on this great journey of life by learning from each other.'

'What shall we call you Lord?' asked Oswald hoping to divert Eanfrith, for it was clear that this old man was far cleverer than Eanfrith, and Eanfrith was in danger of making himself look like a fool.

'I am referred to as Father, because we are a family here and I am the head, the Father of our family, metaphorically speaking. I hope you will feel as if you are *part* of our small community, certainly, as long as you are here, we will endeavour to treat you as such. You are free to come to me at any time if you are concerned in any way or even if you merely wish to talk. I love to talk, my weakness I'm afraid,' and he lifted his hands and frowned in acknowledgement of his failure.

'How long will we be here – Father?' asked Oswald adjusting his seating position.

'Ah…' the Abbot smiled, at Oswald's awkwardness, 'now that is a difficult question, when you have learned enough, shall we say,' he offered ambiguously.

'Does that answer your question?'

Eanfrith's frustration manifested itself by him banging his fist on the table causing the plates to leap in the air. The Abbot never flinched, but both Oswald and Oswiu jumped in time with the platters.

'I am now twenty-one and a man, a King... I know all I need to know.'

The Abbot bowed his head respectfully, 'I am honoured that you are amongst us, Lord, no doubt I can learn much from you, perhaps you will help me with my knowledge of Saxon ways. I speak a little of your tongue, but I am ignorant of so much about your people. If I am to be a friend of your people a greater knowledge of them and their ways can only help me, to that end we are indeed honoured and privileged that you are here.'

'Where are we to sleep, Father?' Oswald once again stepped in quickly, before Eanfrith had a chance to further shame himself by his hostile behaviour.

'I will leave you now, but when you have eaten, Brother Aidan will show you the rooms we have prepared for you.' One of the young men who had brought the food to them who was standing behind the Abbot bowed. Oswald thought this monk was slightly older than himself, perhaps seventeen. Oswald smiled congenially at him. 'Because of your seniority, Lord Eanfrith, you will have a room to yourself and you two young Lords, will share a room. We thought that Lord Oswiu might benefit from the comfort of your company, Lord Oswald. You will be in a hall where there are other young men, who are studying to become full members of our community.

'Their wish is to devote their lives to God.' '*Your* god,' Eanfrith asserted.

'Yes, forgive me, I refer to *my* God.'

'Thank you... Father, that is kind,' Oswald said speedily, Eanfrith did no more than give a brief grunt. It was clear to

Oswald that this man was not easily provoked and was equal to the hostility Eanfrith was exhibiting.

The three princes ate in silence. While they ate, the monk named Aidan, stood with his back to the wall and never uttered a word. The silence in this place was so insidious that Oswald felt overwhelmed by it. He kept thinking about his name, "God Rules", it made him tremble at the thought, how was he to understand such a thing, what did it mean? Suddenly, he wanted to shout out – to bring some release from the deafening noise in his head, – *but* – he did no more than smile at Oswiu. He wondered if his brothers were feeling the same as he. He glanced at Eanfrith, but he seemed only concerned with the mete before him. Oswald remembered Helen saying to him that he *thought* too much, perhaps he did.

Once they'd finished the meal, Aidan, with a graceful sweep of his hand, indicated that they were to follow him. He took them to a small dwelling with two floors. There were stone steps leading up to the second floor at one end, which overlooked the space below where there were several sleeping places laid out for the night. Oswald assumed, as he looked down, that they must be for the other young people, who the Abbot had mentioned. He thought that they probably cleared away the space in the morning.

They were indeed to be privileged with their own individual rooms. The rooms were basic without adornment, each enclosed with a rough looking door. The boards on the doors had wide gaps between them; they had obviously dried out and shrunk since the doors were first made. The walls were plain white limewashed and the only decoration was a cross, painted on the wall. There was none of the brightly painted decoration depicting animals and elaborate patterns on the walls with which he was familiar. Oswald guessed the cloth bags that were to be their beds were packed with hay or perhaps even wool. He'd seen that there were many sheep on the island, and there were drab wool rugs to cover them if they were cold; the same as they'd seen laid out downstairs.

Oswiu lay down on his bed and smiled for the first time. 'This is really quite comfortable Oswald, and it's warm too.'

'I hope that Eanfrith feels as you do,' Oswald whispered, hoping that his voice didn't carry to the next room. He knew that Eanfrith had a wooden frame bed at Bebbanburg; he didn't lie on the floor like a servant.

'Are you missing your mother, Oswald?' Oswiu asked sadly, his smile having been no more than a fleeting expression of comfort.

'A little, but we have each other, and I was told that I would see her often; I will remember that promise when I think of her. It has been a *long* journey from Bernicia has it not, I think about our people there. I hope that King Edwin treats them kindly. Together, we will make the most of what we have here, daily supporting, and encouraging each other. Agreed?'

'I will do my best Oswald, but I feel lonely, I wish my mother was here with us. I know she will be missing me too. She gave me this little bag filled with lavender,' Oswiu held the small bag up for Oswald to see, 'she said I must remember her when I smelt it. She always smells of lavender, doesn't she?'

'That's true, but you know her better than me. She will be with you every moment in her thoughts, I'm sure of it, and you will see her when we go back to Dunadd.'

Oswald unwrapped his belongings and amongst them was his prized sword.

'You have brought your new sword. I didn't know that. Do you think you will need it here?'

'I know not, but this sword is more precious to me than you can ever imagine, it will never leave my side as long as I live.'

Chapter 9

Death of a Queen

Over the last year, Oswald had been to see his mother several times because she was ill. He was ever more worried about her deteriorating health, which she could no longer pretend was as it should be. He knew she was unwell and had been since they'd travelled from Bernicia, perhaps even before that and he'd found it particularly distressing on this visit, to see the marked deterioration in her health.

He was quiet as they sailed home to Iona and leant back against the side of the curragh with his head hung between his legs in despair. When they beached, he leapt wearily from the boat without a word, paused for a moment and made his way at some pace up to the monastery.

Brother Aidan had to walk quickly to catch up to him. 'You have been very quiet on the journey home,' Brother Aidan panted as he spoke. He was usually a man of few words, so Oswald knew these were words spoken with kind intent.

Oswald slowed his pace, looked into Aidan's eyes, and spoke in a soft tired voice. 'Forgive me if I have given offence my friend, it was not my intention. I'm concerned about Mother, no doubt you realise that. Each time I leave I wonder if it will be the last time, I will see her, and that is so hard, I can't do anything, you see.'

'I know… it is the hardest thing when we see those, we love suffering. We might not *always* understand another's anguish, but we all have mother's whom we love and losing one's mother is a very painful thing. You are my dear friend too, so believe me, I care how you feel.'

'Thank you, Aidan, you are always understanding. Yes, it's true, our mothers are indeed special, but you have never mentioned your family, and I have never thought to ask. I'm ashamed that our conversations have always been about my concerns.'

'I never saw it like that, Lord. My life is not about me, my friend; it is about my Saviour, who made Himself known to me when I was a small boy in Hibernia. I was only perhaps – seven or eight. Since that day, He has consumed my life, and in that – I have – *found* – life, in such abundance I could never have imagined that it was possible.'

'You are a very special man, Aidan, and I believe the gods have bound you and me together in some way for a reason.'

Aidan didn't reply, he merely smiled, touched Oswald's shoulder and they walked on without further comment. At the door of the building where they slept, Oswald paused and stroked his chin thoughtfully.

'You go on Aidan, I will join you shortly.'

Aidan dipped his head and went in. Oswald stood for a moment longer, as if unsure what to do, turned and walked to where he hoped that he might find Brother Ségéne. He went into the building and asked a monk if he'd seen Brother Ségéne, the monk nodded in the direction of the Brother's cell. Brother Ségéne, was one of the most senior monks and had his own place of work where he also slept, which they called cells.

Oswald knocked and a voice bade him enter.

'Brother Ségéne.'

'Ah, Prince Oswald, come on in, you've been very much in my thoughts, so you have,' Brother Ségéne said rising from his chair. 'Be seated – how can I help?'

'As you know, I have been to see my mother.'

'Yes, the Abbot told me where you were. I gave Brother Aidan some mead for her, the honey in it has healing properties, and it may bring her some relief, it will do no harm. How was the Queen?'

'Thank you, he did give it to her – She is ill, as you know. I fear she is going to die, her skin was an awful shade of yellow and she is so thin, her eyes were as white as white could be.

They have tried all manner of things, but nothing seems to make any difference.'

'That is sad. I met the Queen once, when I went to preach on Coll; she was a very gentle, gracious lady. I'm very sorry, Oswald. You could have stayed if you had wished.'

'I know, I know, in truth – it was difficult to leave her, but she has old friends around her and my brothers. I was worried about Oswiu; here on his own, he needs my company.'

'It's true, how was he when you returned, I have been keeping an eye on him, but sure enough he misses you?'

'I have not yet seen him; I came first to see you Brother. I think Brother Aidan will go to him, Oswiu likes him.'

'I have noticed, Brother Aidan is a good soul and has a kind heart. I pray daily for your mother my friend, as I do for you all.'

'It seems *your* god is not any better at answering our requests than mine is.'

'So, it might appear. I agree that it is difficult to believe in any being, real or imagined, if that being does not touch our lives here and now when we have needs. We all want to ease the hurts of the people we love. That is the hardest part of loving, suffering with them. Caring so much we would give our own lives for them, if we could. This is the measure of real love, putting others before our own wants.'

'Brother Aidan has just this moment said the same thing to me.'

'Yes, he would, he has a rare love for God. I believe that the only thing that God asks of *us* is to believe that He loves us – just as we are, because we can never be as we should be. Isn't that what we all need to hear sometimes, from those we love, that they love us unconditionally. Forgiveness is at the heart of my God. As I have told you before the central message at the beating heart of the Christian faith, is about a *relationship* between the Creator and the created: my Creator and me, and my God wants such a relationship with everyone, no matter how lowly and unworthy one is or feels. From what you tell me, your gods only have time for those who succeed, the great warriors, not those who struggle in this life.'

'I don't seem to know anything anymore, but we all want to feel well and happy and we will follow the one who we think can best achieve this. Perhaps *your* god is the *only* god, I know not the truth of it. I do know that *you* are different, different from anyone I have ever known.'

'Is that a commendation or a criticism, my friend?' Ségéne laughed. 'Let me share some good news, your brother Eanfrith has accepted our Christian faith and was baptised while you have been away.'

'Eanfrith!'

'Yes, he has not progressed with his studies as *you* have; perhaps he was too old when he came. He wished to return to Dunadd as a Christian. You look surprised, Oswald.'

'I am, he has never shown any great understanding or interest in your faith.'

'Mmm, in truth, just how sincere his commitment is, I do not know, but it is not for me to judge another. Time will tell; God is not fooled by man. I will pray for him.'

'When will he leave?'

'He has already gone, a curragh towing barges with timber for the ongoing work landed and he returned to the mainland with them.'

'I don't know what to say,' Oswald could do no more than shake his head slowly from side to side.

'Then say nothing my friend. Go and see Oswiu, perhaps we will talk more on the morrow when you have slept.'

Oswald stared at Brother Ségéne for a moment, turned, reached for the door handle, and left without further comment.

Oswald wearily climbed the stone steps to his room; the door was open, and he saw Aidan sitting next to Oswiu on his bed.

'*Oswald*,' Oswiu, leapt from his bed and jumped into Oswald's arms. 'You are home, I'm so pleased to see you.'

'Come, sit down.'

'Has Brother Aidan made known to you of our time away?'

'Yes, I'm sorry to hear about your mother, Oswald.'

'Thank you; tell me, what do you know of Eanfrith?'

'He has become one of the Christians and returned to the fort at Dunadd.'

'So, I have been told by Brother Ségéne; I went to see him before I came here to you. Thank you, Brother Aidan, I'll stay with Oswiu. We have much to talk about, you must be tired too,' Oswald said, turning his attention to Aidan.

'Thank you, Prince Oswald, but I will go to Abbot Fergno first before I make for my bed, he will want to know how the Queen is keeping, as I see it.'

Oswald stood and embraced Aidan then sat down again beside his brother as Aidan left. He told him about his fears for his mother's health. Changing the subject once more, he asked Oswiu what, if anything, Eanfrith had said to him. Oswiu told him, that Eanfrith had said that he now believed in the Christian God and was going to be baptised and then he would return to Dunadd as soon as it was possible. He returned two days past when a trader landed on the island.

'Mmm, it seems sudden; he never mentioned anything about his thoughts to me. He always seemed to be antagonistic towards the Christian God.'

'Yes, I was as surprised as you are.'

As the time passed, Oswald was becoming ever more fluent with his new language of Hibernian, and of course, it was Ségéne's native tongue, so he was delighted with Oswald's progress. The studying was not a problem, Oswald actually enjoyed the work, as did Oswiu, and they would engage in discussions about their studies even in their spare time.

Eventually the inevitable word came to him via Brother Ségéne, his mentor who'd become more like a friend – Queen Acha had died. Oswald found it difficult when his mentor explained that he and Oswiu would have to attend the burial without any of his new friends from Iona, because the Christian monks could not be part of the pagan ritual.

The preparations for Oswald and Oswiu were made quickly and as they stood before the boat, Brother Aidan pushed a small piece of polished stone, in the shape of a fish, into Oswald's hand.

He explained that he had found it on the beach on a day when he had been wrestling with a particular thought about God and had carried it in his pocket since. 'Holding it in my hand reminds me of my creator and that he works all things together for good for those who love him. I want you to know that though we have been forbidden by the Abbot to go with you in body, I will be with you in spirit.'

Oswald smiled, touched by the kindness of this gentle monk and put the stone in his pocket.

For the first time, Oswald was conscious of an internal challenge to his thoughts and beliefs. He couldn't talk to Oswiu at this moment, his thoughts were too muddled to tell them to someone else, he could only stare at the rolling sea as they sailed steadily on towards the island of Coll. Strangely it was as peaceful as the monastery out here this day. All that could be heard, as Oswald stood holding the main shroud, was the odd cry of a lone seagull and the creaking of the mast and rigging as they moved leisurely in harmony with the wind and the waves,

His hand felt the stone in his pocket. There was so much about this Christian faith, which seemed to make sense, and more and more of his long-held pagan beliefs, which did *not* make sense anymore. Somehow, the Christian God seemed so much bigger, even bigger than Wōden. *His* beliefs had always been based around fate, the whim of the gods, what would be would be; it was simply down to fate when this, or that happened. The Christian faith, as far as he could understand it, was about a relationship between man and this God. Man had been separated from the Christian God because of his "Sin". Sin, that's what they called it, it wasn't a word that he'd really thought about before or understood. It seemed to mean that we were not living our lives as was intended and falling short of the best God had for man.

Apparently, man had chosen to reject God in favour of his own way and this "Jesus" had come to restore that broken relationship and *would* – do so if we would only let Him. Oswald couldn't quite understand the need for Him to die, however, this man came and was tortured to death. If nothing else, Oswald could understand by this action, how much mankind had meant to Him. Now mankind had once again access to this living God, *because* of this Jesus' death on a cross.

'OSWALD!' Oswiu shouted.

'Sorry Oswiu, did you want something? I was thinking,' and as soon as the words left his lips he had to smile – for he could hear Princess Helen's voice teasing him, saying that he thought too much.

'Here, why not try something to eat,' Oswiu passed him some bread and goat's cheese.

'Ah, thank you, Oswiu, what would I do without you?' Oswald smiled at him as he bit into the cheese.

Chapter 10

New Life

It was good to see Cedric and Hrodulf standing on the shore to welcome them, even though the purpose of this visit was one Oswald did not relish.

'I've missed you my two young Princes,' Cedric said sadly, wrapping them both in his arms. Whilst Cedric held them, Hrodulf laid his hands on their heads and greeted them with his blessing.

The funeral rite would be tomorrow, Cedric informed Oswald as they made their way to the village. A tomb had been prepared, and a wooden room had been built where all that was necessary for the afterlife would be placed, such as food and drink for the journey and some of her most precious personal items of jewellery and trinkets as was befitting the great queen she was.

The next day Queen Acha was laid inside the room and it was sealed, and finally it would all be covered with soil and turf to form a protective mound.

As Oswald stood with Hrodulf and Cedric, watching the closing of his mother's tomb. Cedric leaned close to him and said, 'Your mother commissioned me to tell you the story of your birth mother. I made no mention to her about your father being Lord Wulfstan. She always thought that your father was her husband King Æthelfrith. I told your mother not to worry, that I'd already made everything known to you. At first, she was surprised, and then she was pleased that you had never treated her any differently, in spite of your knowledge. She said to tell you how much she loved you, that you could not have been more precious – had you been her own.'

Oswald's head bowed and he felt the tears, which had until that moment been held on the edge of his eyelid, gradually overflow and trickle down his cheek. He was glad that she was at peace after all her suffering over the last years, and he asked the Christian God – if He would recognize that she had done her best and that He would forgive her pagan beliefs, and his too, she was innocent, a lady without guile.

At that instant, it came like a bolt of lightning from the heavens, it struck him so forcefully that he actually staggered and nearly fell. Cedric instinctively reached for his arm, assuming he had been overcome with grief, but it was not grief, it was the complete opposite to grief. He was engulfed in what seemed like a cloud of love. He *knew* at that second, that the Christian God was real. He didn't know why, or how, or what had happened, but he knew that something irreversible had taken place and his life would never be the same again.

Cedric kept asking him if he was all right, he even shook him slightly, but he couldn't tell Cedric, not at this moment, he would never understand, but he *hoped* that Oswiu would. He could see so clearly now that the grave goods would not provide for his mother's afterlife, that was man limiting God to his understanding. Their human offering merely affixed what was of this life – to this life, and in the end, they would all be swallowed up by the ground, as would the *earthly* body of his mother.

He understood that this hope he now felt was beyond the physical world of touch and feel, that in him was living a new creation, which was eternal and would not perish; *he* was *more* than that which walked and breathed this day's air. He couldn't understand it, perhaps he never would, but he was certain that he had been touched by the living God, as certain as night followed day.

There was a burning feeling inside, his face felt flushed, strength seemed to be flowing into his arms right down to his fingertips, he flexed his hands. He was alive like never before, as if his life was suddenly filled with the brightest colours.

He wanted to shout it to all who were standing there. "GOD RULES", that was actually his own name, God would rule in *his* life from now on, he swore it. He would not be defined by his title, or parentage, how his life had played out, or the things that had, or *would* happen to him, *he* would be defined by who he was in the Christ God.

On the way back to the village, Oswald asked Cedric what he would do now that the queen was dead. He said that he would stay here until *he* and Oswiu had finished their time on Iona then he would return to Dunadd with them.

'Did you know Eanfrith is to marry one of King Eochaid Buide's daughters, Princess Edlin?'

'No, you are better informed than I am, Cedric. I don't recall this daughter, *Edlin* did you say? I never heard Princess Helen mention such a sister.'

'Edlin, I'm sure it was. Do you remember the name Hrodulf?'

'As far as I remember it was as you say.'

Oswald shrugged his shoulders, 'it's all news to me.'

'I imagine we get more traders here than on your island, there are more people here to trade with.'

'When is this marriage to take place?'

'I know not, but I imagine that we will be sent for, they will want Bernicia to have as many of her people there as possible, few as we are. I thought that Eanfrith might have come here today, and he could have told us for himself.'

'I wondered if he would come, did you send word to him?'

'Yes, he knew, right enough.'

'Will Hrodulf stay here too?'

'Aye, we have nowhere else to go and we are both getting older,' he smiled. 'We will farm and fish, it's not a bad life, we'll take turns at being the king,' he smiled again, 'but as I have said, we will be there for you when the time comes, never fear.'

Oswald wondered what he meant by, "When the *time comes*", but he didn't pursue it. It began to rain as they walked back; stirred up by the westerly wind off the sea, it was bitterly cold, and the rain cut into Oswald's face like shards of ice.

They began to run, 'Quick lad, let's get into the hall and drink some of the Celtic *water of life*, before we catch a dose of the ague. It will melt the ice in your veins, aye, and dry the wool on your back too.' Cedric laughed as they entered the rather dark dank hall. It was like the barrow they'd only just left, and a shiver ran through Oswald at the thought of his dear mother all alone.

Oswald put his nose to the earthenware cup Cedric had passed into his hand, the fumes made his eyes water. He nervously sipped it and gasped, it took his breath away. Cedric was right, whatever was in this pale-yellow water, it either warmed you, or numbed your senses, so you simply forgot that you were cold in the first place. Oswald wasn't sure which it was.

Oswiu couldn't get to his feet to wave farewell he'd been carried to the awaiting curragh. He was now lying awkwardly on some curled-up rope as they were pushed away from the small jetty, and the men began to unfurl the sail. He looked as if death would be a mercy to him and Oswald was feeling only marginally better. A night of drinking the Celtic water of life, or uisge beatha as they called it – to celebrate the journey of Queen Acha to the afterlife, seemed to be bringing anything *but* life to the pair and Oswiu only had one cup of the elixir the whole night. Oswald had only a little more than Oswiu and still, he didn't know how he could possibly survive until they reached Iona, so ill did he feel, and he slumped down next to his brother and closed his eyes.

Chapter 11

Return to Dunadd

It was mid-afternoon before they arrived home at Iona.

It appeared that while they'd been away, Abbot Fergno had also been informed of the forthcoming marriage. He'd been sent word that Eanfrith was to marry, and Oswald and Oswiu had been instructed to attend by Queen Bebba, as part of the royal Bernician family. Oswald couldn't take in the information at this moment, so thick was his head, he needed to sleep, but he knew he would look forward to going once he had recovered.

He wondered if Helen was yet convinced that she would marry him, and he managed a token smile at the thought. She'd probably forgotten him by now; young girls were ever imagining they were in love and thinking about marrying. He thought that she might not recognise him with his new beard, thin as it was, he was proud of it.

As they approached the village of An Crionan, [18] where they would leave their curragh and walk the short distance to the fort of Dunadd, Oswald could see the people waiting for them. He hoped one of those hands waving would be the hand of Princess Helen.

His eyes burned as they scanned the faces through the evening haze, *yes*, she was there. His heart leapt as he saw her smiling. He knew that it was foolishness, they had only known each other for no more than a week, but she was there and smiling, that was enough for his heart. He was fifteen now, she would be fourteen. Queen Bebba was there and already Oswiu was calling to her, it had been three long years.

The boat settled in the same spot where it had sailed from all that time since. Even the sharp stab of pain, as he looked to the spot where he'd hugged his mother before they'd set off that day, did not tarnish the excitement of their arrival. Oswald playfully pushed Oswiu and jumped from the side before him, splashing, up to his knees in the cold water. Oswiu jumped next to him and was pleased to see that he'd drenched Oswald, but it didn't matter, nothing could spoil this day.

'Mother…' was all Oswiu could say. She was standing with his sister Æbbe who seemed every bit as excited as Oswiu as he ran into their arms.

Helen and Oswald briefly hesitated now that they were in touching distance of each other, but for no more than a moment and then they too embraced, she even kissed him.

'Oswald, you can't know how happy I am. This moment has been in my every thought ever since I knew that you were coming to Edlin's wedding and before if I'm being honest. Are you happy too?'

'What do you think? Look you are all wet now because of me, I'm sorry, I will get my own back on Oswiu for this,' he laughed.

'I don't care how wet I am, it took me all my time not to swim out to meet you,' and she kissed him once more. 'Your face looks different…' she rocked her head slowly from one side to the other as she looked at him.

'Do you like it,' he said proudly.

'It's wonderful you are a man now,' that was the perfect answer to a young warrior. 'Come let's walk on ahead so we can talk, you can tell me all your thoughts, or have you ceased all your thinking?' she teased and they both laughed.

'Before we rush off, I must speak to the Queen.' Oswald turned to Queen Bebba. 'My Lady, it is good to see you looking so well,' he said bowing.

'Oswald… it is good to see you, you have grown into a man since we last met.'

'I have missed you too, *Swald*,' Æbbe said jumping into her mother's welcome, and he smiled at her use of his pet name.

'You've grown, my favourite pest,' he said laughing and wrapping her in his arms. 'But I will leave you for a short while, I am going to walk ahead with the Princess, we will talk later,' and he smiled once more.

'I have much to tell you Helen,' he said to her in her own native Hibernian.

'*Ohh,* very good, you surprise me. Your Hibernian is better than my Saxon.' 'Nonsense you speak very good Saxon.

'My other news is that I have become a Christian.'

'Really!'

'Yes *really*, I have been a Christian for over two months. I have actually been baptized, not once, but twice now, thanks to Oswiu,' and they laughed once more.

'I was sorry to hear that your mother died Oswald. I so wanted to be there for you, but father said it was not my place to go, it was very sad. I have some memories of my own mother dying, but not so many. Most of all I remember how frightened I was. I thought that's what people you loved did; they died and left you. I was afraid to even like anyone for a long time. I want you to know that you can tell me how you feel, *if* you wish, it really matters to me, I want to share everything with you.' Oswald didn't answer her, but he squeezed her hand for he knew she was sincere.

'Did you know Cedric and Hrodulf are here?'

'Thank the Lord, I hoped for that. I wonder why they did not come to the shore to meet me?'

'That is my fault, I'm sorry. I told him how much I love you, and Cedric said he would not take the moment of your arrival from me, that he'd wait at the fort to welcome you. He is the kindest, and beautiful of men, no wonder you love him,'

With that news, Oswald took Helen's hand and they laughed as they ran towards the fort.

Oswald saw Cedric at the gate with a big smile on his face and outstretched welcoming arms. Hrodulf was by his side and Oswald ran into them wrapping them in his arms.

'You get bigger every time we meet Lord, you're almost as tall as me now,' said Hrodulf.

Eanfrith had not gone to the shore to welcome Oswald, but now walked towards them.

'Do you not have a greeting for me, your King, brother?'

Oswald released Cedric and Hrodulf and bowed to Eanfrith, who nodded his approval.

'You look well, I have heard that you have become a Christian, Eanfrith.'

'Yes,' he shrugged his shoulders, 'All gods are much the same, are they not?'

'No, not in the case of the Christian God, He is like no other.' Eanfrith narrowed his eyes warily, and looked suspiciously at Oswald, but said no more. 'I have become a Christian too,' Oswald said glancing at Cedric, whose smile left his face on hearing Oswald's confession.

'I see that you yet have my sword, at your side,' Eanfrith now cast an eye in Cedric's direction, but said no more. Oswald did not respond. Eanfrith would never have this sword, that his father had called "Dream World".

'Walk with me, I will introduce you to your new sister to be, this will be the binding of our two great houses. It will make me stronger when we return to take Bernicia from the usurper, *your* uncle. She is the daughter of King Conadd Cerr, who rules jointly with King Eochaid Buide, I don't think you have ever met him. The two kings are close kin.'

Oswald only listened as he followed Eanfrith. He'd understood that Eanfrith's wife to be was the daughter of King Eochaid Buide and wondered why he could not place her, now he understood. Helen held onto his arm without saying a word. Why do you always have to be like this Eanfrith? Oswald thought despairingly.

They walked the short distance into a longhouse and a girl lifted her head and smiled. She looked surprisingly like Helen; this must be Princess Edlin thought Oswald as they neared the girl.

Eanfrith bowed, 'My Lady, this is my brother Prince Oswald. Oswald, this is Princess Edlin.'

'It is an honour to meet you my Lady, this is a very important time for you, you are welcome into our family.'

'Thank you, Prince Oswald, I hear that you are a scholar, how kind of you to greet me in my own language,' she cast her eyes at Eanfrith, who had struggled with the work of learning Hibernian and insisted she spoke Saxon.

'I'm sure you will want to find out where you are to stay. I think your friend will help you,' she glanced at Helen and they both smiled.

'I will show the Prince, we will see you at the night's feast, Edlin.'

'Yes, we will talk more then.' With that, Helen took Oswald's hand and led him out of the longhouse.

'She seems nice.'

'She is, we are good friends.'

'How old is she?'

'Seventeen.'

'What do you think of Eanfrith?'

She was hesitant… 'Honestly – I don't like him much, I'm sorry to say this as he is your brother, forgive me.'

'It's all right; I know that he can be difficult to like sometimes. I don't think he likes himself very much. He has always wanted people to respect him, but he is not a bad person. I have learned how to deal with him over the years and we get along tolerably well, as long as he has not to compete with me. I usually let him win, it makes for a better relationship.'

'I will try to like him for your sake and for Edlin. It is their marriage on the morrow and our Priest will give them God's blessing.'

Helen took Oswald to where he was to sleep. She said that she had things to do for Edlin.

'I will see you at the feast,' she kissed Oswald and left him. Her timing was perfect, for Oswald saw Cedric coming towards him, and he knew he would have to face his displeasure.

'Cedric.'

'Prince Oswald.'

'I imagine I am facing a storm because I have become a Christian.'

'No, I understand how difficult it must be for you living with all those priest-monks on that island. I would probably have done the same in your position.'

Oswald was at first stunned by Cedric's ready acceptance. Then he realised that Cedric thought that he was merely being pragmatic, to make his life less complicated on Iona.

'Cedric, I think that you have misunderstood.'

'Misunderstood, in what way?'

'I am not merely being practical and doing what would make my life less complicated or that I have collapsed under pressure,' Cedric narrowed his eyes wondering what Oswald was about to say, in his heart not wanting to believe what he feared. 'I have actually given my life to the Christian God.'

It took a moment for Cedric to respond in a calm measured manner. 'You *really* believe in this half-eaten god!'

'Yes, I do.'

'But you know fine well that Wōden would gobble up what's left of him in one mouthful. *Wōden* is the god of gods.'

'I understand what you say Cedric. If you will listen, I will tell you about this God I now follow.' Cedric could only stare, it was clear that he couldn't quite comprehend what Oswald was saying. 'All you have ever taught me is the same as this God says to me. All I could hear from this God's teaching about how to live my life, I have heard from you. Often, I could not understand what you were saying, but now I can, because of this God.'

'You are confusing me Oswald; you have grown too clever with words. You have sorely troubled me son, you know you are everything to me. I would have killed anyone else who talked to me as you have. Ah, it will pass, you have just spent too much time with all this foolishness filling your head,' Cedric said, trying to reassure himself and bring some comfort to the disturbance in his thought world. Oswald understood and chose not to pursue it any further.

Chapter 12

Eanfrith and Edlin

In the evening after they had eaten, Oswald and Helen walked down to the seashore. The night was still with hardly a breath of air. They could hear the revelry they'd left behind them at the fort, floating on the warm night air.

There had been much drinking and feasting, the people were happy. For Oswald all was tinged with sadness, he grieved for his mother, for his home in Bernicia, for his loss of identity, and the uncertainty of his future.

'You are thinking again,' Helen squeezed his hand.

He looked down at her, 'I was thinking how fortunate I am to have someone like you to care for me.'

'Ahh, you were, were you! Does your newfound faith permit telling lies?' she smiled.

'Ha, it's the truth, I am fortunate.'

'But… that is not what you were thinking,' she said shaking her head in disbelief.

'I will have to be careful. Clearly, along with your many talents you have special sight too,' he laughed. 'In truth, I was thinking about all the uncertainty of living, for myself in particular.'

'Oswald Leodwalding of Bernicia, life is simple. When you return from Iona we will be married, have lots of children and live happily ever after, and that's the end of it.'

Oswald laughed, 'of course, whatever was I thinking about, life is that simple, foolish me. Come on, I'll race you to those rocks,' and he pushed her and ran off. When he reached the rocky outcrop, he turned, bent forward with his hands on his knees and panted.

'You cheated, you will never get to heaven,' she called out as she neared and ran into his arms giggling.

'Come on sit down. LOOK, can you see them?' He blurted out pointing.

'WHAT?'

'Dolphins – look – several of them.'

'Oh yes, I see them, how wonderful.'

They were absolutely captivated by the splendour and grace of these beautiful creatures, leaping and diving, in – and – out of the water with barely the slightest disturbance to the surface.

They both stood to catch a last glimpse of the display as the dolphins disappeared into the distance.

'I don't remember seeing dolphins so clearly before, Helen.'

'No, a rare sight, I wonder what they were thinking,' she teased, and he laughed at her taunt.

'Now there's a thought…'

'Ahhhh, you are impossible, come, we should go back it is getting dark and I must speak with Edlin about the morrow's employment before we sleep, in case there is something she needs me to do.'

'Can I say – how difficult it will be to return to Iona after the wedding? I have so enjoyed the time with you.'

'Don't talk about it, I am absolutely dreading it.' They continued towards the fort in silence for some time.

A grasshopper clicking in the long grass distracted Oswald and suddenly he was aware that there was a competition going on to see who had the loudest click. They stared into the long grass, but neither of them could spot the culprit who'd started the game.

'I pray Helen, that we are not amongst the grasshoppers at Eanfrith's wedding on the morrow, all trying to click louder than the next man. I have found that such gatherings with powerful people present an irresistible opportunity to show that you are better than your enemies and friends.'

'Not just men, women too,' Helen added.

'Aye – women too.'

Oswiu shouted to them as they entered through the gates, he was sitting on a bench with his sister Æbbe. Oswald and Helen sat down beside them.

He and Oswiu had not yet spoken about their time on Iona and this was an opportunity to tell Helen and Æbbe of their life there, about what they did in their studies, the monks, and their daily life.

Oswald told them of his weapon practice with his tutor Brother Ségéne, both he and Oswiu smiled at the expression on their faces.

'Brother Ségéne was not always a monk, he was once a warrior of some note and an accomplished swordsman.' He hesitated – then told them of his new faith and all listened intently. Obviously, the undoubted conviction with which he spoke captured their attention, especially Æbbe. Oswald was actually struggling to tell his tale because of her constant interruptions, wanting even more detail.

He could see that Æbbe was mesmerised by his confession.

Helen apologised to them but said she must go and see Edlin. Oswald also took his leave, as he wanted to see Eanfrith before he settled for the night.

'Please don't go yet Swald, I want you to tell me more.'

'I'm sorry, Æbbe, my beautiful sister, I would like to stay, but I must go. I promise that I will tell you more before I return to Iona.' She was about to argue, but he pointed his finger at her, narrowing his eyes and she resisted her natural inclination to insist, and he smiled and kissed her.

'She loves you, you know.' Helen said quietly as they walked away.

'Ha, I know, and I love her too.'

'But you are an easy man to love, Oswald of Bernicia.'

'You think so do you?'

'I think so.'

Oswald knew that feelings of love and emotions were considered an absurdly flimsy reason for a marriage, which was a match for life. People grew and changed, the binding needed to be something of a more lasting nature. To that end, the two families of Queen Bebba and King Conadd Cerr would have agreed a marriage contract on the betrothal of their children. Even though Eanfrith was not Queen Bebba's son, she was the Queen of his father. The actual marriage ceremony was of less relevance.

Nevertheless, Helen was excited to see them on the morrow; the whole day would be one of spectacle where all would assemble in their finery.

As the couple stood in the midst of their family and friends at the door of their small place of worship, Oswald had to say that Edlin was very beautiful indeed. She wore a white veil of the finest material kept in place on her head by a circlet made of interlaced strands of gold. Her tunic was made of the most beautiful deep blue wool, which signified her purity. It was tied at the waist by a belt, finely plaited from strips of leather with jewels hanging from it. On her breast, she wore two swags of rare coloured glass beads and in the centre of them, a gold and silver brooch set with red garnets.

Eanfrith was equally richly dressed, with a finely woven purple overshirt, Oswald knew that purple was the most expensive of dyes, worn only by kings. It was embroidered on either side of the v-shaped neck around the collar, cuffs and at the hem, with rich gold and silver thread. At his waist, he wore a broad leather belt with a magnificent enamel and gold buckle. Attached to it was a bone-handled short seax, beautifully inlaid with gold wire, all of which befitted the heir of the royal Bernician King, Æthelfrith.

They exchanged gold rings, which sealed the betrothal contract after which their priest gave his blessing and prayed over them sprinkling holy water upon their heads and anointing them with oil.

In the evening, there was music, dancing and feasting under the stars. Oswald didn't think that he had ever seen Eanfrith look so happy and he was happy for him. Perhaps this would be the making of him and once and for all settle his insecurities.

Whatever Oswald's doubts, he had to say he'd enjoyed the whole occasion, not least the time spent with Helen.

On the morning of their departure, he begged his leave of Helen, saying he must spend some time with his sister Æbbe before he left. Helen understood and reluctantly let him go, she knew that the moment she was dreading was all but upon them.

Oswald found Æbbe sitting by the fort well, she saw him coming and smiled.

'Thank you Swald, I thought that you'd forgotten me and were going without saying goodbye.'

'Now, would I do that to my baby sister, though in truth you are not a baby now.'

'You will always be my Swald. I wanted to talk more to you about your newfound faith. You can't know how my heart sang as you shared your story on the day past. The more you talked the more I wanted to hear. You left something burning in me and I wanted to know this Christ God too.'

'It is not a secret for only a few, but it is a gift, free for all. I can't explain it Æbbe, you can tell this God just how you feel, and He will answer you, I promise. When I return you can tell me your story, for I know this God will have spoken to you.'

She could only stare at him in disbelief. 'Is that really the truth? But I must have to do something to please this God!'

'No, believe me, all you need to do is ask, that will please Him more than you can imagine. As I have said, it is His personal gift for you, Æbbe. Come wave goodbye to me then find a quiet place and talk to Him. You can talk to Him at any – time or any – where, but sometimes we have to be in a quiet place to hear Him.'

He took her hand and they walked down to the shore and the awaiting curragh. Helen was already there, she saw him coming and she wiped her face on her sleeve. Oswiu was there with Queen Bebba, as was Cedric and Hrodulf. This was a hellish moment; it could be two years until his return.

He released Æbbe's hand and went to Helen, she tried to smile, but as he tenderly touched her cheek with the back of his hand she burst into tears and clung to him sobbing uncontrollably. Even Cedric was moved to gently lay his gnarled old hand on her shoulder.

'Go Lord, I will take care of the Princess,' she released Oswald and leaned into Cedric's arms. Oswald hesitated for what seemed like forever, turned, and waded into the water. He paused for a moment longer then clambered into the curragh, steadied himself, reached over the side, took Oswiu's hand and helped him onboard.

Once again, there was the familiar sudden jerk as the little craft was freed from the wet sand to begin its wearisome journey back to Iona.

Oswald saw Helen turn her head, but she was unable to wave.

The fort at Bebbanburg 600 AD

Chapter 13

Call to Arms

Oswald had adopted some of the monk's ways during his time spent amongst them, it was unavoidable. But now he found that he sought out time on his own to reflect on his Christian God, and what following Him might mean for his future. Being born into a royal family had responsibilities and duties that could not be swept aside by personal desires. He owed his allegiance to Bernicia and Eanfrith, but what a joy it would be to be free from these burdens. The monk's practice of solitude and meditation allowed a person to just "Be" – what a liberation that was.

He'd discovered fishing; though he'd been brought up by the sea he'd never bothered before, but now he understood that such an occupation was well suited to solitude and thought, and the early morning was ideal for the purpose. He narrowed his eyes as the bright sunlight glinted off the smooth golden surface of the water drifting lazily in and out of the rocky inlet where he was fishing. There was a slight haze this morning as the night air was warmed by the early sun. His peaceful contemplation was ended when he heard someone call his name, he turned to see Aidan walking with some haste towards him and waving something in his hand. Oswald laid his fishing pole down and stood, shading his eyes with his hand, he tried to see what Aidan was waving with such urgency.

Aidan and Oswald had become close friends over the last years. Aidan was older, but that didn't seem to make any difference. At first it had, in the beginning Oswald was a little intimidated by him, thinking Aidan aloof, but he discovered that Aidan was in fact shy and preferred to be quiet, actually *needing* time on his own. The years together had slowly moulded them into a pair who understood each other, and their friendship had deepened.

'Brother Aidan,' he called, 'why such haste at this early hour?'

'The Abbot has had some news, and I was told to bring it to you with all haste,'

'News!'

'Yes, from Dunadd, a boat towing a barge loaded with timber arrived last night they unloaded and brought this document, but it never reached the Abbot until this morning he'd spent the night in prayer and fasting. He has only the hour past read it and sent me with it for your immediate attention.'

'Sit down my friend, it must be of some importance to take you from your early morning vigil.'

Aidan slumped down on the rock and passed the parchment to him wiped his brow and lay back, propped up by his arms.

Oswald took it, sat next to him, and unfolded the missive.

'Mmm,' he frowned as he read it. 'I am to return to Dunadd. Finachnae mac Báetáin [19] some called him Fiachnae Lurgan; High King of all Dalriada [21] is raising an army to attack King Edwin at Bebbanburg. I know of this High King, but I've never seen him, he was a constant thorn in my father's side.'

'Yes, I know of him too, he comes from the north-east of Hibernia my homeland and is part of the same family as King Eochaid Buide here in Alba, which is all part of the one kingdom of Dalriada. The Abbot told me that he thinks that your brother Eanfrith will see this as an opportunity to rid himself of the usurper King Edwin, regain his throne and take the gospel to Bernicia.'

'Mmm, I imagine so,' Oswald pondered, wondering what implications this would have for him. As far as he knew, he'd never met his uncle Edwin and had to confess to a certain curiosity about the man. He couldn't help wondering if his uncle knew the tale of his parentage and what had become of the great Wulfstan and Queen Aefre.

'Wulfstan and Aefre,' he spoke softly their names and felt suddenly – unaccountably sad for this mysterious couple that had lost their lives because they'd loved each other.

'The Abbot sent me; the curragh is yet waiting to take you to Dunadd. If you wish to go with them, you must make haste.'

'I must go, if this is truly a chance to regain our lost kingdom, we are bound to take it. I'm not sure that will be how King Lurgan sees it. Why would he risk his men for our sake? I doubt Eanfrith has given that question much thought.'

'I cannot say, but Oswald... I would counsel you to be cautious, the High King is powerful, and I've heard he's cunning.'

Both rose to their feet, Oswald paused for a moment and stared out to sea, turned, nodded to Aidan and they set off towards the monastery at some pace, leaving his fishing pole where he had laid it. So, *this* was how it was to be, called into service to restore a kingdom of flesh and blood rather than the kingdom of his new master. How quickly the peacefulness of contemplation is broken when a war is declared.

'Oswiu must come too; we will pack quickly and go. I wish you were coming Aidan,' Oswald added as they walked. 'Who knows when we will meet again?'

'*God* does my friend, He knows everything He is never surprised,' Aidan said stumbling as he stepped on a stone with his bare foot. 'Unlike me,' Oswald caught his arm and steadied him.

'I should not imagine that an army would wait for the two of us even though we are Princes of Bernicia. Will you explain to all our friends here, especially Brother Darragh, that we did not have time to say farewell?' Oswald asked puffing.

'Don't be anxious, my friend – I will attend to everything – never fear. You must go now, or you will not reach Dunadd before dark.'

Oswald rushed into their rooms shouting for his brother. 'Oswiu, Oswiu,' Oswiu ran into the building behind him.

'What's happened? I was outside in the garden and I heard you shouting.'

Oswald stopped halfway up the stone steps to their rooms, '*Oswiu*, thank God, come, pack your possessions, as quick as you can I will tell you as we go.'

Oswiu did as he was bidden without question and followed Oswald up the stairs to their rooms. They began to fill bags with their clothes and belongings. Finally, Oswald took a deep breath, and buckled his sword to his side.

Aidan was at the door as they came out loaded with their bundles and he embraced them both.

'Can you manage, do you need me to carry anything?'

'No, no, it's not far to the shore Aidan, we will be alright.'

'I will, pray for you both, I promise you. May God go with you and be assured of my *daily* prayers.'

'Thank you, Aidan, I will miss you. Come, Oswiu, down to the beach, Aidan says the curragh is waiting.'

Aidan nodded, 'GO.'

The two ran with their belongings the short distance down to the curragh. When they reached it, they waded into the water, the boat was already bobbing free of the shore.

They threw their belongings onboard and clambered in after them. No sooner were the two of them onboard, then the men pushed the curragh away from the beach with their oars and the sail was hoisted. It was instantly filled with an obliging gust of wind from the lee, which blew them into the open bay and away from the rocky outcrop.

'Now, are you going to tell me what this is all about brother?'

'Sit down and steady yourself first…' Oswiu seated himself as Oswald instructed, leaning back against the side. Oswald sat opposite him. 'King Finachnae mac Báetáin, do you know him?'

'I'm not sure, should I?'

'He's the High King of Dalriada from Hibernia.'

'Ahhh yes... I thought I'd heard the name before; didn't he fight against father?'

'Yes, that's him, he must be at Dunadd, we'll know better by nightfall. He is preparing warriors to march on Bebbanburg.'

'Will he want the sons of King Æthelfrith with him?'

'That was my first thought too. I suspect that he hopes that it might be to some advantage to having us with him when it comes to conquering the Bernician people and the fort at Bebbanburg. I doubt that he does it to restore the kingdom to the sons of his old enemy, if that's what Eanfrith expects and it may well be. Eanfrith wants Bernicia and that might cloud any clear thinking. We will just have to wait and see. I suspect that we'll have little choice either way.'

There were many ships of various sizes along the shore when they arrived at An-Crionan, but there was no one there to welcome the little craft this time as it ran up the beach, apart from the odd guard. Oswald was first over the side leaping into the shallow water. Oswiu passed their belongings down to him, and then he too jumped from the curragh. They bade farewell to the men in the boat and made haste to the fort as best they could with their load, leaving the crew to secure the boat.

The guards at the gate recognised Oswald and Oswiu, so they were able to run into the fort unimpeded. They ran up the steps onto the highest level where they knew Eanfrith was most likely to be. There were warriors everywhere, laughing, talking, eating and drinking. Oswald was thankful that he could now at least understand their Hibernian tongue; he could see that such ability would be a great advantage if they were indeed to travel together and attack the Bernician capital.

'Where is Prince Eanfrith?' Oswald called to the first person he recognised, who happened to be the Briton Daffyd who Cedric had befriended; he was at this moment leaving the dunghole.

'Prince *Oswald!*' Daffyd looked surprised, 'Prince Eanfrith is in the longhouse, Lord, where I'm going,' he pointed. 'Come, I'll take you.' Daffyd signalled to a slave, the man came to him and Daffyd told him to see that the Prince's bundles were put somewhere that was safe for the moment. The slave bowed and Oswald and Oswiu passed him their belongings.

'Stay with them,' Oswald commanded him.

'*Oswald*, brother, good tidings, is it not,' Eanfrith rose unsteadily from his seat on seeing his two brothers entering the longhouse. 'I am delighted to see you, what do you make of this good news, brother? An invasion, all that we hoped for.' Eanfrith was in good humour, clearly the worse for ale; he even embraced Oswald and Oswiu. '*Ale* for these noble Bernicians,' he called out.

There were many new faces unknown to Oswald and Oswiu. Ale was passed to them and Eanfrith began to introduce them to the nobles around him. 'More good news too, I am to be a father, the gods have blessed me, a future king for
Bernicia. What do you say to that?'

'The *gods*... What about your new faith?'

'Ahhh, who cares about the Christian God?'

Oswald looked at Oswiu but said nothing. He hoped that Eanfrith might be in a more reflective frame of mind on the morrow.

Oswald guessed that King Finachnae mac Báetáin was the giant flame-haired warrior surrounded by several important looking men, amongst them King Conadd Cerr and King Eochaid Buide. Oswald knew they would be stirring up the blood of warriors ready for the fight, with stories of great deeds of valour, and the promise of riches for all.

Oswald asked Eanfrith if Hrodulf and Cedric had been told of the gathering, Eanfrith said that they had been sent for and he expected them any day, probably on the morrow.

The place was mayhem, the noise was deafening, and it had apparently been like this for days.

'You stay here Oswiu; I'm going to see if I can find Princess Helen,' Oswald shouted. 'Don't get drunk, you are not used to strong ale any more than me. Remember how you felt that night on Coll when mother was laid to rest.'

Oswiu nodded, 'I shall not forget that in a hurry, I would have welcomed death's merciful hand, but it never came.'

Oswald could see how easy it would be to get caught up with the atmosphere in the hall this night and live to regret it the next day. Oswald shrugged, resigned to what would be, he was about to leave the hall having asked several warriors and servants if they knew where Princess Helen was, when he spotted her sitting alone against the wall with her head between her legs.

'Helen, what's the matter girl?' she looked up, giving him a glazed look of utter bewilderment.

She looked flushed and was sweating, he realised that she'd been one of the innocents who'd been swept along by the euphoria of the coming adventure.

'Oswald,' she said as he tugged her to her feet, slung her over his shoulder and carried her into the yard to the well, ducking her headfirst into a barrel of water. Her arms flayed wildly at the indignation and she struck him in the mouth with her fist, he immediately tasted the metallic tang of blood on his tongue.

The shock of near drowning was enough to bring her abruptly to her senses.

'Swald… they said you were here I never saw you,' Æbbe ran at him and almost knocked him over, fortunately he managed to brace himself in time to withstand the impact.

'Oswald,' Helen said once more, he and Æbbe knelt down next to her and she wrapped her arms around his neck, then pushed him from her, was violently sick, and collapsed into a heap on the ground sobbing and groaning as she held her stomach. He dipped a corner of her shawl into the barrel, sat by her side, rested her head on his lap and tenderly wiped her mouth and face. Once again, she clung to him and renewed her sobbing. He was content to hold her until she had calmed. Æbbe could do no more than look on unsure how to assist her brother.

'Oswald, I'm *so* sorry, I feel so ill.'

'I think that it's normal, but you will recover. There will be many who will feel as you do on the morrow, aye and far worse.'

'I do love you Oswald, I'm so pleased to see you, but I am ashamed for you to see me so.'

'I'm sure you are, it's not the welcome I'd expected, but don't worry I'm yet happy to see you,' and he smiled as he lifted her from the ground, cradling her in his arms. He carried her to her roundhouse, the place was empty, and he laid her on the first bed he found.

'Stay here, I will bring a maid to watch over you. You wait with her Æbbe, until I return.'

'Don't *leave* me Oswald!'

'I must, I will return in a short while, your father and brother will kill me if I'm found here alone with you,' he said looking down at this girl with totally different eyes, she was no longer a girl, but an extraordinarily beautiful woman, and she – loved – him.

Once Oswald was satisfied that Helen was safe, and cared for, he went to find Oswiu and was relieved to see that his experience on Coll had been remembered after all. It was a different story with Eanfrith; he was now laid under the table where Oswiu was seated.

'He's well enough Oswald,' Oswiu reassured him; I dragged him under the table for his own safety.

It was a greatly chastened Princess Helen Oswald was presented with the next morning. Oswald and Oswiu were among the rare early risers, there was food aplenty and they ate heartily before Oswald made his way to Helen's roundhouse.

The Princess was seated on a stool before her maid looking none too pleased to have a comb dragged through her tangled hair. She saw Oswald as he entered but cast her eyes to her feet.

Oswald crouched down before her and looked up into her face.

'What must you think of me?' She said in a low quiet voice.

He took her hands in his, 'I think that I love you.'

She smiled, shook free of her maid and hugged him.

Chapter 14

Siege

The army made good time as it travelled southeast from Dunadd, Oswald and Oswiu had kept well clear of the leaders for most of the journey. Oswald settled in his mind that he would let Eanfrith enjoy all the adulation of being the Lord and King of the Bernicians. He didn't long for or need any of that kind of thing; he knew such was a fickle measure on which to base one's self-worth. He and Oswiu had both been made known to the High King and that was enough for them.

Oswald was as yet unsure of the High King's true intention – for the present – he would be satisfied with watching and listening, Brother Ségéne had always told him that it was no accident that God had given man two eyes, two ears and only *one* mouth. Clearly, the Christian God hoped that man should do twice as much looking and listening as talking.

The army was assembled for the night on the edge of the great purple moor with a view all the way down to the coast and Bebbanburg; it must be all of twenty leagues, thought Oswald. The view was magnificent and said all there was to say about why his heart loved this place.

There was much talking and good spirited humour amongst the warriors as they sat in their small groups. For this night, Oswald would be content to sit quietly rubbing his sharpening stone along the edge of his Ulfberht. He spat onto the stone once more, paused, and glanced up at Cedric, who was seated a little way from him with his forearm resting on his raised knee and his back against a large rock. He munched slowly and deliberately on an apple whilst gazing into the distance towards his home where he'd lived since, he was a boy. The last six years away from his home he had only tolerated. Oswald tried to imagine what he was thinking. Every so often, he noticed that Cedric would massage his left arm and flex his fingers. Clearly, he was in some discomfort. Oswald wondered if he'd injured it on the way here, at least it wasn't his sword arm, which might have been a real problem. Men were going to die in a very short time and that would be all the more likely if a warrior was carrying an injury, especially in his sword arm.

Cedric being Cedric, he would never make a fuss over a simple pulled muscle, if that was what indeed it was, but it was clearly troubling him it hadn't been the first time Oswald had seen him doing this. He'd been quiet and at times irritable on the journey east, not like his usual self, for some reason he preferred to keep his own company.

Oswald had tried several times to engage him in conversation, but to no avail. In the end, he had left him in peace, but there was something disturbing him of that Oswald was *absolutely* sure. Oswald was far too close to him not to notice this strange uncharacteristic behaviour.

Oswald had asked Hrodulf if he knew what was troubling his friend, Hrodulf had merely shrugged his shoulders.

'Who knows, you know Cedric, he's not one to complain. He'll be fine, don't worry Lord, it's been a long journey and he's no young chicken, I'd guess he's tired as I am.'

'Mmm,' Oswald knew all that Hrodulf said was true, but it didn't satisfy him. No longer was Cedric the indestructible warrior of former days; it didn't take much exertion these days before he was panting like a winded old nag. Their roles were reversed now, Oswald wasn't exactly sure to a day when it had happened, but it for sure had happened.

He would watch out for Cedric, as Cedric had always watched out for him. That would be Oswald's work for the rest of Cedric's days, but Oswald knew that he would need all the skills and sensitivity he learned from his friend Aidan on Iona, to carry out that occupation with any measure of success. He knew without the *slightest* doubt Cedric would be at the *very* best difficult, if he thought that he was a burden to *anyone*, never mind to Oswald.

'He shouldn't have come Hrodulf, I tried to tell him, but I knew as I was speaking to him, I was wasting my breath. He was coming home to his "Din Guyaroi", as he ever insisted calling it, and that was the end of it.'

'I didn't even *try* to dissuade him Lord; we have been as one man for so long, if he is cut, I will bleed, and it is the same for him. That's just how it is when warriors become as close as we have been over the years, and closeness is invaluable in battle. So, I know when to speak and when not to waste my time.'

'This I do ask of you Hrodulf, stay close to Oswiu and me, once we set off on the morrow, I want him near me every moment.'

'Do you really need to tell Cedric and me such a thing? We will die by your side. I thought you knew that,' and he slapped Oswald's back and he laughed. 'Awe, don't fret yourself, I understand your meaning.'

'Well, let us hope and pray that it doesn't come to anyone dying.'

It was a cool clear night and there were a million stars dancing in the heavens. Oswald could only stare in wonder at God's creation, as he lay with his head resting on his rolled-up saddle blanket. God had spoken, and it was so, that is what the scriptures said. Oswald prayed that the creator God, who had brought so much to life, would be with them on the morrow in the battlefield where they would be faced with taking life away from his countrymen. Would the Christian God protect a warrior in battle? He had been confident that Wōden would.

He knew he must get some sleep, no one knew what the morrow held for them, but it would be all the better faced if they were not tired, and to that end he pulled his thick cloak over his head, prayed, and thought of Helen's tears when he'd left Dunadd.

She'd begged him not to go, but that was never a possibility, and he guessed, in her heart of hearts, she knew that, but it had been a difficult parting for both of them, nevertheless. God willing, when he returned, they would marry.

There was a fine mist when he awoke, not *too* bad, it would burn off once the sun got up, but it was enough to wet the belongings they'd left unprotected.

Oswald shivered as he pushed the damp cloak from his face, sat up, stretched and yawned. He was glad that he'd wrapped his sword in the waxed cloth he'd brought for the purpose. He'd never used his father's sword in a real battle, but Brother Ségéne said he was a born warrior, and that he'd never known anyone with his natural ability. Oswald knew that the next few days might prove the truth or lie of that high praise.

They ate the last of their dried meat; there were no fires, they didn't want to take the risk of being seen by any of the Bernicians loyal to Edwin, though none really believed their presence would have escaped the ears of King Edwin, no, Edwin would know.

Cedric was slow to rise, Oswald was watching him like a hawk, but no one made any comment. Oswald noted that he'd slept in his mail and wasn't sure how to read that, perhaps he wanted to be prepared for a surprise attack – or – more likely he was too weary to remove it and didn't want to have to go through the trauma of having to put it on this morning, exhausting his now limited recourses of energy.

'Remember, stay close to me young Prince and learn how a real man fights,' was Cedric's morning greeting. He actually smiled as he mounted his pony, which pleased Oswald. Oswald returned his smile and led his pony to where Cedric was waiting, he tapped Cedric's leg and beckoned him with a twitch of his finger, and Cedric leant down to him.

'How do you feel about making war on our own people, Cedric?' Oswald whispered.

'I will be fighting warriors who want to stop me entering my home, they will never be the Bernicians, I know.'

'That's one way of looking at it I suppose, I'll try to keep that in mind, though with a little effort, I may be able to pick holes in that argument.'

'Aye, I dare say, but you would be wise to heed my advice, you don't need confusion in your head when someone's about to gut you.'

Oswald smiled and nodded. He and Oswiu mounted their ponies and fell in behind Cedric and Hrodulf, as they headed down the long sloping road to the sea and Bebbanburg. It would be midday before they reached to coast, no point in rushing, Edwin would see them coming.

It was King Finachnae mac Báetáin's intention to assault the fortress from the south seaward side; the walls were lower there. No doubt, Eanfrith had suggested that approach, but as they neared the beach, Oswald felt pangs of uncertainty about the decision, for there was little cover.

The fortress looked fearfully imposing before them as they dismounted. Oswald wondered if they would camp and attack on the morrow, but no, there was a sudden yell and the warriors began to run with pole ladders towards the wooden walls. Oswald was compelled to run with them and was no more than a pace behind Cedric. He couldn't help noticing Cedric's erratic gate, he was staggering and stumbling, he looked as if his legs were out of control, he would fall any moment, Oswald was certain.

Another yell went up, 'SHIELDS,' it sounded even more frantic than the first, not a second too soon. The ladders were instantly abandoned as a cloud of arrows rained death upon them. Some were not quick enough and fell with the look of hedgehogs. Cedric fell head first into the sand, unable to raise his shield, but by some miracle, he was only struck with one arrow, a flesh wound in his shoulder, nothing serious.

Oswald, Oswiu and Hrodulf leapt as one to cover him with their shields. They stayed covered by their large war shields until the deluge ceased. Cedric never moved. Oswald dragged his arm from the straps of his shield.

'*Quick*, turn him over,' they did as Oswald said and Oswald rested Cedric's head on his lap, Cedric's lips were purple, he slightly opened his eyes and smiled at Oswald.

'It's over son...' he spoke in a whisper. His voice was so quiet Oswald had to press his ear to his lips to hear him, but then the words were only for him anyway. 'Never was a father prouder of a son,' his said in a whisper, he paused and gave a shallow gasp. 'You may not be my flesh and blood, but you're my son, right enough,' he coughed, and a trickle of blood ran from the corner of his mouth, 'there will be more than me laid out in this sand afore the day's end, but I'm happy to lie here son. Mind – don't lie me next to one of them monk priests from Iona,' and he smiled weakly, coughed once more, closed his eyes, his lips moved, but there was no sound – it was over… Oswald was trembling, his teeth were chattering, he couldn't control himself.

Suddenly another cry went up, 'BEHIND US.'

Oswald shook his head and stared with disbelief, there seemed to be hundreds of warriors coming at them from out of the sand dunes. They turned as quickly as they could and tried to form some sort of shieldwall, but it was hopeless, King Edwin's men were upon them. The half-formed shieldwalls fell apart, it was hand-to-hand fighting, Oswald and Hrodulf stood shoulder to shoulder and another warrior leapt next to them, it was Daffyd, and the three of them stood back to back and formed a triangle with Oswiu and Cedric in the middle. All Oswald's training and natural talent were needed for this; his first blooding. They fought for more than two hours; the sand was red with blood.

Eventually, Edwin's men began to lose ground. The four comrades had never moved from the spot, the dead were heaped around them. Finally, the Dalriadans began to take control of the ground and Edwin's men were forced to turn tail and run, but King Finachnae mac Báetáin had paid a terrible price for his rash assault on the fort.

He didn't know what this feeling was, was it grief, or exhaustion? Who could tell, but Oswald knelt, clasped Cedric's hand, pressed his forehead to his chest, and wept.. Hrodulf crouched next to Oswald put his arm around him and wept too.

All their vain hopes dashed in a single afternoon. After all the distance that they'd travelled, it was over in just *one* afternoon's fighting. Oswald could not believe the stupidity or was it the arrogance of kings who believed their own lies, that they were wiser, and divinely greater than mere mortal men and certain their gods would be on their side because even they were dazzled by their greatness. That bloody lie, yes, and *bloody* lie it is, this red sandy ground bears witness to that truth, and is here for all to see how noble kings stand humbled by their vanity. Let them, who profess such nobility, fall prostrate before those who are subject to them, or at the very least hang their heads upon their chests in shame.

The darkness had lowered her sombre cloak upon this day's malediction, before Oswald was able to take in the true scale of the catastrophe. He didn't know how long he'd been sitting there. He'd never moved from Cedric's side he and Hrodulf were both seated together on the sand, simply staring at the body of their dead friend, oblivious to the hell world around them. Oswald looked up and saw Eanfrith talking to Oswiu; he'd never given him a thought until this moment, but on seeing him, he was glad that he had survived, though at this moment he may well wish himself dead. There were groups of warriors all around standing talking, clearly almost as dazed as he was.

The next day was spent digging graves for some innocents to find in years to come and wonder why so many bodies were buried there. The truth of the forgotten graves would be that history had not time to record the slaughter upon her slate, so fleeting was the moment.

Oswald and Hrodulf laid Cedric to rest, and Oswald lashed two pieces of driftwood together to make a cross, and hung upon it the Thor's hammer, which Cedric always wore around his neck. Oswald remembered Cedric saying that he would let the gods decide who welcomed him into their hall; it was all down to their charity in the end.

It would be as he wished, but Oswald would pray a Christian prayer that one day he would have a proper grave in a Christian holy place, and there he would rest until the final day of resurrection. [23]

The Dalriadans withdrew to safer ground to decide on the future of the expedition. It was decided by the kings that their numbers had been so depleted that any chance of victory was now hopeless.

Eanfrith stormed out of the tent, he was furious, cursing and swearing, and slashing with his sword at anything in his way. Oswald was concerned and understood
Eanfrith's utter frustration and the despair that he felt, at possibly never regaining his kingdom.

Oswald would go to him when he'd calmed and endeavour to inject some hope into his despair.

Chapter 15

The Unforgiving Master

Before Oswald this day was a more subdued band of warriors than the ones he had seen, but a few days past, in the great hall at Dunadd. Those warriors were drinking and feasting, they were giants amongst mere mortals; nothing could ever bring those warriors to their knees.

It was *difficult* to believe that these bedraggled specimens of mankind; *he* was now a *part* of, were the same people. It was a heart-breaking, miserable sight, to see these defeated and broken shadows setting their foot on the road back to Dunadd and shame.

These three kings were not carrying gifts heralding the birth of a new and glorious kingdom; they were not even riding near to each other. This disaster had driven resolute wedges of blame and contempt between them.

Then there was Eanfrith… poor Eanfrith; Oswald's heart reached out to him, for he wore the heavy mantle of rejection, even his own people hated him, or he thought it to be so. In the evening he sat alone, he was at this moment no more than the feral wolf, separated from the pack, left to die, knowing that he was not wanted and detested by all. He was the embodiment of their tribulation, the living-breathing reminder of their tormentor, the *King* of *Bernicia*.

Oswald tried several times to talk to him, but Eanfrith didn't want his comfort at any price. He saw Oswald's attempt at kindness as no more than cynical mockery, delighting in his suffering. Oswald thought it the saddest thing for a human being to actually think he deserved the cruel treatment he was given. Wasn't that a lie to be fought in the heads of the followers of the Christ – that they were unworthy of forgiveness and redemption? He knew that one thief on his cross at Calvary had accepted Christ's forgiveness and the other rejected it.

Both might well have deserved all that was meted out to them, "But" that was not the issue, the issue was, were they prepared to receive the undeserving forgiveness that the Christ God was offering? Only one of the two thieves were humble enough to reach out and take the gift.

Always a simple choice, the two trees in the garden, good or evil, light or darkness, truth or lies, life or death, Barabbas or Jesus. Brother Ségéne said that all down through the ages God yet offered man that simple choice, the Christ God, or the world.

Eanfrith simply could not grasp hold of that hope. He could not, or would not, see the mutilated hand of the Christ God reaching out to him, and was content to wallow in the misery of his human condition.

Oswald recalled that Brother Ségéne had often said, failure put a man on his knees, but defeat left a man face down in the dirt. Not only Eanfrith was in such a place of desolation at this moment, it was the condition of the whole army.

Those who were yet able, would have to raid and forage as they went on their way, and pray God, that they showed mercy to those who could no longer fend for themselves. Oswald knew that victory had many fathers, but defeat was an orphan.

All had been brothers as they travelled south, but now Oswald saw only orphans without any family connection to the land of milk and honey. It had not yielded its riches to these warriors from the north, not – as they'd expected. There was no milk, for the pasture had been scorched by the heat of man's impulsive folly, and the honeybees searched in vain for a flower, which had not been corrupted by the stench of fresh blood.

Oswald wondered if King Edwin had any idea whatsoever that his nephew had been at the gates of his fortress, or if he even knew of his existence.

Out of the blue Oswald wanted to know every detail of the lives of his mother and father, Aefre and Wulfstan, but it was too late, their tale had been laid to rest with Cedric, now no one would ever know the truth, it would be hidden in the folds of the shroud we call history.

The mighty fort of Bebbanburg was yet clearly in view when Oswald drew his pony to a standstill, he stared at the reins in his hands resting on the upstand of his saddle. Oswiu came to him.

'What ails you brother, you're not carrying some hurt are you?'

Oswald lifted his head and stared at him.

'Hurt…? Aye, and deeper than any slash from a war axe, or even from the keen edge of an Ulfberht.'

Oswiu nodded slowly with heartfelt understanding, 'You refer to Cedric; I take it, brother?'

'Aye – Cedric – and I have had a hundred other nicks to my heart these past days. This is our home Oswiu, this is where we belong, these are our people, and we may never see this place or them – again. The pain is hellish, and it consumes me.'

'Is there a problem, Lord?' Hrodulf's voice broke innocently into Oswald's grief, lacking any awareness of his condition at this moment.

Oswald responded without turning to him,

'I'm going back, Hrodulf!'

'Back…back where? Not to Bebbanburg!'

'Aye.'

'No Lord, I forbid it,' and Hrodulf snatched the reins from Oswald's hand startling Oswald's pony, which skittered and tugged at the rein.

'You forbid it! I must, I need to be alone and say goodbye. I will soon be with you again, fear not, but I must do this.'

'No, I cannot allow it, if you go, I'm going with you, Lord.' Hrodulf's pony twisted and turned as if it was part of his anxiety.

'You are a good man Hrodulf, but I need to do this and do it alone,' and he gently reached across and withdrew the reins from Hrodulf's hand.

'Lord – I beg you not to take part in such folly…'

'Did you not hear me? I have got to, Hrodulf.'

'If that be your resolve, I will wait here until you return. I will give you one day only – then I will come for you. If you place any worth on my miserable hide, you will return before the day is out. Let that consequence be upon your conscience.'

'You are a rebellious huscarl to threaten your Lord and master so unashamedly, but if you insist, so be it.'

'Hrodulf's right Oswald, it is foolishness, but I do understand. I will wait here too; remember Eanfrith and me, and what about Helen, how would your careless folly satisfy her? At the very least think of her, if your thoughts extend to no other.'

'I must do this, for the very reasons you say I should not. I'll return, you can pray for me, Oswiu. Remember that incredible gift that is ever at hand.'

With that, he tugged on the reins, the little pony resisted but for a second, and then obediently turned back towards the fort.

Oswald walked his pony in the shallow water as it rolled gently up the sand. Though he could readily see the fort over his left shoulder, there was no sign of any action that might endanger him. They were sure to have seen him. He wondered if the very boldness of his lone appearance caused them to suppose that this was some sort of trick. Perhaps they thought his mount was not flesh and blood but a wooden horse, the like of the beast in Helen's tale of a horse filled with men about to sneak into the fort and overwhelm them. For whatever reason, there was no sign of activity, threatening or otherwise.

He rode to the far end of the beach to the black rocks, dismounted and sat down upon them. He stared at his home, never blinking, as if trying to burn the sight before him into his thought world, every slope, tuft of grass and stone, imprinted forever. When he was satisfied, he mounted and rode once again along the beach, past the fort and on into the dunes to the holy place where his dearest friend lay. He slipped from his pony and quietly knelt by the grave for some time, and finally he closed his eyes and began to pray…

'Fæder ure þu þe eart on heofonum… [24]

Hallowed be thy name, Thy kingdom come, Thy will be done, on earth as it is in heaven. Give us this day – our daily bread and forgive us our wrong-doings as much as we forgive others. Lead us not into temptation but deliver us from the hand of the evil one, for Thine is the kingdom the power and the glory forever and ever, without end. Amen.'

He slowly opened his eyes, it was almost dark now, he didn't realise he'd knelt there for so long. The fort was slipping from his sight in every sense. He mounted once again and returned to where he'd left Oswiu and Hrodulf. They stood when they heard him, Oswiu ran to meet him, and Oswald slowed and walked his pony wearily towards them.

Every homeward step was a miserable one; the weather even reflected their misery for it rained incessantly. There were daily fights and arguments between the men. Wounded men died and sickness began to spread amongst the defeated warriors as untreated wounds became putrid and their suffering was increased.

Oswald found little comfort in that his part in the conflict had been noted and those who were witness to his courage as a warrior began to call him by the Hibernian name of Lamnguin or "Whiteblade" [25] because of the way the light flashed off the blade of his Ulfberht in the heat of battle.

At last, the fortress of Dunadd was in view, Oswald was torn as they approached. On one hand, he was pleased that he would be once more with Helen, but on the other, there would be a reckoning for their failure, maybe even war throughout Dalriada. One thing Oswald was sure of, this debacle would not obligingly drift away from the memory of the families who'd paid the ultimate cost, of the life of a loved one.

The praise and deference he was being subjected too did little more than embarrass him. That people older and with years more experience should bow to him was not right.

Hrodulf had tried to explain to him, that people were suffering unbelievably, and they needed something of worth to hang onto and identify with.

'At this time Lord, the gods have chosen that to be you, and you will have to learn to live with it. I have known men it has destroyed because they began to believe that they were above others. Guard against that Lord.'

'I hear you Hrodulf, I commission you to be the weight around my ankles.'

Hrodulf smiled, 'I think you know Lord I am equal to that task,' and he reached across to Oswald and they clasped hands.

'This will be your first test, no cheering as we enter, I notice, bad news travels faster than a straight arrow.'

If anything, Hrodulf was overestimating their welcome, women and children scuttled out of sight, fearful of what would happen now the army had returned.

King Eochaid Buide dismounted and looked around the yard, eventually a stable boy came hesitantly to take the rein of his horse. On another day, the King would have severely upbraided the boy for his tardiness, but today he merely handed the reins to him and said naught.

Oswald looked around, expecting to see Helen; she must surely know they had returned… he twisted in his saddle, she was there, a door only just opened, and he saw her beckon him. For the flash of a single moment he forgot all about his aches and pains, he swung his leg over his pony's head and slid his bottom from the saddle. Glanced around the faces of the jaded warriors and made his way casually to the roundhouse. The door opened before him and closed as if by magic and he felt her lips press to his. Oswald wrapped his arms around her, and she pressed close to him arching her back. He tenderly kissed her throat and she melted as she felt the tension of days of anxiety fall away from her. They had spoken not a word of greeting; their lips said all there was to say. Helen laid her head against his chest.

'I have missed you my beautiful warrior, thank God He saw fit to wrap you in His arms and keep you safe.'

'It was hellish Helen; the whole adventure was a disaster from the moment we got to Bebbanburg.'

'We know, riders came the day past and told us, but we were also told of our new hero for all to sing of in new spun ballads.'

'Hero!'

'Oswald of Bernicia you fool, he was all the messengers could talk of once they made known to us the terrible losses. This Oswald killed one hundred warriors by himself, they were but flies before his "Whiteblade", so we were told.'

He laughed without humour; 'the number has doubled since we left Bebbanburg.' She could only smile troubled by his sad face.

The laughter quickly drained from Oswald's face when he spoke… 'Cedric died.'

She pressed her hands against his chest pushing from him to arm's length and stared into his face in horror.

'NO, not Cedric, my dearest, dearest, beloved,' she drew herself to him once more, wrapping her arms around his neck and pressed her cheek to his. 'I am so sorry, he was your father, I know the love between you. What happened, were you there?' She took his hand and they sat on some sacks of grain, 'Tell me, this is so sad.'

He leant forward resting his elbows on his knees and hung his head. Helen pressed close to him gripping his arm.

'Yes… I was there, I was following him, we were running up the sand dunes, it was utter folly, it all just happened. It was exhausting, even my legs were on fire, and then to make things worse they released a hail of arrows that fell from the sky like a black cloud of death. One struck his shoulder, but it was only a flesh wound, nothing really, it barely broke his skin. Suddenly he began to stagger and stumble, it was most odd, and then he suddenly folded forward into a heap…'

Oswald's voice trailed off to a tear-filled whisper as his emotions took control of the vivid memories. He paused… taking a deep breath to steady his voice and then he shakily continued. 'He couldn't go on, Helen, he tried to raise himself, but he couldn't, he tried, he really tried Helen, but he just couldn't. My hero, who I thought could do anything, couldn't even raise his head. All he had left was said with a soft sigh, "It's over, son".'

Oswald cupped his face in his hands and sobbed, Helen hugged him and cried too.

After a time, Oswald wiped his face on his sleeve and took another juddering deep breath before he spoke again. 'Thank you, Helen, I thank you for your love. I daily thank God for you. You have been here for me from the very first night I arrived, that is a very precious thing.'

'Not really, I knew I was going to marry a hero, who slew two hundred giants with a single flash of his blade,' she nudged him and smiled.

Oswald smiled at her attempt to bring some cheer to him and he kissed her once more. Helen released him and lay back on the sacks and Oswald looked down at her.

'Will you marry me? Princess Helen of Dalriada.'

'I will, Oswald Leodwalding of Bernicia.'

'I shall have to speak with your father and perhaps Eanfrith, but first I want to return to Iona and see Brother Ségéne and Abbot Fergno, would you mind if I did that?'

'Not at all, but I'm afraid we have had news that Abbot Fergno has passed away. Brother Ségéne is now the Abbot.'

'Really, this is a time of great change, Brother... But Abbot Ségéne forever would say to me, that God never awakes in the morning and is surprised by the day's events.'

Oswald had talked to Princess or *Queen* Edlin, as Eanfrith insisted she be called, but she'd said that Eanfrith had barely spoken ten words to her since he'd returned from Bebbanburg.

Oswald tried to explain to Edlin how Eanfrith thought and why he'd felt as he did. After all, at this point in time, it must look to him as if his kingdom was gone from his reach forever, and the truth, as painful as it was, might well be that it had indeed gone forever.

It was a little easier for Oswald at this moment, because he had his forthcoming marriage to distract him, but he knew that when he reflected, as no doubt Eanfrith did, on what the future might have in store for him, and the kingdom of Bernicia, his mood was none too different to Eanfrith's miserable condition.

There were no tears this time from Helen when he set sail for Iona, as she would be fully distracted preparing for his return and their wedding. In fact, on this occasion, she nearly pushed him into the curragh. They both laughed and kissed. She waved until she could no longer see him, then she ran home.

Her cousin Queen Edlin would be like a mother to her in this time of preparation and Helen vowed she would enjoy every moment. Oswald would never regret that *she* was his wife.

Helen shared Edlin's sorrow for her husband, but Helen was sure he would get over his disappointment *and* he may well yet be King of Bernicia. It was confusing to her for Oswald had said that he was not in fact entitled to call himself King, not until the Witan, their governing assembly, had decided and to make him their King. At this time, he was no more than the de facto king, and for all his assertions, Oswald knew that Eanfrith understood that, but for now, they must all move on.

Both Oswald and Helen were surprised how quickly the adventure had been forgotten. King Finachnae mac Báetáin had returned to Hibernia, and slowly the fort was returning to something approaching normality. Oswald prayed that King Edwin might not allow his victory over the Dalriadans to make him over confident and imagine that he would attack King Eochaid Buide and conquer Dalriada. Thus, adding to his empire, but for now Oswald had other concerns he was slightly nervous about meeting his old friend, wondering if he had changed with his new position.

Chapter 16

Abbot Ségéne

Oswald leapt from the curragh, it had become a well-practiced manoeuvre, and walked, the now familiar, short distance up to the Monastery.

Once he had made his numerous greetings, to old friends, he made his way to see the *new* Abbot.

He knocked nervously on the worn oak door, just below the familiar well-polished brass cross, where countless knuckles had no doubt rapped over the years, fearing as *he* did at this moment, that they were to be admonished for some infringement of which they were *ever* guilty, being part, as they were, of God's fallen creation.

A monk opened the door just enough to see who was there.

'Ah… Prince Oswald, it's yourself then, is it not, come in, come in,' the rather small young man said with a strong Hibernian accent. 'It's a fine t'ing to see you again, so it is, you have been expected so you have.'

Oswald smiled at the young man whom he'd known and liked, for several years. The Abbot's room hadn't changed since the last time he'd been here to see Abbot Fergno.

It was plain with whitened walls and a well-polished wooden floor. There was always a sort of sweet musty smell about the place, but it was yet warm and inviting. On the wall by the door where he'd entered, hung a large wooden cross facing the Abbot's work table, which was covered, just as it was in Abbot Fergno's day, with rare books, parchments and writing materials. In the wall adjacent to the table, there was a glazed window overlooking the bay. No doubt, it served to give an inspirational, if somewhat distorted view of the world outside, for it was difficult to make out much if anything that lay beyond it, but at the very least, it provided some light for the Abbot to see his writings.

'Welcome Prince Oswald be seated,' the voice said, as the smiling face of Abbot Ségéne, [8] looked up at him. 'You may leave us brother Darragh,' the monk smiled once more at Oswald, genuflected before the cross on the wall, and left. Opening and closing the door, with such practised skill that the only sound was the faint whisper of the hem of his habit brushing over the floor.

Oswald sat on the bench in front of the table. The friendly welcoming face of the new Abbot set Oswald at his ease.

'I am delighted you could come Prince Oswald, I longed to see you and hear your news, this is the first chance we have had to talk together and renew our old friendship since your disappointing travels to your homeland. As you can see, I have now become the Abbot of Iona.'

'Should I congratulate you Father?'

The Abbot laughed, 'Too early to say my son, perhaps no one else wanted the work.'

'I know better, as do all who live and serve here. I consider that I have been fortunate during our time together to have learned much from your wise counsel.'

'You are kind; I am honoured by your generous opinion. Abbot Fergno talked a great deal about you, before he died. He had huge hopes that you might one day take the Gospel of Christ back to your own land of Bernicia. Did you know this?'

Oswald smiled. 'He made some mention of such, but I never took him seriously. It's difficult to imagine oneself as someone worthy of such godly employment, not when I am ever conscious of my failings. Next to the men of God here, with whom I have spent so much time these last years, I fear *I* would make the poorest courier of the Christian faith.'

The Abbot lifted his eyebrows but made no comment. 'How old are you now, Oswald?'

'I'm eighteen, Father.'

'It seems a long time since you first came to Iona. You were, what some may call, a pagan then.'

'Yes indeed, it all seems a lifetime since that first day. I can yet remember how anxious we all were.'

'Are you continuing as strong as ever in your faith I take it, after... what is it... six years?' The Abbot asked glancing at a parchment before him and focusing on the date written there by touching it with his forefinger. 'Though you do not come so often now, you are always welcome.'

'Thank you, Father, yes, I came here first in 617, not long after I arrived with my family at the Dalriadan court. I *should* say – I'm yet a Christian, Father, I suppose I am anyway. I have been baptised and follow the Christ's teaching. Sadly, that forever annoyed my friend and mentor. There was never a man, I would set above him as an example of how one should live one's life, save you Father,' the Abbot's eyes lit up as he smiled.

'You do me great honour to number me alongside your friend, whom you held in such high regard.'

'He was a man, who actually lived by the ideals of what *you* teach here, though he worshipped Wōden, and I doubt he would ever have seen the need to convert to a lesser, *weaker* god as he understood the Christian God.'

'A *weaker* God you say!' The Abbot asked lifting his eyebrows once more, 'I should have liked to meet such a man,' he continued with obvious sincerity.

'I would have like that too. I asked him to come several times, but he would not. He always said *he* could have taught me all I ever needed to know, and my time here was naught but to humour King Eochaid Buide and those of his Dalriadan court, and it served only that purpose, no more than that.'

Abbot Ségéne smiled, leaning back in his chair, 'and what do *you* think, Oswald of Bernicia?'

Oswald hesitated for a moment, *what did he think...* that was an interesting question... 'I have learned how to read and write, understand number and to speak Hibernian, and it is with all gratitude to you Father.' Abbot Ségéne sitting back in his chair with his hands on his chest, and his fingertips pressed together, bowed his head in acknowledgement of Oswald's kindness. 'I can see the value of such ability. I will never doubt that the Christian God is the only true God, I daily grow closer to Him, and I am told that He died for my sins, but what that means is as much of a nonsense to me as it ever was, the more I think about it the less I understand it. My friend Cedric told me that Wōden rewards us with an afterlife too, without the peculiar need to be killed and then to rise again. No one can kill Wōden in the first place, or so my friend would say. Who then is the greatest? It is said that my father Æthelfrith massacred 1200 Wealas Christian monks who had gathered to *pray* to their God against my father's victory. I don't know how truthful that number is, tales and numbers often grow with the telling.'

The Abbot smiled sadly and shrugged his shoulders. 'Yes, I remember Augustine's grim warning when he said, "if the Wealas don't wish peace with us; they shall perish at the hands of the Saxons".'

'But what does that say about the Christian God's ability to stand against the followers of Wōden? I have found that to live a life worthy of the "Great Hall", always brings respect from the best of men. Men whom I hold as good men, who have lived honourable lives, *such* is the life I would hope to live. Cedric, the friend I speak of, said that the gods could argue amongst themselves who would welcome him into their homes when his time came, there is little he could do either way, it would be down to their charity in the end.'

The Abbot listened intently, struck by Oswald's bold honesty and self-confidence. He was clearly a young man who had thought about life and was not afraid to voice his opinion, and not in a defensive arrogant way. The Abbot knew from the past, Oswald was open and equally responsive to sincerity and honesty. He would be no blind follower who believed everything he was told on face value. What was said had better stand up to the vagaries of this world. Abbot Ségéne pitied the teacher who was standing before this young man and was not teaching from a position of deep personal faith, but he'd always known that about Oswald. He was no ordinary young man; if it had been his calling, he would have been the Abbot of Iona. This young man had the mark of greatness upon him; Abbot Ségéne was not in the slightest doubt of that, and yet he was blest with the grace and humility, which would never yield such presumption.

The Abbot now leant forward, rested his elbows on the table before him, and steepled his fingers lightly against his lips, hesitating for a moment before he spoke…

'Mmm, I have it in my mind that when we face the Creator of the world to be judged, as surely the Holy Scriptures tell us that one day we will, one fellow will say, "I am a follower of Jesus," and God will ask him if he is such a man, why did he kill the innocent? Why did he steal food from the hungry? Why did he lie, cheat, and undertake all manner of calumny against his fellow man? Then the Judge of all may well say, "Depart from Me, I never knew you". There may be another who stands before God, having come through the same door as the previous fellow, for there will only ever be one way to enter into the Father's presence. That we may be able to come near to the Father was made possible at a fearful cost. He might call the Father of all by another name, for example, "Wōden", but it may just as well be a name not yet thought of, and the Father of all may see in the man's heart His own reflection, and welcome that man into His eternal presence. It is my humble opinion, for my opinion is worth no more than yours, that it is not what we say that defines us, my dear Oswald, but what we do. In the book of the most holy Saint James, it is written, in essence, what we believe in our hearts will determine how we live out our lives. Perhaps it is possible that the truth is sometimes written upon a man's heart, but he does not recognise the writer. What do you think?'

Now it was Oswald's turn to smile, 'I think my friend Cedric, the man of whom I have already spoken, would have done well to meet with you, Father, for he had said the same thing to me many times. Perhaps he worshipped the same god as you, when all is said and done.'

'Perhaps he did. I would very much like to have met this man. Now, may I ask, how are your brothers, are they men of established faith?'

'Who can truly see into the heart of another, Father, for sure I cannot?'

'Very true, my son, very true, out of the mouth of babes and children... you shame me,' the Abbot laughed heartily.

'For what it is worth, in truth I'm not sure what Eanfrith truly believes, he has been baptised, as you know, if that is the measure of a man's belief, but he never talks about his faith. Oswiu and I talk much about our new faith and our sister Æbbe loves to talk with us. She is Oswiu's full sister. We wanted her to marry Prince Domnall Brecc, King Eochaid Buide's son, so that our two royal families may be more closely bound together. Eanfrith has already married one of King Conadd Cerr's daughters, Edlin, and they now have a son, Talorcan,'

'So, I have heard.'

'But Æbbe would not hear of it. She said she wants to give her life to God. Perhaps the truth of it is that she didn't like the prince's freckles,' both the Abbot and Oswald laughed.

'I hear also that you are to marry, is this so?'

Oswald blushed for no good reason, 'Indeed I am Father.'

'Then you have my blessing, it's not good for man to be alone, for that reason our loving Creator gave Adam a wife. So, the scripture tells us, unless your life is given solely to God as mine is, but to correct myself, I am not alone either I have a like-minded family all around me. You have a different path to tread, I think.' The Abbot hesitated, then once more rested his elbow on the tabletop, and slowly stroked the curve under his bottom lip with the tip of his forefinger. 'I think my young prince, that you have an important future in service to the Church.'

Oswald listened with intense interest, curious to know what the Abbot was about to say. Could God use a warrior as a missionary? Not being the king, or even of pure royal blood, he was not in a position to lead the people like King Eochaid Buide or even Eanfrith, should he be restored to the throne of Bernicia. Was the *Abbot* intending to raise an army, he wondered?

'You will find that the Church can be of great assistance and strength to those rulers who likewise give support to the furthering of the Gospel. Perhaps you will bear that in mind, "If" you decide to return to your kingdom of Bernicia.'

'I will indeed keep that in my thoughts, Father.' Oswald frowned and wondered if the Abbot's words were merely passing observations or a clear offer of support, but why make such a proposal to him rather than to Eanfrith. Was it possible that he had already had such a conversation with Eanfrith?

'I have heard tell of an island off the coast of... is it Bebbanburg, you call your capital?'

'Yes, some call it that now; to others it will forever be Din Guyaroi. The island is named Lindis Feorna, [9] by the Bernicians, called by you Britons, "Metcaud".'

'Indeed, Metcaud, the very one, it is almost a perfect image of this island of Iona, I'm told.'

'Not quite, but there are similarities.'

'An ideal location for a Christian heart in which to take the good news to the pagans of Bernicia, is it not? However, that is a thought for the future. I must thank you for coming to see me, Prince Oswald. I understand that you are unable to stay long on this visit, which is our loss; you have many who love you here and want to spend time with you. I hear King Eochaid Buide has a high opinion of you as a warrior prince. I have heard that they are calling you "Whiteblade", because of the flash of the steel from some mystical sword you own,' the Abbot laughed. 'I'm pleased that all my hard work was not in vain.'

'Yes, Father, that is true. As you know the sword was a gift from my father... He is part of it and lives in it,' Oswald answered as he rose from the bench. 'I have learned much from King Eochaid Buide, he makes his kingdom rich by trade rather than by warfare and expansion as my father King Æthelfrith did.'

'Always have an ear to learn, my son. You are joining us for our meal and staying the night with us I hope?'

'Indeed Father, but I must return to Dunadd with the morrows tide.'

'Thanks, be, we will talk more this evening, you ever challenge my complacency. It is very easy to become accepting of the dogmas in a close community where one's beliefs are never challenged and refined. You are a breath of fresh air, straight from the Almighty Himself, my young Prince. I have missed you. Alas, there are very few who do not show complete deference to my opinions, wherever I go. Let my blessing go with you Oswald of Bernicia,' and the Abbot reached across the table and laid his hand upon Oswald's. 'May He who is able, keep and enrich your endeavours and straighten the path you set your foot upon, be with you and remain with you always.'

Oswald, bowed and kissed the Abbot's ring of office, rose from the bench, and left.

Chapter 17

Bride and Wife

It had become Oswald's normal practice to rise before first light and find a space to be quiet, outdoors whenever possible suited him best. It was simply how he lived; it had been a way of life for many years now. He'd discovered the disciplines of the monastic life were more than simple rituals;

they had a valid claim to benefit man in all walks of life. Certainly, as far as he was concerned, such time spent alone with his God helped clear his mind and set him on a right footing for the whole day.

This morning he was lying on the grassy slope that surrounded the high part of the fortress, and it suited his purpose perfectly. He could see over the ramparts and into the distance, for as far as his sight would carry him.

Suddenly his warrior instinct was awakened, he ceased his breathing and tried to slow down the beating of his heart. He became conscious of a barely perceptible change in the gentle whisper from the grass off to his left.

He understood more and more what Cedric had been teaching him since he was a boy, about the art and qualities of being a great warrior. "Awareness was the backbone of any great warrior's armour," he would say.

Oswald's hand lightly touched the hilt of his seax, and he tentatively caressed the smooth leather with his fingertips. He knew he could remove it from its sheath, and slice through a man's throat in the blink of an eye.

He turned his head fractionally and, to his relief, he saw no more threat than his young sister Æbbe coming slowly towards him, with a large smile on her face. Raising himself onto his elbows, he returned her smiled and she waved.

'Oswald, I have been looking for you and I caught sight of you up here. I was afraid that you were sleeping, and I didn't want to wake you, I'm sorry if I have disturbed you.'

'Well here I am, you have no idea of the danger you placed yourself in sneaking up on me – and – when have you ever worried about disturbing me first thing in the morning, might I ask?' she laughed, for she knew as long as she could remember, her day had started by seeking out her brother Swald.

She sat down beside him, 'I'm sorry Swald but you did look to be asleep or in prayer, and truly I didn't wish to startle you. I would have waited quietly until you were able to talk to me. *But* forget all that, now I see you are indeed awake, and this is a beautiful day – are you excited about this most important day, of days, Brother?'

'I am, what about you? Oh, and please do be seated,' she laughed and pushed him. 'As a matter a fact, on this beautiful day, I was this moment thinking about *you* my dearest sister, if you must know.'

'You were! You're teasing me, I should think that your baby sister would be the last thought on your mind this particular fine morning.'

'It is the truth. I was thinking about you... I am concerned about your wish to join an order for women yearning to give their lives solely to God, known as brides of Christ. Are you yet certain that you want to give yourself wholly to God forsaking all others? You could have married Prince Domnall Brecc if you'd wished; he wanted your hand, you could have been a Queen one day, and yet still be a devout follower of the living God. In the role of Queen, you could affect the lives of many by the choices made for your kingdom and changed them for the better.'

She smiled, 'You of all men should understand, that to give my heart to God will be as real to me as is your commitment to Princess Helen.'

'Yes… I understand that, believe me, but you are only twelve, are you certain what you feel is really a calling from God to join an Abbey? I don't mean to insult your sincerity, but there are many changes in your life at this moment, when you move from child to woman. Nevertheless,' he shrugged, 'you have time yet to change your mind. Have you talked to Eanfrith as head of the family?'

'*Eanfrith!*' she laughed. 'My dearest sweet Swald, you are so kind, to everyone; in fact, you are the kindest person I know.

'Æbbe, your reaction was *unkind*, and you know it. Eanfrith tries and needs our support at this time not our mockery.'

'You're right, I'm sorry.' She said bowing her head. 'In all honesty, I have not spoken to Eanfrith, but let me settle your fears – the decision I have made – is the way for my life. I have thought of it constantly since you told me about your newfound faith. It is for me. My future is to give my life fully to God.' He looked at her and lay back, resting his head on his hands. Æbbe wrapped her arms around her knees and stared into the distance; they were silent for some time. 'I am honestly sorry I have disturbed you. I imagine you were with God. I'm ever selfish, forgive me, but I just wanted to have these last few moments with my big brother before his life changes forever.'

'I will yet be here my dearest Æbbe, I'm not going away,' she turned to him and smiled. 'Don't be afraid, Æbbe; none of us knows what is ahead of us. Fear enables some people and it disables others. I saw that when we fought at Bebbanburg, but I have a feeling that fear with not hinder you. However, my dearest Æbbe, much as I would love to sit here all day with you and chatter, I surely have other matters that make demands on me this day.' He leant over, kissed her, stood, and dragged her to her feet.

Oswald walked carefully down the incline, and leapt over a low chestnut paling fence, at the bottom of the grassy slope and lifted Æbbe over it.

'I will have to leave you now Æbbe, and ready myself to meet my bride, I would not like her to think that she is being joined to an impoverished beggar.'

'Not Helen, she knows she is marrying my brother, the most handsome man in the whole world,' she laughed, kissed him and walked off. Oswald watched her go, she turned fleetingly, and he lifted his hand in acknowledgement.

Oswiu was waiting for him in his roundhouse, his clothes were hanging ready for him and there was a tub to bathe in, before he dressed.

'Ah, Oswiu… sorry I'm late, your sister wanted to talk. I will bathe and you can remind me of all I need to know.'

'There is plenty time. Abbot Ségéne, has arrived, he wishes to personally bless your union with the Princess. We came looking for you and wondered if you had perhaps run off,' Oswiu smiled. 'He is now with the King, Helen's father that is.'

'I wondered if he would come, that means a great deal to me, they must have sailed through the night. I hope that the priest here is not offended,' Oswald said as he climbed into the tub.

Eventually, after all the work and anxiety of the now tired servants, some of whom had worked through the night, *and* Oswald's restless pacing back and forth, for what seemed like hours… it was at last time – and the two young people faced each other and held hands.

Oswald's eyes met Helen's; she looked very nervous, he thought, even more so than he.

She was indeed nervous, more than he could ever imagine, fearing that *he* might have regrets with his choice of a wife. At this moment, she was filled with self-doubt. She was endeavouring the best she was able, to hide her fears from all watching. She had wrestled all night with her worries about their union; she thought that she was perhaps not beautiful enough, clever enough, or interesting enough for a man of such increasing importance as he. He was now a hero, revered by men, a scholar, and handsome above any man she had ever known, whilst she was feeling, – so very plain and uninteresting, for such a man as this.

The eyes of this innocence girl staring fearfully at him, touched, and warmed him, and he smiled, and in the tenderness of that smile all the words – she ever wanted to hear were spoken into *her* heart. She knew, and she would never doubt again, he *loved* her.

'He – loves – me,' she whispered under her breath. The tension drained from her, all she wanted at this moment, was to fall into his arms and dwell there forever.

Words were said and promises made, and then suddenly, she was conscious of the Abbot binding their hands together with his scarf and blessing them. She thought if heaven were more wonderful than this moment, leaving this world behind would be a glorious thing indeed.

The one dark spot on the day's celebrations was Helen's father, he was pale, and he looked so tired. Oswald knew that he'd not seemed well since they returned from Bernicia. That ignominious defeat had taken a heavy toll on him, as it had on all the other leaders. On the surface, it was if it had never been, never was it mentioned, not even in whispers behind closed doors.

Though there had been some "Slight" improvement with Eanfrith's health, he remained withdrawn. Oswald felt that the weight was shared unevenly by Princess Edlin, he was desperately sorry for the Princess, and felt that he should have been able to do more to alleviate her suffering, because he was, after all, Eanfrith's brother. They had only recently been married, no more than some three years past, their son Talorcan was now toddling and trying to speak. This *cloud* of failure and depression tormenting Eanfrith was not even in the sky that day they were married, never mind constantly hanging over their heads as it now was.

Oswald had thought time and again, of the self-worth their marriage had brought to Eanfrith, he'd been a different man, until Bebbanburg… All had changed from that day, and he was now in a worse state of self-doubt, than he'd ever been.

Neither Oswald nor Helen guessed that within three weeks, her father would be dead and buried, and her brother Prince Domnall Brecc, would be the new King of Dalriada alongside King Conadd Cerr.

Helen was distraught when she was told. She and Oswald had been to see where his mother had been laid to rest on the island of Coll. It was important for Oswald to take her, and she wanted to go, never thinking that whilst they were away, her own father would die.

In some sense, there was even worse news to come; the Dalriadans were going to war in Hibernia, and Oswald would be expected to go with his followers, to fight against Maelcaich and the Irish Cruithne. The Cruithne were a people much like the Picts in their own land of Alba.

Ever since Oswald had fought at Bebbanburg, warriors had turned to him. Warriors would align themselves to any athelings that they thought worthy and able to advance them. Now that Oswald was the son of the King, his power and wealth had increased. Oswald was ever conscious of the threat he now posed to King Domnall Brecc, and King Conadd Cerr, though they never seemed to see it as a problem to them, it appeared as if they had complete trust in Oswald's loyalty. Oswald wondered if he would be so generous of spirit if he were in their place. However, they would expect his support now, and he would have to give it, which only served to cause more distress to Princess Helen, she'd convinced herself that Oswald would be killed, and she would lose her beloved husband after waiting all these years to be together.

Oswald's faith in the goodness of God never wavered, 'God is daring us to trust Him, Helen. Trust that whatever circumstances unveil themselves before our eyes, that He loves us and that He will never flee from us. God will never leave us or forsake us, Helen. I am absolutely certain of this truth, and when you cannot believe this, let *my* faith uphold you.'

As with every war since the beginning of time, there was great activity prior to the event. Weapons were to be made and repaired; some stores were to be gathered, though they would forage for most of their needs as they travelled. More curraghs would need to be built, that was one of the beauties of the little craft, it was simple and quick to construct.

Oswald was now one of the respected leaders, which he thought absurd, but what he would bring to this venture would be a cool level-headed approach. The folly of Bebbanburg would never be repeated, *not* whilst he was in any form of command, and *that* he swore.

As the day of their departure approached, Helen could hardly eat or sleep. This was a level of anxiety she had never imagined possible. She endeavoured to hide her fears from Oswald, so that he might not be distracted, but she knew he understood, and his calm consideration for her was beyond any love she'd seen or known. This man's connection to his God was almost priest-like.

Chapter 18

Warrior

Helen watched Oswald as he stared at the table, moving his food from side to side on his platter with the point of his knife.

She was gripping her fists tightly under the table, pressing them into her lap, so that he would not be witness to her struggles and be distracted from his work.

Merciful Father, I can't hold my tongue. Help me, help me, I must be strong, the tension was travelling up her arms, she was shaking, he would notice, he must notice. *Help me* Father, she prayed.

She tried to breathe deeply and slowly. With all the strength she could muster, she asked, 'Is all ready for the journey on the morrow?'

He made no response; clearly, he'd never heard her, '*Oswald...*'

'Sorry, Helen... did you speak?'

She breathed deeply once more before she answered. 'I asked – if you were content that the army – was ready.' He still didn't look up. She sat waiting; his silence was the torment from Hell.

'You seem troubled, Oswald.'

'Do I? Mmm, in truth, I am troubled, I have little confidence in our leaders, they are not real warriors; they are traders. All I hear is indecision, sometimes I think that the only warriors here are Hrodulf and me.'

'But you are one of the leaders, have you told them of your doubt and fears?'

'Both Hrodulf and I have tried to tell them, they listen, but are not able to hear; your brother Domnall Brecc is a fine man, but no Cedric or Hrodulf. Ohh, to have such a man with us, and King Conadd Cerr, if anything, is worse than your brother.'

Helen's shaking was now replaced by a limp despair; she was barely able to remain upon her seat.

'Will you still go?'

'Aye, I must, but I will make sure that my men are well led. We will not be slaughtered as we were at Bebbanburg. I'm already preparing for defeat before we set off, that does not bode well for us. Perhaps we will prevail and find that those who oppose us are led by incompetence as we are, but I fancy that will be a vain hope, for I have no faith in this venture. As you know the scripture teaches us that faith produces hope, all the hoping in the world will not produce faith.'

'Dear Father in heaven – how will I live until you return?' Helen cried.

Her heart now reached Oswald for the first time, and he looked up and smiled; now conscious of her fears.

'Forgive me Helen. I am burdening you with my selfish concerns, and filling your world with unwarranted doubt and fear, I will return and with an army, you can be assured of that. You must have no worries for my men, we will not turn from the fight, but we will not die mindlessly either. Pray for the others who are led by the two Kings,' and he rose from his seat, went to her and embraced her, pressing his lips to the top of her head.

'I will pray for you all,' she said.

Come the morning light, the men and their families were on the beach, there were no ponies as the curraghs were totally unsuited to transporting them.

The plan was to sail up the River Bann as near as they could to the inland lake of Lough Neagh and then go on foot to Muine Mór. [26]

Oswald's fingers slipped reluctantly from Helen's and he walked into the water to the awaiting curragh. He reached up to the frame on the side of the boat, as he was about to haul himself onboard, he paused and rested his head against the side. Suddenly he pushed himself away from it, strode out of the water, and back to Helen, wrapped her savagely in his arms and kissed her, as if he would merge their spirits into one, to spiritually multiply their strength.

'I *will* be back, never fear,' he whispered into her ear. '*Remember* – if He is for us, none can stand against us,' he turned and waded once more into the water to the awaiting boat and slung himself up and into it, as easily as mounting his pony.

The friends and loved ones of the warriors watched the boats slip silently away from the shore, as they, like phantoms from the spirit world, were gradually swallowed up before their eyes, into the shimmering morning haze.

Helen stood alone, separated from the others. Æbbe had watched her for a while wondering whether-or-not to go to her. In the end, she'd decided Helen may well want to be alone with her thoughts at this moment, and she would go to her later.

Helen stared into the distance long after the crowd had dispersed. She swept strands of hair from her eyes, which had been disturbed by the light breeze and were now held to her face by her tears. She lifted her shawl over her head, to hide her private grief, and made her way slowly back to the fortress.

By nightfall, the army was in the mouth of the River Bann, and from there, they would travel south down the river, their curraghs were ideal for this purpose.

It was already dark and King Conadd Cerr wanted to press on, but Oswald argued that they were better to rest with the sea at their back and lay low for the night and then travel cautiously on the first light. He said it was utter folly to drive an army forward in the dark, in what was unknown territory. He thought that they needed to travel the next stretch of their journey in the one day and with speed.

Any delay once they had set foot on the journey south would extend the time King Mael Caích had to decide how to defeat them.

The only advantage they had was surprise, to attack quickly, before the Hibernian Cruithne warriors had time to assemble a credible defence. Once they had started south, they *had* to complete the journey without any delay.

If they went on now, they would need to stop and rest and that would give the Cruithne time to prepare for they would soon know that they were there and travelling south.

No, Oswald *insisted* once they started, they must reach their destination with all haste and strike quickly. This was not a fortress like Bebbanburg, where it would have been wise to consider their options before they attacked.

King Conadd Cerr listened, but he would not be persuaded, they *would* go now and rest before the battle.

Oswald despaired, they had made his decision for him, and his only focus now would be the safety of the men who looked to him. He was compelled to trust their guides as they made their way towards the inland sea of Lough Neagh, for he'd never been to this place before.

At midnight, King Conadd Cerr decided they would rest, so that they would be fresh for the battle if it came on the morrow. He was told that they were yet some way from the great lake, not far from a place; the guides were calling Fid Eóin. [27] They drew their curraghs into the bank and pulled them ashore for the night. Once again, Oswald begged them not to take the boats out of the water, to re-float them would take time and time they might not have.

Oswald was *convinced* that the Cruithne people would have seen them by now, and King Mael Caích would most certainly have been told of their army. Oswald was furious; at what he thought was a gift to the enemy, this would give them vital hours. He knew that King Mael Caích would now have the advantage, extra time to assemble his forces and select the point of contact. With his already superior knowledge of the landscape, he would know every hill and vale to use to his gain.

In fact, all the advantages for battle lay with the enemy, whichever way Oswald thought about it, all he could see was that they would be giving their enemy the upper hand. With every step nearer to the conflict, he became more certain of their fate.

Oswald and Hrodulf spent most of their night in preparation. They made sure that their men were all at the rear of the army and able to escape if they were attacked and overwhelmed, some even slept in the curraghs. Oswald was certain that any hope of surprise was now lost to them. He would leave *his* curraghs in the water with men guarding them. His men would not have to waste time in having to re-float them.

At first light, they began to ready themselves for the next stage of their journey. Oswald was anxiously trying to put himself in the shoes of King Mael Caích and think what he would do in the King's position.

Hrodulf knelt down next to Oswald, as he was speaking to the Briton Daffyd, and said in a low voice, 'They are here Lord; I know it, assemble the men around our boats, and have them prepare. I have no idea of their numbers, but I fancy they will outnumber us, or they would not be so bold as to attack us.'

'Hell's teeth, you see to that Hrodulf, I must warn Helen's brother King Domnall Brecc, *if* he will listen, the *fools,* they could get us all killed.'

'NO, he's not worth it, Lord! He had his chance, don't risk...' but Oswald had already gone.

Oswald had no sooner reached King Domnall Brecc, then suddenly they attacked, charging with their long spears as if men possessed. King Domnall Brecc was frozen in panic. Oswald grabbed the neck of his mail and literally dragged him choking and coughing, back to the river bank, and behind their shieldwall; they were the only ones in any semblance of order and able to offer some resistance.

Hrodulf had done well, his old friend Cedric would have been proud of him;
Daffyd was also a man who knew his business; no wonder Cedric had liked him. Oswald pushed King Domnall Brecc to the ground and forced his way into the shieldwall.

This was Oswald's first shieldwall, but he knew what to do, he had stood behind the master and learned all there was to know; this was second nature to him.

There were just too many Cruithne warriors; the Dalriadans were being slaughtered. Oswald caught sight of the fallen King Conadd Cerr out of the corner of his eye; all that was recognisable was his torn purple cloak. His head had been almost completely severed.

It was all Oswald saw, a seax came over the top of his shield and nearly poked out his eye. He only managed to avoid it by a spilt-second reaction, and at the same time he ducked, he drove his Ulfberht underneath his shield and into the belly of his assailant. The man's eyes bulged in utter disbelief as Oswald dragged his sword free, and he slid down the front of Oswald's shield into a heap at his feet.

This sword came alive in this situation; its ability to bend was such an advantage in close quarter fighting. You could easily find a sword torn from your hand because of its lack of flexibility or even worse; it would shatter on the first contact with metal.

'Every second man drop out of the wall and close-up, NOW!' Oswald yelled.

The ones who'd dropped out were to get the boats ready. The wall closed immediately they'd stepped from it, sealing the way to the boats. They had trained and practised all these manoeuvres in Dalriada, and they worked seamlessly.

Oswald had learned from the Bebbanburg disaster, that organisation and discipline was the way to win battles, and he'd decided that day, he'd not repeat the same mistakes of a band of warriors operating as individuals.

Oswald yelled again, 'every second man drop out of the wall – and close up, NOW!'

There were bowmen at this moment standing in the front of the boats. When the final men in the wall ran to the riverbank, they would be covered by them.

'NOW!' the wall broke for the final time and they backed as one to the boats, bending low so that the bowmen had targets. Swisssssh, an arrow shot passed Oswald's head so closely that the goose feather fletching brushed against his face.

The last men from the wall waded to the rear of the boats and climbed in, whilst the archers pounded mercilessly those who came at them.

As they pulled into the centre of the river, Oswald could see that the Dalriadans they'd left behind were being slaughtered, but he had saved his men and others besides.

They needed now to make their escape up the River Bann, and return the way they'd come from the sea, and as quickly as they could.

There was nothing Oswald could do for those left behind, he could only watch. The only other option would have been to stay and die with them, a pointless death.

'You did well Lord, *he* would have been proud of you, I know it.'

'Thank you Hrodulf, but it need not have been like this, another utterly humiliating, stupid defeat, a total waste of life.'

'Aye… I know that, Lord, but take it from one who knows, every battle I have walked away from has been a victory, as far as I'm concerned.'

'Now that did sound like Cedric, that is something he would have said,' and Oswald gave a weak smile.

Hrodulf shaded his eyes with his hand, 'They don't seem to be following us. I don't think that they will have had time to organise a boom across the river to trap us, so we may be free.'

'Let's hope so Hrodulf, what a waste…'

King Domnall Brecc now stood and rested his arm on Oswald's shoulder.

'Sorry Oswald, we should have listened to you – *and* – thank you for my life. I will not forget the risk you took for me and I swear this before God.'

Chapter 19

Land of the Living

Oswald led his men sombrely away from the shore and up to Dunadd, they were all that was left of the warriors who had gone to Hibernia, and died at the battle of Fid Eóin. For such a number they moved silently. The warriors dispersed, equally silently once they'd entered the fort, all but Oswald, he saw Eanfrith sitting on a bench at the door of his roundhouse. Eanfrith wearily lifted his hand in greeting and Oswald and King Domnall Brecc walked to where he was sitting and sat down beside him. Eanfrith made to stand, but Domnall touched his shoulder and he stayed seated. Eanfrith looked frail he had lost much of his strength and bulk because of his inactivity since Bebbanburg. He was clearly weak, but Oswald could see his health was improving the fact that he spoke to them, was a good indicator. He had on previous times; scuttled inside whenever someone went too near.

'How goes it Eanfrith?'

'I feel much improved Lord; it's good to see you Brother. No need to say ought, I can see that it did not go well for our army.'

'We missed your strong arm.'

'I'm strong right enough, at least in that I was, just like father, but you are *brave* that's the difference between us,' Eanfrith said in a soft resigned voice with empty eyes that stared straight through Oswald. 'You are too harsh on yourself, what happened at Bebbanburg wasn't your fault. We were led by men who should have known better. Next time it will be different.'

King Domnall Brecc looked down, for he knew his father had been one of the leaders responsible for the shame at Bebbanburg.

'Do you think that there will be a next time, Oswald?' asked Eanfrith.

'For sure, and I would be your general if it was your wish. The King here has said, when we feel the time is right, he will raise an army to help us regain what is ours.'

'You would do that for us Lord?'

Eanfrith turned to the King in astonishment.

'I am now in Lord Oswald's debt and I will do my best to make right the grave state of shame I find myself in.'

Eanfrith visibly brightened at these welcome yet unexpected words of hope.

'I am learning much from the needless mistakes.' Oswald confessed to him, to add honesty to the encouragement. 'Mistakes can be a rare teacher, you learn, or you suffer, until you do, and I have witnessed many mistakes.'

King Domnall Brecc lowered his head once more, though Oswald had meant no insult or attempt at shaming him; he was merely trying to be encouraging to his brother Eanfrith.

As Oswald was speaking, he glanced over Eanfrith's shoulder and saw Helen step outside her doorway, no doubt alerted to the return of the army, by the disturbance and influx of warriors. She saw Oswald and quickly ducked back inside their roundhouse.

'I will leave you now, but we will talk later, I have just seen Helen behaving rather suspiciously.' The King turned to see where Oswald was looking.

'Yes, you should not be sitting here idly chatting with me, she'll think you are in no hurry to see her, and I'm guessing that falls short of the truth by the length of a straight arrow's flight.'

Oswald stood up stretched his neck from side to side and back and forth, it felt stiff. He'd pulled it to his certain knowledge when he dragged King Domnall Brecc to safety at Fid Eóin. He squeezed Eanfrith's shoulder and went to where he'd seen Helen.

He opened the door and walked in. She had been hiding behind the door and pounced on him, laughing with a mixture of raw hysteria, and relief.

'Oswald Leodwalding how dare you keep us waiting. You can't imagine what it's been like, waiting here and not knowing. Was it a great victory?'

'Nothing like, we were slaughtered.'

'Dear God, what about my brother?'

'Fear not, he is safe, but his men suffered a mighty number of causalities.'

'But you escaped.'

'Yes, I was not about to see my men die for nothing, once was enough for me.'

'I prayed for you every moment, we needed you home safe and sound.'

'What do you mean, *we* needed you home?'

'Your wife and your son...' Oswald stared at her, his face was at first expressionless and gradually it was transformed into a smile.

'Did I tell you what a wonderful person you are? This is the best news to hear after all I have been witness to, believe me,' he said tenderly embracing her. 'When, will all this happen?'

'January next year, so I'm reliably informed.'

'Come, we must tell Hrodulf, who else can we tell, Eanfrith and Edlin, Queen Bebba, your brother and of course, Æbbe.'

'Actually, I have already told Edlin, I had to. I was so worried that I could not think straight, please forgive me.'

'Of course, I forgive you, how could you suffer to keep this to yourself?'

Over the next months, there was more unrest within the greater kingdom of Dalriada; it seemed to Helen, her husband was constantly away from Dunadd she saw so little of him.

Oswald Whiteblade's courage and leadership was on the lips of all, but that brought little comfort to her.

This was also a time of renewal for his brother Eanfrith who was once again fighting alongside him and Oswiu. Eanfrith would never inspire men like his brother Oswald, but for now, he seemed satisfied with this. Oswald thought the renewed optimism of returning to Bebbanburg had worked in him a message of hope and a future.

The hooves of Oswald's pony clattered on the stone steps up to the highest level of the fort at Dunadd. They'd never been intended for such a purpose, but Oswald drove the little animal up the incline onto the top and leapt from the saddle followed closely by Oswiu.

He had been out hunting with King Domnall Brecc, and his brother Oswiu, when a rider had been sent for him with news that his wife, Princess Helen, was about to deliver their child, and he was to return immediately.

He'd no need of direction he could hear Helen screaming before his feet had touched to ground. There were women milling around everywhere, he was forcibly barred from entering the birthing area.

'God in all His mercy, what are you doing to her?' he yelled.

'Be calm, brother nothing can be achieve by your distress,' Oswiu laid his arm on his chest and directed him to a chair.

The noise went on for hours, or so it seemed. Eventually there was a brief moment of silence, and then the cry of a newborn child was heard, and he breathed the greatest sigh of relief, fell to his knees and gave thanks to God.

He was told that he had a son, and all was well, he should wash and change ready to meet the newest member of the Leodwalding dynasty.

There was a tub provided and he was bathed, he merely lay in the tub with his eyes closed giving thanks to his God and allowed the servant girls to do their work. Once the dirt of the hunt had been removed, he was dressed and taken to see his wife and new son.

The cowhide drape was drawn back to allow him to enter the birthing chamber and he was greeted by a servant offering him his son to admire. Though there were candles, the light was poor, it was dark now, but Oswald was able to see the child well enough and he thought him something of a wonder to behold. Oswald lightly touched his cheek with the back of his finger, the babe trembled, and Oswald smiled. He gazed at the babe sleeping in her arms tightly bound in swaddling, so he resembled a little parcelled-up moth in his chrysalis. His eyes were closed, and his tiny eyelashes glittered as if sprinkled with gold as the glow of the candlelight brushed over them. There were the most delicate violet shadows beneath them, and his skin had the pale bloom of lavender. His breathing was so soft that Oswald could barely hear it, confined as he was within the layers of wrapping.

He knew that many children did not survive infancy. Only the strong survived into adulthood, the struggle of living had begun this day for his son, he laid his fingers lightly on his yet bloody head and prayed that God might keep him and bless him.

Oswald turned to the bed, and the servant curtseyed, saying, 'my Lady is very tired Lord.'

'Hmm, no doubt,' Oswald went to Helen, knelt and took her hand. Her eyes flickered and she smiled, he leant forward and kissed her lips, they were dry and rough.

'He is beautiful; we will call him *Æthelwald* the name means masculine and ambitious, leader, that's what I want for our son. I want him to be ambitious, not to be resigned to things the way they are, a man who can change things for the better, a man who inspires and a man whom men will follow.

Helen smiled weakly, 'Like his father,' she whispered.

'More like his mother, I hope. I know myself and I would not wish my son to have my shortcomings. How do you feel now my brave wife?'

'Tired, happy, more than that I can't say, I have never been a mother before. I'm glad to have given you a son for our first born, *Æthelwald*, a fine name.'

'Yes, you have made me a proud man, but you must rest, I will be near at hand, never fear, we'll have a lifetime to talk,' and he reached once more to her, kissed her and left.

He'd been several times to see her through the night, but he didn't disturb her, she was sleeping.

When he went at first light, she seemed disturbed, she was sweating; there were beads of sweat standing on her forehead.

'Help me Oswald, I'm so hot, bathe my face.'

'WATER,' he called out, 'COLD WATER.'

A servant entered with a bowl and cloth. Oswald took the cloth from her and dipped it in the water while she held the bowl. He drew back the bedcovers, but he instantly recognised the putrid smell.

'Dear God in heaven, get the Cunning woman, quickly girl.' The girl ran out and he continued to bathe Helen with the cool water, he didn't know what else to do. He knew that this was serious, Helen was writhing and twisting now, she was rapidly becoming delirious; she could no longer hear him.

It only took moments before the girl returned with the Cunning woman, *and* the priest.

The old woman who'd seen it all before said it was the birth flux, and there was naught she could do only wait, keep her warm and pray for the fever to break quickly.

'This day will tell you the will of God, Lord,' was her best miserable offering, as if the God he knew would want this.

The old priest, Father Adam, anointed Helen with oil and prayed for her, but such was her agitation she knocked the small flask of holy oil from his hand. Oswald tried to grab it, but it splashed all over him and ran through his fingers.

'Don't worry about that Lord, I will leave you now, go to the church and pray for her, and you.'

'Aye, aye, pray for us all, the child too. Will you baptise him now Father?'

'Yes, I will attend to that, tell me what he is to be called?'

'Æthelwald.'

In the evening Helen stilled, she seemed at peace after all her striving. Oswald held her in his arms hardly able to hear her above the sound of the pulse pounding in his head... *her* breathing was shallow.

Finally, she gave a long – soft – sigh, it was almost, a sigh of relief, and her face relaxed.

Oswald couldn't quite comprehend the moment; how could this be? What had happened? How could she be here, then not here? All he could do was stare at this person who held his heart in her hands, none of this made any sense, this surely couldn't be the end…

'I mean Lord Jesus, I love her, she can't, *not* be here. She's part of me, it can't be; it just can't. How can I live without hearing her laughter, seeing her smile, not for a day, a week, a year, but never, ever again?'

He was squeezing and kissing her hand and pressing his lips to it, tears streamed down his face onto her fingers. A hand touched his shoulder and Æbbe knelt by his side, she was in tears too.

'I'm so sorry, Swald.'

He shook his head in disbelief, he was unable to speak. Never in all his life had he known pain the like of this, he was even struggling to breathe.

Eventually, his heart spoke. 'Never again, never again, never again.'

Æbbe didn't know what he meant, it was the sound of some darkness from within, but there was a tragic finality in the moment which was hell on earth for all those who loved another, as Oswald, her Oswald, had loved this woman.

How could a human being recover from such invisible pain as this? No salve other than God's peace could bring relief, true relief that is. Time alone would not heal this, deaden it, hide it perhaps, but heal it, no.

She would be here for her beloved brother, she would pray when he could not, and she would love him when he could not love. People did not like Oswald they loved him, and Oswiu knew that, he was such a man that had cared for others and they now cared for him. It was unusual for a warrior, to show weakness and vulnerability not the obvious qualities of a hardened man of war, but with Oswald his weakness, his humanness seemed to be his strength.

Poor Eanfrith had to undertake greater and greater heroic deeds for men to take any heed of him, whilst Oswald showed weakness and men would die for him. It was such a contradiction of all that made sense to normal human thought.

God ministered to Oswald through his friends, none more than Oswiu and Æbbe. Æbbe, in particular, seemed to have the measure of his needs. She understood when to speak, when to hold him and when to stand back. Perhaps it came from the heart of her love, whatever was to be the truth, she was one of those people who understood the deep, unseen needs of others, as if she had special sight.

He sat on his hunkers holding his son to his breast, watching her feeding the chickens, with grain and kitchen scraps from a basket under her arm. He was sure she'd chosen the right path; to give her life completely to God would be the only way for her. It was who she was, and who she would be, for the rest of her life. [28]

'God bless you my dearest sister…' he spoke softly into the hair of his son.

Æbbe told Oswald that Helen had merely left the land of the dying for the land of the living. He remembered Helen saying, on their wedding day – "If heaven is better than this moment, it must be a glorious place indeed". Wherever heaven was he knew she would be there, and he thanked God for allowing him a brief moment in eternity with such a beautiful person. He knew of all men how blessed he had been a yet was.

Chapter 20

News from Bernicia

Oswald was seated with his back against the wattle and daub wall of his roundhouse. He shuffled slightly trying to find a comfortable spot where there was not a hardened stalk sticking annoyingly into his back. It was a warm sunny day, and perhaps after the long endless wet winter this would be a summer to remember. However, in truth, Oswald had too many dates to remember and the balance was now weighing down on the side of the dates that he would rather forget. He thought it odd, as he read his book; that a man's life, with all its trials and heartaches, in the end, amounted to no more than a list of dates. Would that be the sum total of his legacy to his son Æthelwald, he wondered.

He was struggling to concentrate on the text he was reading, he felt sleepy with the heat of the day. Abbot Ségéne had loaned him a book on the lives of the holy men of old; it was rare and very costly. He knew how privileged he was to have been trusted with this holy book. It was an open display of the high regard in which he was held by the Abbot, who had been his special friend since he first set foot on Iona.

Oswald thought for a moment, was that in 617. He wasn't quite sure of the date; it seemed like a lifetime ago. He smiled in the light of his thoughts; his life was already assembling its dates. Abbot Ségéne had once said that time, was no more than us passing through eternity.

Oswald had been many times to see Abbot Ségéne, especially since Helen had died. He was ever encouraging when Oswald was in deep despair. Often his life without Helen became too much for him; it was a little better now. The times between the dark days of hell were longer, but no matter how he tried, the pain of losing her would forever catch him when he least expected it, and it could literally bring him to his knees. It was an actual physical thing, as if a knife was stabbing into his heart; the pain was so intense he would sometimes find himself having to hang on to a post, or a wall, to prevent collapsing into a heap, and he would have to pant to regain some control of his breathing. These were the worst of days when hope was lost to him, and he could see no future, then he'd remember the Abbot saying that he'd seen a sign above his head saying, "There is something in your future worth living for".

Oswald glanced up from his book at his future for now, his son, Æthelwald. He was a mixed blessing, if the truth were known, "Wald" as Æbbe insisted on calling him. Oswald smiled; Æbbe had clipped the names of the people she loved, for as long as he could remember. She only came home very occasionally, now that she was at the Abbey. He missed her company even more since Helen had died. She had the unerring ability to make complicated things seem simple.

Æthelwald was nearly two and was forever doing something he should not be doing. He demanded fulltime attention in this world of fascinating things to touch. Princess Edlin, had taken on the day-to-day care of him, and Eanfrith seemed happy for her to do that. Eanfrith and Edlin had only the one child, their son Talorcan, who was six now. Even at this moment as Oswald watched him, Æthelwald was tormenting a new kitten which seemed to have made Oswald's roundhouse its home and was content to endure Oswald's continuing presence.

Yes, Æthelwald was a mixed blessing, for he was the image of his mother. Sometimes that was a great comfort insomuch that through him he felt as if Helen was yet in reaching distance, just behind a veil, her smiling eyes looking out at him from their son's. On another day to see Æthelwald's beautiful face, was a torturous memory of things lost.

Abbot Ségéne had said to him once that the pain he was suffering was all part of the love he'd had then. The pain now was a measure of their love, both extremes of being human.

Hrodulf had called Æthelwald's cat Cedric, he said his hair was the same nondescript untidy mess that Cedric's always was, and the name had stuck.

Suddenly Oswald's contemplations were broken when Æthelwald shrieked, flopped down holding his bloody finger in the air. Clearly, Cedric had tired of the game and needed to establish who was in command. Cedric had found a position of calm, after his initial shock when Æthelwald shouted, and was now sat on a nearby post licking his paw and attending to his ruffled appearance.

'Lord,' a voice called, Oswald turned as he bent down to pick up Æthelwald and saw a servant running towards him. 'The King wishes to see you; he has had important news. I am to fetch Lord Eanfrith and Lord Oswiu too.'

'And where is the King?'

'He was at the hightable in the longhouse, when he bade me find you, Lord.'

Oswald called to a servant and told her to watch and care for Æthelwald until he returned.

Oswald saw King Domnall Brecc standing at the entrance to the longhouse waiting for him and looking like Cedric when he had his tongue in a bowl of cream.

'Oswald, have you seen Eanfrith?'

'No, I came straight here.'

'I have just received news that your nemesis King Edwin has been killed by King Cadwallon ap Cadfan of Gwynedd. I was told he is now ravaging the land. It appears that his tyranny knows no bounds.'

Oswald was speechless, his uncle dead, he couldn't believe it. He'd never expected this; he was totally unprepared. He had yet to make a comment when Oswiu and Eanfrith came. In contrast to Oswald, Eanfrith needed no time to consider what this might mean. His immediate thought was that they must go now with an army and claim back his birthright.

'One moment, we need much more information before we rush off and risk ending up with the same disaster, we were part of last time.'

Eanfrith looked crestfallen at Oswald's less than enthusiastic response.

'Of course, Brother, we will need to plan carefully, but it is good news, nevertheless, is it not?'

'On the face of it, it sounds very encouraging, but this might be our last chance, therefore we need to be sure how we will approach this. I am assuming that you will allow me to lead the men as you suggested sometime since.'

'Indeed, you have the greatest number of followers, it would be only sensible for you to lead in any battle.'

'*And I* have not forgotten my oath to you Lord Oswald; I promised you support and I meant it,' King Domnall Brecc pointed out.

'That is very generous Lord. Who brought the news?'

'The fellow is inside I have seen that he has mete and drink. He'd ridden hard, spreading the news so *we* might be prepared in case we in the north are attacked next. This King of Gwynedd wishes to be King of the whole of Briton, so it is said of him.'

'First, with your permission, Lord, I will speak with this rider and find out exactly what he knows.' Oswald turned to Eanfrith, 'Perhaps brother you might rally together our Bernicians and tell them the good tidings, while I talk to this messenger.' Oswald didn't want Eanfrith confusing the man with his overbearing excitement. 'You come with me Oswiu,' Oswald said quietly tugging at Oswiu's sleeve.

Oswald spent some time making sense of all that the messenger had to say, until he was clear in his mind what the situation was really like in Bernicia.

When he'd first seen the messenger, he was surprised to see a monk, who'd apparently been travelling in Bernicia, spreading the message of the Christian faith, when the death of King Edwin was made known to him.

'And what should I call you brother?'

'I am known as Brother Edgar, I take it that you are the famed Whiteblade.'

Oswald laughed, 'I think that is really my sword, Dream World, you speak of, but some call me that, it's true.'

'Your fame has spread throughout the north, Lord.'

'That may well be so, but it's you who are of interest here, tell me what you know.'

The monk told his tale in greater depth than he had to King Domnall Brecc, for Oswald was familiar with the names of the people and places in Bernicia, so he had a greater grasp of what was said. It appeared that this King Cadwallon ap Cadfan of Gwynedd, with his fearsome reputation was not occupying Bebbanburg, but merely ravaging the north.

As Oswald listened, he began to think that this really could be an opportunity to retake Bernicia. If the people were suffering under this tyrant, surely, they would be ready to join a force led by their own people, sons of the great King Æthelfrith.

Yes! This could be the God given opportunity they'd been waiting for, to return to their home, Bernicia, this was a chance to grasp with both hands.

Oswald swore that he would lead this invasion, no matter what Eanfrith said. He knew Eanfrith could never do it. Oswald would be content to allow Eanfrith to be the figurehead. He was sure that Eanfrith would be happy with that, and he was certain that *he* would forever have Oswiu's support.

King Domnall Brecc was as good as his word, he gave funds and men; those added to Oswald's own followers made for a formidable force. Even yet Oswald was not about to rush south he insisted that his army trained and practised, at first there were mutterings. This was not the way of warriors, but such was Oswald's charisma that they submitted to his will.

The time to march came, they would take Bebbanburg, it would be their heart, and from there, they would drive out King Cadwallon ap Cadfan of Gwynedd from the whole of Bernicia and reclaim their homeland.

Oswald rose early, as was his practice and went to Helen's grave. He took a small bunch of forget-me-nots with their delicate blue flowers, laid them reverently on the small mound and sat down cross-legged staring at her name on the stone marker. It was an ornate cross, exactly as he had wanted. The stone had been intricately carved by the mason with well worked familiar Saxon patterns of knots and snakes, enforcing their never-ending theme, reflecting both Oswald's and God's eternal love.

Yet there were tears, it would be so difficult for him to leave her here when he was in Bernicia, perhaps one day he would have to leave her for good and he didn't know how he would do that. Never to be this close again, it was a hellish thought and he leaned forward on his clenched fists and sobbed. There were moments of panic when his memory of her face became faint as if behind a veil, these were moments of great anxiety, but the moment would pass, and he would find his peace once more. He still couldn't believe she had gone and lifted his eyes heavenward as if hoping for one more glimpse, he would take that, just one glimpse, but it seemed that it was not God's way. Then he lowered his head sadly and prayed.

Hrodulf saw him coming down the slope; he knew where he'd been, as did Oswiu and Daffyd their new comrade and friend.

'*Lord*,' was all Hrodulf said bowing and squeezed his shoulder as he came to his side. 'We are ready – this day will see men place their foot on the road to victory, I know it Lord, I feel it in my blood.'

'If it is God's will, it will be so Hrodulf, in Him I trust and though a host encamp against me we will not be overcome.'

'That's sounds good to me, Lord. I will take that from any god, even the Christian God.'

Oswald laughed and slapped Hrodulf's back.

'No wonder you and Cedric were such friends you were one and the same.' Oswald glanced at Edlin with Æthelwald in her arms and went to her. Æthelwald reached for him and he took his son from her, lifting him high in the air. Æthelwald giggled. Oswald lowered him gradually until their noses touched, kissed him, and returned him into the arms of Edlin. 'Take care of him, my dearest sister Edlin, be sure to tell him all about his mother.'

'I will, and his father too.'

'Aye, and his father, but it is my hope that I will see him again,' he smiled and kissed Edlin.

Oswald was the last to mount; Eanfrith was in high spirits as he led the army away from the fortress of Dunadd, southeast to Bebbanburg and their home of Bernicia.

Brother Edgar would ride south with them and Oswald was glad of his company. They were much of an age; he had been for a time on Iona, so he knew many of the people whom Oswald was familiar with, which bonded Oswiu and Oswald to him.

As they neared the borders of Bernicia there were many signs of raiding, houses burned, animals and humans slaughtered, grim sights for the warriors. Oswald hoped and prayed that he could contain them as their anger grew. He had to trust that the discipline he had attempted to instil within them would hold fast when they met with King Cadwallon's men, which they would sooner or later.

Oswald spent much of the journey talking with Eanfrith; the nearer they got to Bernicia the more Oswald could see the old Eanfrith emerging. He said he would restore the old gods to their place of honour and with them the greatness of Bernicia as it was in his Father's Day. If Eanfrith noticed the despair in Oswald's eyes, he chose to ignore it. He was not going to be dissuaded from his restoration plans by Oswald, but Oswald knew that Eanfrith only saw life through the narrow vision of his *wants* and could not cope with that larger picture, which may present a more unfavourable view, bringing with it a challenge to his vision.

Oswald was quite at a loss, he didn't try to challenge Eanfrith, as it seemed he had not learned anything from their previous venture to Bernicia. Eanfrith would never be able to hold onto this kingdom no matter how he wished for it.

There was much unknown before them, but Oswald feared *most* the foolishness of his brother. He talked with Oswiu, but neither could settle in their minds Eanfrith's total lack of understanding or leadership, yet their leader, he was determined to be.

The fortress was in view now as the army stopped in more-or-less the same place as it had when they last came to challenge King Edwin. Oswald leant forward onto the upstand of his saddle, and eased his backside from his seat, it was hot and sore, he needed to dismount and stretch his legs while he took in the vista before him.

'We will dismount and spend the night here. We all need to gather our thoughts and be refreshed. From now on we will be in constant danger.'

'I'm not sure about this Oswald, we should strike whilst the iron is hot.'

Oswald paused, straightened himself, and looked Eanfrith in the eye. 'Eanfrith, I was not offering a suggestion that we might stay here for the night, for your approval, let me make it quite clear, *this* is what we are going to do.'

Eanfrith visibly drew back, clearly shaken by the force of Oswald's declaration. From this point on, if there *had* been some doubt before, there must be *no* doubt now, Oswald was in command, and Eanfrith was not. Even if he were *King* Eanfrith, what was to happen in the days ahead, would only happen on Oswald's yea or nay.

Oswald walked to the edge of the camp with Oswiu and they stared into the distance.

'We are here once more Oswald, I doubted that we ever would be.'

'Yes, I wondered too, many times, but as you say, we are here and I am not leaving, but that we are the victors. I will, by the grace of God have Bernicia returned to our Leodwalding family. This is where my son Æthelwald, will grow up. I will extinguish those fires of burning lives and homes that we see in the distance and light a fire for God which will *never* be extinguished.'

Oswald left the last task of the night to Oswiu, which was to see that guards were in place and the list of changes and times had been made clear to those guarding the camp.

Chapter 21

The King is Dead

Oswald sat for some time on his mount staring at the fortress, no one said a word to him. Oswiu watched him out of the corner of his eye, he dares do no more; Oswald never blinked. The only movement to be seen was the rhythmic flexing of his jaw muscles. Even his horse stood statuesque, apart from the occasionally flicking of its ears.

'So, God, it has come to this, the gates of the city of our birthright are before us. We are come as an army to claim it back, but what of the people inside, our people, do they not have a right to expect their king to protect rather than destroy them? Eanfrith desires to enter his kingship on the tails of a great battle – but what would be his legacy? Show me the right of it all God.'

There was a moment when Oswiu thought that Eanfrith was going to speak to Oswald, but he must have thought better of it.

The whole army waited for his instruction; finally, he tugged on the rein and turned to face his warriors.

'I will ride up to the gate of the fort and speak to their leader.'

'*Lord!*' Hrodulf pushed his pony forward, 'that's too dangerous, let *me* go, I will tell them whatever it is you want to say.'

Oswald looked at him and formed a soft smile on his lips. 'No, I thank you for your concern my friend, but I will do it,' and he turned his mount, trotted along the beach and up to the gates of the fortress and stopped.

All Oswiu could hear was the surf tumbling up the beach and rolling back again dragging the soft sand with it. Horses and men were standing in total silence.

'I am Prince Oswald of Bernicia, son of the great King Æthelfrith, a fair and generous Lord.' Oswald called up to the guards, 'who ruled and lived in this fortress. Now you Bernicians, whom he loved, cared, and died for, close your gates to his sons. We are the rightful heirs of his kingdom, and we have travelled far to free the noble people of Bernicia from a tyrant and oppressor, not to enslave you, and this is how you treat us, you shame us. Fear not, we will not molest you our brothers, instead we will return from whence we came in great sadness.'

'Prince Oswald, is that really you?' A voice called from the ramparts.

'I am Prince Oswald, who is this, who addresses me?'

'I am Ælfweard, the friend of Cedric, do you remember me? I was ill when you left with your mother the Queen those many years since and could not go with you. I thought that I was dying, don't you remember? You came to me and wished me well.'

'I remember an Ælfweard,' now it was Oswald's turn to look surprised. 'If you are whom you say, why are these gates barred?' 'We fear Cadwallon ap Cadfan, he is destroying Bernicia, though he has not tried to attack us yet, we are ready.' Ælfweard disappeared from view, a shout was heard, and the heavy oak gates began to slowly swing open. Oswald narrowed his eyes when he saw this old man standing before him, bowing.

Oswald walked his horse forward to the man and the man stood up.

'Ælfweard, it is you!' Oswald said leaping from his horse and embracing him. 'How I rejoice to see you my old friend, I thought you long departed from this life. Praise be to God, this is a great blessing indeed to find old friends here in Bebbanburg, now I know I am truly home.'

'Do you remember Godric?' Ælfweard swept his hand towards Godric standing nearby.

'Of course, I do, you look well Godric.'

'We are the only two boyhood friends left now, once there were five of us. We two, Cedric and Wulfstan, who you never knew, he was the greatest of us. If I'm not mistaken that is his sword you now wear.' Ælfweard said twisting his head to better see Oswald's sword, 'a gift from Cedric I dare say, you must be a great warrior Lord, for Cedric to give you that holy sword.'

'You said there were five of you!'

'Aye, so I did, sadly there was Lord Wulfstan's traitorous brother, who we never speaks of, forgive me Lord I can't bring myself to utter his name.' There was a moment of tense silence until Oswald spoke.

'I will call the others,' Oswald walked back outside the gate and beckoned
Eanfrith, Oswiu and Hrodulf to join him.

They hesitated, looked at each other then rode forward up the bank and into the fortress.

Once they had nervously dismounted, Oswald introduced Eanfrith to the fort defenders, though most there already knew him.

'This is your new king,' and the defenders dutifully bowed, but Oswald wondered if Eanfrith would be truly accepted.

He knew that it was important that any claimant to the throne as rightful heir, in the Saxon world, should have been born while their father was king.

Unfortunately, Eanfrith was born before Æthelfrith was the king; he was born whilst King Hussa was on the Bernician throne. Even if he had been born when Æthelfrith was on the throne, he would yet need the final approval of the Witan before he'd be accepted.

For now, it appeared as if those here in the fort, were simply relieved, and prepared to see them as a gift of hope, when there seemed to be no hope. Oswald could understand that they would initially accept Eanfrith; time might have a different story to tell, much would depend on how Eanfrith acted. However, there would be an initial period of grace.

Over the next months, King Cadwallon ap Cadfan of Gwynedd continued his raiding. Oswald had tried to engage Cadwallon's forces, but he had never been successful they had always managed to evade his efforts to confront them.

The chase had led Oswald to the northwest, Cear Luel [29] where the old Roman Wall ended. He was seated at the table in his tent writing when he received the stunning blow. Godric, old as he was, had ridden through the night to bring him the news. Godric had been given the task because Oswald knew him of old, and the nature of this message must not carry with it any shadow of doubt. Godric came into the tent with Hrodulf and bowed. Oswald pointed to a chair, he could see that Godric was exhausted; Godric bowed once more and sighed as he sat down.

'Bring refreshment for this warrior.'

'Thank you, Lord.'

'Now, then Godric, what brings you all the way from Bebbanburg, not a ride for a man of your years?'

'Bad news Lord.'

Oswald didn't answer; he lay back in his chair and gestured with open palms for Godric to speak.

'King Eanfrith… has been murdered by King Cadwallon.'

Oswald's sat up straight in his chair; his face was as stone.

'Go on,' Oswald's spoke without emotion, steady and measured.

'Cadwallon summoned King Eanfrith to the Roman town of Corbridge, on the northern edge of our Bernician kingdom, under a flag of truce. Eanfrith went with a twelve-man guard of warriors, treasure and hostages as is customary, under the assumption that Cadwallon wanted to negotiate some sort of peace settlement. We were told that Cadwallon had them decapitated and their heads displayed on spiked posts.'

Throughout this distressing report, Oswald yet never moved, apart from clenching his fists so tightly his hands were white. He was furious on several accounts. One – Eanfrith had made great play of rejecting the Christian faith and restoring the pagan gods to Bernicia. In Oswald's eyes that made Eanfrith and the whole kingdom vulnerable. This was deeply offensive to Oswald who was a devout Christian. Secondly, Oswald could not believe Eanfrith's stupidity, he should never have gone to meet with Cadwallon, never mind with only twelve men. He ought to have known what a foolhardy venture that was, at the very least Eanfrith should have discussed his intention with him before he did anything. This madness could well result in a victory for Cadwallon, for who else had the ability and resources to defeat Cadwallon, but them. Such thoughts must have been predominant when he contemplated this flagrant demonstration of his contempt for traditions of battlefield conduct. The man was without honour in any shape or form, he was no more than a thief and a brigand.

Oswald decided that his army would follow the Roman wall across country to Corbridge, where his spies told him Cadwallon and his forces were camped. It would be three days of strenuous travel before they fought the battle, but Oswald was certain he would not make the same mistake as King Conadd Cerr made in Hibernia, when they were brutally defeated at Fid Eóin. No – once they set off, they would not be camping overnight to give Cadwallon time to prepare his defences, where Oswald stopped would be the place to do battle.

Oswald would expect support from Royth, son of Rhun who had also been tormented by Cadwallon.

Oswald had demonstrated great political foresight, when he'd arranged the betrothal of his brother Oswiu to Princess Rhieinmelth, the daughter of Royth. He had not long been betrothed, but that union brought with it forces from the northeast, and the fine horses they now sat upon, which had been a gift from Royth, son of Rhun.

Oswald gave an impassioned speech at the betrothal of the two, to ensure Royth's support when the defining battle came, as he was sure it would.

'Will the warriors of Rheged stand by their allies against the perfidious apostate, Cadwallon, who like a cursed whelp seeks only to destroy the north parts of our island with rapine and slaughter. Will the King cement our friendship in the name of the True God by honouring the betrothal in Christ, of our brother Oswiu to his daughter Rhieinmelth, agreed upon in the time of our fathers.'

Arranging the betrothal of Oswiu was not difficult, for he was a Prince of Bernicia and as such, a person of great consequence. It was said of him that he was tall and handsome, pleasant of speech, courteous of manner to both commoner and nobleman alike, and loved by all because of his great dignity.

Although Oswiu had already fathered a child with a beautiful Hibernian Princess, called Fina, it was not seen as any hindrance to the advantages of being betrothed to a Leodwalding atheling.

Oswald had become a formidable leader, and was now, since the murder of his brother Eanfrith, the King of Bernicia in all but name. His fame as a fearless warrior had spread throughout the north. Adding the gilding to his fame was his overwhelming charisma, known integrity, and political understanding, which made him both an implacable friend and enemy.

To some, the connection between the legendary Hibernian god, Nuada Airgetlám, who'd lost an arm in battle, which was then replaced by a silver arm – and the similarities of Oswald's name of

Whiteblade or "Whitearm" was not missed. It was also said that when his beloved wife, Princess Helen, was on her deathbed, she'd poured holy oil over his right arm.

Oswald knew his friend Abbot Ségéne never missed an opportunity to add mystique to his protégé's story. He had once told Oswald that the Church could be a powerful ally. Oswald had not fully understood at the time, what the Abbot had meant, but he did now, and was content to allow the stories to be told. Not only was he now seen as a warrior and a king in waiting, but also a holy man, and an anointed servant of the Living God.

Travelling near the great wall made the journey quick and relatively easy. The route had been maintained as a way of travelling across country by traders, shepherds and drovers alike.

The mid-summer rivers yet ran with ale coloured water draining off the high moors. At Greenhead's narrow pass, Oswald sent scouts ahead of his force for it was the ideal place for an ambush. However, their spies returned informing them that there was no such ambush waiting for them. It seemed that Cadwallon was blissfully unaware of Oswald's oncoming force.

Oswald was greatly encouraged from the reports that Cadwallon seemed oblivious to his presence, for he was sure that his army would have been seen by now. He concluded, that it could only mean that the local people knew of him and wholly supported him.

Oswald picked his spot for the fight, he was sure that God was with him. The battle would take place at Hefenfelth [30] they made that their camp for the night and set about preparing for the morrow's battle.

While Oswald slept that night in his tent, he had a dream, he dreamt of Colm Cille a man he'd never known. [31] The Saint shone like an angelic beauty, he was so tall his head seemed to touch the clouds and as he stood in their camp, he covered it all but for one corner with his shining robe. Colm Cille spoke to Oswald in the dream just as God had spoken to Joshua, saying, '*be strong and act manfully, behold I will be with you.*' The saint also said, '*This night go out from your camp for the Lord has granted you that your foes shall be put to flight and Cadwallon, your enemy shall be delivered into your hands and you shall return victorious after the battle, and reign happily.*'

Oswald awoke trembling; he was sweating. He wiped the back of his hand across his forehead to clear the sweat from his eyes. He'd never had a dream so stunningly clear as the one he'd been awoken by; he was in a state of utter bewilderment. There was an earthenware jug of cold water by his cot and he filled a bowl and washed, but the dream would not leave him it was so vivid he felt that he could have reached out and touched Saint Colm Cille.

Oswald awoke his leaders to tell them of his dream. The sleepy confused men Christian and pagan alike, were to a man touched by the telling of Oswald's vision and felt the powerful encouragement it engendered.

'You must tell the men of this Lord; it will bring great encouragement. We are all men the same. When the hour of the battle draws near, fear and doubt touch every man. Believe me Lord, I am too old, and have been here too many times, not to know the truth of it.'

At first light, Oswald repeated the tale of his dream and the men listened intently. As he spoke aloud the words of Saint Colm Cille, *'Your enemy shall be delivered into your hands and you shall return victorious after the battle,'* he felt with deep conviction that his life as a warrior was pleasing to God. He did not need to fear that the manner of his birth was a hindrance to God, for had he not said through the Saint he would reign?

So powerfully did Oswald feel God's blessing that he had men erect a wooden cross on the site so that all might see that they, these Bernician warriors, fought for the Living God, his God, and his priests blessed the cross and prayed for the warriors.

After the priests had blessed the cross, the warriors launched their attack on the camp of Cadwallon, near Hagustaldesham [32] Oswald's warriors achieved almost total surprise. The Britons were forced to run, with the Bernicians in hot pursuit, the Britons were eventually trapped and massacred, along with Cadwallon himself, and his most faithful warriors who'd surrounded him at a place called Divelis. [33]

Oswald thought that they had probably hoped to cross the river and escape onto the moors. Even though Oswald's force was smaller than the Briton's, they had overwhelmed them, the defeat was total, there was no mercy shown, their bodies were left to rot in the bloody river where they'd been killed. This was a great victory by any standards and Oswald knew it would be talked about for many years.

After the battle, Oswald knelt in his tent and gave thanks to God for His kindness to the Bernician people.

Chapter 22

A New Friend

Oswald was now the King of Bernicia; he'd been crowned at Caer Urfa [34] at the eastern end of the great Roman Wall. It had been a windy day at the end of Winterfilleð [35] when he had been proclaimed King of Bernicia on a hilltop called Lawe Top, some now called the hill, *Oswald's* Hill, in memory of the great occasion.

He had wanted to return to his capital of Bebbanburg as their undisputed King, the son of the *great* King Æthelfrith of

Bernicia and confirmed as his rightful heir by the Elders of the Witan.

Oswald felt to be a man chosen by God; he had never sought any of this. Abbot Ségéne told him that the Christ was called the son of David, but he was not in fact the descendant of the great King David. He was *God's* son, conceived of the Holy Ghost.

The Christ had taken on David's name from his adopted father's line. Oswald felt his lineage was in some way similar, because his father was not actually King Æthelfrith. His father was the Lord Wulfstan who was exalted by all who knew him, and his mother was Queen Aefre, but he, Oswald was known by all as the son of Æthelfrith and always had been.

The names of his mother and father, and their love, forever touched Oswald's heart, they, their names, and their sacrifice would be forgotten. The little he knew of their story was that two people had loved enough to lay down their lives. They had done no more than that, they had not wanted such a love; they'd tried to run from it. Unlike the Christ, Oswald reflected, they, their names, and their sacrifice would be forgotten.

Cedric had told him that he set no one above his father Wulfstan, that his honour, goodness and kindness was an example to all, this had been the testimony of all those who'd ever known him. God in His goodness had seen fit to have mercy upon them and *he* had been blessed because of them. As with David and Bathsheba, God had seen fit to give them a son and make him the great King Solomon, famed for his wisdom and wealth. So also, God had made him, Oswald of Bernicia son of Wulfstan and Aefre, a King, and he would serve God as long as he lived. He, by the grace of the Living God, would bring Christianity to all he ruled; his would be a Godly kingdom, a light in the pagan darkness of Briton.

Oswald sat at his work table tapping the soft feathered end of his quill on his lip, contemplating the events of his history that had brought him thus far, sometimes of great joy, but there were others of yet unbearable sorrow. The pain of losing his beloved Helen ever tormented his heart. He looked around the room, it was incomplete, as would every place be, where he set foot, or laid his head at the end of a day.

'Dear God, how lonely I am, forgive me.' A quiet voice in his head reminded him of a piece of scripture from the prophet Joel, *"I will restore to you the years that the locusts have eaten"*.

Suddenly, there was a scratching sound at the end of his long worktable, and he turned his head to the sound, it took a moment for his tear-filled eyes to focus. There was a large black bird, a Raven, pecking contentedly at a plate of half eaten food, which had not yet been cleared away by his servant.

It was the strangest thing, and then he remembered how in the scripture story God had sent ravens to minister to Elijah when he was distressed. Was this God's way of speaking to him, and telling him He knew of his need, and He would feed him?

Oswald was in this moment lifted from his despair and gave thanks. The bird looked at him as if it might speak, cocking its head first to one side, and then to the other. Oswald gently set down his quill, and slowly reached out his hand to the glossy black bird, but it was startled and flapped its wings, then it settled once more and came to him laying its beak in the palm of his hand. He gently touched the tip of his finger to the crown of its head and the creature seemed perfectly content. He smiled, for he was sure that he'd made a friend this day.

He decided in that moment that he would write to his friend, Abbot Ségéne and ask his advice about how best to further the gospel of the Christ God in his kingdom. He remembered that they had talked about the island of Lindis Feorna or Metcaud, as the Abbot called it. Perhaps the wily old fox always had such a plan in mind Oswald thought, pausing and smiling. In any event, Oswald knew that his friend would be able to advise him.

Oswald had heard that his uncle King Edwin had tried, even if it was half-heartedly, to set up some Christian work. Alas, the Bishop who had been set the task, whose name seemed to have been lost, was lacking in any ability to reach the Bernician people. It had been said of the Bishop, that his manner was one of threatening and bullying; suffice to say; the mission had failed miserably.

No matter how he tried, Oswald was unable to find out any detail, where the fellow had come from or to where he had gone.

While Oswald waited for the reply from Abbot Ségéne he decided to travel around his kingdom and also to those minor kingdoms of which he was Overlord, such as the kingdom of the West Saxons.

Oswald had heard that there was a Christian work being done, with some success, in the royal house of Gewisse and he wanted to encourage and lend his support to it.

He'd been told by Abbot Ségéne that a bishop called Birinus had been sent from Rome. His original commission entailed preaching to parts of Briton where no missionary efforts had reached, and it may have included instructions to reach the Mercians in particular. However, at this time, he had gone no further than the West Saxon kingdom of King Cynegils.

King Cynegils seemed content to allow Bishop Birinus to preach the faith of the Christ God to the people of the West Saxons.

It was also rumoured that King Cynegils wanted the support of the new king of Bernicia to help him secure his kingdom against the Mercians, clearly Oswald's fame as a holy warrior king, was spreading throughout Briton.

'Yes!' Oswald decided, as he sat at his table with his new friend, that was where he would make his first visit, and then he would wend his way slowly up country back to his home, visiting the people of his new kingdom and establishing his rule. It had been a long road to this place in his life, but he believed that God's timing was always perfect. He'd had much to learn and when he looked back over the way he'd travelled, he could clearly see the hand of God.

If King Edwin had not forced them to flee from Bernicia, he knew that he'd never have gone to Iona. That he'd never have met Abbot Ségéne, never learned how to read and write, never learned the art of warfare, at the expense of other kings, never found the most Holy God, and he'd never have discovered how *He* could hold and support a human being through even the blackest torments of life.

He'd found a God who'd chosen to make His home in the suffering degradation of mankind, so that He could share in man's most desperate moments. A God, who would not turn from the rejection, failings and torments of His creation, a God who had sent his only Son to redeem His wilful and rebellious children. He knew now that his weakness was God's strength, and so when he was weak, and all was against him, God was at His strongest.

'In thee have I trusted, let me never be confounded.'

Oswald was setting off into a new world, and for the first time he would be leaving the old world behind, starkly highlighted by the waving hand of Hrodulf. He could not call on him forever, he was old, and this was a long journey, He'd earned the time to be at his ease. When he argued, and he did argue with Oswald, his challenge was not to his King, but to his friend for that's what Oswald was to him. Oswald had learned how to fight; now he needed to learn how to stand and rule. The two had been through so much together, they'd love the same people, Oswald could ask no more and Hrodulf could give no more.

Oswald did however leave Hrodulf with a smile on his face, saying that he now had a greater responsibility than caring for him.

He was to care for his new friend, "Theophilus", friend of God, his raven, who followed him everywhere.

Oswald tried to smile at the thought of leaving; thankfully, he still had Oswiu by his side, but he was leaving Æthelwald, his son. His birthday was forever a miserable date to remember, but Oswald loved him and he his father, he was a fine boy. Æthelwald had wanted to come with him, but Oswald felt it was too uncertain to risk his wellbeing, Hrodulf would care for him, Oswald knew that.

He recalled how he'd felt when his father King Æthelfrith had left on similar journeys as the one he was undertaking, but these sacrifices were part of being King and he would accept them as such.

The journey took five days, longer than Oswald thought it would, he was overwhelmed by the reception he received from villages on his way. People were calling him a saint; they'd heard stories of how people had been healed by merely getting close to the wooden cross he'd erected at Hefenfelth, where he'd defeated King Cadwallon and his army.

It was said that one day a horseman was riding near Oswald's cross when his horse began to feel great pain. It rolled in agony on the ground, apparently dying, but at the sight of the cross, it was immediately cured. Its owner told the story at the nearest inn, and the people there decided to take a paralysed girl to the same spot. She was cured too.

It seemed that everyone they met had heard of his vision of Saint Colm Celli and how he'd told Oswald, that the victory against Cadwallon would be his.

Oswald was certain that the majority of people he met would not be followers of the Christian God, but that did not appear to make the slightest difference. People who were sick pushed towards him hoping for a chance to touch him. Even as he travelled, the stories followed in his wake, of how people had been healed after touching him or his clothing.

Oswald was mightily relieved when he finally dismounted at the court of King Cynegils, but even there, people treated him with a reverence, that such as Abbot Ségéne would not be unfamiliar.

King Cynegils and his family came out of their longhouse to greet him, even Bishop Birinus had come to meet him and he went as far as to kneel before Oswald. Oswald was so confused by this absurd treatment he could only stand in silence smiling like the fool he felt.

'You do us a great honour Lord; we are blessed amongst men that you should come to visit us. The Bishop here tells us that God's hand is upon you and that it is a sign from the true God that I should be baptised.'

'And what do you think, King Cynegils? It is not for me to instruct you, it's you who must decide what God is saying to you, but we are tired from the journey we will talk on this later, might we bathe…' Oswald was distracted from the embarrassment he was feeling when he caught sight of a beautiful young woman smiling at him.

King Cynegils gave orders to servants to tend to the needs of King Oswald and his men and then he turned once more to Oswald and began to introduce his family to him. The beautiful young woman was his daughter, Cyneburh. Oswald could only stare at the woman. She was uncannily like his beloved wife Helen, and this, was almost a repeat of the day when he first arrived at Dunadd, all those years past. It was not until Oswiu tugged at his sleeve that he realised he was yet staring at the woman.

Servants led them to the house where they would be staying and a very fine house it was, Oswald could plainly see how he was to be treated by King Cynegils, for all was done to impress upon him the honour in which he was to be held.

Chapter 23

Cyneburh

Oswald lay down on his cot, with his head resting on his linked hands.
'This has been a strange adventure Oswiu, has it not?'

'Certainly, strange for me, I have never known a saint before, let alone touched one…' Oswiu ducked as one of Oswald's gauntlets flew past his ear and he laughed.

'This is difficult enough for me without your input, brother, pass me my gauntlet and be glad it was not my seax.' Oswald was struggling to turn the last days travelling here into anything approaching a jest.

'I'm sorry, Oswald, but I'm laughing, in an attempt to keep myself in some world of reality, while we make our way through this maze of unravelled lonnens, in which we now find ourselves,' Oswiu said passing the gauntlet back to Oswald.

'I know what you mean, Oswiu, it's beyond anything I've ever heard of.'

Oswiu sat down on his bed, 'I wish Abbot Ségéne was here to ask, perhaps he'd be better equipped to understand all this than we are.'

'Who knows, on another line of thought, what did you make of King Cynegils' daughter, Princess Cyneburh?'

Oswiu narrowed his eyes and looked suspiciously at Oswald who was staring nonchalantly up into the rafters. 'Why do you ask?'

'Oh – no particular reason, Brother, merely making conversation, no more than that… It's strange that she is not wed though, she is surely past the age when she would expect to be wedded, and she has tolerable features.'

'Perhaps no one wanted her,' Oswiu suggested teasingly, whilst tugging off his boot and massaging his toes. He could be obtuse too, if that's what Oswald wanted.

There was some activity outside, and Oswald lifted his head to see what it was, just as servants carrying a large tub came through the door.

'Lord, your tub…' the fellow said stating the obvious. 'We'll fill it in a minute, Lord, can we gets anything else for thee?' the man said nervously, never lifting his head.

'Not now, we'll bathe first.'

Two servants entered with towels, they obviously had been set the work of bathing them. Whilst several others trundled in and out with large jugs of steaming hot water, Oswald undressed.

Clearly, they were to be bathed and dressed under the supervision of these diligent servants.

'We have more servants here than at home, Lord, and prettier too.' The girl preparing to scrub Oswald smiled at Oswiu's comment.

'Indeed.'

Once they were both bathed, and dressed, they were shown into an attractively decorated hall with the usual painted patterns on the woodwork, and hunting scenes on the walls. They were taken to the high-table and Oswald was given the most elevated seat, which surely was where King Cynegils would normally sit.

He wasn't sure exactly why he was being treated with such excessive deference. Was it because he was their Overlord or because they thought him some great holy man or did King Cynegils merely want to ensure his support against his Mercian enemies?' It was unsettling and he felt uneasy, but then he shrugged, what did it matter anyway.

A servant drew back his chair so that he could take his place at the table then he pushed it carefully under him. Once Oswald was seated, the others there took their places. King Cynegils sat to his right and his wife next to him, beside her their son Cwichelm then Oswiu. On Oswald's left sat the Princess

Cyneburh, then Bishop Birinus. She bowed her head respectfully and smiled as she took her seat.

Oswald was slightly amused by the seating arrangements. He was surprised that he was seated next to the Princess, he would have expected to be seated between Prince Cwichelm and the King, but he knew well Prince Cwichelm's history with Bernicia. He had not travelled all this way, without being well informed about the places and people he was going to encounter. If they took him for a naive saint, they were in for a rude awakening.

He knew fine well that King Cynegils had been concerned about the rise of Bernician power in the north. King Cynegils had ceded the northern half of his kingdom to his son, Cwichelm, effectively creating a buffer state in the process. He also forged a temporary alliance with the Mercians who were equally concerned about the growing power of the Bernicians, and this alliance was sealed by the marriage of Cynegils' youngest son Cenwalh, who was noticeable by his absence this night, to the sister of King Penda of Mercia.

In 626, the hot-headed Cwichelm launched an unsuccessful assassination attempt on King Edwin of Bernicia. Oswald smiled as he recalled the tale he'd been told. Edwin subsequently sent his army to confront the West Saxons and both sides clashed at a place called Bēamford [36] over to the west of Briton. With the Mercians at their side, the West Saxons had a far larger army than the Bernicians, and went into the battle with complete confidence, but they were defeated due to poor tactics. Oswald had been told that the Bernicians had dug into the side of a place called, "Win Hill" and when the West Saxon forces started moving forward, they were met by a barrage of boulders that had been rolled from the Bernician position above them.

This had been a humiliating defeat for both Cynegils and Cwichelm, and they subsequently retreated within their own borders. The following years saw the Mercians take advantage of the weakened West Saxons by taking the old Roman towns of Gloucester, Bath and Cirencester from them.

The assault today was a subtler form of attack, and one, to which Oswald was not averse. He for one, was no more likely to object to the attention of a beautiful young woman, than any other man would be, suppose he was a saint. He a saint, 'Ha,' he actually made himself laugh at the absurdity. The Princess frowned, no doubt wondering about his seemingly unwarranted amusement.

Oswald saw her narrow her eyes as she glanced at him. 'Forgive my rudeness Princess; I was merely laughing at myself, and how people apparently see me. I am really such an ordinary fellow.'

'Can a King be so ordinary Lord? Perhaps because you see yourself in such a manner, it makes you anything but ordinary.'

It was now Oswald's turn to be taken aback, but he was not afforded the time to think on what she had said. King Cynegils stood, lifted his drinking cup, banged on the table and the hum of chatter and laughter quickly died.

'Let all who are gathered here, drink to the health and future of the great Warrior and King of Bernicia. We welcome you, King Oswald, and all here in this hall are pleased to share this humble feast with you.'

At which there was raucous banging on the tables and cheering. Oswald did no more than lift his silver cup and dip his head in acknowledgement and respect of the greeting. Once the guests had settled again to their seats, Oswald turned to the Bishop and asked him to bless their mete. A faint smile touched his lips as those who had eagerly began to feast slowly set down the mete they had only just picked up.

The Bishop stood and gave thanks for the mete, bowed to Oswald, and took his seat once more.

There was ale for all, but for them fine wine was on offer; the Princess lifted the jug and set it to his cup for his approval.

'Do you wish for wine, Lord?' Clearly, she was serving him as a demonstration of humility to their Overlord.

'You are very kind Princess,' he nodded, and she carefully filled his cup. 'Tell me about yourself, Princess.'

'What is it you wish to know Lord?'

'Whatever you wish to tell me, what do you enjoy doing for example?'

She hesitated; Oswald could see she was finding his directness difficult. 'I like riding Lord, I ride most days.'

'That's good, so do I, will you let me join you on the morrow? You can show me your home.'

Her eyes brightened, 'If you wish it, I would be delighted to, Lord.'

'I wish it,' he laughed, and she smiled too, showing beautiful even white teeth framed by the most perfect red lips.

As he leaned forward and set his cup to the table, he thought, this was the most honest laughter he'd had since Helen had died.

The following morning Oswald was up bright and early, it was a fine day and he would hold Princess Cyneburh to her promise that she would go riding with him. It would be an ideal opportunity to find out about the West Saxon kingdom and its people.

Oswald was reluctant to admit to himself, never mind his brother Oswiu, that on this particular morning he wanted to know more about Princess Cyneburh than the West Saxons.

Oswald was slightly unsettled as he sat at the table for the breaking of his night's fast. He tried to enter into the conversation with others who had gathered around him. All seemed eager for his company, but he'd hoped to see Princess Cyneburh and as of, yet she had not shown her face. Perhaps he had made her feel too uncomfortable at the feast the night past and she wanted to avoid him.

The brightness of his awakening mood was rapidly disappearing into an altogether gloomier, overcast day.

He wondered where Oswiu was, he'd told him that he wanted to see the smith before he came to break his night's fast, but he had not as yet appeared.

As Oswald was leaving the hall, a servant came to him and bowed.

'Yes!'

'The Princess has asked me to make it known to you Lord that she is at the stables if you yet wish to go riding with her.'

Suddenly, Oswald's gloom was dispersed by a ray of sunlight.

'Take me to the Princess.'

When the stables came into view, Oswald could see Princess Cyneburh standing by two fine mounts, dressed for riding. As he approached them, both horses snorted and pawed on the floor of the yard, eager to be off.

'My Lord,' she said bowing. 'I hoped that you yet wish to join me.'

Oswald bowed to her, 'Indeed, I assumed that you had either forgotten or were otherwise engaged. However, I'm delighted that was not the case.' Oswald nodded to four warriors and the maid who were clearly there to accompany them.

Oswald mounted, he was known as an accomplished horseman, and he'd been given a fine steed.

As they rode from the fort gates, he glanced at a flock of crows taking flight from a fallow field and flying ponderously across the smoke-streaked blue sky before them. All seemed well with the world this fine morning.

They were clear of the fort and the nearby sleepy village before they spoke.

Oswald brought his horse nearer to Cyneburh's and they slowed their pace to a trot. The two horses shook their heads and snorted rattling their harnesses, clearly wanting to press on, not yet ready to walk, but like Oswald, Cyneburh was quite able to establish that she was in command of her mount, not the mount in command of her.

They were now leisurely walking their horses along a riverbank.

'Tell me Princess, how can it be that someone such as you are not wedded? Forgive me if that is too personal a question.'

'I might ask you the same, Lord.'

Oswald nodded his head, 'Indeed you might, Princess.' His happy mood had now been changed by a simple question, his smile now left his face and he stared into the distance. They rode on in silence for some time; all the while, he strummed his fingers nervously on his thigh, wondering what to say. Most avoided asking such a question of him, so he'd never had to say much about his feelings for Helen. It was something too painful to face up to, so he pushed it to one side, he knew he'd never moved on, he clung to her memory, it was all he had. This woman had innocently confronted him, and he had not been prepared for the challenge.

'Might we dismount for a while and sit on the riverbank,' he asked, trying to sound perfectly at his ease.

'If it is your wish, Lord.'

Oswald dismounted first then reached up to aid the Princess, she rested her hands on his shoulders and he lowered her to the ground. He laid his cloak on the sward, took her hand and she sat down, he seated himself next to her, drew his knees to his chest and wrapped his arms around his legs.

'Have I offended you, Lord?'

'No, no, forgive me... I – *have* been married – and I have a son of some ten years, ten years,' he repeated. 'Has it really been so long, – my wife...' he bowed his head, 'was called Helen,' he said in a soft voice. 'She died when my son was born. I have never really talked about it before this moment, to my friend, the Abbot of Iona, perhaps, *but* not to anyone else, that seems odd now I mention it.'

'Clearly it was a love match, Lord.'

'Yes – a love match. We'd been in love since we were young, no more than children, I guess,' he gasped and tried to control his speech. 'Aye – we were in love.'

'I was betrothed once, to a Prince from Mercia. The threat from Mercia is ever a concern of my father's, but the man caught some flux or other and died before we were wedded.'

'Now it is I who should ask for your forgiveness, I'm sorry to hear such a thing.'

'No need, I had but met him once, there was no love there. If I may say more,' she smiled and lowered her voice, 'you will see now what a rebellious, traitorous daughter I am, when I make known to you that my father hopes to foist me onto the King of Bernicia.'

'*What, me!*'

'You see – such foolishness.'

'Forgive me, I meant no insult. I would see that to be an honour,' and he smiled at her and touched her hand. From that moment on their talk was easy, this was a long-forgotten experience for him. In fact, he could only ever remember really talking to one woman, Helen, and of course his beloved Æbbe.

'Perhaps we should return, I'm not usually gone for such a time.'

'My fault, come Princess, let us ride back, perhaps we will keep our conversation to ourselves, that those concerned may wonder.' She laughed, they both laughed, he stood, reached down to her, took her hand, and raised her to her feet.

When they rode into the fort, the first-person Oswald saw was Oswiu, who nodded most knowingly at him, much to Oswald's infuriation. Oswald dismounted and lifted Cyneburh from her saddle; she bowed and left, escorted by her maid. Oswald paused, took a deep breath and walked to where his brother was smugly sitting.

'Was that a pleasant ride Brother?'

'Yes, I learned a great deal in casual conversation, things that I would not have learned in a more formal setting.'

'Is that so.'

'You forget brother, that kings have the power of life and death over their subjects.'

Oswiu laughed, 'Come, share what you know over a jug of ale, my King of
Bernicia, I am your most humble subject.'

When Oswald saw King Cynegils next, he took Oswald aside clearly wishing to talk with him in private. Oswald prepared himself for the offer of his daughter in marriage, but nothing could have been further from the subject of an earthly marriage.

King Cynegils asked him if he would honour him by standing as his godfather at his baptism. Oswald was quite speechless at first, eventually saying to a nervously waiting King Cynegils that it would be an honour to stand with him.

Oswald knew that this would be all that Bishop Birinus could have hoped and prayed for, the conversion of a King often meant in practice, the conversion of a kingdom.

Chapter 24

Warrior – King – Saint

Oswald was cautious about the integrity of King Cynegils' conversion after his experience with Eanfrith who had merely used the church to his own ends and then when it suited him, reverted to his pagan past.

When he mentioned his doubts to Bishop Birinus, the Bishop asked, who were they to judge the heart of another man?

At the very least, the Bishop was now able to preach the gospel freely and that was something of a miracle in itself.

On the day of the baptism, the weather was kind to them, and the sun shone for this new child of God, who this day would enter into the hope of eternity through this outward confession of a spiritual reality. This earthly king would now take on a new heavenly robe of righteousness.

Oswald prayed with King Cynegils, as his role of godfather dictated and assured the King that he would continue to support him in prayer, in the years to come. Whatever was the truth of this moment, Oswald had to admit that King Cynegils' confession of faith seemed sincere.

Dressed in a short-sleeved white robe King Cynegils was led into the river. Oswald smiled as he saw fish scatter before him, he remembered the fish scattering before the boat when he first went to Iona. King Cynegils knelt, holding his crown before him, clearly placing under God his kingship as well as his humanness.

Oswald stood on the riverbank holding towels. The Bishop scooped up water in a silver dish and poured it over King Cynegils' head, saying, 'I baptise you, Cynegils of the West Saxons, in the name of the Father, Son, and Holy Ghost.'

As the King walked out of the river towards Oswald, he nodded towards his assembled household who one by one followed his lead and were baptised. During the day the whole of the King's family and household were baptised into the Christian faith, including Princess Cyneburh.

At the feasting that night, Oswald decided to ask the Princess if she would return to Bernicia with him as his wife and Queen.

On asking her, her immediate reaction was to laugh. Over the weeks Oswald had been with the West Saxons, they had become easy friends, but this was a surprise. Her first thought was that he was teasing her, in the light of what she'd told him of her father's hopes. Oswald's disappointed face quickly dispelled that thought.

'Lord, forgive me for my cruelty, you are *truly* serious, aren't you?' Now she was solemn too and stared into his eyes. 'If I was to choose a husband he would be in your image, my dearest Oswald and Lord. If it is truly your wish, then it is mine also.'

'Then it is decided,' and he embraced her, 'Princess, I cannot tell you how happy you have made me. I must talk with your father.'

This was all that King Cynegils had hoped for and he duly thanked the Christ God.

Oswald would return to Bernicia with his new Queen and an ally secured in the south.

As Oswald's entourage travelled slowly north, they visited town after town and village after village. Their subjects fell down before them, offering flowers and gifts and begging that he might pray for their sick.

These were good days and both Cyneburh and Oswald prayed each morning and night giving thanks to God, they could be in no doubt that their subjects saw him as a saintly person.

The first sight of Bebbanburg was all that Oswald said it was, it was more beautiful than Cyneburh had ever imagined it could be, set as it was in the rolling landscape of Bernicia, which sloped and meandered lazily down to the coast with its sandy beaches and blue sea. The view was simply stunning.

'Oswald, it is magnificent, I know that I will be happy here.'

All that Cyneburh said pleased Oswald for he loved his home.

They rode up the hill to the fortress and into the yard, standing there to greet them was none other than his old friends Abbot Ségéne and Brother Aidan from Iona. Oswald leapt from his horse and excitedly embraced them both. He didn't know where to start so much had happened since he'd last seen them.

'One moment,' he reached up to Cyneburh and lowered her to the ground. 'This, my friends, is my new Queen, Cyneburh, a child of the Living God, from the West Saxons, daughter of the newly converted King Cynegils.'

The Abbot and Brother Aidan bowed respectfully.

'I am honoured to meet the two men of whom my husband speaks so highly.'

'We have all been friends for many years my Lady, I pray that we might be numbered amongst *your* friends.'

'Then your prayer is answered,' she said laughing.

'Come, we have much to speak of, I am delighted to see you here, when did you arrive? I never expected such honoured guests.'

'Five days past, Lord, but our time has not been wasted,' Aidan told him.

'See to it that we have mete and drink in the hall,' Oswald ordered a servant as he passed.

'This is much grander than I am used to Oswald,' commented Cyneburh as she walked, and looked at all before her.

Hrodulf quickly joined them in the hall and with him came Oswald's son Æthelwald who leapt into his father's arms. Hrodulf embraced Oswald and Oswald introduced him to Cyneburh, he bowed to his new Queen and the Abbot.

'How are you my fine boy, I have missed you. I want you to meet a very special person whom I love and know you will grow to love too. Now take your arms from around my neck and, as I know you can, bow respectfully to this lady who is now your new mother and Queen of Bernicia.'

Æthelwald did as he was bidden, but with reservation, clearly, he was not sure what this meant. Oswald was distracted for a moment then lifted Æthelwald once more onto his lap and turned his attention to the Abbot and Aidan.

Oswald said that he never imagined that the Abbot would come in person and to bring his old friend Aidan was more than he could have possibly hoped.

Abbot Ségéne told Oswald that Aidan was now a Bishop and that he'd been working in Hibernia. He had left that work to bring the gospel to Bernicia.

'Have you been to Lindis Feorna yet?'

'Indeed, we have.'

'What did you think, Bishop Aidan?'

'We think it ideal, the perfect location to set up a community and we will reach out from there to the people of Bernicia.'

'We will need help and funds for the work,' added Abbot Ségéne.

'Fear not, you shall have all that you require. For this work of God is dearest to my heart.'

That night Oswald was so utterly overwhelmed by the joy he felt, he was unable to sleep. He walked and talked, sat, lay next to Cyneburh, then rose and walked some more, all the while she lay in their bed wrapped in his joy, how she loved this man.

Then he paused and lifted his finger to his nose as if struck by a sudden thought, and went to a small chest, opened it and withdrew something from it.

'I have something very special for you, it belonged to my mother, she never wore it, she once told me when I was young, younger than Æthelwald is now, that it had actually belonged to her sister. She said that the man she loved had given it to her. That meant nothing to me at the time, but it does now, I understand completely what she was saying and the significance of it.'

Oswald came to Cyneburh with his hands cupped together. Slowly he opened them like a clam revealing its pearl, but when Oswald's hands opened inside was the largest most beautiful emerald, she had ever seen on a gold chain.

She gasped, pressing her hand to her mouth. '*Oswald*, I have never seen anything like it in my life, it is beyond beauty.'

'Let me fasten it around your neck, where it belongs.'

'Where did it come from?'

'In truth, I know not. My mother, Queen Acha never wore it as far as I can recall, she showed it to me only the one time, when she told me it belonged to her sister. My mother, Queen Acha died on the island of Coll off the west coast of Alba, when I was living on Iona with the monks. Her belongings were packed and stored at Dunadd and I never opened them until they were brought here and that's when I found this, and I remembered what she had once said to me.'

'I am so honoured, that you should give this to me.'

'It is more precious to me Cyneburh than you could ever imagine, as you are. It was given by a Lord Wulfstan to the Lady Aefre and they mean everything to me.'

'Who were they?'

'I will tell you the tale sometime, but not today.'

These were the happy years; Bernicia became a thriving kingdom with stability and wealth. Oswald's goodness and generosity as a King and ruler spread to all corners of Briton.

The work on Lindis Feorna was all Aidan and he had hoped for, they had been joined by more monks from Iona, all able and familiar with the work. Aidan's gentle self-effacing manner had suited the Bernician personality perfectly and they were growing to love the man.

Oswald was sorry that Cyneburh was not allowed on the island, they followed the same rules as the community on Iona, but Oswald told her in detail every stage of the work. He even made sketches for her so that she would have a better understanding.

One Easter feast at Bebbanburg where he'd invited Bishop Aidan to dine with him, a servant came to Oswald and told him there were beggars at the door asking for food. Oswald not only told him to feed them, but that the silver platter before him should be broken up and given to them. 'How can any man dine on such when there are men starving?'

Aidan had been so touched by
Oswald's demonstration of kindness, that he had grasped his hand and prayed that it would never know corruption.

Oswald lifted his eyes from the letter he was reading and looked to Cyneburh who was busy with some needlework, by the window, 'I have had some disturbing correspondence from your father, Cyneburh, it appears that King Penda of Mercia is making war on the West Saxons, and I am sworn to help your people as their Overlord. I must raise an army and go south to give support as I have promised, and as soon as I can.'

'When, will that be, Lord?'

'It will need to be done as quickly as I can, otherwise it might be too late. Who knows how long I will be gone, but I must go as soon as I am able to.'

The last few days had been hectic, but all was ready now. Oswald strode to his horse with the appearance of more confidence than he felt. He had rarely been separated from Cyneburh since they'd first met, which made this parting all the more difficult. She clung to his arm as he walked, and Æthelwald who was now eighteen walked alongside them. Oswald was fully dressed for war, when he reached his horse, he paused with his hand on the saddle then turned to Æthelwald withdrew the Ulfberht from its frog and passed it to him.

'I will leave this precious thing in your safe keeping, Son, it means too much to me to risk it being stolen on my travels.'

'But Father…'

'Hush, I have other swords, but this one belonged to your grandfather, your mother here will tell you all, when she has a mind to. She knows all the history of this sword and its owner.'

He wrapped Cyneburh in his arms, she reached up and touched a grey curl on the side of his head with her finger, and then she quickly withdrew her hand and cuffed a tear from her cheek. He lowered his head and tenderly pressed his lips to hers. When he tried to turn, she clung to him and refused to let him go…

'I can't do this Oswald, the pain is more than I can bear,' she whispered into his ear.

'My dearest Cyneburh, you are the Queen of Bernicia and you will be strong for Bernicia.' He kissed her once more, smiled weakly, and gave her to Æthelwald to hold, 'Take care of your mother, my Son; I leave all in your hands. God bless and keep you both.'

'And you my dearest most precious husband.'

Oswald wearily mounted his waiting horse, leaned forward and patted its neck, nodded to his wife and son and he rode out of the gates, down the bank to the beach where his army eagerly awaited him.

Once he was with them, they moved off along the sand, southward, just as he had done so many times before. As the fort was about to disappear behind the sand dunes and out of his sight, he stopped and turned, while his army, rode passed him.

Finally, he was alone, and he looked back towards the great fort of Bebbanburg. A gust of wind blew the silk scarf Cyneburh had tied to his arm and it fluttered before his eyes, and from it he caught the fragrance of her nearness. He knew his beloved wife Cyneburh, and his son Æthelwald would yet be watching, though he could no longer see them. It was strange – thought Oswald, as he looked back. As he gazed at the fortress, silhouetted as it was, against the grey streaked Bernician sky. This view before him seemed to symbolise and contain, most of his life, if any single view could, that is.

Strange... *strange* the things you remember, he thought. He thought of the people he'd known and loved, none more than Cedric, and his beloved Helen. The places, the moments in time burned into his heart forever, whilst others just fade into the mist. He'd always known he'd lived a life different from other men. He reflected on when he was a boy and saw no path before him. He'd simply taken one step then another, ever rushing to a place he knew not where, and now he looked back and saw that each step he'd taken was a choice, to go left, or go right, to go forward or even not go at all. He could see so clearly now that every day one had choices to make, between right and wrong, love and hate, to forgive or not to forgive. Sometimes even between life and death and the sum of those choices, was the measure of a life lived.

He lowered his head; he could choose even now to ride back into the arms of his wife and son. Man's right to choose was God's costly gift to His children, which had ultimately cost Him His life.

Oswald knew that his mother and father had made choices, and each choice had played its part in *this* moment. He stared for a little while longer, searing the image into his mind, until the tears in his eyes made the edges of the skyline blurred. Then, with a heavy heart, he made the choice to honour his word – against the choice presented by his heart; slowly he turned his pony, and rode off...

Love is more than the time spent between hello and goodbye.

Author's Notes

KEY:

[1] **Elne:** Saxon measurement 1 elne or ulna equals three feet/914.4mm (later yard)

[2] **Ad-Gefrin:** So-called by Bede, "Now known as Yeavering" is a twin-peaked hill near the river Glen in Northumbria, England, to the west of the village of Woller, and forming part of the Cheviot Hills. The hill, 361 metres above sea level, is encircled by the wall of a late-prehistoric "Hillfort", a tribal centre of the Votadini called in Brythonic and Old Welsh Din Gefron, from which the name stems from the Old English Geafringa.

The hill fort encloses an area of approximately 12 acres. It was enclosed by stonewalls, which was upwards of 10 ft (3.0 m) thick, having four entrances into it. One of which is defended by a guardhouse. Within this area is an inner fort, excavated out of the rock, of an oval form, measuring 13 ft (4.0 m) across at the widest part. On the sides of the hill, and in a high valley between the Bell and the next hill, called Whitelaw, there are many remains of stone huts rudely flagged. Some of them are in groups surrounded by rampiers (ramparts), and others isolated. Barrows, too, are numerous here. In the Annals of Cambriae, nearby River Glein is recorded as the site of the first of King Arthur's legendary twelve battles.

[3] **Din Guyaroi:** In 547 A.D. the ancient British coastal stronghold of Din Guyaroi (Bamburgh) on the North East coast was seized by the Angle chief called Ida the Flame bearer, who probably already had a foothold in the Tyne, Wear and Tees region. The name of this emerging kingdom, Bernicia, was probably an adaptation of an existing Celtic name and would come to be synonymous with the North Eastern region in the centuries to come. The rivers Tyne and Wear probably lay at the centre of this kingdom, which included most of present Northumberland and extended southwards to the Humber. Ida had conquered huge areas of land in the North East by 550 and was now undisputedly the most powerful leader in the northern Angle Land (later England). In 593, Aethelfrith, the grandson of Ida the Flame bearer, became the new King of Bernicia.

[4] **Bebbanburg:** It is clear that the name Bebbanburg was acceptable to the Æthelfrithlings, in that it stayed attached to their main royal fortress and still does.

Aethelfrith and his sons are the ones who made Bernicia into a kingdom. Prior to Aethelfrith, Bernicia was little more than a Saxon stronghold, surrounded by Britons. It makes sense that Bebba was the queen of Aethelfrith and critically, I believe, for the name to have stuck on the fortress her son must have been a long and foundational king. Now, we know that Oswald's mother was Acha of Deira, so it can't be him. This really leaves us with King Oswiu, who reigned for 28 years. Oswiu is an ideal candidate for a son of Bebba who fixed her name to the fortress permanently.

[5] **Leodwalding:** were an Anglo-Saxon aristocratic clan in Northumbria who claimed descent from King Ida of

Bernicia. They played a prominent role in eighth century Northumbrian politics, providing several kings and prelates.

[6] **Atheling:** Old English for prince or lord.

[7] **Abhainn Dubh:** River Forth in Scotland.

[8] **Abbot Ségéne:** Was a kinsman of Clom Cille (*Saint Columba*) He is credited with playing an active role amongst the Irish churches. It is tempting then to see Ségéne as the motivating force behind the Bernician conversions since he and Oswald enjoyed a close friendship, he had known Oswald while Abbot Fergno was head of the Iona community. It was through Ségéne that Oswald learned to speak fluent Irish.

[9] **Lindisfarne:** Today, often referred to as Holy Island, called by the Britons Metcaud.

[10] **Dunadd:** Originally occupied in the Iron Age, the site later became a seat of the kings of Dal Riata. It is known for its unique stone carvings below the upper enclosure, including a footprint and basin thought to have formed part of Dal Riata's coronation ritual. It is near Kilmartin in Argyll and Bute, Scotland on the west coast near Crinin Canal. Dunadd is one of the most significant archaeological sites in Scotland, and one of the most important early medieval sites in Britain. The site was excavated in 1980-81 by Dr Alan Lane of the Department of Archaeology, University of Cardiff.)

[11] **Welsh:** 607 A.D. And her Æþelfried lædde ferde to Legaceastre & þær ofsloh unrim Wealana. & swa wearþ

gefylld Augustinus witegunge he cwæð, "gif Wealas nellaþ sibbe wið us, hie sculon æt Seaxena handa forweorþan."
(Translated) 607 A.D. And this year Ethelfrith (Æthelfrith) led a troop to Chester and there murdered a huge number of Welsh people and thus was fulfilled Augustine's prophecy when he said, "if the Welsh don't wish peace with us, they shall perish at the hands of the Saxons".

[12] **Poet:** Replaced Old English **scop** (which survives in scoff). The name was used for all sorts of writers, and composers of works of literature.

[13] **Eostre:** (*Ostara, Easter, Idhunn*): is thought by some to be the spring maiden. She is compared to Idunna, the goddess of vitality and health and is said to keep the apples that furnish the gods with eternal life. As the goddess of natural beauty and life just beginning, she is seen as ever jubilant and frolicking. The only account of her existence is made by Bede in the Reckoning of Time, and the modern holiday of Easter is named for her. It is still debated whether-or-not Bede is correct in his conclusion that she is a goddess worshipped by the Anglo-Saxons.

[14] **Celtic knots:** are complete loops without any beginning or end; this unending style is called pure knots. The knots vary from simple to complicated ones. The use of only one thread highlights the Celts' belief in the interconnectedness of life and eternity.

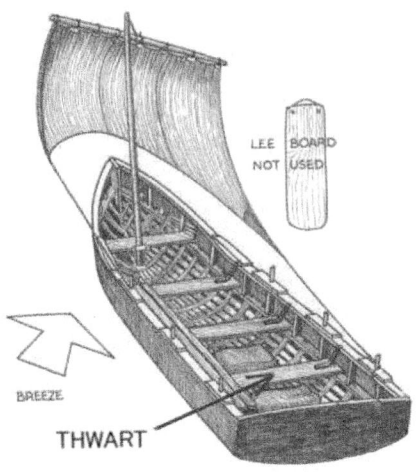

[15] **A Curragh:** was an Irish boat, which could carry at least twelve people. It was made of oak laths and tarred canvas. The boats were very flexible and needed special oars with very thin blades to prevent too much stress/torque on the side of the boat frame.

[16] **Thwart:** a board that spans the boat and serves the dual purpose of distributing the load on the structure by tying the sides together, and at the same time, creating place for crew and passengers to sit. (See above)

[17] **Muile:** The island of Mull off the western coast of Scotland.

[18] **An Crìonan:** Crinan is a village on the west coast of Scotland. The Crinan Canal is a waterway with one of its outlets at Crinan, linking Loch Fyne with Loch Crinan.

[19] Sluagad Fiachnae meic Báetáin: No historical sources for Fiachnae's life now remain, excepting a few bald entries in the Irish Annals. Several later traditions and a lost poem called Sluagad Fiachnae meic Báetáin co Dún nGuaire i Saxanaib. The hosting of Fiachnae mac Báetáin to *Dún Guaire* (**Bamburgh** in Northumbria England) in the kingdom of the Saxons) suggest that he was a significant figure in his time. He campaigned against King Edwin of Northumbria and perhaps also his predecessor King Æthelfrith. He may have captured Bamburgh, - or only besieged it circa 623.

[20] Sutton Hoo Helmet: In 1939, with World War II about to begin, archaeologists in Britain were excited by a discovery from 1,300 years ago.

Inside a grassy mound at Sutton Hoo, in Suffolk, they unearthed the remains of an Anglo-Saxon ship, possibly the tomb of a 7th-century nobleman, thought to be King Rædwald.

The wooden ship had rotted away, but its outline, and some of the treasures buried with it remained. Among the gold, silver and iron was a sword, a shield and this warrior's helmet, probably the most famous of all Anglo-Saxon museum treasures.

[21] Dál Riata (also Dalriada or Dalriata) was a Gaelic over-kingdom that included parts of western Scotland and north-eastern

Ireland, on each side of the North Channel, which connects the Irish Sea to the Atlantic Ocean. In the late 6th – early 7th centuries it encompassed roughly, what is now Argyll in Scotland and County Antrim in the Irish province of Ulster.

[22] Ulfberht:

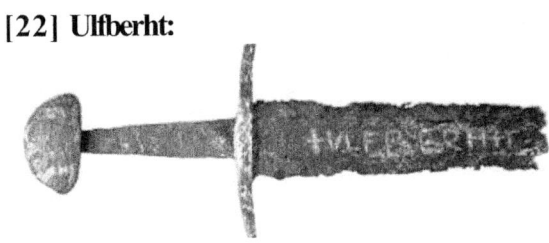

Ulfberht is a name given to unique Viking swords. The high-quality steel they used remained unparalleled until the Industrial Revolution. 171 such swords have been found so far, but only a few of these have been proven authentic Ulfberht swords. The earliest Ulfberhts date from circa 850.

Little information is available about the fabrication of the Ulfberht sword. However, modern tests reveal that genuine Ulfberht swords were forged from crucible steel, which is the purest form of steel. While most medieval weapons were made of soft iron with little carbon, an Ulfberht had a much higher level of carbon and less slag.

This made the weapon stronger, more flexible, and therefore less likely to break and easier to remove from enemy shields. The technology was likely acquired by Vikings who travelled to Central Asia. Using speculative techniques, modern-day blacksmith Richard Furrer made a replica of an Ulfberht. He can be seen making it on "You Tube".

https://www.youtube.com/watch?v=fTlmrAh1oHI

The Ulfberht gave those who wielded it, a significant advantage, and was probably carried only by elite warriors and chieftains, a high-status symbol of great expense and prestige.

Porsche, GUCCI, ROLEX, or Aston Martin would make a similar statement today.

Although of similar size and shape to a common Viking sword, the Ulfberht was far more durable, and penetrated armour more easily. The characteristic identifying mark is the metallic inlay "+VLFBERH+T" on the flat of the blade close to the hilt (the variation "+VLFBERHT+" was inlaid in swords made from lower-quality steel, much in the same way a Nike, or Rolex brand may be copied in today's market place). The sword's primary purpose was to break through an enemy's shield and chain mail armour. An Ulfberht's blade was very flexible compared to other weapons of the time and would not break or be held fast as easily when slicing into wood, striking steel, or even flesh, thus giving the swordsman opportunity to move on quickly after cutting down a foe.

"Ulfberht" is possibly a Frankish word whose meaning is unknown. The inscription "+(U)VLFBERH+T" used Latin letters.

The most common hypotheses are: that it was the name of a sword smith who passed his craft on to apprentices or family members, or that it was the name of a group of craftsmen. The word is possibly a compound of the elements *Ulfr* "Wolf" (old Norse) and *beraht,* "Light, bright, shining" (old high German, old Saxon).

In May 2008, at Christie's, £9350 was paid for an original Ulfberht sword in excavated condition, circa 950 AD.

[23] **Burials:** The remains of 110 individuals have been found in the sand dunes near Bamburgh Castle in
Northumbria. In 2016, they were laid to rest in St Aidan's Church in Bamburgh more than 1300 years after they died. By

taking DNA from their teeth at least one of the skeletons, can be identified as having lived on Iona, possibly a monk.

We also know, that one of them was a warrior named Cedric and a prayer was answered. It must be true it's in the story.

[24] **The Lord's Prayer:** "Old English" is a version of English spoken from approximately AD 450 to about 1100 and was in use in much of England and southeast Scotland. It also known as "Anglo-Saxon", and is a combination of the Germanic based languages of Old Norse and Old Frisian, and Latin.

(note: the old English "þ" is pronounced "th")

Fæder ure þu þe eart on heofonum;
Si þin nama gehalgod to becume þin
rice gewurþe ðin willa
on eorðan swa swa on heofonum.
urne gedæghwamlican hlaf syle us todæg and forgyf us ure gyltas
swa swa we forgyfað urum gyltendum and ne gelæd þu us on
costnunge ac alys us of yfele soþlice.

[25] **Whiteblade:** Oswald was known as Oswald **(Lamnguin)** Whiteblade the name is Irish and must have been given to him during his exile amongst the Scots between the age of twenty and thirty, when he returned to Northumbria.

[26] **Muine Mór:** Moneymore in Ireland (from Irish: meaning "Large thicket or large hill") is a village in County Londonderry, Northern Ireland. It is situated within Mid-Ulster District. It is an example of a plantation village in Mid-Ulster.

[27] **Fid Eóin:** the exact location of the battle is unknown.

In the Chronicon Scotorum (Author: unknown)

Anal CS629

The battle of Fid Eoin in which Mael Caích son of Scannal, i.e. the king of the Cruithin was victor. The Dál Riata fell, and Díucaill son of Eochu king of the Cruithin people fell, and Aedhan's descendants, i.e. Rigullan son of Congaing and Faelbhe son of Eochaid and Oric son of Albirit, heir designate of Saxan, with a great slaughter of their followers.

[28] **Saint Æbbe:** Abb or Ebba is sometimes known as Æbbe the Elder to avoid confusion with a later Saint Æbbe. She lived from 615 to 25 August 683. Æbbe was born a princess, the daughter of King Aethelfrith of Bernicia and his wife Acha of Deira. Aethelfrith had married Acha in 604 after invading Deira and becoming the first King of a unified Northumbria. In 616, the deposed King Edwin of Deira returned from exile and defeated Aethelfrith to become the second King of Northumbria. Aethelfrith's children, including Æbbe, were sent to safety in the court of King Domnall Brecc of Dalriada. While in exile they were converted to Christianity by the followers of Saint Columba.

[29] Cear Luel: modern day Carlisle in the North of England.

[30] Hefenfelth: Heavenfield in where Oswald camped in Northumbria England.

[31] Colm Cille: Saint Columba of Iona.

[32] Hagustaldesham: Hexham in Oswald's Northumbria.

[33] Divelis: Is now called Devils Water, near Hexham in Northumbria.

[34] Caer Urfa: South Shields is a coastal town at the mouth of the River Tyne at the eastern end of the Roman Wall. It had been a supply depot for the wall when it was a border defence of the Romans.

[35] Winterfilleð: The Anglo-Saxon lunar month corresponding to **October** was *Winterfilleð*, according to the Venerable Bede.

[36] Bēamford: They clashed at the Battle of "Win & Lose Hill" Modern day Bamford in the Derbyshire peak district.

Oswald's Time line

- 603: King Ælla of Deira must have died and **Æthelfrith became king** and drove out Edwin King Ælla's.
- 605: Born: 605ish.
- 605: Battle of Degsastan… *(Wulfstan & Aefre Die)*
- 606: In 611 Æthelfrith defeats **Ælla** (Æthelfrith must have killed Ælla) King the now King of Deira and marries Acha, Edwin's sister.
- 610: Æthelfrith marries Bebba, possibly a Pictish princess.
- 611: Oswiu is born to Bebba.
- 612: Æbbe Born to Bebba.
- 616: Æthelfrith killed at the battle of the river Idle by Edwin & King Rædwald of East Anglia.

The Story begins in 616…
(Age) Date
- (11) **616**: Oswald and his family escaped to King Eochaid Buide, who Colm Cille had prophesied to his father would be king at the Dalriadan court. (Oswald would be 11ish)

Æthelfrith's eldest son's mother (born around 590AD) was most probably Pictish and may well have been related to King Eochaid Buide, one of two possible reasons why they went to

Æthelfrith's enemy for shelter. The other reason is that Queen Bebba, who married Æthelfrith, may well also have been related to King Eochaid Buide.

- (12) **617**: Oswald went to Iona to study, Acha went to live on Coll. Bebba, may well have stayed at Dunadd the court of King Eochaid Buide.
- (12) **617** The Abbot of Iona is now Fergno Brit, probably a Briton. (Died in 623)
- (15) **620**: Eanfrith marries a Pictish princess, Edlin (Invented name) possibly King Eochaid Buide's daughter.
- (17) **622**: Eanfrith has a son, Talorcan, who becomes King of the Picts.

While no historical sources for Fiachnae's life now remain, excepting a few bald entries in the "Irish Annals", a number of later traditions and a lost poem called Sluagad Fiachnae meic Báetáin co Dún nGuaire i Saxanaib (The hosting of Fiachnae mac Baetain to Dun Guaire (Bamburgh) in the kingdom of the Saxons) suggest that he was a significant figure in his time, campaigning against King Edwin of Bernicia and perhaps also against Edwin's predecessor King Æthelfrith. He may have captured Bamburgh - or only besieged it - circa 623.

- (17) **622**: Oswald offers his sister Æbbe in marriage to Prince Domnall Brecc (King Eochaid Buide's son, nicknamed "Freckled Donald") of Dalriada, but she refuses and enters the Church.
- (18) **623**: 617 The Abbot of Iona, Fergno Brit, died.

- (18) **623**: Abbot, Ségéne replaced Fergno Brit and was one of the longest serving Abbots of Iona. He served until 652. (29 years)

- **(20) 624: In my story, Oswald marries Princess Helen.**

- (23) 628: King Eochaid Buide died now 45. *(Born 583 he would have been 33 when he met Oswald)*
- (23) 628: Oswald fought with the new King Conadd Cerr in Ireland against Maelcaich, at the battle of Fid Eóin. King Conadd Cerr was killed in the battle and was succeed by his brother, Prince Domnall Brecc.

- **(24)   629: Helen Dies in childbirth.**

See note: Age (31) in 636.
In my story Oswald's son Æthelwald born, in 629 this would make him 19 when he became king which has been suggested by some scholars.

- (28) **633**: King Edwin killed by Cadwallon of Gwynedd & Penda of Mercia when they invaded Northumbria.
- (28) **633**: Æthelfrith's eldest son Eanfrith returns to claim his throne. As soon as he becomes king, he renounces his Christian faith and returns to his pagan ways. He befriends Cadwalla or Cadwallon, *(As with all the names of this time there are many differing*

spellings) and is tricked, by going to Cadwallon with only 12 men to negotiate peace and is murdered.

- (29) **634**: Oswald's raven comes on the scene.
- (29) **634**: Oswald becomes King. There is a tradition that Oswald became king on what is now known as the Lawe Top at South Shields, in the olden days it was known as Oswald's Hill.
- (29) **634**: Oswald takes an army to defeat Cadwallon and meets him at Heavenfield (Hefenfelth). The Welsh army advance north from York. Oswald positions his smaller army beside the Roman wall about four miles north of Hexham. He has a vision in his tent of Saint Columba who assures him of victory. Oswald erects a cross. His army faces east with Brady's crag on one side and the wall on the other which creates a narrow front for Cadwallon's army.
- (30) **635**: Oswald marries Cyneburh, *(Only once her name appears and that is as Kyneburga in Reginald of Durham's 12th century writing)* the daughter of King Cynegils Wessex in order to expand his territory and Christianity. Oswald stands as godfather to King Cynegils. I suspect Oswald's wife's name would have been spelt with a "C" rather than a "K" thus my different spelling. In 1938 Henry Bosley Woolf showed that Old English female names have a high probability of *alliteration* with their father's name, and that is what I have assumed. It is not difficult to see the connection to the 12th century spelling.
- (31) **636**: Oswald and Cyneburh have a son *Æthelwald*. Æthelwald begins to rule in 651, which means he would only have been 15 years old. This has led some

> to wonder if he was the son of a relationship born whilst Oswald was in exile at the Dalriadan court.
- (32) **637**: Oswald sent for Aidan, he comes and blesses Oswald's arm, which is said to be then incorruptible.
- (33) **638**: Oswald conquers Edinburgh and his brother Oswiu marries
  Princess Rhiainfelt, the last princess of North Rheged
- (38) **642**: Oswald now 37/38, is killed at Masterfield now Oswestry in Shropshire…

St. Oswald subdued the kingdom of the Mercians and drove the pagan King Penda into exile in Wales. However, in 642 Penda gathered a large heathen army and, allying himself with the Welsh ruler of the mid-Severn valley Cynddylan, he unexpectedly attacked Oswald near Oswestry. "But the man of God," writes Reginald of Durham, "hitherto renowned for his honour as a soldier, refused to consider flight, in case he should seem a man unskilled in the conduct of battle. He considered it dishonourable to be found vanquished and disgraced at the end, when hitherto he had appeared to all to be a vigorous and victorious warrior. And so, he summoned a small force of soldiers and proceeded to commit himself to Christ, gladly choosing to die for the honour of the Lord and the faith of the Cross, and for the salvation and freedom of his Christian people... He therefore advanced to battle with great confidence, seeing that he was summoned by the Lord's mercy to a martyr's crown. Penda had gathered a large force of the heathen, and suddenly advanced to the field of battle, where he slaughtered a great number of the Christian people together with their holy and most Christian king. "Bede records that when the saint "saw that he was surrounded by enemy forces and about to be slain, he prayed for the souls of his army; and this is the origin of the proverb. 'God have mercy on their souls,' said Oswald falling to the ground.

Penda took the saint's head and hands and fixed them on stakes for a whole year, to be an object of derision and scorn. His head was later retrieved by his brother Oswiu, and was placed in St. Cuthbert's coffin, where it still remains. His right hand - the one St. Aidan had blessed - was placed in a silver casket at Bamburgh, where it remained completely incorrupt until at least the twelfth century, as both Abbot Aelfric and Simeon of Durham attest. At the place where he died - praying, with arms outstretched, for the souls of his men - many miracles were wrought.

In the year 697 Queen Ostrythe of Mercia, who was the saint's niece, and was later murdered herself, decided with her husband, King Ethelred, to transfer the relics of the saint to the monastery of Bardney in Lindsey (Lincolnshire). But the monks of that monastery, entertaining a grudge against Oswald because he had once been king over that region, refused to allow the relics through the monastery gates. So, they remained on a wagon covered by a tent throughout the night.

However, during the night a great column of light was seen stretching from the wagon up to heaven, which was visible throughout Lindsey. Chastened, the monks brought the holy relics inside the gates, washed them with reverence, and placed them in a specially constructed shrine in the church with a gold and purple banner over it. The water used in the washing was poured away in a corner, but the earth, which had received it was found to have the power of expelling demons.

Other books by this author:

Restoration (Book 1)

This is a saga; spread over two novels telling of impossible love, its path travelled, and the tension between relationships, honour, pride, privilege, resentment, hate, and forgiveness.

Acceptance (Book 2)

The series plots a family's journey through the period of history from 1900 to 1946 the fears, sadness, and uncertainties of two world wars with their lottery of life and death, the only constant is love and the product of love, hope. Set in the North East of England.

The Man Who Lived In A Book

A murder mystery set in the Marshall Islands. You may well solve the murder but miss the mystery.

Detective Inspector Tyyamii has a great future, how would you like to be his assistant in the Marshall Islands?

Swallows Leave In Autumn

Set in the North East of England with its miles of beautiful golden beaches, blue sea and historic castles, the home of international author, Sebastian Swan.

Tom Jackson decides to step out of the "Rat race" and rent a cottage in a quiet fishing village on the north east coast of Northumbria. He'd recently resigned from his job as a schoolteacher. Work he had grown to hate.

Tom had a first-class honours degree in fine art. His lecturers told him he was "Exceptional".

He was now going to try to make a living as an artist and see if "Exceptional" would sell enough paintings to put bread on his table.

One summer's evening Tom was sitting on a bench, relaxing mindlessly in the sun watching the swallows swoop back and forth, as they sliced through the sunlight before him. Glancing along the beach his eye caught sight of a young woman in the distance. She drew nearer and nearer, walked up the path to where he was seated, sat down beside him and smiled. This was to be the moment his life changed forever.

Tom never imagined what he would have to face. They came from different worlds, which inevitably brought conflict to their relationship. They were to discover the sharp reality that "True love" can be a very painful path to tread.

Sebastian Swan invites you to walk, laugh, and cry with them.

International Author Sebastian Swan's latest page-turner.

The Colour of Envy (Ulfberht Book 4)

Set in the Reign of Henry II.

On hearing of the fortunes to be made at the tournais in France, a young knight, Richard Maillorie, sees a way to restore his family's fortune and becomes a friend of the great William Marshal. On his return from France, he meets the beautiful Julianne and a complicated journey of love and jealousy begins.

Driven by Honour (Ulfberht Book 5)

A sequel to "The Colour of Envy" a chance to follow the lives through the history of three kings culminating in

the reign of King John accredited with the title of the evillest King in history.

The Price of Honour (Ulfberht Book 1)

The setting is Bernicia, circa (Northumbria) 600 AD

Wulfstan, a young warrior known throughout the north for his bravery and honour, is asked to seek a bride for his King, Æthelfrith. She is the beautiful Princess Aefre, the daughter of King Ælla of Deira.

The gods pour on them their magic potion and their future is sealed.

Are they wicked, or merely playthings of the gods, and to be pitied? You decide.

The Carnelian Ring

SAS Captain Robert Mallory and his wife Maggie, invite some old friends, Keith, and Irene, around for lunch. During the meal, the conversation soon focuses on a ring Robert found that morning in the garden. Keith is intrigued, but Robert tells him he must not touch it for fear of being injured, for he suspects that the ring holds within it the strange power of Synchronicity.

However, Robert does not heed his own advice.

Resulting in him being faced with an impossible choice.

Plato said, "time is an imperfect reflection, it is merely the moving image of eternity".

If the reader has any comments about the book, the author would be pleased to hear from you.

sebastian.dave.swan@gmail.

Printed in Great
Britain
by Amazon